Patricia Kennealy was born in Brooklyn and grew up in North Babylon, New York. She was educated at St Bonaventure University and Harpur College, taking her degree in English literature. For three years she was the editor-in-chief of *Jazz & Pop* magazine, a national publication devoted to rock and progressive music in the late 60s and 70s, and she has written extensively in the field of rock criticism.

She is an award-winning advertising copywriter; a former record company executive, and a member of Mensa. In 1970 she exchanged vows with the late Jim Morrison, leader of the rock group The Doors, in a private religious ceremony. Her leisure pursuits include riding, fencing and playing the violin.

She lives in New York City. Her ambition is to christen a warship. *The Throne of Scone* is her second novel, sequel to *The Copper Crown* (1984).

By the same author

*The Copper Crown*

# PATRICIA. KENNEALY

# The Throne of Scone

A Book of *The Keltiad*

**GRAFTON BOOKS**

A Division of the Collins Publishing Group

LONDON GLASGOW
TORONTO SYDNEY AUCKLAND

Grafton Books
A Division of the Collins Publishing Group
8 Grafton Street, London W1X 3LA

A Grafton UK Paperback Original 1987

ISBN 0-586-06832-5

Printed and bound in Great Britain by
Collins, Glasgow

Set in Times

To my mother and father

# Notes on Pronunciation

The spellings and pronunciations of the names and words in THE KELTIAD are probably unfamiliar to most readers, unless one happens to be thoroughly steeped in things like the Mabinogion or the Cuchulainn cycle. The Celtic languages (Irish, Scots Gaelic, Welsh, Cornish, Manx and Breton) upon which I have drawn for my nomenclature are not related to any tongue that might provide a clue as to their derivation or spoken sound. Outside of loan-words, they have no Latin root as do the Romance tongues, and they are in fact derived from a totally different branch of the Indo-European linguistic tree.

Therefore I have taken certain, not always consistent, liberties with orthography in the interests of reader convenience, though of course one may deal with the names any way one likes, or even not at all. But for those who might like to humour the author, I have made this list of some of the more difficult names, words and phonetic combinations.

One further note, to those (and they are legion) whose Celtic linguistic scholarship exceeds my poor own: The words used herein are meant to be Keltic, not Celtic. I have appropriated fairly even-handedly from most of the Celtic languages – and from Elizabethan English and Lowland Scots (Lallans) as well where it seemed good to do so – both archaisms and words that are in common modern usage, and in not a few cases I have tampered with their meanings to suit my own purposes. Therefore do not be unduly alarmed should familiar words turn out to be not all they seem. Words may be reasonably assumed to change over time and distance; Keltia is very far away by both measures, and who is to say (if not I) what words they shall be speaking and what meaning those words shall have.

But just in case that does not suffice to avert the wrath of the purists, I hereby claim prior protection under the Humpty-Dumpty Law: 'When *I* use a word . . . it means just what I choose it to mean – neither more nor less.' Now you are warned.


## Vowels

Generally the usual, though *a* is mostly pronounced 'ah' and *i* never takes the sound of 'eye', but always an 'ee' or 'ih' sound. Thus: 'ard-ree' for *Ard-rígh*, not 'ard-rye'. Final *e* is always sounded; thus: 'Slay-nee' for *Slaine*, not 'Slain'; *Shane* is pronounced as in English.


## Vowel Combinations

*aoi:*     'ee' as in 'heel'

*ao:*     'ay' as in 'pay'

*au:*     'ow' as in 'cow', never 'aw' as in 'saw'; thus *Jaun* rhymes with 'crown', not with 'fawn'.

*ae, ai:*     'I' as in 'high'. Exceptions: the proper names *Aeron* and *Slaine*, where the sound is 'ay' as in 'day'.

*á:*     The accent gives it length. Thus, *dán* is pronounced 'dawn'.

*io:*     'ih' if unaccented. If accented (*ío*), then 'ee'.

7

## Consonants

c:      always a 'k' sound. (To avoid the obvious problem
        here, the more usual *Celt*, *Celtic*, *Celtia* have been
        spelled *Kelt*, *Keltic*, *Keltia*, throughout.)

ch, kh: gutturals as in the German 'ach', never 'ch' as in
        'choose'

g:      always hard, as in 'get' or 'give'

bh:     pronounced as 'v'

dd:     pronounced as 'th' in 'then', not as in 'thin'

## Some of the more difficult names

Aeron: AIR-on
Aoibhell: ee-VELL
Gwydion: GWID-eeon
Ríoghnach: REE-oh-nakh
Caerdroia: car-DROY-uh
Taoiseach: TEE-shokh
Sidhe: shee
Annwn: annoon
Nudd: neethe (sometimes spelled Neith)
Sorcha: SURR-uh-kha
Taliesin: tal-YES-in
Kynon: kinnon
Pryderi: pree-DARE-ee
dûhín: doo-heen
Irin Magé: EE-rin MAH-gay
Scone: properly, skoon, but, as you please

# Characters

## Kelts

AERON AOIBHELL, High Queen of Kelts

GWYDION AP ARAWN, King of Keltia, Prince of Gwynedd, First Lord of War

MORWEN DOUGLAS, Duchess of Lochcarron, Taoiseach of Keltia

ROHAN, Prince of Thomond, Aeron's brother and heir

SORCHA NÍ REILLE (Sarah O'Reilly), former Terran

DESMOND, cousin to Aeron, son to the late Elharn Ironbrow

SHANE, cousin to Aeron

INDEC, an Abbess-mother of the Ban-draoi

BRONWEN, a Ban-draoi novice

SABIA NÍ DÁLAIGH, friend to Aeron

GRELUN, an officer in Gwydion's service

POWELL, Prince of Dyved

PRYDERI, Lord of Caradigion, his son

CARADOC LLASSAR, High Admiral of the Keltic starfleet

GWENNAN CHYNOWETH, Captain of the flagship *Firedrake*

DENZIL CAMERON, commander in Rohan's service

STRUAN CAMERON, his brother, Master of Horse

FEDELMA NÍ GARRA, Fian general

DONAL MAC AVERA, Captain-General of the Fianna

HELWEN DRUMMOND, Kin to the Dragon

CUMARA, a merrow

ALLYN SON OF MIDNA, a lord of the Sidhe

DECLAN, brother to Aeron

FIONNUALA, sister to Aeron

GAVIN, Earl of Straloch, Lord Extern
KYNON AP ACCOLON, Kymro and traitor
RÍOGHNACH, Princess of the Name, sister to Aeron
NIALL O KEREVAN, Duke of Tir-connell, her husband
KIERAN, brother to Aeron, twin to Declan
EILUNED OF GARIOCH, his wife
MELANGELL, cousin to Aeron
SLAINE, cousin to Aeron, sister to Desmond
ITHELL, a woman of Upper Darkdale
GWYN AP NUDD, King of the Sidhe
ETAIN, his queen

## Terrans

HACO GREX, Terran Ambassador to Keltia
THOMAS DE VALADON, consul
DEONORA MARONCHUK, consul
WARREN HATHAWAY, Lieutenant, FSS *Sword*
ATHENÉE MIKHAILOVA, Ensign, FSS *Sword*
SARAH O'REILLY, Lieutenant, FSS *Sword* (now Sorcha ní Reille)
THEO HARUKO, Captain, FSS *Sword*; deceased

## Coranians

JAUN AKHERA, Emperor of the Cabiri
STREPHON, his grandfather and predecessor as Emperor
HELIOR, his mother
SANCHONIATHON, his brother
TINAO, his mistress
HANNO, Captain-General of the Imperial armies on Tara

GARALLAZ, aide to Jaun Akhera
IRIN MAGÉ, chief priest of the Cabiri order
INDARRAK, servant to Tinao

## Fomori

ELATHAN, King of Fomor
CAMISSA, his queen
TALORCAN, his half-brother
BASILEA, Queen-Dowager of Fomor, Elathan's mother
RAUNI, sister to Elathan
THONA, concubine to the late King Bres, mother to Talorcan
BORVOS, captain of Elathan's guard
TREIC, his lieutenant

the hollow
mountains

mount kcicia

mount army

the scar

north plain

the avon cut

the rimm
of hells

the great glen

drum wood

moymore

Throneworld (tara)
Northwest Continent

the hykes of ra

# In *The Copper Crown*:

It is the Earth year 3512. The FSS *Sword*, a probe ship from Earth sent out to make diplomatic first contact with alien civilizations, arrives unknowingly in what turns out to be Keltic space.

An interstellar kingdom comprising seven star-systems, Keltia was founded in 453 A.D. by Kelts from Earth led by St Brendan the Astrogator. It is ruled at present by the young High Queen Aeron, who, seeing in the *Sword*'s arrival a chance for Keltia to re-establish friendly relations with the world from which her people came so long ago, sets about achieving an alliance.

Aeron's wish is by no means universal, however, neither within her own realm nor beyond the Curtain Wall, the psionically-maintained forcefield that conceals Keltia from the rest of the galaxy. The Cabiri Imperium and the kingdom of Fomor, ancient and bitter enemies of the Kelts, have been informed of the contact with Earth by the traitor princess Arianeira, sister of Aeron's consort-to-be, Gwydion; and now Jaun Akhera, heir to the Cabiri Emperor Strephon, and Bres, the king of Fomor, join forces to invade and occupy Keltia before Keltia can ally with Earth.

Theo Haruko, the Japanasian captain of the *Sword*, and his lieutenant Sarah O'Reilly, who by now have become Aeron's friends, discover to their horror that Hugh Tindal, one of their fellow crewmen, has been seduced into joining Arianeira's treasonous plot. But before they can tell Aeron of this, Arianeira uses black sorcery to breach the Curtain Wall and let in the Imperial and Fomori fleets.

In the savage battles that follow, the Kelts, though successful in space, cannot throw back the invaders from the Throneworld of Tara. Aeron herself engages in a fierce dual of vengeance with Bres, the Fomorian king, who has just slain her friend Haruko, and who, three years before, ambushed the starship carrying her parents and her first consort, Roderick, all of whom perished.

She kills Bres, whose son Elathan, now King, immediately withdraws from the war and takes his armies home to Fomor; Elathan had been opposed all along to the war with the Kelts, to the angry disgust of his father and his half-brother, Talorcan, and now that he has become King he can do as he wishes. Aeron, however, has been terribly wounded in the fight with Bres, and she is saved only by the sorcery of Gwydion, who uses his considerable powers to create a magical pool to heal her of her injuries.

Caerdroia, the Keltic capital, finally falls to Jaun Akhera's own desperate use of sorcery – which art Aeron has steadfastly refused to employ in resistance – and Aeron, Gwydion and Morwen, the Keltic prime minister, are all taken prisoner by the Imperials.

Arianeira, however, repents of her treachery, and, with Gwydion's complicity, arranges an escape for Aeron and Morwen. Although Aeron refuses to leave without Gwydion, at last he manages to trick her into going, and she and Morwen flee. When Jaun Akhera discovers that the Queen and her prime minister have both fled the City, and that his supposed ally Arianeira was the one who effected their escape, he is enraged, and fully intends to kill Arianeira for her betrayal. But Arianeira has already killed herself to atone for her treason to Aeron, and to thwart Jaun Akhera's vengeance, and she dies in her brother Gwydion's arms.

The planet Tara remains in Imperial hands, with Jaun Akhera and his brother Sanchoniathon in occupation of Caerdroia – and with Gwydion as a willing hostage. He does so to keep Keltia for Aeron and in hopes of organizing a resistance; before the City's fall he dispatches the royal family and others – including the Terran lieutenant O'Reilly, who has elected to remain in Keltia after the *Sword*'s return to Earth – to parts unknown for sanctuary.

After a long and terrible flight over the mountains, in deep snow and bitter cold, Aeron and Morwen manage to reach a secret spaceport where Arianeira has hidden Aeron's starship *Retaliator*, and in that ship they escape from the planet and from Keltia.

They are bound on a long and difficult quest, even the reality of which is uncertain: to find the lost and legendary Treasures of Keltia, taken away from the kingdom fifteen centuries before by the great King Arthur himself – magical weapons that will enable Aeron to win back her realm from Jaun Akhera, and, if such is her final choice, to destroy Jaun Akhera and win an empire of her own for herself and for Gwydion. But first she and Morwen must find Arthur . . .

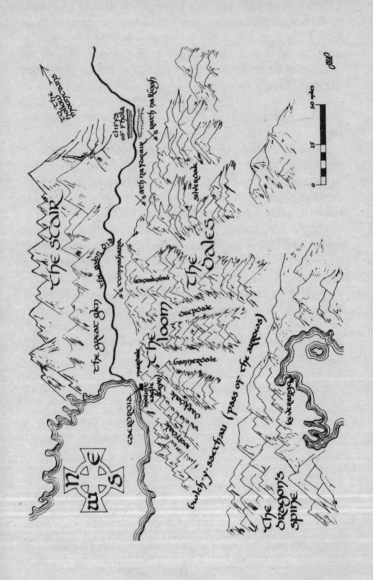

*Ni bu Arthur ond tra fu.*

('Arthur himself had but his time.')

# PARTIAL DESCENT
### of the Ard-Rían Keron
#### from the Royal and Noble Keltic houses

**House of Dôn    House of Arvon**

Gweniver = Arthur Morgan

Gwrgalarch = Arvon Arcuryp = Maboc

Aravwen = Macsen Lloyd
(1) Maravaun = Semple

Gweyr (2) Maravaun = Semple

Brennya = Keiros    Maraghal = Cormac
(not every generation shown)

**Princes of Gwynedd**
(not every generation shown)

Gwydion

---

**(House of Dân**
(Royal line of Doibhell))

(not every generation shown)

Malen = Brendan 176r Doibhell

Keron XVI    Enryre = Iachlar nan Cathal

Declan VIII Raoull II Aoyaray X    Tigernach = Sorcha

Kerrebec or Gwalarm = Keron Kra IV

Brion or Brenny = Lessaruna V

Brendan XVII = Elowen

Síoda = Declan IX

Klaoan = Rofan

Aulteun = Fionnbarra XIII

Graesan = Dorfe VI    Comp Luneð

Gwynene = Lessardan III Revlin Durfac Elfaen

Morlaus Tanfyrg Eogyn Keina Emer = Fionnbarra XIV Orlaith Deian

Aeron Rofan Ríoghnach Keren Sechan Fionnuala

Telery = Rhydian
Lords of Powys

Lords of the Isles

Glesyn = Somharle

---

**Lords of Brecorieð**

Brydoan = Mauwyn Coronwe = Fiona

Gwennan Aífas = Farrell Copall

**Princes of Lenystr**

Morlaus Tanfyrg Eogyn Keina Emer = Fionnbarra

(In early generations,
not all issue shown)

# Rígh-Somhna: The Royal Family of Doibhell and Collateral Kinships

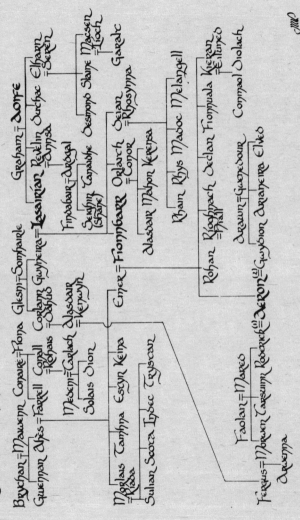

# Chapter One

In the days following his coronation, Elathan of Fomor had had little time to call his own. The Iron Crown of his ancestors had been set upon his head, the fealty of his barons had been accepted, the body of his father, Bres, had been placed in the dim dusty vaults beneath the palace with the fifty-four kings and queens who had preceded him as monarchs of Fomor. Time now to begin to rule, not merely to reign.

In truth, there was much that had need of being ruled, and well did Elathan know it. In his first hour as king, he had taken a decision that would without question shape not only his own reign but the destiny of Fomor for generations and reigns to come: Thousands of star-miles away, upon the Keltic throneworld of Tara, Elathan had called his armies from the war with Keltia – had whistled them off like hounds from the hunt – and against all advice had quit the war, taking his forces home to Fomor with the body of his father. But the war had gone on all the same without him, a war neither of Elathan's making nor to Elathan's liking – a war begun in treachery by Jaun Akhera, heir to the Cabiri Imperium, and joined in by Bres out of vengeance and a long, long hatred.

A shadow of sorrow crossed Elathan's face at the thought of his father. They had never been close – Bres had reserved such affection as he could feel, or show, for his youngest child, his blond daughter Rauni, and for Talorcan, his son by his longtime concubine Thona – and in these last few months they had been not merely estranged but actively antagonistic. All the same, Bres had been Elathan's King as well as his father, and the loss was a real one.

Well, Bres was beyond all vengeance now, slain upon Tara by the Keltic queen herself, in a combat that had put paid to a quarrel seventy years old, and had nearly put paid to Queen Aeron as well. But she had not died: She had been taken prisoner by Jaun Akhera, and then she had escaped – fled off-planet; her friend and First Minister Morwen Douglas with her and all the Imperial fleets after her.

And they had not found her! Elathan felt a surge of elation at the thought: hopefulness that she would continue to elude capture, and no astonishment whatever that he should feel so.

He would not mind an escape of sorts himself: to flee the Court and his capital of Tory, to slip away to his favourite country seat in the southern hills – no attendants, no courtiers, no guards, just him and Camissa his lady. They had been happy there before – before Bres had seen fit to throw Fomor into unholy alliance with the Imperium and vengeful war with the Kelts – and they would be happy there again; though of course any such idyll would now have to wait until after their wedding, and that itself would have to wait on the six months' official mourning for Bres. But after that . . . The thought of Camissa brought a peace to his spirit and an ease to his bearing, and he smiled.

The chamberlain who had stood so patiently before him all this while took the smile as recognition, and coughed discreetly.

'The ambassadors from Alphor wait outside, Majesty. Shall I show them in?'

Elathan came back into the present with a start, nodded reluctant assent and rose from the ivory chair as the door opened on the Coranian envoys. He had been dreading this official encounter since the day of his crowning, had put it off, in fact, as long as he had dared: but he could keep Strephon's minions waiting no longer, not without risking insult – or retaliation.

He had broken with protocol so far, however, as to receive them here, in his private office, at his desk with all its working clutter, instead of in the Presence Chamber as was customary. It was a subtle reminder – not too subtle, he hoped – that the ambassadors would be certain to pass on home to the Emperor Strephon.

He watched them as they came gliding across the room. It was the dead of winter here in Tory; yet the Coranians had defied the bitter cold and leaden skies to appear in full regalia of their home planet: long, ankle-hobbling skirts of intricately pleated white linen over narrow trousers of rich figured cloth, chests half-bared under short jackets, gold-embroidered sleeveless coats falling below their knees. Upon their heads were small shapeless caps like velvet bags, banded with jewelled cords, and their gold-capped slippers too were velvet. Their garb looked extremely foreign by contrast to the simply cut robes of the Fomori; their faces were gilded by the variable sun that had made their homeworld of Alphor by turns into a freezing desert and a burning waste. Beneath the velvet caps, their hair was thick, straight, dark.

They stopped on the other side of the desk and bowed deeply to Elathan as the chamberlain withdrew. He returned the obeisance with the curt nod of a sovereign, concealing his distaste, and indicated that they might sit in his presence. But they carefully waited until he had resumed his own chair before they did so.

'My lords,' murmured Elathan, freeing them to speak.

'We extend the felicitations of the Cabiri Emperor Strephon, long may he reign, to his noble cousin of Fomor,' said the emissary who seemed senior of the two.

'And, of course, the Imperium's deepest sorrow for the untimely demise of Your Majesty's royal father, in so abhorrent a manner.'

Elathan did not reply at once. 'We thank our cousin Strephon for this earnest of his sympathy and concern,' he said then. 'You are here to take up your diplomatic duties, my lord – ?'

'I am called Emen Gaitz, Majesty,' said the ambassador, looking more than a little chagrined, for Elathan should certainly have known his name, and, the envoy almost instantly realized, undoubtedly did . . . 'May I present my colleague Chamara?' he murmured, chastened.

'Your credentials?'

Silently Emen Gaitz extended a gold diptych to Elathan, who broke the thin seal and gave the contents a cursory scan.

'Your Majesty will find all in order . . . We are indeed appointed duly by the Emperor to the court of Fomor, but we have also another errand, of somewhat more delicacy, entrusted to us by another member of the Imperial family.'

Elathan, frowning slightly, set the diptych aside and leaned back in his chair, steepling his long fingers under his chin and waiting for them to continue.

It was Chamara who now took up the conversation. 'We know well of the high regard,' he began, 'in which Your Majesty of Fomor is held by His Highness Jaun Akhera, the Imperial Heir, and, feeling certain that this regard is fully reciprocated – ' Here he faltered, for Elathan's face was completely devoid of expression, but he rallied and went on. 'We have in any case been instructed by Her Imperial Serenity the Princess Helior, acting for her son Jaun Akhera, to inquire respectfully of

Your Grace if you would not deign to reconsider your position, and reopen hostilities against Keltia.'

*Keltia* . . . The word buzzed in Elathan's ears like a bee-bird, made the room swim before his eyes. What in the name of all gods did he have to do, to prove to folk that he was sincere in his stated policy, that he *wanted* to be friends with the Kelts, and with Aeron . . .

'The Princess Helior, no less than her son, is surely aware of the circumstances under which I recalled my armies from the Keltic war. What could Fomor possibly hope to gain by resuming the ill-considered fight that killed her king?'

'Among other things, lord, vengeance for that king's death,' said Emen Gaitz eagerly. 'It was Aeron Aoibhell, Keltia's own queen, who struck down your royal father. She is now, as Your Grace knows, a common fugitive, and Jaun Akhera holds her throneworld in the teeth of everything the Kelts can throw against him.'

'And that says much for Jaun Akhera. But that is still no good reason, in fact no reason at all, why I should bring my armies again to a fight I had no wish to be part of in the first. I said so to Jaun Akhera himself, long before battle began, and again after the death of my father.'

The envoys looked uncomfortable. 'The Princess Helior prays you think of future friendship, lord, if nothing else,' said Chamara after a while. 'Jaun Akhera is of Your Majesty's own age, and he looks to you – as friend, contemporary and future ally – for assistance. Your late royal father – '

'My late royal father,' said Elathan, an edge to his voice now, 'was the one who wished for a war of vengeance upon the Kelts; my father, lord, not I. That feud is now ended, at least as far as I am concerned, and I think I may speak in this matter for the Queen of Kelts

25

as well. I say this once only: I will not reopen the war with Keltia under any circumstances, and if Aeron Aoibhell lives to return to her kingdom, and takes it back again from Jaun Akhera – as I am firmly convinced she shall – then it is my declared intention to make peace with her, monarch to monarch. House to House, person to person. The enmity between her family and mine has gone on long enough, and has cost of royal blood more than enough. Past time to bring it to an end.' He rose, and they scrambled hastily to their feet. 'If there is no more we must speak of?'

They smoothed the pleats of their clothing, smiling professionally, spreading their hands in indication that their speeches were done.

'Well, then. I accept your duty as envoys, and I look forward to seeing you here at Court. As to the rest of what we have spoken of today – you understand we have not spoken of it. I give you good day, my lords.'

He fell back into his chair as the doors swung closed behind the Coranians; and so he did not see the man who loitered alone in the great open hall beyond the study doors, and who now, with a quick furtive glance around, fell into step as if by purest chance with the Imperial envoys.

They stopped, startled, and began to bow to the new-comer as formally and respectfully, though less deeply, as they had bowed to the King of Fomor himself. But he cut their obeisances off and conducted them quickly out of the hall, glancing around yet again to be sure that none had seen them go. Once safely out of sight of the royal environs, he turned to them, smiling winningly.

'Ah, sirs,' said Talorcan, half-brother to Elathan, son of Bres and his legal concubine the Lady Thona, 'would it please you to speak further of your true business here at Tory? For I,' he said, 'may be of assistance to you in

26

such matter, and – howsoever my royal brother may decide – I would not turn down the friendship of the next Cabiri Emperor. Shall we speak more of this in my chambers?'

'Aeron? Do you sleep?' Morwen Douglas, Duchess of Lochcarron and First Minister of Keltia, stood in the doorway of the starship cabin and smiled indulgently at its occupant.

The one she addressed lay curled up on the blastcouch in an attitude full of elegance, long slim legs crossed at the ankle and drawn up slightly, red-gold hair draped over her like a coverlet. Aeron Aoibhell, High Queen of Keltia, Morwen's foster-sister and onetime sister-in-law, stirred, stretched and sat up all in one fluid movement.

'Not now . . . Any road, I am all slept out. Let me take the ship for the next watch and what is left of this one. I feel a need to take counsel of myself, and that is easier done at the helm than lolling here.'

Morwen's smile widened. 'Well, should Her Majesty need other counsel – I will not say wiser counsel – let her not forget she has to hand the services of her Taoiseach. But I think I will sleep now a while myself; besides, you are the only one here knows where we are bound.'

'I have told you where we are bound.'

'Oh, aye: We go in search of Arthur – a king dead fifteen hundred years – and in search of the Thirteen Treasures of Keltia – which may or may not exist, and which he may or may not have taken away with him. Not the most certain of destinations.'

'Perhaps not. But if Your Grace of Lochcarron will delay your rest until you have read a little in this' – she tossed to Morwen a small book bound in dark-blue leather, and rose from the couch as she spoke – 'you will shortly have a better idea of where we are bound. That is, if you truly wish to know?'

Morwen snatched the little volume from its arc through the air. 'I am not entirely sure just yet . . .'

When Aeron, grinning at her friend's exasperation, had gone past her, headed for the command cabin of *Retaliator*, Morwen looked down reluctantly at the silver-stamped blue leather cover.

'"Preithi Annuvin,"' she said softly and reverently. 'From the hand and harp of Taliesin ap Gwyddno himself . . .'

She shook her blond head and dropped down on the blastcouch. Almost the only thing Aeron had as yet chosen to impart to her was that this book would be their map for the desperate quest ahead. For this journey they were now embarked upon was not one of pleasure, nor of choice, nor even of their own planning. It was flight plain and simple: flight into exile, flight arranged at the cost of others' lives, to save their own lives and to seek help that would save their kingdom.

And – again according to Aeron – this bard dead for a millennium and a half would guide them . . .

'Oh gods, Aeron,' said Morwen, looking after her friend. 'I pray you know what it is that you do.'

She leaned back against the pillows in the hollow left by Aeron; unfastening the silver clasps of the little book, she opened the blue leather covers and began to read.

In the Keltic capital of Caerdroia, in Aeron's tower bedchamber overlooking the sea, Gwydion put aside the book that had been in his hands, rose, and walked to the windows that gave on the city. His eyes, ordinarily so all-seeing, saw Caerdroia no more than they had seen the pages of the book, for his mind – and his heart – had fled

28

many light-years away, moving with *Retaliator* as she sailed into the unknown.

Yet for all his skill and power, he could not see that ship with any sight; she, and those who sailed her, had passed beyond the reach of telepathy and prescience and even hope. All he could do was yearn; and that, for the Prince of Gwynedd and the King of Keltia, was not permissible, not now, and never for long.

But in truth he had not found his self-chosen captivity as onerous as he had expected to. Having resolved to remain as hostage in Caerdroia – as he had patiently explained to both Aeron his consort and Jaun Akhera his captor – he had not for one instant regretted his decision. He had stayed so that Aeron would have a kingdom to return to; as First Lord of War on the royal council, as Pendragon of Lirias, leader of the Dragon Kinship, and, most of all, as Aeron's chosen lord, he was the logical one to remain.

And both Jaun Akhera and Aeron had perfectly well understood his reasons, though Aeron had fought bitterly against his decision, and had had in the end to be tricked into flight . . . But she would have died on the scaffold had she stayed, and Morwen with her; and that he could not have borne. So he had seen to it that she fled, and his sister Arianeira – she who had betrayed her Queen, her brother and her country into Imperial hands – had arranged the escape before killing herself, all in atonement for her treachery . . .

The wind through the open casement stirred Gwydion's dark hair, and his handsome face showed for a moment his despair. Well, things had gone as they were fated, and more folk than Ari had met their dán in this quarrel. Unbidden, the face of Theo Haruko formed before his eyes: Haruko, the Japanasian captain of the Terran embassy ship that, only months before, had rediscovered

Keltia for the first time in three thousand years; Haruko who had been his friend – and Aeron's.

A wave of pain swamped all his defences at the renewed thought of Aeron, and this time he let it take him. For all his passionate relief that she at least was beyond Jaun Akhera's reach, the doubts he had held at bay for a month now crowded around him like camurs ringing a wounded stag. Was she safe, was she well, was she even alive . . . She was clever and courageous, right enough, a true Aoibhell and a true monarch; but would that be sufficient for the task she had accepted and the path she had set herself to walk? *Ah, Aeronwy* – Gwydion leaned his forehead against the sun-warmed stone of the window embrasure – *gods with you, cariad . . .*

He did not turn as, deceptively casual, one of the omnipresent guards peered through the doorway to see what their royal charge was up to. Though never was Gwydion unwatched by at least four sentries of Jaun Akhera's personal troops, few demands were made upon him, and he had all the leisure he could wish to read, or play his beloved telyn, or walk in the palace gardens with Aeron's wolfhounds – and his Coranian guards. Even the wolfhounds, though, had managed to escape from Turusachan: After a few weeks' pining, they had fled one night to hunt their absent mistress, and now Gwydion walked alone, and wished he could have followed.

He had even on three occasions been permitted the extraordinary grace of riding out from the gates of the City, under heavy escort, north to the Avon Dia and east as far as Miremoss. The liberty had been granted under the guise of necessary exercise, but Gwydion knew very well the hope that had been in the Marbh-draoi's mind: that this brief taste of greater freedoms would push his recalcitrant prisoner in the direction of collaboration – or at the very least away from recalcitrance.

Gwydion laughed, a little bitterly. Pity it was that Jaun Akhera and so many of his closest advisors were such proficient sorcerers. Otherwise, Gwydion had shape-shifted long ago, and been away from Turusachan in form of a hare or sea eagle or some other creature both swift and natural to the region. *Or even another wolfhound to run with Ardattin and Cabal* . . . But a spell of such power and complexity required time and effort both; he would have been detected long before his power could have been called in, and he would have been summarily, and unpleasantly, stopped.

So Gwydion remained, turning away all Jaun Akhera's overtures of friendship with the same grace and good humour as he used to turn away Jaun Akhera's threats; and nothing changed.

It was the height of the rainy season in that part of Alphor where lay the Imperial city of Escal-dun. Persistent rains from a grey sky had turned the endless sands beyond the city walls into a quagmire; within the high streaming aurichalcum walls, the mood of the city's inhabitants was as grey.

'But why will you not! Girdle of Auset, the boy is my son, your grandson – you yourself named him etcheko-primu, Imperial Heir!'

Even the thick doors emblazoned with the gold Imperial eagles were not proof against the bitterness of that cry; beyond the doors, the guards kept impassive faces and studied not to hear, knowing only too well that their lives most surely hung upon that tacit ignorance.

Within the columned stoa, a woman in clear bright red paced back and forth, in her anger vivid against the rainlight. Her thick black-brown hair was cut precisely even with her shoulder-blades; around her slim neck was the narrow gold collar worn by members of the Imperial House of the Plexari. Her name was Helior.

The father she so passionately harangued lay, as was his habit, on silk pillows piled thick upon the longchair of solid gold. He was an old man, bald, his skin furrowed and dewlapped with great age, though its texture was still that of a young man's; his eyes that had once been clear amber-gold were paled now to the colour of citrines seen through moving water. Those eyes were at this moment bent narrowly upon his eldest child, and they held annoyance, amusement and indulgence in equal proportions.

'That I did,' said Strephon with a snort. 'The Cabiri Emperor may choose his heir as he pleases, and once you yourself had resigned your rights in favour of your son – or are you regretting *that* decision? – No, I thought not; in any event, Jaun Akhera was the only logical one of your brood to choose. As for your brother's spawn, the less said the better, though there will be trouble there later on. Young Akhi will be well able to deal with it.'

'If he lives to come home again from Keltia!' snarled Helior. 'Why you ever permitted him to proceed with that invasion I shall never know – a sleeveless errand if ever there was one . . . But once you did commit him to it, my father, it seems to me that the course of honour would have been to support him in his need.'

Strephon shifted on his pillows, dabbling his fingers in the ornamental carp-pool.

'Honour doesn't enter into it. Jaun Akhera knew there would be, after my initial – investment, not one smallest flitterworth of additional help from me. Besides, if he cannot manage to turn things around for him in Keltia with the seventy legions he has remaining after Bres's defection' – the Emperor's voice gave particular emphasis to the number – 'then he richly deserves whatever fate the Kelts may deal him, and I shall look elsewhere for

32

another, and worthier, heir. He was careless enough to allow the Keltic queen to escape, and her chief minister with her; and he must be made to bear the consequences of that lapse.'

Helior, who had been drawing breath for a bitter refutal, angrily clamped her lips together. That point could not be argued, and her father knew she knew it: Aeron Aoibhell and Morwen Douglas had indeed managed to elude her son and all seventy of those crack legions; had from all reports made a harrowing march through snow-mountains to a remote spacebase – garrisoned by Imperial troops! – and had stolen a ship from under the noses of those troops and got clean away off-planet . . .

'And he was also careless enough to permit his own hand-picked ally, the Princess Arianeira, to betray him in turn as she had betrayed her Queen; it was she who arranged Aeron's escape.' Strephon shook his head, but his eyes under lowered lids watched his daughter's every move. 'A sad and sorry performance.'

'He succeeds in keeping caged an eagle indeed – Gwydion Prince of Gwynedd,' returned Helior with considerable sharpness. 'That one is no peacock-princeling, nor plumed bustard either.'

That was certainly true enough, conceded Strephon privately. Gwydion of Dôn was not only Keltia's chief warlord but the consort of Keltia's queen, and, as a hostage, worth several planets at the most conservative reckoning.

'That was well done, I admit it freely. But of little use in the long run if it lures not Aeron back again to Keltia . . . Still, we shall see. And now – ' He fluttered jewelled fingers in the air, and Helior curtsied deeply, hands crossed on her breast.

Outside in the broad hallway, she stood a moment in

thought, then hurried in a rustle of silk towards the family quarters in the palace's garden wing used by her son – and shared by him with his mistress, the Lady Tinao.

Aboard the Earth ship *Sword*, nothing stirred; nothing save the banks of light and complex circuitry, blinking erratically to life in waves of incomprehensible patterns, switching themselves on and off, monitoring course and velocity, correcting where necessary.

The blinking banks monitored other things as well: the lives of the six people who lay in motionless stasis in the coldsleep cabins. Two of these were Terrans: Warren Hathaway and Athenée Mikhailova, ship's officers, two of the three remaining survivors of the original embassy probe mission that had brought the *Sword* to Keltic space. Their companions remained in Keltia: Captain Theo Haruko, dead in a hero's grave in royal ground; Hugh Tindal, dead for a traitor in an unmarked ditch, and Sarah O'Reilly, very much alive, and, since she was hunted for by the agents of Jaun Akhera, safe in the custody of the Ban-draoi Sisters, hidden away in a convent on the planet Vannin.

The other four sleepers were Kelts, Aeron Aoibhell's ambassadors to Earth: her sister the Princess Fionnuala and her Council minister for out-Wall affairs, Gavin Earl of Straloch. One was a bard: Morgan Cairbre, sent on the mission as master-spy as much as master-bard. And the last was a warrior: Emrys Penmarc'h, a lieutenant in the service of Gwydion, and one who was Kin to the Dragon.

The *Sword* was on course to Earth, programmed to intercept, if possible, the Terran embassy ship which was even now sailing to Keltia with a full consular aboard her, to take up Queen Aeron's invitation to open negotiations for full diplomatic ties between Earth and Keltia.

And that fact was what had brought about the invasion of Keltia by the Cabiri Empire and its ally of necessity, the kingdom of Fomor: the fact that these two powers, Keltia and Earth, kin from old, were after three thousand years of separation now minded to reconcile. *That* neither Fomor nor the Cabiri Empire could countenance; and so Keltia had come to be betrayed and invaded, never knowing if indeed the same fate had not been visited upon Earth; and the six aboard the *Sword* knew nothing of any of it. When the Terran embassy ship was within hailing distance, the droids would awaken them; until that time, they slept peacefully on.

Not far from where Gwydion Prince of Dôn had just laid aside his book, Jaun Akhera, Prince of Alphor and Imperial Heir, slammed a palm down in irritation upon the touchboard of the computer that formed the top of his desk. The screen lighted like a aurora, then with a wheezing noise died away into blankness.

Jaun Akhera stared at it a moment longer, then looked up to meet his brother's eyes.

'I am sorry, Akhi,' said Sanchoniathon, turning one palm outward helplessly. 'But there is nothing to be done. There will be no more help from Strephon; our mother has tried and failed, and even that message was not got to us without great difficulty. We are to do whatever we must with whatever is left to us.'

His elder brother swore briefly. 'Apparently! Hanno?'

Jaun Akhera's captain-general came to attention where he stood prudently nearer the door.

'You know the situation as well as I do, my lord,' he said. 'While we hold this planet, and the City, we are safe; but no more than that. The Keltic starfleet will not venture inside the Criosanna, for fear of what we might do to those of their people under our hand. But beyond

Tara's moons it is a different story, and outside this system – ' He shrugged, palms open in the same gesture of futility Sanchoniathon had used.

'Outside this system, we are defeated, or near enough to it. Not acceptable.' Jaun Akhera had begun to pace by the windows that overlooked the sea. 'Who leads the Keltic fleet since Elharn was slain?'

'Prince Rohan is in command, but the new High Admiral to take Elharn's place is called Caradoc Llassar. He is a veteran of the Halistra conflicts – you remember, that Keltic protectorate system the Phalanx so long coveted – and every bit as devious as his predecessor.'

Jaun Akhera swore again. 'And what of Aeron?'

Hanno and Sanchoniathon exchanged quick dreading looks. Neither man had wanted to have to answer this question, and both had known it would certainly be asked . . .

'There is no news, Akhi,' said Sanchoniathon carefully. 'None but what we already know: that she and Morwen are undoubtedly off-planet, as Gwydion has claimed; and that, five days after we took the City, her personal ship was stolen from a spacebase a hundred miles to the south of here.'

'A spacebase guarded by troops of my own household division!' Jaun Akhera was furious all over again when he thought of it. 'Well,' he said after a while, 'from the claw we may judge of the tiger – or the She-wolf. If she lives, she will go on what way she has begun; of that, at least, we *can* be certain. Where do you think she is likely to go?'

'Earth,' said Hanno. 'Perhaps she is even there by now; it would depend on the sort of transport she may have found herself. If she is indeed the one who stole *Retaliator* – her own ship, after all, and I must say I cannot imagine who else would have, or could have, done it – she will have certainly come to Earth by now, if that ship is as fast as everyone seems to think it is.'

Jaun Akhera snorted. 'It is; Gwydion enjoyed telling me so much too much for it not to be true.'

'Well, what then? We cannot move from Caerdroia, and we cannot take the war beyond this system.'

'What then?' repeated Jaun Akhera. 'If we cannot take the war elsewhere, perhaps we can make it come to us . . . Since we can get no help from without, as my grandfather has declared, then we must make shift to get help from within. I will see what may be done to find some.'

# Chapter Two

Sarah O'Reilly stood on the edge of the little landing-field, possessed of such an impatience and excitement that she resembled nothing so much as a racehorse held in before the start. Her feet did a little shuffle in place, her face was lifted eagerly to the sky, and her brown hair – she had been letting it grow in Keltic fashion since her arrival on Tara, and it was now down past her shoulder-blades – blew behind her on a warm wind.

Try as she might, she could not manage to control her anticipation. *The Sisters would not approve*, she thought a little guiltily. *They have been trying so hard to teach me control and restraint, and now, as soon as a little of both is called for* – But that was not strictly true, and she knew it. It had not been a person devoid of self-control who had been communications lieutenant aboard the probe ship *Sword*, and no unrestrained individual had been the friend of Theo Haruko, and certainly the Ard-rían of Keltia herself had not chosen one lacking in self-discipline to be her personal squire . . . O'Reilly felt the familiar tug of anxiety at the thought of Aeron, and those other friends now bound for Earth on the *Sword*, and the renewed pang of loss for Theo her captain. *I have not forgotten you!* she cried to those ghostly presences so real before her. *Oh, I have not forgotten . . .*

Then all the fretful shadows vanished, as out of the low clouds a familiar silver ship came in a flashing curve, dropping fast and steep and coming in to land a hundred yards away. The high keen of the thrusters died as the power was cut; then as the doorseals opened, O'Reilly was free to run forward at last.

A tall man emerged from the portal. Dark-haired, dark-moustached, clad in the brown uniform of the Fianna, he staggered a little as O'Reilly threw herself into his arms.

'Softly, anwylyd,' he protested with a smile. 'Have the Ban-draoi sisters not been teaching you patience and purposeless waiting?'

'A neat trick,' said O'Reilly with some bitterness, 'for such as can manage it. I think I shall never be among them. Oh, I have missed you, Desmond – '

'And I you.' Desmond Aoibhell bent his head to kiss her then. 'But it has not been so long, considering. I may be Aeron's cousin, but that means only all the more duties in her absence for me and the rest of the family; she leaves a gap is no small task to fill. Also is there a war on, as you know.'

'It has been three weeks! Quite long enough. Besides' – she fitted herself under his shoulder as they walked from the field, slipping her arm around his waist beneath his cloak – 'most of the time I do *not* know what is happening with the war; and if the Abbess Indec knows, she does not always see fit to tell me. Though God knows why she might think *I* should be spared such knowledge . . . no one else in Keltia is. It's bad enough I have to stay here at all.'

'You know very well why you were sent here to Glassary,' said Desmond, tightening his arm around her shoulders. 'Aeron thought to keep you safe, for that Jaun Akhera was searching for you and your fellow Terrans, and this seemed to her an excellent place to do so. Any road, you suggested Glassary to her yourself.'

'Oh, I know – it's just that it's very hard for me to sit here safe and healthy and happy, while the rest of you are . . .' O'Reilly gestured with her free hand, and on her face now was bitter disdain for her noncombatant status.

'Well, I am here now.'

'So you are.' She leaned close into his side again, ashamed of her outburst, ashamed still more that she had allowed him to see it.

'All the same,' continued Desmond, 'I would not be here even yet, were I not on a scout's errand for Rohan, and as it is I can spare only a few hours. But I would not have passed so near to Vannin without seeing you.' They had come to the shell-paved road that climbed to the Ban-draoi convent of Glassary, its buildings of cream-coloured stone low-set, square-built and solid on its hill in the middle of the island. 'Very little else is new,' he added, anticipating her questions. 'Still no word of Aeron and Morwen; the Imperials still hold the Throneworld; Gwydion is still the Marbh-draoi's prisoner in Turusachan – though that last at least may soon change.'

O'Reilly's head snapped up, her eyes sparkling with sudden hope. 'A rescue? You will get him out?'

'There is – a possibility, which is all I may say of it, even to you.'

'I see – and I *am* glad.' She sighed and moved away a little. 'Are you hungry? Do you wish to bathe and eat now, or later, or what?'

Desmond laughed. 'Or what? Might we go somewhere private and talk a while, you and I? There are some things I wish to speak of are best spoken of outside convent walls.'

O'Reilly blushed. 'I know just the place.'


Aboard *Retaliator*, Morwen sat with her chin in her hands and her elbows on her knees, staring disconsolately at the little book on the bed before her with an expression that

40

needed no gloss. Aeron, coming in, saw the look and smiled.

'It is no real scholar's matter, Wenna. You need not strike so hard to crack the nut.'

Morwen cast her a baleful upward glance. 'Easy for one who has studied at Seren Beirdd to say so. Well then, ollave, translate the words of Taliesin to simplicities that a poor ignorant cumal such as I might understand. No doubt I am not so learned, as I might be, or apparently should be.'

'Nay, sulk not. We will puzzle it out together.' Aeron took the book and turned it so that both of them might read. 'Now, we know that Taliesin ap Gwyddno was Arthur's oldest and most beloved friend; they had been boyhood playfellows in Arvon, Druid schoolmates later on, though Arthur went to Dinas Affaraon to study with the Pheryllt for the rank of master-Druid and Taliesin's first love was ever bardery. Still they remained close, and when Arthur began his great labours Taliesin was the first comrade he called to his side.'

'And one of the last to leave him, if we can believe this.' Morwen indicated the book with a jerk of her delicate chin.

'Oh, but I think we must. Do not forget, he was the beloved of Arthur's sister, Morgan, and she so great a sorceress as would have seen the least little shadow of a lie in his face, and read it in his heart . . . Nay, what Taliesin has set down here is pure truth. It remains only for us to sort it out. It is couched in the highest style of the ríogh-bardáin, and damnable difficult.'

'Not so for – ' Morwen caught back her thought before the name was out.

'Nay,' agreed Aeron quietly, her face expressionless. 'Not so for Gwydion. But he is not here, and so you and I must do our own poor best. Come then, my Taoiseach, let us read.' She opened the book to where she had placed her sgian as marker. '"Three times the fullness of Prydwen we went into it; except seven, none returned from Caer Sidi."'

The words of the wild, ancient chaunt echoed in the cabin, sounding huge and cold and full of mystery out there among the stars. Morwen felt the fine hairs on the back of her neck begin to rise; she hugged herself for comfort, hands rubbing her upper arms, suddenly chilled, as Aeron's voice went on and on, as strangely changed and charged as were the words themselves.

'Three times the fullness of Prydwen we went into it.
Except seven, none returned from Caer Sidi.

Am I not a candidate for fame, to be heard in the chaunting?
In Caer Pedryvan four times revolving,
The Shout above the Abyss, when was first it heard?
Is this not the Cup of the King of the Dead,
Ridged round its edge with pearls?
It gives no life to a coward, nor to one forsworn.
A sword of light to a seeker will be given,
And before the portals of Uffern the horns of light shall burn.
And when we went with Arthur in his splendid labours,
Except seven, none returned from Caer Vediwid.

Am I not a candidate for renown, to be heard in the singing?
In Caer Pedryvan, in the Isle of the Strong Door,
Where twilight and black dark come together,
Is not bright blood the guest-drink offered?
The point of the lance of battle lies lapped in fumes of sleep,
When shall it waken?
And the bronze lid of Fál's eye, when shall it open?
Three times the fullness of Prydwen were we that went on sea;
What time we went with Arthur of glorious memory,
Except seven, none returned from Caer Rigor.

No praise give I to the lords of swords,
For beyond Caer Wydyr they saw not Arthur's might.
In gear of battle stood they upon the walls,
But hard it was to speak with their watchman.

Thrice the freight of Fairface were we that went with Arthur;
Save seven, none returned from Caer Coronach.'

Aeron's voice, clear and steady until now, faltered suddenly, as her eyes ranging forward perceived the text to come. Morwen glanced anxiously, and curiously, at her, but Aeron was already continuing as if the tiny break had not been.

'Complete shall be the prison of Gweir in Caer Sidi,
Through the spite of Pwyll and Pryderi.
Few before him went into it, the sea's blue chains to hold him fast.
Before the Spoils of Annwn shall he sing,
And until the end of time shall he be a bard for it.
Three times the fullness of Prydwen we went into it;
Except seven, none returned from Caer Sidi.'

So the poem ended, and there was silence in the small cabin, and for long moments neither woman stirred.

Then Aeron: 'Oh but these are wingèd words! Gwyn son of Nudd has sent us well . . . Did you hear, Wenna? Did you hear where we must go?'

'I heard naught save a tale of death and dolour,' said Morwen flatly. 'Seven alone escaped from a mort of caers with baneful names – oh, Aeron, what guide is this, there is nothing here for us! Look, he speaks of *Prydwen*, even, as if she sailed oceans, not space: He says "were we that went on sea." How is that to chime with our course, or our need?'

Aeron riffled the stiff parchment pages. When she spoke again, she seemed to change the subject.

'What means the word "morimaruse" in the tongue of the Prytani?'

Morwen looked hard at her – had Aeron lost her wits for true? – then answered with some bewilderment.

43

'Well, "mar" means "death", so that "i-maruse" is "of the dead" or "of death".'

'So. And "mor"?'

'In all our tongues, "mor" is – ' Morwen stopped abruptly. *Gods, my own nameword, and I did not make the leap to it* . . . '"Mor" is to do with the sea. Oh, Aeron, can this be so?'

'Gods willing. Do not forget, the maker of this poem was both bard and Druid. He would not have made so important a chaunt accessible to the casual reader. Nay, the sea Taliesin speaks of here is the Morimaruse itself.'

Morwen felt a chill touch her again at the name. The Morimaruse, the great galactic dust-sea that they had been on course for ever since they had passed the Curtain Wall . . .

'And the caers?'

Aeron clasped her hands behind her head and leaned back against the metal brattice.

'Ah. That is rather more problematical; and more difficult to construe, for the poem is ancient and has been much broken and repieced over the centuries. But when first Gwydion told me of Gwyn's message to me, that I must remember *Prydwen* and the lost Treasures, I straightway thought of Taliesin and this same poem. You know the poem itself was lost for some hundreds of years; any road, we gave much study to it when I was at Seren Beirdd for my schooling, and I have never forgotten it – far less the turn it gave me when first I read it, like a hare leaping over my grave . . . So, before Caerdroia fell, I sent to the Bardic Library and brought away this book.' She drew a light fingertip over the silver-stamped device on the leather binding: the Gwynedd stag. 'This copy came down in Gwydion's family for many generations; maybe even from Taliesin himself, he was an ancestor of their House . . .'

'Surely you have not carried it with you all this time? How did you get it from Caerdroia?'

'I did not,' said Aeron levelly. 'Ari did. Gwydion had told her of the book and the prophecy alike, when they held their ruseful meeting to plot our escape from the City. I found the book here in my cabin that first night.'

'That was – ' Morwen fell silent, knowing Aeron knew her thought: *That was nobly done of Arianeira, her last debt of repentance fully paid* . . .

'Aye. Aye, it was . . . Well, to return to the poem, I think each one of those named caers has meaning; more to the point, meaning for us. I think they are places within, or perhaps beyond, the Morimaruse. Planets, maybe, at least some of them; or they might be clearings, as it were, within the dustclouds of the Sea itself. Any road, they are every one of them places where Arthur brought war, and so only seven returned.'

'Seven: Taliesin, and who else?'

'Their names come in another poem,' said Aeron. 'But those others were three women and three men: Tanwen of Dyonas, and Ferdia son of Kenver, and Daronwy the daughter of Anwas; the two sons of Geraint, Sgilti Lightfoot and Anghaud Holdfast; and Elen Llydawg, Elen of the Hosts, she who was one of the greatest generals Keltia ever had. Seven returned, and spoke no word of Arthur or his fate; at least, they did not that we know of. But they founded the order of the Dragon Kinship, in celebration of their fellowship and in memory of their Arthur. They were great souls and true ones, and they went well on a fearful road. Yet for all that, they have but little to do with our hunt. Taliesin alone has left the trailmarks we must follow.'

'But where shall these marks lead us?'

'Ah, now at last we come to it!' Aeron sat forward again, leaning over the book in a posture almost bouncing

45

with eagerness. 'Here is how I do read it: It is pieced all awry, as I said before, and so the first parts in sequence of time come not first in the poem. Where Taliesin speaks of Caer Sidi – that means Spiral Castle.'

'The Morimaruse again? Caer Sidi is also the name of an island stronghold on Dyved.'

'I know; but that place had its name much later than this poem, most like even took its name *from* the poem . . .'

'So, the Morimaruse.'

Aeron nodded. 'From above the plane of it, the Sea is a giant dust-spiral, a galaxy in small. Now, Caer Wydyr – Glass Castle, where warriors stand upon the walls and it is difficult to converse with the sentinel. That I think to be a space-station, or perhaps a ship, deep within the Morimaruse. Soldiers *would* man the walls of such a station, or the defences of a ship; and a reflective hull could well be described as glass-like. It would be hard to speak with the watchman because he would not only speak a foreign tongue, but in posture of war he would surely refuse to respond to hails from an enemy starship.'

'Very clever. A ship sounds the more likely; if only for that surely the existence of a space-station within the Sea would have been widely known to military intelligence.'

'Not of necessity. Do not forget, all this was in a time before the raising of our Curtain Wall, in a period of fierce wars in many galactic sectors, not just our own little squabbles with the Coranians and Fomori. Intelligence-gathering might well have been hampered by the fighting; any power could have built a station in the Sea and managed to keep it secret from its enemies. Still, I think you have the right of it here, and Taliesin does speak of another ship over against *Prydwen*.'

Morwen's eyes sparked. 'The flagship of the Coranian invaders, that Arthur lured away from Keltia – '

' – and dragged with him into the Morimaruse. Coming from the Battle of the Roads of Camlann, he knew there was no way else to destroy the enemy command and keep Keltia safe. So he engaged the alien ship with *Prydwen* and took both craft into the Sea, not knowing if ever he would sail out again. That is when he sent his famous message back to Keltia, telling all our people that he would come again when he was needed.'

'And then?'

Aeron shrugged. 'Who can say? Seven returned, that is all we have been given to know. Though not, I think, all we are going to know . . . But there is so much more here, Wenna, that I have not begun to uncipher: He speaks of a sword of light, and the Cup of the King of the Dead; then later, of a sleeping spear and a lidded eye. What are those but the four chief Treasures – Sword, Spear, Cup and Stone – those very ones Gwyn has set me to seek? But here now, in the second dwned, you can see much has been lost: "In Caer Pedryvan, in the Isle of the Strong Door, where twilight and black dark came together/Is not bright blood the guest-drink offered?" That can only mean Fomor: "twilight" and "black dark" signifying the Fomori and the Coranians, who made common cause against us in Tory itself. "Pedryvan" means "four-cornered tower", an old bardic usage for "prison", and the tradition is strong that Arthur went to Fomor – also Caer Rigor – to free Keltic hostages captured by the Fomori in the raid on our trading planet of Clero that was provocation to the war itself. He could have done so only had he come safely through the Morimaruse, and on to Fomor. That would explain, too, why *Prydwen* was three times her fullness.'

'Because the rescued prisoners made up those numbers.' Morwen was beginning to catch some of Aeron's excitement.

Aeron noticed it. 'Nay, Taoiseach,' she cautioned with a laugh, 'you are to play anti-advocate for me; keep your remove yet a while, as loyal opposition.'

'As Your Majesty will have it. Oh but Aeron, it does fit so pat together!'

'It does, which is why we must take greater care than we might like in the glossing of it. But after that, I can make out no more at present. Where, or what, might be Uffern, or the horns of light, I know not.'

Morwen leaned back on the pillows and studied her friend's face. 'I am wondering,' she said after a while, 'what is this doubt I sense from you concerning the Treasures. And I mind me of something you did say back at the very start of this flight, before even we had passed the Curtain Wall.'

'And that?'

Morwen drew a deep steadying breath against the storm she felt sure was about to break over her head, and plunged in.

'You said that this time it was not like Bellator; that it would not be vengefulness to use the Treasures to save Keltia, or to win back the Copper Crown. If you truly think this, then why do you have this doubt?'

'For one who prides herself on being no sorceress,' said Aeron, her voice carefully casual, 'you can manage a clever piece of kenning when you put your mind to it . . . What is it you would know, Wenna? No gaudery on it; just let you ask straight out.'

'Well, then, remembering how it was with you after Bellator – where you yourself did admit you used your magic unlawfully to revenge – how can you be sure that your using the Treasures against Jaun Akhera is not a sin of the same degree, and will not bring down upon you a like punishment, or even a worse?'

Aeron's eyes met hers full on, and Morwen flushed

48

and looked away. 'There is not much could be more plainly put than that,' said Aeron evenly. 'Do you think *I* have forgotten Bellator, Lochcarron? That I have not thought of all this long since, and more beside?'

'Aeron, Bellator all but destroyed you. To give up your life for Keltia is one thing, and any of us would gladly do as much; but I will not have you give up your soul for it. And if that is the choice, by all the gods I will do whatever I must to stop you.'

The green eyes glinted. 'Would you? Well, since I will do whatever I must to achieve this errand, let us only hope you and I may never come to such a contest.' The eyebite faded, and Aeron's face softened. 'Ah, Wenna, you see how already things are twisted? But to answer your question, I do not know. To use the Treasures against Jaun Akhera may well be a worse sin even than Bellator, and it may also be that, in the end, I shall choose not to take the advantage the Treasures would surely give me, over the Marbh-draoi or any other enemy. But I will have that choice to be mine alone to make. My chiefest task – and yours while you are with me – is to find the Treasures and bring them home to Keltia. Once that is accomplished, it is another matter altogether, and I will deal with it when I must, and not before.'

Morwen nodded, but did not look at her friend. Presently she turned a page of Taliesin's book and pointed to the last verse of the poem.

'And this?' she asked. 'It seemed to me you liked not to read it. It is not like the other dwnedau.'

She had thought only to divert Aeron's attention from the ground of their disagreement to something less painful. To her astonishment, it looked almost as if Aeron flinched as she glanced at the page; in any case, she did not answer Morwen for several moments.

'Nay,' she said then in a quick, controlled voice. 'It is

not; rather, it is a prophecy, and for that it gave me pause.'

*More than pause, I think* . . . 'It speaks of a prison in the sea, seemingly,' said Morwen, pondering the words again as she spoke, 'by the malice of Pwyll and Pryderi, for one called Gweir. What ill can there be in that?'

'Pwyll – latterly the name is turned as Powell – and Pryderi are names traditional to heirs of the Dyvetian ruling house; as you know, the present Prince and his son are called so.'

'And Gweir?'

Again Aeron seemed to gather herself for speech. 'Gweir is an ancient short-form of the name Gwydion.'

Over the past months, Rohan, Prince of Thomond, heir-presumptive to the Throne of Scone, had spent nearly every waking hour in the same place: the bridge of the Keltic starfleet's great flagship, *Firedrake*. He left it only to sleep, and that briefly; his meals too were taken there for the most part, usually standing and always hastily.

He stood now near the viewport, watching the skirmish being fought off the cithóg side of the huge ship. Even as he watched, a brace of cursals harried the Imperial convoy that *Firedrake* was pursuing, and a Keltic destroyer overtook some slower-moving Coranian gunships, disintegrating a luckless straggler into a billion flaming sparks. Rohan was surprised at the wave of fierce satisfaction that swept over him, and thoroughly alarmed at the flavour of exultant righteousness that it carried. *By Lugh himself*, he thought, *but there will be no more of that* . . . Once rooted and growing, such an evil blossom would be near impossible to prune away. His sister had learned the same lesson, but at terrible cost; to herself still more than to others . . .

'Rohan? Cousin – '

Rohan spun around at the sound of his name and the surprise of the family appellation, stared blankly for an instant at the young man who stood a few feet away. Then he took two quick strides forward and enveloped the newcomer in an enthusiastic hug.

'Shane! You!'

Shane Aoibhell returned the embrace. Like Rohan, he was a greatgrandson of the Ard-rían Aoife: Their grandfathers, and Desmond's father, Elharn, had all been brothers, though Shane's grandsire Revelin was the only one of the four sons of Aoife who yet lived. Shane himself was a few years Rohan's senior, a few inches shorter, but otherwise the two might have been brothers themselves rather than second cousins; they possessed the same regular features, the same red-brown hair and hazel eyes, though Shane's were flecked with gold where Rohan's shaded to green. Of all the rígh-domhna, Shane's family branch were the least frequent visitors to their kinswoman Aeron's court, and he himself came least of all. Not even the historic arrival of the Terran probe ship had bestirred him to leave his own lands, and only Aeron's summons to him to take his seat on the Privy Council had brought him to Tara, where he had not long remained; by choice he lived a quiet country life on the planet Kernow with his parents and his young sister, Tanaidhe, and his presence here now boded ill.

'Ah, Shane, I can hardly believe it is you! It has been so long since you roused yourself from Sawnas – ' Rohan held his cousin at arm's length, then hugged him again. 'You look very well. Come now to my cabin; you must eat, and rest for a while, and we can talk privately there.'

Shane shook his head, following Rohan off the bridge into the turbolift, aware of the curious glances cast their way by kerns and officers alike, all of them wondering what was Shane's errand to his cousin, for only an urgent matter would have brought him.

'Rest must wait its time, and I am not hungry. My grandfather sends me, Rohan, and the errand has urgency. He had words for Aeron's ear, and now he bids me say them to you or to Gwydion . . . Sorry was I to hear of my uncle Elharn's death,' he added. 'Ríoghnach spoke of it to Tanai, and she told our parents. Is there news of Aeron?'

'There is not. Save for one brief coded transmission announcing their escape, we have had no word from either my sister or Morwen since they fled from Tara.'

Shane's face darkened. 'That is what my grandfather thought – feared, rather.'

Rohan touched a stud, and the lift doors hissed open. 'Does Revelin think that the Ard-rían was wrong to leave?'

Shane smiled slightly, hearing the warning: *Ard-rían*, not *Aeron*. 'Nay, not a bit of it. In truth, he would have liked her to have fled far sooner than she did. He thinks her conduct, in battle as well as after, was most irresponsible and careless of her own safety, far too much so for a High Queen. Which may or may not be true, but that is not why I have been sent.' They had entered Rohan's quarters on the main crew deck, and now Shane seated himself in a low chair and leaned forward, face troubled. 'You know that we hold, through Findabair my mother, significant lordships on Gwynedd and Dyved? Well then, my mother has heard from her rechtairs in both places certain very grave and very alarming rumours. She spoke of these at once to Revelin and to my father, and so I am sent to tell you.'

'What rumours?'

Shane set aside the quaich of ale Rohan had poured for him. 'Someone unknown has been making very probing inquiries into the loyalties and attitudes of certain of the more powerful Kymric lords. Into their social and financial positions, their warrior status and political affiliations and number of fighters under arms – and into whether they might not be entirely averse to a certain degree of collaboration with the Coranian.'

Rohan stared at his cousin, a wave of horror and disgust rising up that nearly dizzied him.

'You truly had not heard this?' Shane was saying. 'Nay, I see that you had not . . . Well, I am glad, at least, that one of the family was the messenger to bring this news. You will look into it?'

'I should say so! I will wish to speak to those rechtairs of Findabair's, and also I should like to contact Revelin. Who were the lords in question? I gather no one was able to learn names?'

'Unfortunately, that was the one thing my mother's retainers could not learn. And be sure that if they could have, they would have; their families have been in service to hers for generations, and *their* loyalties, at least, are beyond question.'

'Aye so.' Rohan ran a hand through his hair. 'It is the Marbh-draoi himself, of course. It can be no other.'

'His position on Tara is so uneasy,' ventured Shane. 'So he looks for collaborators on other planets?'

His cousin nodded. 'I should be interested to learn who it was that he has approached. I can think of a few possibilities myself, though I like not to think of it at all. But it was very well done, Shane, to come yourself; this was a matter better not left to transmissions.'

'Then how will you contact my grandfather and the others? You yourself cannot be spared from *Firedrake*, and I must return to my home – I would not leave my family alone in such a time.'

'Nay, surely not; return now, but I may command you

53

back in a time of greater need. If I cannot go myself, though, I know who it is that I shall send.' Rohan punched up the bridge on the cabin transcom. 'Rohan to Caradoc Llassar: a priority message to Desmond Aoibhell, at Glassary on Vannin.'

# Chapter Three

Camissa hurried purposefully down the long bright corridor leading to Elathan's study. She was dressed in blue silk girdled with silver, her black hair intricately massed at the back of her small head; her eyes were nearly the same colour as her gown. She nodded cordially, if a little shyly, at the many who drew respectfully aside for her, some even essaying small bows, or quick bobs too sketchy to be called curtsies; for though she was not yet Queen of Fomor, as Elathan's betrothed she merited more courtesy than previously – for now her affianced was King.

Knocking on the study doors, she went in unannounced. Elathan, who had been sitting brooding on the recently departed Imperial envoys, cheered up at once, and held out a hand to her.

'You took your time in coming,' he complained with mock annoyance. 'Your mantlemaker, no doubt, takes precedence over your King?'

She laughed and came to stand behind him, resting her chin on top of his head, her arms around his neck.

'Today she does, yes; it is she, not my King, who is sewing ten thousand pearls onto my wedding-cloak – at His Majesty's own request, I might remind him.'

'This is true . . . Well, will it be ready for our wedding, then, this over-decorated garment?'

'I think so.' Camissa sounded complacent. 'There are yet ten full months to the day; and sometimes I think ten minutes too long a time to wait.' She added, uncannily echoing his own earlier thought, 'Could we not go away for a few days, you and I, go south to the Mirregaith just ourselves? Belerion will be lovely right about now; it is just spring there – new flowers, soft weather.'

'That would be lovely,' he agreed, tempted anew. 'And we shall have many springs there, I promise. But for now, we must stay here in the cold, snowy Arregaith, and entertain – or endure – our guests. Also, it is too soon after – well, it is too soon.'

Camissa brushed her lips over the dark blond hair. 'Ah, love, I know; too soon after your father's death. But it is mostly for that I did wish to get you out of Tory, to have some time away to – to heal a little. You have endured much these past few weeks.'

He turned her hand over to kiss her palm. 'That was a loving thought. But private needs and sorrows must wait upon public duties – yours as well as mine. We shall have to begin to learn that a little better for the future. And there are so many offworlders here to pay their respects and present diplomatic credentials. I have to receive them all.'

'Spies, most of them, and very tiresome.'

'Undoubtedly spies, and exceedingly tiresome; but I must receive them all the same . . . How is my mother?' he asked suddenly, twisting in his chair to look up at her. 'I have not seen her for some days, and she does not return my messages.'

A peculiar quiver passed over Camissa's face. 'The Queen Basilea is still overwrought by your father's death,' she said. 'She prefers you do not see her until she is once again mistress of herself.'

Elathan looked alarmed. 'I had not realized her grief had so affected her. Perhaps I should go to her in any case – '

Camissa threw out a hand, caught it instantly back again. 'Nay, love, if you must know: My lady Basilea does not grieve, at least not for that her husband is dead.'

'I do not understand.'

'Elathan, she is not glad that Bres is slain, but neither does she weep for it. It is that which so distresses her: the fact that it does *not* distress her.'

There was silence for a long moment. 'I knew, of course,' said Elathan after a while, 'that my parents had not been close of heart for many years. Still, they were royal partners, sharing companions, parent-figures to all of Fomor.'

'And as such does the Queen sincerely mourn him,' said Camissa with conviction. 'But Bres the beloved is lamented by another.'

'Thona! Gods, I had forgotten all about her since the funeral – ' Elathan rubbed the big coronation ring upon his thumb; it was still so new as to not yet be part of his hand. All these years he had carefully kept it secret from his mother that that Lady Thona, Bres's legal concubine since before Elathan's birth, had been not merely the tolerated mistress of his royal father but someone who stood to Elathan as a much-loved aunt, or stepmother even, who gave him unfailingly and unstintingly all the affection and indulgence and understanding that Basilea could not, or would not, bestow upon him; and to whom he gave in return the love and trust his own mother turned aside.

And, for her part, Thona had put Elathan, son of the man she loved and his rightful queen, above her own son, Talorcan. Though Bres, to please his lady, had made Talorcan a legal heir, confirming his demiroyal status according to the Fomori succession laws, so that he stood in line to the throne behind Elathan and Rauni and their now-dead brother Tharic, Talorcan had grown up despising his father and detesting his half-brother: hating Bres for not marrying the woman he loved so faithfully, for tossing crumbs of favour to Talorcan as a begrudged

57

birthright; hating Elathan for being the right heir to the kingdom, for stealing the affection of Thona from her own son.

'I must go to Thona,' said Elathan, all thought of his mother vanished now, and Camissa nodded understanding. She alone among the Queen's ladies knew of the special relationship Elathan shared with his father's concubine. 'I have been so busy these past weeks – but that is no excuse at all. I forgot her, and I should not have.'

'She will understand.'

'She would, and a far worse lapse than that. But that is her special grace, and no apology for me.'

'Not even for the King of Fomor?'

'The King!' Then over the sudden blank surprise came the still more sudden remembrance that *he* was the King of Fomor, and he threw her a rueful smile. 'Especially not for the King . . . I will see you at dinner, lady.' He kissed her hand; she brushed her fingers lightly over his lips as if to capture another, and curtsied as he left the room.


When the door of his chamber was safely shut behind him, Talorcan motioned his companions to proceed through to the inner rooms; once they were all safe within he carefully secured doors and windows both.

That done, he turned to his guests with a smile. 'I will not waste what time we have, my lords, in social ritual. I tell you straightway that I know of the message that you, Emen Gaitz, and you, Chamara, have carried here – never mind how I know – from Alphor to my brother the King.'

Emen Gaitz, smiling gently, spread his hands and bowed. 'Most assuredly you do, my lord Talorcan; that is hardly a secret of state! We were privileged to convey the condolences of the Imperial family to the kin and subjects of his late Fomorian majesty Bres, and to present our diplomatic credentials to King Elathan.'

Talorcan's eyes hooded briefly in exasperation. 'Do I look like one of your tame apes? The message I speak of is the one entrusted to you not by Strephon but by his charming daughter the Princess Helior, on behalf of her son Jaun Akhera. You besought my brother, in Helior's name, to reopen the hostilities against the Kelts, as an assurance of friendship between him and Jaun Akhera.'

'Even if such a thing should be,' said Chamara carefully, 'I hope I do not offend if I ask what concern is this of your lordship's?'

'None at all, strictly speaking. Except that if one son of Bres has already declared himself no friend to the Imperium, that is no reason to expect a matching unfriendliness from the other.'

A little silence took the room. Emen Gaitz fingered the jewelled buttons of his coat. 'We took the liberty of studying you, my lord,' he said then, and his voice was subtly changed, 'before we came to this planet. Your personal history, your relationships with your father and brother, all such things.'

'How foresighted the servants of the Plexari!'

'If we wish still to remain their servants . . . But I think that the more accurate word would be "practical". The Emperor Strephon likes to be prepared for all possibilities however remote, and his daughter has naturally inherited his carefulness.'

Talorcan laughed in real amusement. 'Naturally . . . Well, let me make things as clear as I can, so that you may pass it all on to Her Serenity: There is no way in all the hells that Elathan will ally with Jaun Akhera. He fought our father every step of the way on joining the invasion of Keltia in the first instance, and the first thing he did as king was order our armies home – as you know.

There is no way he will change his mind, and no one who can sway him to do so.'

'The Lady Camissa?'

'Hardly! As far as politics go, there is not a pin's worth of difference between them. Besides, her enthralment is such that she would not sway him even if she could. No, what my royal brother wants is friendship with Keltia, and friendship with Keltia's queen.'

Chamara leaned forward, intent on the answer. 'Do you believe, my lord, that this theoretical and wished-for friendship could change into something more – active?'

'Such as military and political partnership? Nothing likelier. If Elathan does not stand aside completely from this war, then he will join in again; and this time he will be at Aeron's side as her ally, certainly not – as Jaun Akhera hopes – at her throat as her enemy. If nothing else, you may be sure at least of that.'

The two Coranians exchanged glances, and Talorcan peeled a pear with great show of unconcern.

'Would he try then, do you think, to sway the rest of the Phalanx?' asked Emen Gaitz.

Talorcan nodded, spoke round the mouthful of pear. 'Not only would he try, he would be far more successful at leading those sheep than ever Bres was.'

'Yet it will be many weeks, perhaps months, before Elathan is confirmed as Archon of the Phalanx. You know as well as anyone that quite possibly he may not be confirmed at all: The position is hardly hereditary, many other princes covet it and Elathan is full young for it.'

'Maybe so,' said Talorcan, unimpressed. 'But Fomorian kings have always had the odds in their favour, to be Archon, and Elathan is well liked by the rulers of many of the smaller systems.' He dipped his fingers in a silver bowl of rosewater and dried them on a silk cloth. 'I do not ask you to decide anything tonight, my lords. That would be premature in the extreme, not to mention potentially dangerous. But if you should find, upon consultation with each other and with the Princess Helior, that a guarantee of alliance – contingent upon proper Imperial support, of course – from the Fomorian king would be a thing worth having; and knowing that you will never get such a guarantee from the one who at present occupies the throne . . . well, I ask you to remember I am your servant, my lords, and my duty and respect to Her Serenity. – No, I think it would be best if you were to leave this way, by the garden-walks. Good night, and safe faring, to you both.'

Alone in his room, Talorcan allowed himself a wide and pleased grin. They would tell Helior of his offer, and, he was sure, she would at once perceive the possibili-ties, and accept. If she acted swiftly enough, he could be King of Fomor within weeks. And the new King would require a suitable consort . . . Talorcan's smile grew wider. Camissa would be Queen of Fomor, right enough; but, if Talorcan had his wish and his way, her King would not be Elathan.

Outside, in the dark gardens, the two figures passed quickly by, the sound and sight of them covered by wind and misty rain. When they had gone, the gardens stood empty again. Then a cloaked figure emerged from the little marble summerhouse, stood a moment looking after them, then watched Talorcan latch the garden-doors of his chamber after them and the shutters close off the lights from his room.

Within the shadow of her cowl, Camissa's face was troubled. After a moment, herself a wraith upon the wet mossy paths, she made her way back to the Queen's wing of the palace and her own chambers. She had come out

61

into the gardens in the rain to ease her mind of doubts; and had found instead only more questions to vex it.

But next morning all seemed well, and her fears and doubts as insubstantial as the mists of the night. Now there was only brightness, and the afternoon sunlight lay in golden pools upon the velvet in Camissa's lap. It was her wedding dress, in the traditional shaded blue worn by Fomori royal brides – palest water-ice at the throat darkening through flaxflower to indigo at the hem – and now she was putting gold wire stitches into the deep sapphire of the flowing train.

'And so you see,' she was saying, bending intently over the tiny golden flowers she was embroidering, 'I did not know quite what to do. I surely did not wish to bring it to Elathan . . . But the Lord Talorcan is your son, after all; and since I had no proof of anything, I thought it best – well, not *best*, but most acceptable of all the things I might have done – to speak first to you. Was I wrong to come here? If so, I am sorry,' she finished hurriedly, and lifted her face to meet Thona's sympathetic gaze.

Thona shook her head, then put a comforting hand over Camissa's, squeezing briefly and with real affection, before returning to her own stitching on another corner of the forty-foot train.

'Not for me were you wrong, child.' She was a handsome woman of late middle age, with light eyes and clear skin and a dancer's carriage. Her grey hair, unbound in the privacy of her chambers, was loose around her like a snowcloud, fine and soft and thick, falling nearly to her feet.

'No, Cami, you were not wrong,' she repeated. 'But what do you think my son may have been up to?'

'Who knows? Except maybe those ambassadors . . .' Camissa lifted her hands to shrug; the velvet, freed, slithered down over her knees to the floor. She hauled it up again, and wound the gold thread round her needle to stab the cloth for another Sintran knot. 'Beastly fiddly things . . . But they *were* the Imperial ambassadors,' she said, returning to her tale as if to another thread of her embroidery. 'I was not mistaken in that, and they were surely in Talorcan's rooms, and most surely of all none of them wished it known that any of them had been there.'

'Perhaps Talorcan merely wished to question them further on what they had said to the King earlier.'

Camissa looked up, surprise and compassion in her face, for that was the first time she had heard the Lady Thona call Bres's son and successor by the title that had been her lover's. But the even-featured face was sweet and strong in its repose, reflecting only her absorption with her sewing, and there had been no catch in the low voice.

Truly, Camissa mused, Bres's loyalty – indeed, his fidelity – to Thona had been remarkable. She had been his contracted concubine since the day she had turned eighteen; but, obedient to his parents' arrangements, Bres had wedded Basilea, making her his queen. The Lady Thona, outwardly unruffled, had countered in her own good time by producing Talorcan, a full year before Basilea gave Bres his legitimate heir in Elathan. And in all the years since, living in the same palace and in the same uneasy peace with Basilea, Thona had consistently turned aside all the Queen's growing spite and jealousy – *perhaps understandable jealousy*, thought Camissa loyally, for she liked Basilea, and had served her as lady-in-waiting ever since her arrival at court – with the sweetness and gentleness that had held Bres through a lifetime.

Yet strangely it had always been Elathan, child of the woman who hated her, who stood higher in Thona's heart than the child of her own body, and why that should be so – Camissa pushed the needle once more through the thickness of the velvet, stabbed her finger and swore mightily.

Thona laughed. 'Queens may think such things, but they may never, never speak them; no, nor kings neither . . . Get it all said now while you still may.' She folded aside her section of the train, coming back to the problem Camissa had laid, like the velvet, in her lap. 'Well, it is true my son is a meddler, and that he has been from a child; but he is not, I trust, a traitor and a plotter. Not that I do not think he could be so, if he chose to be, or were brought to it – You were wise to speak to me of this, and not to tell Elathan; I shall watch, and you as well, but no more than that for now. Things in this kingdom are far too unsettled for such dangerous rumours to be set afloat.'

'Has my lord been to see you yet, madam?' asked Camissa after a few minutes' steady quiet stitching. 'He told me that he would come.'

'And come he did.' Thona's face lighted with such a smile that the younger woman suddenly thought she understood, a little, why Elathan loved this lady better than he loved his own mother. 'And he was so gentle, and so very kind . . . I am to be allowed to remain in my own dear place' – she looked around her, a small wave to indicate the beautifully furnished chambers – 'by his special grace and favour. He will make a fine king, that young lord of yours. Bres, dearly though I loved him, could often be . . . well, no matter.'

'Has Elathan spoke to you of his wish for peace with Keltia?'

'He has, and I think I was never prouder of anyone in all my life, to hear him speak so.' Thona's countenance, bright enough before, suddenly blazed with the strength

64

of her loving pride. 'The thought that that ancient grievance might be put at last to rest, and that he could be the one to make that peace, for himself as well as for Fomor – the joy of that thought fills my heart.'

Camissa murmured hesitantly, 'My lord told me that there had been a private cause for the quarrel's beginning, some personal discord between his father and King Fionnbarr of Keltia, though he did not say just what.'

All the brightness died on Thona's face. 'I am not the one to speak of that,' she said, softly but firmly. 'Even Elathan does not know the true tale . . . If you wish to hear the truth of it, the only one still alive who may rightly tell it is the Queen Basilea.'

'The Queen!' Of all the names Thona might have mentioned, that one Camissa had never dreamed to hear, and her mind leapt giddily to impossible possibilities. She glanced again at Thona, saw with utter confusion that Thona had risen from her chair and was curtsying, head bent and hand to breast; and she turned round in her own chair. She was out from under the blue velvet, and curtsying herself, before she could even think about it.

Basilea, Dowager Queen of Fomor – widow to Bres, rival to Thona, future mother-in-law to Camissa – stood in the garden doorway, and on her face was no merry look.


When word had been brought to her of her husband's death beneath the sword of the Queen of Kelts, Basilea had received it in silence and stillness, only the momentary lowering of her eyes giving evidence that she had even understood. That regal control had not faltered, not even when – especially when – a fortnight later, the battered remnants of the Fomori fleet had begun to limp home, the flagship bearing both the dead King and the new King first among them.

Basilea had met the shuttle at the landing-field, and first of all in Tory had done reverence to her own son as he emerged from the craft. In the days that followed, and the months those days had since become, she had played her part as Queen-Dowager with dignity and dry eyes, at least for her people to see; but even her ladies marvelled that she did not lay aside that queenly stoicism in private, and allow herself to grieve.

But now that composure seemed well and truly broken, as Basilea looked long and coldly upon Thona and Camissa as they remained still dipped in court curtsies before her, not daring to rise until she bade them.

'A fine domestic scene, for the next Queen of Fomor . . . Oh, rise, the pair of you, it makes my head ache to watch you.' Basilea latched the door behind her, and swept past Thona to the seat Camissa held for her. 'So, my young madam, you have come here for the quality of the needlework? Or are there other reasons? Does my son know you are here?'

Camissa flushed, but spoke without nervousness. 'Majesty, he knows – and he also approves,' she added, unable to forbear the taunt and the petty triumph. She was meanly pleased to see Basilea briefly catch her lip between her teeth.

'The Lady Camissa felt the need of an explanation,' said Thona blandly, 'of the causes of the feud between his late majesty of Fomor and King Fionnbarr of Keltia.'

To Camissa's astonishment, if there had been displeasure and animosity on Basilea's face before, now there seemed to be guilt, and secretiveness, and, most amazing of all, a kind of furtive fear, in the look that the Queen-Dowager turned on the royal mistress.

'And did you see fit, my lady, to enlighten her?'

Thona shook her head, not looking at Basilea. *Deliberately not looking at her*, thought Camissa wonderingly.

'If there is need for the future Queen to know, then no doubt she will learn in good time. If not, are past bitternesses not best left in the past?' Thona raised her eyes to meet the Queen's, and what understandings, what history of compromises and tradeoffs and emotional barterings over the years, went into that glance Camissa could not begin to comprehend, and would have been embarrassed to try.

But Basilea seemed satisfied. 'Indeed they are, madam. Take care, then, you leave them there.' With a swirl of skirts she was gone, before the other two could move from their chairs.

After a long silent moment, Camissa dared to look again at Thona. And again she was astonished: On the older woman's face, as she gazed after Basilea, was an expression of purest pity, and on her cheeks were slow tears.

# Chapter Four

'The latest figures, Akhi.'

Sanchoniathon, for no other had been willing to accept the task, stood holding out to his brother a slice of clear crystal. It contained, as he had just announced, the most recent information on the Imperial position on the planet Tara, and the information was not good.

Jaun Akhera, who had ignored both his brother's words and the proferred computer-billet, raised his head at last, and, for all their closeness, Sanchoniathon quailed just a little at the look in the golden eyes.

'Despite your delaying tactics, yours and the good Hanno's, I have already seen them . . . Sancho, what am I to do? I have redeployed our legions here on Tara – several times, in fact; but we can barely manage to feed them properly. I have pulled such fleet strength as we still have into a ring to defend this system. . .'

'And it holds!'

'Oh yes, it holds – but Rohan jabs through it as the fancy takes him, then scampers away again before we can catch him.'

'One day he will overreach himself within our grasp, and we shall have him.'

'Maybe so. But until that hypothetical day, I seem to find myself lacking promising alternatives.'

Sanchoniathon sighed. 'Akhi, I do not know how to advise you. You have had counsel from all of us over the past weeks.'

'I surely have; very little advice, one way or another,

has *not* been given.' Jaun Akhera swung his chair sideways, to stare out at the sea beyond the windows. 'Well, I have made some inquiries in what I hope shall prove profitable directions. Also I have thought of putting it about that if Aeron does not return within a set span of days, or if, in her continued absence, Rohan does not give over the fight, I shall make an end of Gwydion.'

Sanchoniathon stared at his brother's elegant profile. 'Has your mind softened completely?' he whispered, aghast. 'Gwydion is the only bargaining counter we have.'

'We have the City – '

' – which its inhabitants have been quietly deserting, or had you not noticed how many fewer Kelts are abroad in the streets of the Stonerows these past weeks? In spite of curfews and patrols and everything else, they somehow keep finding their way like ferrets through the City walls themselves.'

'And we have the planet itself, where all those folk you speak of have dispersed themselves.'

'You know perfectly well,' said Sanchoniathon with considerable heat, 'that Gwydion's value is more than people and planet together. I like the idea not one bit, and surely it is a step we are very far from needing to take. Just now you mentioned inquiries you had made; what of those?'

Jaun Akhera's manner grew suddenly reticent. 'I do not choose to say any more of that just yet. As for the other, perhaps it *is* a step we need to take, to force Aeron's hand.'

'Even if she is still within our reach, which we do not know, she will never respond to simple threats and bullying.'

'Not if the threat were to herself, no, I agree that she would not; but neither will she suffer the thought of her

69

lord in peril . . . Well, perhaps you are right. But, Sancho, if I must spend him to come at her, I will.'

'I think,' said Sanchoniathon with slow distinct vehemence, 'that if you bring harm upon Gwydion it will be the worst mistake you ever made, and lead only to utter disaster in the end.'

Jaun Akhera looked up at him without lifting his head, and the skewed steady gaze soon had Sanchoniathon fidgeting with discomfort. But he could not leave until he was dismissed.

'You know you are always free to speak your mind to me, my Sancho; and your advice is, as always, well reasoned and most temperate. It is what I love you best for. But I have had enough of moderation, though, and when I require further advice of such a nature I shall ask it. Now leave me a while.'

The sun dipped, and above his head the frescoes faded, but Jaun Akhera sat on alone in the darkening room. In spite of what he had so blithely asserted to Sancho, he knew in his heart that such a threat as he had promised was no more than a pointless boast. There was no real reason, having spared Gwydion all these months, to put an end to him now. Sancho was surely right, and Aeron long gone from Keltia, far outside the reach of blandishment and intimidation alike. No reason at all – save vengeance, or pique, or the chance of providing an object lesson thereby for other obstreperous Aoibhells, like Rohan, or Desmond, or . . .

The thought of Desmond reminded him of something he had heard, and he tapped out a query-mode on the touchpad on the desk. Data filled the screen, and he paid it close attention: Sarah O'Reilly, Lieutenant, FSN, attached as communications officer to the probe ship FSS *Sword*; now known as Lady Sorcha ní Reille, knighted by the Ard-rían and latterly serving as Aeron's personal squire; rumoured to be romantically involved with Prince Desmond Aoibhell, son to the late Elharn . . .

Presently Jaun Akhera sat back again, and now he was smiling. Perhaps he was not so devoid of possibilities as he had thought. One Terran in Keltia – how hard could she be to find?


'I come if not as a friend, lord, then as an honest emissary,' Sanchoniathon was saying. 'My brother is growing desperate; as a swordsman you know that it is the opponent at bay who is the most dangerous, because he is the most unpredictable, and has the least to lose.'

Gwydion watched his visitor with no apparent emotion. 'What would you of me, Prince Sanchoniathon?' he asked after a while. 'As Keltia's First Lord of War I must surely be in favour of anything that chips away at Jaun Akhera's hold upon this kingdom. That has never been a secret. Am I to take it that you think by warning me of your brother's difficulty, I might be made to reconsider my attitudes? After all this time, do you read me so lightly?'

'No . . . no, I had not thought that. But Akhi – but my brother has other plans.'

'I do not doubt it,' said Gwydion. 'What he is doing is not new – and it will never be old.' He rose, and Sanchoniathon realized that he was being dismissed. 'But I thank you for the warning all the same. You may think it no compliment, but you are more unlike your brother than you know.'


In the long blue summer twilight of Vannin, Desmond and O'Reilly walked hand in hand along the shores of the sea-loch. Above them, the walls of the convent of Glassary receded slowly behind a frieze of ancient chestnuts. The air was cool for summer, now that the sun was low, and save for the lapping of the little waves on the stony shingle, all was still.

O'Reilly had spent the past few minutes in anything but stillness, weeping uncontrollably, in total, no-longer-to-be-resisted capitulation to the upheavals of the past four months: Desmond's presence, Desmond's absence, her enforced stay in sanctuary, all the griefs of the war. But Desmond had only listened patiently, evening her sobs with a comforting hand, and had led her down to walk by the edge of the water. The peace of the place and the strength of the arm had worked their separate magics, and now O'Reilly was calm again.

'Better?'

'Much. You are very patient to put up with me.'

'What, I!' She heard the laughter in his voice, dared not look up. 'Sari-fach,' he said, turning her to face him, 'think a little, I ask you, about what you have endured in the past quarter-year. Since Fionnasa, you have come to a foreign place, near a thousand light-years from your own home; have been subjected, for the first time in your life, to public curiosity, which is a burden even for those born to it; helped discover a plot of treason to which your friend and fellow officer Tindal was party; have seen your remaining colleagues return to Earth without you, Tindal executed for his treachery, your captain who was your dearest friend killed in battle and your new friend Aeron nearly killed as well; have yourself been sent to yet another strange world for protection against the Imperials who hunt you . . . All this, and you make excuse to me for a few tears?'

'Oh, well, if you put it like *that* – ' O'Reilly managed a shaky smile, and Desmond's heart soared to see it. 'One hates to be hysterical . . . But it hasn't been too easy for you, either.'

'Aye, but at least this is my home, and the trouble not

entirely unlooked-for. Had I been in your boots – sent as diplomatic officer to Earth, say, and things like to your misfortunes had befallen me there – no smallest doubt but that I would be weeping about it too.'

She smiled shyly up at him. 'You have been so kind and patient, ever since Tomnahara. I didn't think . . . I mean, they told me you were – '

'That I was not the easiest of folk to deal with? Well, that is true: It is hard for me with strangers, and I think it is so with you also. Not that I mislike making friends with new folk, but rather that I find it difficult. A few of my family have that trouble, though mostly not.'

O'Reilly laughed. 'So I've noticed. Is it because the Aoibhells are the royal family, that they have such confidence?'

'That is a part of it, but I think we are no more confident, as a family, than any other of the old Names. The assurance you see is more a function of belonging to a delineated, established group: the Clann, the Name. More that, I would say, than any supposed royal dignity; for even the ruler of Keltia is but first among equals in his or her own clann. Not all the Aoibhells are royal, you know; but whether Ard-rían or sea-crofter, each clann member is a full and equal partner in the clann's tradition and pride. It is a vertical distinction between Names, not a horizontal one between ranks.'

'Well, it's all way beyond me,' said O'Reilly. 'Shall we go back now?'

'A moment yet. I have a thing to say to you, Sorcha; you need not answer me at once, but I wish to leave the thought with you while you are here with the Ban-draoi and have peace and leisure to consider it fully.' As he spoke, he had let his arm fall away from her, and O'Reilly was paralysed anew with insecurity. But Desmond went on as if he had not noticed, so intent was he upon his own thought. 'We have grown close over the past months, and, if the idea does not mislike you totally, I would ask you to consider if you would wed me.'

O'Reilly, who was by now almost ill with apprehension, stopped dead at the water's edge and blurted out the first words that came into her head.

'I've had other lovers, you know.'

Desmond threw back his head and laughed. 'Well, of course you have. So have I, so has every Kelt of marriageable age. That is no real reason; not even, I would bet, on Earth.'

'You'd win that bet,' she admitted sheepishly. 'It was the only thing I could think of.' She looked out over the roughening water. 'What I really mean: I'm a foreigner here, a Terran, even if I am of Irish descent. *You* are a member of the royal family, a prince of the blood: grandson of a queen, nephew of a king, cousin to the Queen that now rules. What's your family going to say – what's *Aeron* going to say, to your alliance with an outworlder of dubious parentage?'

'Ah. I thought it might be something like that.' Desmond took her chin between his fingers and turned her unwilling head until she faced him again. 'Nay, look at me, Sorcha ní Reille . . . True it is that Aeron as Ardrían must give her fiant to any marriages of the ríghdomhna, but why do you fear what she will think, or do?'

'Desmond, she's the *Queen*!'

'Also she is your friend, who loves you dearly.'

'Enough to let me become a member of her family? I know how important family is to Kelts, even had I not just heard a lecture on clann pride.'

'If you wanted to marry *Rohan*, O'Reilly – Rohan who is at present heir-presumptive to the Throne of Scone itself – Aeron would give her loving blessing to you both, though I rather think she would draw the line at Gwydion

74

. . . You do not wish to marry Rohan, do you?' he added anxiously.

O'Reilly shook her head and leaned against him. 'Oh no,' she said in a soft voice, her face aglow with joy and shy pride. 'No, I surely do not . . .'

An hour later he was gone again, not even staying for the nightmeal; there had come an urgent communication from his ship – Rohan requiring his services for an errand he could not speak of even to O'Reilly – and Desmond had returned hastily to his orbiting destroyer, at the last moment putting his seal ring, with its device of a black bull, on O'Reilly's hand.

So now O'Reilly sat at one of the long tables that lined the four walls of the Great Hall of the convent, eating and drinking with a fine abstraction and an appetite to match. From the high table, Indec, with the sharp-eyed solicitude of an Abbess-mother, noted her charge's reverie but did not interfere. If there was a problem, let the lass come to her in her own time and way . . .

With a start, O'Reilly realized that the conversation of her neighbours at table had veered round to the endlessly interesting topic of Aeron. Not that it would have been abstained from out of courtesy to O'Reilly: A few of the Abbess's officers knew of Desmond's flying visits to the Terran they were keeping in sanctuary, but in the main the Prince had gone amazingly unnoticed, and the Bandraoi who was now speaking – one of the senior Sisters, living out a comfortable old age at Glassary – knew nothing of O'Reilly's various royal associations.

'All very well to have a young and dramatic Queen, but the folk like better to see family life at Court.'

O'Reilly leapt into it without even drawing breath. 'What could be more family than six brothers and sisters, and God knows how many aunts and uncles and cousins?'

'Oh aye, but they look for Aeron to produce an heir of her own; though of course the succession is more than assured, especially now with the baby prince just born to Eiluned and Kieran.'

In spite of her annoyance, O'Reilly smiled at the thought of the baby, born a fortnight ago on Caledon, to Aeron's brother Kieran and his wife, Eiluned of Garioch. They had only just heard the naming-announcement, though the baby's saining had been held a week ago: Conmaol Díolach, which meant in the Gaeloch something like 'avenging wolf-warrior'. What a thing to saddle the poor little weevil with . . .

'Oh, I don't know,' she said mildly enough. 'I expect there is plenty of time for that. Anyway, she has wedded Prince Gwydion, so that he will be King.'

Bronwen, a young novice who had been listening to the conversation with a mocking half-smile on her face, now looked openly derisive. 'So she has! The Prince of Dôn is no doubt a great and noble lord, but he is not an easy person, as was her first consort, the Prince Roderick. Now that was a bonny lord and a merry one, and the folk loved him dearly.'

'I have not heard that they do not love Gwydion,' said O'Reilly, feeling a certain grim irritation beginning to build.

'They respect him more than they love him, I think, and certainly they fear his might as a sorcerer,' offered another Sister, in an attempt to disfuse the sudden tension that had gripped the table in O'Reilly's immediate vicinity. 'And that may well be unfair – but they will come to love him in time as they do love Aeron.'

'Ah, Aeron!' Bronwen laughed contemptuously. 'Now we come to it – a queen who brought calamity upon her own people by defying the advice of her counsellors, then could not stay to mend where she had marred. A brave defiance, surely!'

'She defied Jaun Akhera bravely enough upon the walls of Caerdroia, and before that at Rath na Ríogh. I was there, and I saw it.'

'Oh, aye, she can be hard enough when she wishes; no doubt she looked very noble and splendid and above it all – like some queen of the Sidhe paying a visit to the kitchen-middens.'

O'Reilly suppressed a strong wish to stick Bronwen with the table-sgian. 'She did as she thought best.'

'She always does. And while she does it, no mortal and few Immortals can tell her a thing she does not want to hear. But all that family are stuffed full of arrogance; from the first days of Keltia, the Aoibhells have been afflicted with the traha, that overweening pride. Look at Fionnbarr, and Aoife before him, though Lasairían did much as Gwyneira bade him, or so at least it has been commonly held. For the truth of it is that not a soul but told them to go no roads with gallán, to stay behind the Wall; but no, they would not hear, and see now what has come of it. Ard-rígh or Ard-rían, the Aoibhells are pigheads to meddle with the stranger.'

'The present one isn't!' snapped O'Reilly.

'Well, and is she not? See where *her* traha has brought her: a price on her head and the scaffold ready waiting in the Great Square if she dares return, exile gods know where if she dares not.'

O'Reilly could hear no more without outraging the sanctity of the house with mayhem, so she stood up, bowed with barely controlled courtesy to Indec and stalked from the hall.

*Ah, hellfire!* she thought unhappily, kicking at the risers as she went up the stone staircase to her rooms. The traha . . . maybe Bron was right after all. Certainly she seemed to have history on her side: There was Fionnbarr's mysterious quarrel with Bres, pigheaded enough, that had cost everyone so dear in the end; years before that, Aoife's high-handedness against just about the entire known universe; much further back, Lachlan Aoibhell's genuinely pigheaded civil war, which had cost him his life and which in time had taken the lives of all four of his children as well; and now Aeron, who had heedlessly – perhaps even needlessly – risked her own life to avenge dead kin and a dying friend . . .

O'Reilly flopped on her bed, toes prising off her boots, her right hand toying with the necklace she never took off that had been a welcome-gift to Keltia from Aeron herself: a circle of golden shields enamelled with the Ardrían's own badge of a sword impaling the Copper Crown, her motto beneath in tiny letters of gold: 'My Sword Against the Thunder'.

Her eyes fell upon the ring, massive and reaching to the knuckle, on the midfinger of her other hand: Desmond's signet. O'Reilly began to smile, then the smile broadened to a grin and that became half-helpless laughter.

'Some family for a nice Terran girl to be marrying into.'


When Sanchoniathon, puzzled and troubled both, conveyed the request of Powell Prince of Dyved for audience with the Imperial Heir, Jaun Akhera laughed quietly to himself and agreed at once.

He had rather thought that his inquiries in that quarter would bear quick fruit. It had been the Princess Arianeira, of all people, who had first mentioned Powell's name to Jaun Akhera as a future ally, once Keltia had been secured as an Imperial vassal state under the Princess's rule. All that had changed, of course, but Jaun Akhera had not forgotten; so that when he felt himself forced at last to seek Keltic collaborators, Powell's was the first name that had come to mind.

To the casual considerer Powell would not have seemed a likely candidate for treason, but then neither had Arianeira . . . Jaun Akhera rehearsed what he knew of his possible confederate. Powell was lord of Dyved, Ruling Prince of the second most important planet in the Kymric system. More than that, he had been foster-brother to Gwydion's father, Arawn ap Kenver, and after Arawn's death twelve years since, Powell had thought to act as adviser to the Gwyneddan's widow and children.

But the bond had not held, apparently: Gwydion, now Ruling Prince of Gwynedd at the age of thirty, had been already too forceful on his own road to tolerate the interference of an older man, and relations had fallen off rapidly between the two ruling houses.

Or so, at least, Jaun Akhera had heard. He turned his mind from the tangled family affairs of the Gwyneddan royal house, and once more to Powell. Here in Aeron's own study, with Gwydion a prisoner in a tower not very far away, Jaun Akhera now awaited, with eagerness and curiosity in equal parts, the coming of the Dyvetian prince, remembering now that Powell had a son, Pryderi, much of an age with Jaun Akhera himself, who in the inbred and involved Keltic fashion had been a boyhood companion of both Gwydion and the dead Roderick Prince of Scots, Aeron's first consort.

He stretched catlike with anticipation. Perhaps this Pryderi would accompany his father: On balance Jaun Akhera rather hoped so; hoped too that they might get on together – it would be pleasant to have another friend in this terrible place. Again he allowed himself to wonder at the motives that had brought Powell to acceptance of the Imperial invitation. Whatever reasons Powell had for choosing collaboration, though, Jaun Akhera would learn them soon enough.

'May we enter, lord, to put the chamber to rights?'

Gwydion barely glanced at the two servitors in palace livery who stood in the doorway of Aeron's bedchamber.

'As you will.'

The Imperial guards on duty withdrew to stand beyond the door, well out of range of dust and ion-besom. For a few minutes there was silence in the room, as the servitors busied themselves with tidying the clutter and sweeping the broom nozzles over the stone floors. Then the woman-servant approached the bed, her arms full of fresh linens, and Gwydion withdrew to allow her to work.

He was just turning away when a low voice froze him into wary, and astonished, immobility.

'We are here to put more to rights than Aeron's rooms, Gwydion.'

He knew the voice at once, and it took all his control not to betray his joyful amazement. But he did not even look at her when he was sufficiently master of himself again to speak.

'See that you clean the stonework in the pool-room before you leave; you did not so last time, and it has grown slippery to the foot.' But his bardic finger-speech said very different.

*Sabia*?! *Is this truly you?*

'Indeed, lord, I will see to it.' *Oh, it is, Gwydion, and that over there doing so feat a job with the besoms is Grelun. We put a fith-fath upon ourselves that is no magic at all: Who would see Dragon and Fian, and your friends, in the livery of palace servants?*

Grelun and Sabia . . . In Gwydion's most sanguine fantasies he had never imagined so fair and fine a chance,

80

or one more to his liking: Grelun, his sword-arm lieutenant, Summoner to the Dragon Kinship; and Sabia ní
Dálaigh, First-rank Fian, and, after Morwen, Aeron's
closest and most loyal friend. *If I have these two with me,
what might not be managed?* In spite of himself,
Gwydion's smile broke like the sun; though, mindful of
the nearby guards, he quickly composed his features once
more to a mask of bored command.

'And, you over there, the casements too need cleaning;
they are all salted from the recent storms.'

Grelun bowed and went obediently to the windows,
and Gwydion turned again to Sabia, risking a swift glance
at her face, reassured somewhat by what he saw there:
strength, resolve, vivid intelligence, even a spark of love
of the danger.

*M'anam don sleibh, I am glad to see you two; but my
gods, Sabia, the peril you put yourselves in –*

*No time for that. We came only to get you out, my
friend. There are more than just we two in it, and we
would all dare far more than the Marbh-draoi to see you
safe. We have a plan – a desperate one, but the best that
we could manage. Listen, now . . .*

# Chapter Five

The moment he laid eyes on Powell of Dyved, Jaun Akhera knew beyond question that here was a man he could trust. If that seemed an odd thing to think of a traitor – well, Jaun Akhera had been betrayed by his own tools before now. Though he neither spoke of it himself nor allowed those closest to him to mention it, the memory of the Princess Arianeira's untimely repentance was vivid in his heart; but this man, it was plain to be seen, would harbour no such quicksilver remorses. Once decided, decided he would stay – no recriminations or recantations for him. And it would appear that the Prince of Dyved had indeed decided: not so much for Jaun Akhera, perhaps, as against Keltia, and against his fugitive Queen, and against his captive foster-nephew. His reasons for so doing – well, those were, presumably, what he now came here to disclose.

All this passed through Jaun Akhera's conscious mind in an eyeblink, as he watched Powell cross the room. The lord of Dyved was not a tall man, though he carried himself like one, with a compact, powerful build that on anyone less obviously athletic would have been described as stocky. His hair, worn shorter than was usual for a Kelt, was iron-grey, streaked and patched with the black-brown it had been in his youth; his eyes still kept their measured darkness. Pacing behind him, his son Pryderi resembled him hardly at all, favouring instead his mother, Aloïda, with curling gold-brown hair and blue-green eyes, skin tanned to the collarbone and the true Keltic paleness showing at the neck-edge of the silk tunic.

Jaun Akhera rose to greet them, giving Powell the straight-armed shoulder-grip used throughout the Imperium.

'Well met at last, Prince of Dyved.' He nodded past him to Pryderi, who bowed in return courtesy but did not speak. 'And my lord Pryderi . . . Will you join me in some refreshment?'

'I had your message, Alphor,' said Powell bluntly, seating himself before the ornate gold desk and gesturing Pryderi to stand behind his chair. 'I considered it, and discussed it with my son, and then came here to Tara. A thing somewhat tricky in the manage, what with the fleets between here and my homeworld; but, as you see, I have come.'

'You seemed to need little time for considering.' Jaun Akhera passed a gold platter of sweetmeats to Powell, who speared several with his sgian and ate them neatly off the point of the knife.

'Truly. You had done the same in my place, I doubt not; your ruler fled, your Throneworld occupied, your chief warlord hostage. I saw no future there.'

'And yet,' said Jaun Akhera smoothly, 'and yet I hear that Gwydion Prince of Dôn is lawful kin to you, your foster-brother's eldest son. I have been told to the point of weariness that such a bond is sacrosanct among your folk; how is it that it seems not to hold here?'

Powell gave a short unamused laugh. 'Goleor of reasons,' he said, wiping fingers and mouth and knife-blade all on the same silk napkin. 'Well, now. When Gwydion's father, Arawn, broke his neck out hunting, Gwydion was confirmed at once as Ruling Prince of Gwynedd, as was his right, and no one expressed either opposition or doubt. True it was he was very young for it – only just thirty – but he had reached his full majority at twenty-seven and did not have to suffer the guidance of a

regent. As his father's foster-brother, I took precedence
in his family over his next nearest male kin, who happened
to be his grandfather's brothers. Gwenedour, his mother,
for some reason took violent exception to this, though it
is perfectly clear in law, and she knew it as well as any.
Any road, she set her face against me, and she passed
her aversion on to her sons. Gwydion, though he listened
with great politeness to everything I said, paid no attention whatsoever, and went his own gait entirely in the
end, to do exactly as he pleased.'

'How well I know *that*,' said Jaun Akhera. 'Even so,
lord, howsoever much this may have rankled, it is surely
of itself not enough to bring you over to me.'

The shrewd dark eyes turned slowly upon Jaun Akhera,
narrowing as they studied him.

'Surely it is not – I choose to throw in with you because
I see no way Aeron will ever get her throne back again. I
doubt she will even return to Keltia, doubt even if she
still lives. And so, believing all this, I deemed best that I
should be one of the first to accept – how shall I put it? –
the new order.'

Jaun Akhera's face registered quick surprise at such
bluntness, and a kind of appreciation also, which modu-
lated almost immediately into his usual pleasant
expression, and he smiled.

'You are practical, Dyved; not, I think, a typical Keltic
trait.'

'Say rather a realist.'

'Well, no matter the semantics; in any event you seem
to have grasped the situation, and for that I thank you.
May I say you are almost alone among your people in so
doing – '

'Not for long, I think.'

Pryderi stirred restlessly behind his father's chair, and
Jaun Akhera's eyes went to him at once.

'You would speak, Lord Pryderi? Feel free to do so.'

'With all respect, Highness' – Pryderi's mouth quirked at the corners – 'though usually such disclaimer is only preface to genuine disrespect . . . Is it that you think my father is not entirely straightforward in his dealing with you? It seems to me you misdoubt his honesty.'

'Never that. But perhaps it is – a little – that I am not completely convinced of the strength of his new convictions. And – a little – that I think there has been here some selective editing of the truth, or at least of the facts. For instance, the facts concerning the Princess Gwenedour's sudden aversion to your lordship's company after the death of her husband. I have heard that, just possibly, she might have found your attempts at consolation a little – overzealous.'

Powell gave a bark of laughter. 'Ah, I should have known better,' he said, still laughing. 'Well seen, lord, and well put – and not even Gwydion knows those particular facts: Gwenedour never explained to him the reason for her sudden frost. He'd surely have called me out if she had done – and very likely he'd have won, and you would today be lacking a good supporter . . . But part of that realism we spoke of earlier is an honest appraisal of one's own position, and that, Highness, we surely share. You need me, Jaun Akhera, to consolidate your hold on what parts of Keltia you currently control, and to expand, as is doubtless your desire, to control more of it. And in that, Dyved could be a useful base from which to move out to the rest of Kymry . . . As for my part, I need you to consolidate my position in a changed and conquered and Aeron-less Keltia. The Ruling Princes of the Six Nations are, in law and in practice, sub-kings under the High Kingship of Tara; how can we maintain that rulership without one at Turusachan to rule us all? Whether that one be you, or Aeron, or

85

whoever, makes no differ to Dyved. That is not treason, as I see it, but expediency.'

'Let us call it so, at any rate.' Jaun Akhera's mouth smiled, though his eyes did not, and he rose from his chair. 'I have had my wings singed once by a Keltic – abettor, as you will have heard. You must forgive my caution, and understand how I must pick my footing with care.'

Powell nodded. 'I understand very well; my niece Arianeira was ever at the mercy of her emotions, whatever she may have liked to believe.'

Jaun Akhera, who had visibly started at the mention of the Princess's name, recovered himself with a strange smile. 'I had forgotten she too was of your kin.'

'Aye, well, kin only by fosterage – but a changeful habit is no trait of *mine*. I am your man, my lord, if you will have me.' Powell stood up, holding out his right hand, and Jaun Akhera grasped it eagerly between both of his.

'And you, Caradigion?' he asked, his glance going to Pryderi.

Powell's heir struck fist to shoulder. 'I am my father's to command, Prince of Alphor. If he is yours, then I am yours through him.'

'Good – very good. Now, Dyved, your advice on a matter. There have been two notable stones in my boot some months now, and I would attend to them before I am lamed altogether.'

Powell smiled in perfect understanding. 'We speak of Gwydion and Rohan, do we not?' he said. 'Well then, let us see what may be done to ease your step.'

'Have you read this?'

Rohan raised his eyes from the message that had been received by *Firedrake*'s signals room only moments

86

before, and which had been thought by the bards who
took the transmission to be important enough and sensitive enough for the High Admiral himself to bring it to
the Prince.

'I have, athiarna,' said Caradoc Llassar, his face grave.
'As did the bards who decoded it, of course. But no one
else has yet seen it, or heard its import. I came straight
here.'

'That is well,' said Rohan grimly. 'Come with me now
to my cabin, and let my cousin Desmond be summoned,
and Captain Chynoweth, and Donal mac Avera, and any
others you think good. Shane too, if he is arrived from
Kernow. We have heavy matters to speak of.'

'Will you meet him then?' asked Desmond.

In the small conference room adjoining Rohan's chambers were gathered some dozen people, all those whom
Caradoc Llassar had called there, and at Desmond's
words all eyes turned to the Prince.

'Aye, I will.' Rohan fingered the message tablet again.
It contained a communication from the Marbh-draoi
himself – Jaun Akhera, Imperial Heir, mortal enemy,
occupier of Caerdroia, jailer of Gwydion – asking for a
temporary truce and parley between himself and Rohan
as acting monarch of Keltia.

'It is almost certainly only a ploy: some delaying tactic,
or stratagem to learn our strength; but if it accomplishes
naught else for us perhaps it might serve to give us news
of Gwydion and how he is faring,' Rohan added. 'Though
I would give much to know what, or who, put this idea in
the Coranian's head at this time; I'll lay odds he never
thought of it on his own. Also there is, however unlikely,
the chance that he may genuinely wish to come to terms.
He and his folk must surely be feeling the pinch of hunger
by now.'

'Aye, well,' said Gwennan Chynoweth, the *Firedrake*'s captain, 'thank gods most of those who live in the City managed to get safely away out of it, so that they are not starving along with him.'

The others nodded in sombre agreement. Even the Imperial legions had not been able to halt the slow stealthy exodus of Kelts from Caerdroia. Like blood from a secret wound, they had ebbed quietly away by night, week after week, until now the City stood almost empty of all save Imperial troops. The Coranians had indulged themselves in some half-hearted looting, but by now, in dead of winter, food was of more desperate importance to them than gold or coin or jewels. That scarcity was thanks to the work of the strike-and-run skirmishers, Fian irregulars for the most part, who had remained on Tara to harry the Imperial supply lines, swooping down from their hidden bases high up in the valleys of the Loom.

'They did well to destroy the granaries and other foodstocks before they left,' said Denzil Cameron. Now Rohan's chief aide, he and his brother Struan had been two of Aeron's top generals in the fight for Tara. 'Though we shall have much to do after the war is over to get the stores back up again according to law.'

'Worry about the laws when we must,' said Rohan. 'What concerns me most now is Gwydion. Is there no way we can get him out? Fedelma? What say you?'

Fedelma ní Garra, another high-ranking Fian general, shrugged slim shoulders, and cast a guilty glance across the table at her commander, Donal mac Avera.

'We had reports, Rohan,' she said reluctantly, 'that some few of us stayed in the City itself.'

'"Us"! What "us" is this?' Rohan's eyes raked the room with all the laser sharpness of his sister's. 'Have you all gone *mute*? Mac Avera! Answer me!'

'Athiarna?'

Rohan spoke with barely controlled patience. 'Donal, what coil is this? *Who* has remained in the City?'

The Fianna captain-general drew his fingers over his moustache. 'Well now,' he said. 'When Aeron gave the order for the rígh-domhna and the war leaders to flee Tara, the Fianna and the Dragon Kin liked not to leave her and Gwydion and Morwen entirely under the power of the Marbh-draoi. So, some of us – stayed.'

'*Against the order of the Ard-rían?*'

Donal mac Avera was unrepentant. 'Aye so.'

'Who?'

'Of those we know for certain, Grelun and Sabia,' said Denzil Cameron. 'Also my brother Struan, and young Helwen Drummond.'

'*Helwen!*' Rohan was appalled. 'She's a child! A schoolmate of my sister Fionnuala!'

'She is young, to be sure,' said mac Avera composedly. 'But she is one of the most accomplished Dragons to come along in many years. Grelun is not Gwydion's Summoner and chief lieutenant for nothing, and Sabia has both long friendship with Aeron and much experience as a Fian to qualify her for this exploit. I need not speak of Struan's valour to *this* company . . . My sorrow to have defied Aeron's command, Rohan, but the fact remains that now we have four of our own – and our best – inside Turusachan with Gwydion.'

'I have a small feeling, mac Avera,' said Rohan, struggling vainly to suppress a smile, 'that this was thought of long before the City fell, and steps taken to assure it when the time came.'

'Ah, you would win that wager, athiarna!'

'Then an escape could indeed be carried out?'

Mac Avera leaned back in his chair, trying to interpret Rohan's tone and mind and wishes.

'Anything is of course possible, Rohan. As to likely, or

hopeful, or even advisable – those are hawks of quite another feather.'

'But you mean to try.'

'Certainly we will try,' said Fedelma. 'And if Arianeira had not got Aeron and Morwen safe away, we would have affected that escape as well.'

'Am I to take it that you *all* knew about this? That folk had disobeyed Aeron, and remained?' asked Rohan faintly, almost beyond surprise by now. *How had they dared; and how in all the hells had they managed to keep it secret . . .*

'Oh aye,' said Gwennan. 'Well, most of us did. It was not a matter we wished to burden Aeron with, she having things of far graver import upon her mind back then.'

Rohan laughed. 'Nay, of course it was not . . . And Gwydion? You have a stratagem for his escape all devised, I shouldn't wonder – some desperately neat-handed plan or other?'

'Goleor of plans,' said mac Avera happily, seeing that the storm was averted. 'When they deem the time is favourable, they will choose their best; only then will they make themselves known to Gwydion.'

'Chriesta tighearna, Donal, the danger – '

Mac Avera waved it away. 'Oh, danger, surely. No more danger than Gwydion has managed to live with for the past months. Where within the Bawn is there a place where danger is not, these days? Are we not in danger, here in *Firedrake*? Is Aeron not in danger, and Morwen with her, out there gods know where? Besides, those who remained in Caerdroia are all of them warriors, Dragon or Fian or both, and all most readily chose to do so. Indeed, we had many more volunteers than were needed; I have heard of no one who held back the offer.'

*As if that justified everything . . .* Rohan shook his head but did not speak. Across the table, Shane's face was dark with foreboding.

'It will march, Rohan,' offered Fedelma. 'You shall see.'

'I hope so,' muttered Desmond.

'Well,' said Rohan with sudden resolution, 'we can do nothing to help them from here. But perhaps if Jaun Akhera is thinking about a meeting with me, he will have less attention to spare for matters closer to hand. If that betters the odds for Grelun and the others, I would gladly parley with Jaun Akhera for no more reason than that.'

'We accept, then?' That was Shane, who had listened in silence this long time.

Rohan nodded. 'Aye, and you shall be my second, with Fedelma and Cameron. Arrange it with Jaun Akhera's agents; no doubt he will name his brother Sanchoniathon, his creature Garallaz and some other Coranian. Let it be fixed for some mutually acceptable area of space on the borders of the Throneworld system; he will not wish to venture too far from the only secure position he has, and we do not wish to creep too far within his jaws. Tell me what he offers in reply.'

When all had left the room save Shane and Desmond, Rohan sighed and stretched and smiled. 'How is it with O'Reilly?'

Desmond's grim countenance lightened. 'Very well, considering.'

'Considering what?'

'That she is fairly jigging with frustration – earth-nuts on a hot peel are nothing to it – at being forced to remain safe at Glassary while the rest of us adventure to our hearts' content.'

'Would you wish to bring her aboard *Firedrake*? She is a skilled communications officer, and could be very useful; and if it would make you both less fretful – '

Desmond shook his head, though a little reluctantly. 'Nay, she is better off remaining with the Sisters. At least I can be sure she is out of danger there, and not overly unhappy. Indec tells me she has even begun to learn a little magic.'

'What a surprise for Aeron, when she returns,' said Rohan, laughing.

'I have more of a surprise for Aeron than that: I have asked Sorcha to wed me, and she has accepted.'

Shane, who had not met O'Reilly during his brief sojourn at Caerdroia and who had only the barest idea of whom his kinsmen were speaking, thought he had never seen Rohan look so surprised, or so delighted.

'That is fair news indeed, and Aeron will surely think no less.'

Desmond looked steadily at him. 'She *will* return, Rohan. Never doubt it.'

'I know that, cousin. But in the meantime – ' Rohan stood up, and so did the other two. 'Tell Gwennan that her curragh goes now to Droma. We may wait upon the Marbh-draoi's word, but that is no reason to lean upon him the less lightly while we do so.'

# Chapter Six

Tinao was feeding the white birds that lived in the chori-gardens when the door to her chamber swung open behind her.

'Serenity!' Much surprised, Tinao gave the Emperor's daughter the deep obeisance due her rank as princess and her position as Jaun Akhera's mother.

'Rise, child.' Helior laid a light hand on Tinao's bent dark head, then, with much the same gesture, stroked the soft plumage of one of the tame birds, and the creature raised its head-tuft in pleasure at the touch.

From under lowered lashes, Tinao studied the Princess's slim straight-backed figure, the nervous fingers, the elegantly rigid shoulders below the golden collar.

'May I offer you the hospitality of the household, madam? Fruit, sweetmeats, something cool to drink?'

Helior shook her head, the dark hair moving like water over her shoulders. 'Nothing, I thank you. I wish to talk to you. Sit by me.'

Tinao obeyed at once, crossing the room with sinuous grace; gathering her stiff silk skirts beneath her, she dropped onto an ivory stool at Helior's feet.

But the Princess did not speak at once, watching closely the lovely kitten-face lowered with such demureness.

'There has been word from my sons,' she remarked at last, almost casually, and was interested to note the sharp fearing attention Tinao at once accorded her.

'Not bad news, please Auset.'

'Not bad, though not good either; but it is hard enough to get news of any kind out of Keltia, so I am grateful for whatever may come . . . Sancho has been leading raids into the hills near the Keltic capital, to burn out resisters and their hiding-places. It seems he was slightly injured on his last foray.'

Tinao kept her face carefully empty of the sickening fear that jabbed hot irons from within. 'Madam, you said the news was of both your sons?'

'So I did.' All at once Helior wearied of tormenting the girl. 'Do not fear, Jaun Akhera is well. He remains in the City, in no better – but no worse – case than before.'

Tinao's eyes fluttered briefly closed in relief so great she came near to collapsing. She glanced up at Helior, who was again petting the white bird.

'Then he does not ride out as does my lord his brother, in his own person against the Kelts?'

'He does not.' Helior met the dark eyes turned so imploringly up to hers. 'You will have heard, as who has not in this whispering-gallery of a palace, that my Imperial father has refused to send my son any further assistance: no troops, no fleets, no funds.'

'Madam, I had heard.'

'And?'

'It is not for me to question the wisdom of my Emperor, though it seems hard.'

'Nor is it for you to evade the questions of your Emperor's daughter. Do you truly love my son, daughter of Tenjin?'

A blush suffused Tinao's honey-gold skin. 'Serenity, I do; not just for that he is Imperial Heir and shall one day come to be Emperor, but for that he is – '

'For that he is Akhi,' said Helior, but she was smiling. 'I, as his mother, am of course interested to know how you do see your own future with him. Since he has been officially named etcheko-primu and my father's successor, he must one day take a wife worthy of so exalted a rank.

94

Not that your own bloodlines are not ancient and noble ones, of course, but perhaps not quite what might be required of a future empress.'

Tinao's curved ivory nail-shields dug briefly and violently into her palms, leaving little red crescents in the soft skin, but her face remained serene.

'That may well be, madam; but the Cabiri emperors since our very beginnings have also in their wisdom taken co-wives to suit their hearts . . . as did Your Serenity's own father.'

*Well, I asked for that*! thought Helior. But in truth she was glad to know that the girl could both think when challenged and snap when threatened. Both talents would be extremely useful in a secondary wife . . .

'Well said, and I ask your pardon. So, you wish no more than to be my son's left-hand consort, giving place – for all the Imperium to see – to his right-hand Empress?'

'It is as honourable a rank, if not perhaps so public a one. So long as his Empress gave place to me for him to see, what matter if she shares his throne, if I share his bed? My heirs would be just as lawful as hers – but I think I know my lord well enough to say that my heirs would be his only heirs, and I the only one to share his nights.'

'Nicely argued,' said Helior. She brushed a gentle finger over Tinao's cheeks, then stood up, and Tinao rose and fell again in another curtsy. 'You have been open and honest with me, child; I like that well, and I expected no less from the lady my son has chosen to love. So well do I like it that I shall make you a promise. We shall speak again quite soon, you and I, for there is a thing you may help me in – a thing to be done for Akhi – and, in return for your help in that, I will perform what is needed to see you as my daughter-of-love.' She looked down at Tinao with an affection she had not shown

95

before. 'I should like to see my son wed to good political advantage, that is only sensible. But equally I should like to see him take a wife for himself. My father did suggest that the Keltic war could be brought to swift and happy conclusion if Jaun Akhera would wed the Keltic queen' – Helior felt rather than saw Tinao's uncontrollable movement of revulsion and denial, added smoothly, 'though I would sooner see him bed a harpy as that one . . . We have spoken enough for now. I will send for you.'

*Daughter-of-love*, thought Tinao when the Princess had gone. A title reserved for co-wives, not principal consorts. In all truthfulness, though, she had never had any particular wish to be Empress, even had her birth-rank permitted such a possibility, and she was as alive to the sense of such matters as was Helior herself. What the Princess had all but promised was perfectly acceptable to Tinao – more than acceptable – and she hugged herself with pure happiness, hands running up her arms inside the big square gold-embroidered sleeves of her tekka.

A wave of sudden loathing knifed across her mood. So Strephon had suggested Akhi wed Aeron Aoibhell . . . *She is fair enough, I suppose, and a queen besides, but I would see both of them dead and bleeding at my feet first . . .*

'Oh, Akhi,' she breathed aloud, and one of the white birds ruffled its feathers at the sound of her voice. 'Take care, I pray you; take care.'

The *Marro* sliced outward through the Throneworld system the same way she had entered it all those weeks before. Indeed, the flagship's commanders had dared take no other route: For all their efforts, the Imperials had still not managed to break the bardic military codes that would have enabled them to read the mine-maps for this sector of the Bawn; and already on this supposedly peaceful voyage to parley several escort ships had been lost. Hyperspace was likewise denied them, as it had been on the original voyage of invasion, and so the sail to the agreed-upon coordinates, above the plane of the system, was taking the Coranians longer than it had the Kelts, who were free to sail as they pleased.

And it had pleased Rohan to take his shortest way there; so that when the *Marro* came at last to the meeting-place, *Firedrake* was before her. The Keltic ship lay like a great golden dragon couchant in a lair of stars; but a dragon that lay with all its eyes open and watchful, and if it could have lashed its barbed tail, it would have.

'I hate that ship,' said Sanchoniathon, staring balefully at it through the viewport on the bridge's port side.

'I am myself not overfond of it,' agreed his brother, fastening his collar around his throat and slinging on a pleated cloak over his space-armour. 'With luck, or the favour of heaven, we may not be obliged to look at it very much longer.'

Sanchoniathon shrugged, then, as the words registered, turned a horror-filled glance on Jaun Akhera.

'Akhi, you have not got some treachery toward, have you?'

'What, against the *Firedrake*? Certainly not; no, Sancho, nor against Rohan neither. There would be no point, and precious little percentage. I meant only – well, no matter what I meant. Where is Gwydion?'

'Waiting under guard in the main landing-bay. We will go by shuttle to a derelict space-station that cannot have been sabotaged in advance by either the Kelts or ourselves. Garallaz and I have arranged the thing with Shane Aoibhell and the Fian captain Denzil Cameron. The station has been scanned, transgraphed, macrowaved and strobe-probed, and to the best of our knowledge it is safe.'

Jaun Akhera smiled at his brother. 'If you say it, it is so.'

'I like it not,' said Hanno, who stood with the princes on the bridge.

'You have said that before.'

'And I say it again. Is it truly the best arrangement we could make?'

'Yes, Captain-General, it is!' snapped Jaun Akhera, and instantly regretted the lapse of control; he was as apprehensive as the rest of them, perhaps even more so, but his rule was never to let it show. 'Come,' he said, and now his usual mask of poise was back in place. 'Let us call upon Rohan.'

The small space-station, little more than a bruidean or travellers' halt for ships bound to and from Tara, showed everywhere the scars of recent and terrible attack – smashed viewports like spider-stars, huge beams cracked and blackened by laser fire – but the atmosphere was intact and breathable, the gravity still functioning.

Jaun Akhera stepped out of the flexible umbilical and through the airlock into what had once been a lavishly appointed reception area. He was followed by Gwydion, moving with his customary unhurried stride. Sanchonia-thon had remained on board the *Marro*; accompanying Jaun Akhera as seconds were Garallaz, who once before had served him as emissary to the Kelts, a vassal lord called Hurca-mendi, and Inguari, a grizzled general who had been close friend and comrade-in-arms to Jaun Akhera's late father, the overreaching Phano.

In the centre of the adjoining room was a round table, its surface reasonably free of debris. Jaun Akhera swept the dust off a chair with the hem of his cloak and seated himself, motioning Gwydion into the chair on his left.

A very few minutes later, there was a hollow heavy

thud, and the entire station seemed to shudder a little. All knew well what it was: Rohan's shuttle had docked.

He came through the same door the Coranian party had used, nodded once to Jaun Akhera. His gaze moving on, Rohan hesitated almost imperceptibly at the sight of Gwydion, whom he had not expected to see, then took a seat across the table from Jaun Akhera. Shane and Denzil flanked him – Desmond, like Sanchoniathon, had remained on the flagship to command in case of treachery – and Fedelma ní Garra faced Inguari at the door.

'Well met, Prince of Thomond,' said Jaun Akhera easily. He accepted Rohan's equally brief return civilities, studying the Prince with careful attention, for they had never before met in all the months of fighting. During the invasion of Tara, Rohan had been aboard the *Firedrake* serving with his great-uncle Elharn, and had had no part in the fall of Caerdroia or what came after.

*Obviously an Aoibhell*, thought Jaun Akhera, *though he bears only the most superficial resemblance to his sister; well, physically, at least* . . . Jaun Akhera let his head incline slightly to the left.

'Only by means of a threat to the remaining people of Caerdroia, Rohan, do you behold His Highness of Gwynedd so biddable.'

Rohan glanced sharply at Gwydion, who returned the look impassively, his face giving no message that any there could read. Except, perhaps –

'So I see,' said Rohan after a while, as one who had indeed received plain-worded tidings.

Had he? Jaun Akhera wondered. The Kelts and the Coranians both had common ancestry from Atland – root cause of the long, long hatred – and one of the talents both races had inherited from that far-past time on Earth was the gift of telepathy. Not words, as such, but rather the conveyance from mind to mind of image and mood and feeling and emotion; a sense-picture rather than worded thought, though those who were trained to it could not only transmit words but hold conversations. And Gwydion and Rohan had been close friends, members of each other's family, since boyhood; easier for them, no doubt, to read each other's thought than a stranger would find it. But if those two *had* managed to exchange a message . . .

Jaun Akhera put it aside, turned to the matter at hand. 'I suggested this meeting, Rohan, to discuss the possibility of our coming to terms. In spite of your best efforts, your fight is at a standstill. And, in spite of all our best efforts' – he threw Rohan a smile full of charm – 'so is mine. I thought perhaps we might be able to come to some sort of political settlement beneficial to us both, without regard to the current, or future, fortunes of battle.'

Rohan leaned back in his chair, its metal frame creaking faintly as his weight shifted. On the edge of his vision, he was aware of the scowl on Garallaz' face, the small smile on Gwydion's.

'I cannot see how,' he said politely. 'Any conditions you might suggest would have to be accepted by Aeron as Ard-rían, and that is of course hardly possible now.'

'Or by Your Highness, as acting sovereign,' suggested Garallaz eagerly.

Rohan affected innocent astonishment. 'There seems to be some slight misapprehension here. I am *not* acting sovereign. Did you truly not know?'

Jaun Akhera felt as if he had taken a step that was not there. 'Let us play no games, Rohan,' he snapped, concealing a rising terrible suspicion. 'You are heir-designate of Keltia, Tanist by Aeron's own decree. If you are not lord by law in Aeron's absence, who then is?'

Rohan let his gaze slide to Jaun Akhera's left. 'He sits beside you.'

'*You*?'

Gwydion bowed slightly. 'I. I thought surely you knew.'

'Instruct me, then!'

'You were informed, I think,' said Rohan, 'that Aeron and Gwydion had been set handfast to each other? – Aye, so we thought. Well then, in the absence of further ceremony, our succession law holds that pledge binding. Gwydion has been, in fact and in law, King-Consort of Keltia since the day you invaded.' Rohan allowed himself a quick malicious grin that flashed over his face and was gone before Jaun Akhera saw it. 'A long way to come, maybe, to learn this.'

'Oh, be not disingenuous with me, Aoibhell!' Turning to Gwydion: 'You might have made mention of this sooner, Gwynedd. Back at Turusachan, say, and so spared both of us a tiresome trip. So it is you I should be speaking to, then, regarding terms of accommodation?'

Gwydion drew a hand across his bearded chin. 'It is, but even I could accept nothing that would not require confirmation by the Ard-rían of Keltia. And to draw her back here to accept those terms, you would first have to lift the sentence imposed on her and Morwen, and to release me, and to raise the siege of Tara, and to convey all this information to her, wherever she might be, and get her to believe that you truly meant it. Even then, very like she would refuse. Doubtless she has plans of her own.'

'Spare me your irony, Gwydion. We both know full well that Aeron would return in a minute if you called her, and that she would honour any bargain you and I succeeded in striking.'

'Not if I bade her refuse.' Gwydion smiled, for the room had gone very still. 'I can do so, Jaun Akhera; and, Rohan, forgive me but I *would* do so . . . And Aeron would hear me; and hearing, she would obey. Be very sure of that.'

In spite of his anger, Jaun Akhera could not forbear a choke of laughter. '"Obey"! *Aeron*?'

Gwydion nodded composedly. 'It happens not often, I admit, but even Aeron can be commanded in good time; commanded even against her own inclinations and wishes, by one she trusts. Believe that she would obey such a word; believe still more that I would give it.'

The silence was broken presently by Rohan. 'Before we leave this place, Prince of Alphor – for leave we soon must, and I doubt that we shall meet again – I would give you a word of cautioning. Your intrigues are not the secret you think them. I advise you to put no trust in untried horses; very often on such beasts the saddle slips round at the first hard gallop, for they have blown out their girths, and the rider will be off.'

'I do not wish to speak in riddles,' said Jaun Akhera coldly, though he was inwardly appalled. Did these Kelts know everything, then, that passed even in his secret councils?

'Very well so, if you will have it . . . We have had word of your intrigue with certain Kymric lords, whose names I will not defame by mention here: that you have sought their treasonous collaboration.' Rohan carefully kept his eyes away from Gwydion as he spoke. This was the information he had so hoped to be able – somehow – to convey to his friend, the only point and purpose, as far as Rohan was concerned, of this whole travesty of a parley . . . Though, in spite of Desmond's best efforts, he had no more proof now than when Shane had first brought him the news, still Rohan believed, as he had from the start, that the rumours were pure truth; and daring a quick glance at Gwydion he saw that his friend thought so too.

Jaun Akhera, after that first terrible sinking moment, had recovered himself. Rohan's professed reluctance to name names argued less a desire not to dishonour lords of Keltia than an ignorance of such lords' identities. Powell and Pryderi had not been discovered just yet, and perhaps all was not in ruins after all. But he would speak sharply to the Dyvetians upon his return: This farcery had been all at Powell's urging, and no mistake but that Rohan had benefited far more from it than had Jaun Akhera . . .

'That is a damnable lie, Prince of Thomond,' he said, voice clear and precise. 'I came here not to be insulted with unproven tales of subornation and subversion, but in honest proffer of a peaceful settlement between us. Though I have heard,' he added with sudden spite, 'that many of the folk of Tara have come to believe that Aeron will never return to Keltia.'

'That I will never believe,' said Gwydion; he spoke lightly, but his eyes had darkened to storm-colour. 'She shall return, and in her return is your downfall.'

'That the event shall prove.' Jaun Akhera turned again to Rohan. To his surprise, the Keltic prince was smiling. 'This amuses you, Rohan?'

Rohan nodded, and let his grin widen. 'You seem to have little luck with the Aoibhells in parley, Prince of Alphor. I was but thinking of Rath na Ríogh, where you and Aeron had so mutually instructive an exchange . . . But since we speak of things unpleasant, I daresay I need not remind you, Jaun Akhera, of your starving garrisons in the City, or the patrols sent out to forage in the farmlands of Strath Mór who do not return, or those who do return but only in small bloody pieces, or the dwindling numbers of the ship-tally of your armada. Nay, I think you know these figures quite as well as do I. But let that stand as my final word and offer to you, and you may pass it back, if you can, to your so politic grandsir: It shall only grow worse for you. And when Aeron returns – well, my sister can speak for herself, and she will, and sooner than you think.'

The silence this time was long and charged; at the door, Fedelma tapped her fingers upon the hilt of her glaive, and Inguari looking back at her never moved a muscle.

Then Jaun Akhera: 'That may be. But plainly you and I have no more to say to each other. Except that I give you a word of caution in turn: Remember, Rohan, that Gwydion comes back to Caerdroia with me . . . When our ships are both beyond the truce-radius from this place, all will pertain as before, and I for one would have it no other way. Aoibhell, Cameron, I bid you farewell. We shall not meet again.'

Rohan was on his feet. 'Gwydion –'

But his friend's grey glance crossed his in warning, as steel crosses naked steel in salute. Then Gwydion was gone from the room, and his captors with him.

As their shuttle raced back to the *Firedrake*, Shane, piloting the little craft, swore quietly and continuously and evilly to himself. Rohan, in the chair beside him, threw his kinsman an amused look.

'I am sure I am every bit as vexed as you, cousin, but truly you expected nothing else?'

'Nay, nothing else! And nothing less either!'

'Well, perhaps you would have handled things differently.'

'Aye so! And I would have begun by smearing the *Marro* across the stars like flaming clouds!'

Rohan was not surprised. 'And Gwydion with it?'

'I love him dearly, Rohan, but he would be the first one to urge that course upon us, and you know it.'

'I do, and that is why we shall not.'

'Rohan – '

'No more, Shane! I am in no mood for a family brangle!'

Such a likeness to Aeron in a temper came down over Rohan in that moment that Shane, who had indeed been eager for words, bit back a grin and turned his full attention to the controls.

'Still – ' said Rohan, after a few minutes of silent consideration, 'you are not far wrong. We cannot leave him any longer under the hand of the Coranian. I fear what Jaun Akhera may do, either in anger or in vengeance, now that he is full aware of Gwydion's true importance in the kingdom, and that we ourselves are aware of his attempts to suborn our own princes. I think that time mac Avera spoke of is come.'

'That is a thing good to hear,' said Shane. 'But as you yourself did say, Rohan, it was a very long way to come to hear it.'

# Chapter Seven

Alone again in her cabin, Aeron rubbed her palm absently over the worn leather binding of Taliesin's book. So frail a blade this, that she must wield against catastrophe; so small a hope to stake such greater hopes upon. She permitted herself a moment of doubt that she would never, for all their loving bond, have allowed Morwen to see. What if she had been wrong, what if she had in her boundless arrogance and overbearing presumption misread what was written, misinterpreted the words of guidance that had been given her? The *traha* had ever been the tragic flaw of the Aoibhells, but was it not hubris beyond even the *traha* smugly to think herself immune to it?

It was true enough that the King of the Shining Folk himself, Gwyn the son of Nudd, had sent her on this road, telling Gwydion to bid her remember the lost Treasures of Keltia, and *Prydwen* Arthur's ship. Still and all, that did not mean that the Treasures were on board *Prydwen*, or that she was free to use them even should she find them: She had merely assumed and decided, in her pure conceit, that such had been Gwyn's meaning.

Not that anyone else was like to have a better idea than the King of the Sidhe of the Treasures' whereabouts, or their very existence. No trace had been found of them in Keltia in all the fifteen centuries since Arthur had gone away forever, and since Taliesin, Arthur's friend and Morgan's lover, had written his great works.

'"Except seven, none returned from Caer Coronach . . ."' Caer Coronach: Castle Death-song. Taliesin had been among those seven, the only ones of all Arthur's sluagh to survive that last voyage to see Keltia again. None of them had afterwards spoken any word of the latter end of Arthur and his company and his ship; they had resumed their own lives, returning home to their kin and their duties, joining together only once again, to found the Dragon Kinship. As for Taliesin himself, he lived with Morgan until the day she died, and then he cloistered himself in Seren Beirdd and began to write, in praise and in memory of Arthur and Arthur's sister, and he wrote of nothing and no one else until his own life's end. Words of singing lightning; histories of Arthur; accounts of Edeyrn and the Theocracy; the great *Life of Morgan*, who was even then known as Morgan Magistra, and who was now, fifteen hundred years later, beloved and besought in prayer as St Morgan of the Pale; and finally, at the end of that long life, Taliesin's work of greatest mystery, Preithi Annuvin – The Spoils of Annwn – known in the Gaeloch as *The Harrying of Hell*.

And it was straight for that hell that Aeron and Morwen now were heading . . . Aeron took the little book between her hands, rested her chin upon its gilded top edge. Despite all her plausible words to Wenna earlier, she had more doubts about the rightness of her quest than she was at present prepared to admit even to herself – especially to herself. It was right to seek the Treasures, Gwyn would not have sent her after them otherwise; but he had not ratified the corollary of that quest: that, having found the Treasures, Aeron should then have licence to turn them as weapons against Jaun Akhera. Nay, *that* she alone had decided, in her righteousness or in her traha she did not know: and she could as readily *un*decide, if so she chose. But the finding, surely, was what mattered most.

From out of the air came a sudden surge of rightness

and reassurance that swirled around her like an eddy of summer wind, a knowledge that she was following precisely the path that had been put down for her, and her lips parted in an incredulous smile at the strength and joy of the feeling. All at once she was filled with the proud certainty that not only would she and Morwen survive this journey and fulfil their errand, but also they would return to Keltia, and return in triumph too, no matter the snares and traps and springes that lay in the road. Their path was sure. They had only to walk it.

Suddenly ravenous, Aeron took a warm pastai from the wall-hearth and ate it much too quickly, barely savouring its taste, aware of it as fuel rather than food; sipped at a steaming cup of shakla to follow. Unbidden, her thought leapt light-years: to where the *Sword* was on course for Earth, its passengers wrapped in the blanket of coldsleep; her sister Fionnuala, her friend Straloch, her new friends Hathaway and Mikhailova. She had grown very fond of those two Terrans, though she had been closer to O'Reilly, and closest of all to Theo . . .

At the thought of Haruko she smiled, though her eyes had gone suspiciously bright. Perhaps, as he had wished with his last breath, he was already reborn as a Kelt; maybe even as a member of her own family – Kieran and Eiluned's baby was due about now, perhaps already here. For a moment she entertained the idea of herself as the reborn Haruko's aunt . . .

Her thought flipped yet again, to the Protectorates. Her cousin Kerensa had been hastily dispatched there when the Imperials first invaded, to remind those governments of the terms of their treaties with Keltia and to gather what help she could. It would have taken some time to contact all the Protectorate homeworlds, and there would not be much help forthcoming; but even a little was better than none, and with luck all casts would roll out together: help from Earth with Straloch – or rather, the promise of help, for a promise was all she had asked for; help from the Protectorates with Kerensa; and the help she herself had gone to seek, from wherever she must go to find it.

'"Thrice the freight of Fairface were we that went with Arthur . . ."'

'Aeron?' Morwen's voice over the transcom was strangely flat. 'I think you are needed up here.'

Aeron was in the command cabin not a score of seconds later. 'What is it?'

Morwen nodded out the front viewports. Ahead of them lay their first certain destination: the Morimaruse, the giant electromagnetic maelstrom that was the terror of this sector. There were others like it scattered throughout the galaxy, though none so vast or so violent, and the Morimaruse had an evil reputation that its fellows likewise did not share. It was a galactic graveyard for unwary or unlucky starships, and for their crews also: a slow rolling mass of dustclouds laced with flashes of sullen incandescence, a score of light-years edge to edge, its eddies of swirling dust and planet fragments troubled incessantly by soundless stellar concussions, like the summer lightning that is seen but not heard.

Aeron's mouth tightened briefly, but she made no other sign and took her place at *Retaliator*'s controls.

'It will be well, you shall see.' She spoke as much to herself as to Morwen. 'Arthur went into it without a guide and without a choice, and he came safe out again. We have both, and we will come safe out as well.'

Despite her optimism, it took all of Aeron's considerable skills as a pilot to bring them to a place where she thought it least perilous to enter the Morimaruse. According to tradition, Arthur had last been seen heading towards the sea from the direction of the great space battle at the Roads of Camlann. Aeron had therefore calculated his most likely trajectory from that place, and it was this course they had been following all these weeks. But if her skill had brought them there, it was now her daring that was demanded . . .

'Well, then.' She and Morwen exchanged a swift look, and then they were into the Morimaruse.

It was as if they had crossed an inchoate boundary into a universe of dust; all navigational sensors were blanked out as the stars went dead around them, hidden by the thickness of the roiling clouds. They sailed blind for a time; but then, the deeper they went, the more often they began to cross the thin winding lanes of clear space between the sea's spiral arms, and Aeron quickly learned to orient herself by the brief glimpses of the heavens above and below the plane of the clouds.

'Three times the fullness of Prydwen were we that went on sea,' murmured Morwen, looking straight ahead, and Aeron felt an echo, warm and cheering, of that peace that had earlier visited her in her cabin.

'If you are right about the poem, Aeron, we should soon come to the first of the caers.'

'If I am right.'

The ship bounced alarmingly as the space around it was rocked by a nearby explosion, and Aeron fought to bring the craft back under control.

'This is a place where stars are born; it seems they are conceived in as much turbulence as humans.'

'And in as much beauty also – look there.' Morwen pointed out the deosil port, to where, unguessable distances away, an eddy of the spiral had begun to coalesce, falling in upon itself, drawing in closer and finer to glow in the dusty dark. Its contraction had made a clearing about itself, and the light of the nascent star bloomed faint pulsing radiance, like the tinna-galach that danced at night on the marshes of Gwenn-Estrad.

The clouds swallowed up the light behind them as *Retaliator* plunged deeper into the void. They had been going many hours now, for in there they dared travel only at sublight speeds. The clouds around them grew thicker than ever, and far up ahead an astrostatic storm was raging.

Morwen regarded it expressionlessly. 'Do we go into that?'

'Gods, I do hope not.' Aeron's face was showing the strain, physical as well as mental, of holding *Retaliator* to her course; it was no easy line that she had taken, and even the knowledge that she was following Arthur afforded her just now little comfort, and no peace of mind.

'Will you take something to eat or drink? You cannot go on so.'

'I dare not just yet; later, perhaps.'

'Aeron, before very much longer you will fall over at the helm.'

'Then fetch me some appropriate drug to make sure that I do not! Dubh-cosac will do, or that hellbrew Slaine concocts of water-elm and slán-lus . . . Do it!' she snapped as Morwen hesitated, though never glancing away from the screens. 'And do not think to slip me a draught of soporific either; if I fall asleep now we will – '

Her voice broke off. Morwen's head snapped round to her, then her gaze followed Aeron's out the front port.

All around them the clouds had thinned without warning. *Retaliator* was nosing now through the last veils, dust like blowing smoke. Beyond, there was open darkness, with stars above and below, a clearing in the shifting clouds that stretched many star-miles ahead of them, like the eye of a terrene storm.

Aeron had forgotten her fatigue, and was pushing the ship forward as fast as she dared.

'This is surely the place,' she said, voice hushed. 'And we perhaps the first humans to come here since Arthur himself.'

Morwen was as entranced, peering ahead into the spangled blackness, then down at the sensor boards.

'*Is* it the same place, do you think? Will not the clouds have shifted over the years?'

Aeron finished setting the long-distance sensors to pick up any trace of solid artefact, and shook her head.

'Fifteen centuries is the briefest instant inside such a thing as the Morimaruse; it moves all at once around its own axis, and it will not have changed overmuch in so short a time. As for its being the right place – we must find that out as we do go.' She arched her back and shoulders in an aching stretch, and gave Morwen a tired, but happy, smile. 'I could eat now.'

In the deeps of the Morimaruse, *Retaliator* hung motion-less on the edge of the Eye, as they had come to call the eerie lacuna amid the endless dust. Worn out by the effort of getting them thus far, Aeron had finally acceded to Morwen's pleadings and the demands of her own body; she had eaten and drunk, and now she was deep asleep. Morwen had stayed on watch a while, then had done the same, leaving the ship on automatic, hove-to and space-anchored in the void.

Waking suddenly to the sensation of ship-motion beneath her, Morwen rolled over and up off the couch. A quick disbelieving glance at the chronodials set beside the door: nearly fourteen hours since she had fallen asleep. Coming into the command cabin, she saw Aeron back at the helm. All the strain of the previous day was gone from her face, and the green eyes were beryl-bright with excitement.

'Look, Wenna,' she said without prologue. 'The sensors found this in the night.'

Morwen leaned over Aeron's shoulder to read the screens. Plainly, *something* was out there . . . 'What is it, then?'

'Something too small and lacking in density for a planetary body, though very large for a ship.'

'*Prydwen* was large enough – nay, the Coranian flagship!'

'So I think. Or else some derelict, dragged in by the tides.'

'So massive a craft as that would never have foundered like a curragh. However it came in here, it came by design.'

'Ah, but whose design?'

'There is only one way I know to find out.'

Aeron smiled. 'That is what I was so longing to hear you say . . . Set your chair-restraints on full.'

Distances were deceptive in the Eye. They came upon the mystery ship long before they expected to, and Aeron at once sent *Retaliator* into a sweeping reconnaissance circle around the giant hulk.

Coranian, and no question; the lines and armaments bespoke her provenance without a doubt. In her prime, she must have been lovely indeed. She was not lovely now: Ugly black scorches scarred her flanks, jagged furrows ploughed across the once-sleek hull plating, and parts of her life-support enginery had been shot clean away.

Morwen had seen something. 'Move us closer.'

Aeron obeyed: *Retaliator*, responsive as always, rose up from beneath the foreign ship like a dolphin nosing in inquisitively beside a torpid whale. Then she saw what Morwen had seen: On the outer hull below the bridge housing, half-burned away by long-ago lasers, the Coranian ship's name was blazoned in chelofused paint. She had been called the *Marro*.

Aeron pulled herself carefully along, hand over hand, through the snaking attacher tube that extended from *Retaliator* to link the two ships. Both she and Morwen, who followed after, were encased in skiaths, the close-fitting pressuresuit-forcefield worn in hard vacuum, for they could not be sure of finding atmosphere or gravity inside the Coranian ship.

But for the moment, mere entry was the difficulty: The outer doorseals of this earlier *Marro* were rusted and pitted with the wash of a millennium and a half of interstellar dust tides.

Coming up to the spacedoors, Aeron ran her fingers along the edge of the airlock frame. Fused solid, or so it seemed: If she could not find the touchplate she would have to cut through the door, or even through the hull itself, with the small laser handsaw; and even if she did find the mechanism, there was no guarantee it was still operational.

Morwen caromed gently into her. 'Over on the right.' Within the confines of the skiath, her voice rang thin and metallic in Aeron's ear.

Aeron laid a gloved hand in the palm-shaped hollow, almost invisible under the rough patina of rust, and put arm-strength behind it. After a long moment, there was a grinding vibration, and then, inch by slow inch, the spacedoor moved aside.

They stepped through onto the Coranian vessel. Morwen glanced down at her belt-probes: They had been right to rely on the skiaths, for the atmosphere was exhausted of oxygen, and there could well be viruses or other plagues that the probes could not detect. But the gravity was intact, and that meant the ship's power-train was functional: a good sign.

As they walked cautiously along the wide companionways, they saw all around them vivid evidences of the last moments of the flagship's crew; and what they saw affected them deeply. Morwen, who had never thought to feel for any Coranian anything but cold loathing, found herself moved to pity by the sight of these lost ones, their poor dried bodies still as death had found them, either in the privacy of their cabins, alone, or sitting in the common areas with small groups of their comrades. They had not been cowards, either: Knowing themselves doomed, soon to be waterless and foodless and airless, lost beyond hope in the Morimaruse, they had to a man chosen a swifter way home. Coming upon them so, in the final attitudes of their lives, their Keltic foes of fifteen hundred years later paid silent, and ungrudging, tribute to that last quiet courage.

Picking their way like cats through the rusted rubble, they came at length to the bridge. Here, at the ship's heart and head, all seemed at first glance oddly untouched by disaster: uniformed crew still at their posts, lights still blinking – after fifteen centuries! – upon the consoles, and, in the centre of the command deck, the captain himself still in his chair. But as they came closer, the illusion shattered, revealing the dry leathered skins, the clawed hands of a thousand years and more of mummification.

Aeron had been as unexpectedly touched as Morwen by the sight of the Coranian dead; had been moved enough, indeed, to place a silent blessing upon the ship and those who had sailed her – could not harm, might yet help – and now she felt almost as if she had violated some long-protected tomb, some sad hallow sealed away for eons against the tears of time. Years had gone by outside, the stars themselves had shifted in their places, but here these had remained. Though they had been enemies, they had been brave ones; their valour in the end needed neither prayers nor tears of hers to ratify their passing. Yet her logic did not unblur her vision for many moments . . .

Presently she reached out to touch Morwen's shoulder. 'The captain will have left some record, surely,' she said. 'Look among the wallbanks, and I will search the command console.'

She found it almost at once: a thickish crystal rectangle, hand-sized, its interior milky with the data that had been inscribed into the lattice of its molecular structure.

'We must try to run it here,' suggested Morwen. '*Retaliator* has no facilities compatible to such an antique.'

Though she was no computer expert, and would herself have been the first to admit it. Morwen was certainly correct on that count: In the fifteen centuries since this system was new, computer science had evolved almost beyond belief – Keltic computers were capable of original thought, and could be communicated with by telepathy – and by present-day standards the Coranian crystal was hopelessly old-fashioned.

'We can try,' said Aeron doubtfully. She inserted the crystal block into a likely-looking slot in the console beside the captain's chair. There was silence, then the lights dimmed briefly as the long-idle relays came back on-line.

Upon the main viewscreen, a flickering picture was suddenly projected, and they whirled in alarm, hands to weapons, at the unexpected motion, then relaxed a little sheepishly. Though blank in places, for the crystal lattice that held it had deteriorated over the years, the picture was remarkably clear, and they unconsciously straightened to hear the last words of the man who had been Arthur's last Coranian enemy.

He was tall, even though he sat in his command chair for the making of the taped record – even as he still did: black of hair and eye, with the golden skin of a native of Alphor, his face strong-boned and pleasant to look upon. Proud he appeared, and intelligent; calm in surrender, yet not altogether resigned to calm acceptance of the fate he had elected for himself and for his crew; yet not broken by it either; and Aeron found herself wishing that she might have known him in life, and in friendship. Then, over the transcom link, his voice came down to them across the ages.

'I, Jaun-Zuria, son of Errazill and Lsaura, Lord of Vidassos, captain of this Imperial ship *Marro*, leave these words for those to come by them who may. If you are friend, that is good. If you are enemy, that is also good, for my folk and I shall soon be past all such distinctions alike. But, foe or friend, I would ask whoever hears my words to spare, of your honour, a thought or a prayer to our gods and your own.' ('Already spared,' murmured Aeron, and Morwen's eyes closed briefly in compassion, for the Coranian's voice had cracked in pleading.)

But it continued at once in calmness. 'We came into this most evil place by no means unwilling. It was the *Marro* that led the great armada against the kingdom of Keltia and its Wizard-king, Arthur of Arvon. It was he, in his ship *Prydwen*, who locked with us – each dragging the other into this dust-hell, two lions with their fangs fastened in each other's throat. Yet *he* broke loose at the last' – the voice betrayed bitterness, and Aeron's fingers clawed into Morwen's forearm – 'and he escaped, leaving us too crippled to crawl home to lair. We could not even get a message out through the dust, to cry a rescue; and

117

he knew this would be our fate. So, rather than wait to die parched and choking in the dark, we have elected to take our own lives. We shall not destroy the ship, but leave her, and us within, as a marker and a sign, and perhaps in time we shall be found, and so not perish utterly from the memory of the world.'

For the briefest moment, the calm expression shattered, and all the anguish showed clear: for his ship, for his crew, for the homeworld he would never see again, for gods knew what family and friends he had left behind, who would watch for his homecoming in vain – pain and defeat, anger and sorrow, but not for himself, and not one atom of fear. Then the mask was back in place.

'Let you know we did our best. If you are Coranian, you will see that; if you are Kelt, you will have felt it. There is little more I can say, or wish to. But whether it be to you a matter of vengeance or triumph, let you know that Arthur did not escape unscathed. He was a worthy enemy, whatever else he might have been, and we know only that he has gone on to find his own fate at Fomor. As for you – the choice is yours. Follow him, or follow us.'

The screen went dark, and the transcom was suddenly silent. In the great stillness Aeron spoke to the empty screen, spoke across the widening chasm as the centuries rushed back between them, to the empty shell in the chair beside that had housed so brave a soul; spoke as she had spoken to the dead Haruko, and to the dead Roderick, and to her dead parents, the confident and beautiful assurance of the Keltic death-ceremonial.

'Bydd i ti ddychwelyd.' "*There shall be a returning for thee*" . . . She turned to Morwen with a face that shone like the sunrise. 'Then let us follow Arthur.'

# Chapter Eight

'Pardon, Ambassador, but there is a ship approaching on the starboard bow.'

Haco Grex, first Terran ambassador to Keltia, put down his antique silver eating utensils, wiped his lips with a napkin and reached over, with a sigh of regret for the perfectly cooked meal, to activate the transcom.

'Identify.'

'Ensign Alessio, sir.'

'The *ship*, Ensign.'

'Oh. Sorry, sir.' The voice sounded as if its owner were biting the insides of her cheeks in mortification; then, surprise succeeding the embarrassment, 'It seems to be one of ours, sir.'

'Ours!'

'Getting a reading – the diplomatic probe ship *Sword*, sir; Admiralty registry number 7568-DGW, Theo Haruko, captain.'

Grex drew an elegant finger over the neatly trimmed grey beard he had allowed himself to cultivate for this assignment. Among the welter of thoughts that were flooding his brain, one fact stood out with blazing clarity: The *Sword* was the ship that had found Keltia. The ship that had made first contact, only a few months ago, with the Kelts, a race of terranic origin three thousand years ago; and that contact was the reason Grex was now on his way to the Keltic throneworld of Tara, and the court of Aeron Queen of Kelts. But why the *Sword* was here, more than halfway out from Keltia and apparently on an Earth heading, he could not imagine. All his old military instincts were suddenly alive and prickling. *I don't think I like this much – they shouldn't have left before I got there, and they weren't called home either, or the Admiralty would have told me . . .*

'Send them a wake-up call, if they haven't already got one from their ship – they'll have been in coldsleep for a couple of months by now, and they'll need some time to acclimate,' he said presently. 'And match their trajectory to bring us to rendezvous point.' Before he went any farther on his way to Keltia, he was going to get a very much better idea of how things in fact stood there. After a moment's thought, he pressed a button, and the young officer who served him as aide entered the cabin from the office suite next door.

'Excellency?'

'Tell the consuls that I wish to see them.'

The aide looked surprised. 'Is there a problem, sir?'

'Not that I know of.'

When the officer had gone, Grex returned to his dinner, nibbling absently at the excellent baked fish. Well, if there *was* a problem, the sooner his two chief subordinates knew about it the better. He had chosen them himself, for the particular needs of this extraordinary mission; good, solid, dependable, loyal people, with a high degree of perception and just the right amount of flair, whom he intended to push for all they were worth in the weeks ahead.

But no harder than he intended to push himself, of course: He had been a diplomatist forty years now, serving as and where the governments in power had seen fit to send him. On Earth, the planetary diplomatic corps had evolved over the centuries into a service unit largely independent of partisan politics, and Grex's talents had been universally prized no matter who had chanced to be head of state. Unlike most other top-level officers, Grex had come to his position out of an unusual combination of circumstances and experience: academics – he had been chancellor of a great university – and the military, in which he had begun his career, rising to be one of the youngest ressaldar-generals in history. Though he had not come up through the ranks from a young embassy officer as had most of his peers, Grex had the wit and the confidence to surround himself with polished professionals, and he was afraid of neither title nor talent. Witness his personal choice of consuls for the Keltia assignment, for instance; and he had also been a major designer of the probe ship programme, in which his old friend Theo Haruko had apparently played so historic a part. Grex smiled; he would have to tell Theo so when he saw him; there was probably even a major decoration in it for the *Sword*'s captain . . .

For the moment, though, there was little to do but wait. Grex braced involuntarily, and unnecessarily, as he felt the ship beginning to throttle back, dropping down again into space-normal for the rendezvous; then the sensation of drag vanished as the stabilizers compensated. Well, the crew of the *Sword* still had to wake up; and whatever trouble they were bringing, or fleeing, could wait till then. He would have time, after all, to finish his fish.

On pretext of taking the evening air, Gwydion stood on the turret walk outside Aeron's rooms. Behind him, in the solar, Sabia and Grelun were again at their sham drudgery – and their deadly mission, for their errand to him this time was already achieved. As they had brushed past each other only a few minutes ago, Grelun had given him a message in bardic dichtal: The escape attempt would be tonight, in the owl-time hour past midnight.

Gwydion moved a few yards along the parapet, followed by two watchful guards, and sat down on Aeron's little stone bench. As Sabia had admitted, the plan was desperate enough, even for a desperate situation: Under cover of a Fian berserker raid on the front gates of Turusachan, Gwydion and his rescuers would escape down the face of the perpendicular cliffs that overhung the sea below Caerdroia on the west. There they would be met by others aiding the escape, but more than that, Grelun had not said; out of concern either for time or security, Gwydion did not know.

So he conducted himself according to his usual custom: bathed, and read, and ate his nightmeal under the eyes of his guards; and when the summons came at last, he was deep asleep, for once unplagued by dreams. He woke suddenly and completely, to the touch of another's mind on his.

Sabia, clad in the camouflage black of the Fianna, stood by the bed. Two dead guards lay in the doorway where they had fallen, and as Gwydion hastily dressed, arming himself with the weapons Sabia had brought, he could see the bodies of more Imperials beyond the door.

Faint to his ears came the sound of sudden battle: Out at the palace gates, the raid had begun. He half-turned to it, but Sabia's eyes flashed him clear warning, and he followed her out onto the turret walk. As he emerged into the windy dark, three friends came out of the shadows, to greet him with the small grave smiles of feelings that ran too deep for easy mirth: Grelun, Struan Cameron, Helwen Drummond.

He returned their smiles, clasped forearms briefly and silently with Struan, then laid a detaining hand on Sabia's shoulder.

'There is a thing or two I must fetch; a moment only.'

Before she could protest, he was up the outside stair to

Aeron's chamber of magic. Crossing the slate floor, he knelt respectfully to those who watched over that place, then closed his hand over the emerald ring, its stone the size of a kestrel's egg, that was the Great Seal of Keltia. Aeron had set it there, arcanely protected, before fleeing Caerdroia on the first leg of her desperate journey beyond the Curtain Wall. He slipped it now onto the smallfinger of his left hand – *no rings on your sword-hand*, came, inevitably, the old Fian dictum as he did so, and he might yet have to fight before the night was over – and picked up from the altar the other thing that had rested there: the small horn of old gold, coelbren characters etched around the bell, that he had received from the hand of Gwyn himself. Fixing the horn to his belt in a pouch of waterproof leather, he closed the bronze doors behind him and rejoined the others at the base of the stairs.

Sabia was in a fret of impatience. 'I know what you went for, Gwydion,' she said in a voice taut with tension, as the four slipped silently down the outer stairs and into the gardens. 'But no more delays. We are waited for below.'

She led them expertly through the garden-maze, gliding like a footless ghost through the dark, straight to the cliffs that rose up sheer out of the sea more than half a lai below. Suddenly she dropped from sight, as if she had vanished into some pocket in the air itself, and Gwydion, though he knew where she had disappeared to, could not suppress a spasm of vertigo: Aeron could stroll about unconcerned on the lip of a precipice, but Gwydion was one of those who had an active horror of heights, and he had dreaded this moment from the moment he had heard of the plan. But there was nothing else for it. He took a deep breath, touched Aeron's Dragon medallion that hung against his chest, then followed Sabia over the edge of the cliff.

A rough-cut, narrow path snaked its way down the face of the rock, slippery with salt and sea-wrack flung up by the giant waves that came to their long journey's end against those coasts; it was this uncertain and perilous path that Struan and Sabia had argued for as their best way out of Turusachan. But tonight the waves were quiet, only a whisper reaching Gwydion's ears from below. From above – well, there was as yet no cry upon their trail, so perhaps their flight was still to be discovered. *If the Coranians are too busy at the palace gates* . . . Gwydion's mouth tightened at the thought of the Fians and Dragons dying even now to cover his escape, but he could do nothing for them: nothing save to get himself safe away, such was the only thing they asked of him.

Heart pounding with the exertion of the long downward scramble, Gwydion leaned for a moment against a rocky outcrop; then a dim form came into view below him, and he tensed at once, every muscle prepared for attack.

He relaxed again almost as swiftly: The figure before him was a merrow, as Helwen, on the way down, had told him it would be. Of middle height, the merrow was in shape like a human, though slimmer and shorter and lighter of build; but that was where the resemblance ceased. Its skin glowed red as a ruby even in the faint light of the Criosanna, and the coarse, stiff, mane-like hair was the green of sea-foam over sand, or the green of the great kelp-fans that sway like ferns in the tidal swings. And the eyes – the eyes like the inside of an oyster-shell, iridescent as nacre, filled with all the mystery of the wild waters.

The eyes met and held his. 'Quickly, lord,' said the creature, and its voice too was clear and wild. 'The tide is almost at the full.'

Gwydion leapt down to join – him? 'As quick as I can . . . I am Gwydion ap Arawn,' he added.

The sea-being smiled with piercing sweetness, and the pearl-eyes flashed whorls of colour in the dark. 'I know, and I am called Cumara.'

"*Hound of the Sea*" . . . 'My thanks, Cumara, for the risks you and your folk take for me.'

The merrow waved one graceful web-fingered hand. 'Are not the Moruadha Kelts as much as any others? We are something limited in warfare, save in a sea-fight, but at the least we can serve the Ard-rían – and the new King – in this. Also we liked not the Marbh-draoi's overtures to us, that he thought we could be bent to do evil, at his bidding, against Aeron.'

Gwydion chose his footing with care, and pitched his voice with urgency. 'The Marbh-draoi has tried to suborn the merrows?'

Cumara nodded. 'He sent emissaries to Kernow to speak to our chief, and it would not surprise me to learn that he had tried a like tactic with the Sluagh-rón: to set both our races against humans. But Faruane, he who is Morar-mhara among our folk, sent the Coranian camurs about their business. The Three Peoples are not so easily divided.'

Gwydion was silent again, though now with more than merely the strain of the descent. Rohan's information had been correct, then; or at least some of it, since Jaun Akhera had apparently attempted the merrows and the silkies. *Aye*, he thought, *and who else might he not have attempted? Worse, with whom might he have succeeded*?

He turned his head to look behind him on the path for Grelun and the others, and the movement probably saved his life, for a laser bolt flashed past him not a foot from his head, drilling a neat smoking hole through a granite boulder.

'They come hard after,' called Cumara from a little way below. 'We must dive from here.'

Gwydion felt chilled with more than just the cold spray that beat up from beneath. Even though Cumara and his companions had assured the humans of assistance, they were still several hundred feet up the cliffside. He peered cautiously over the rocklip into the darkness. By straining his nightsight, he could just make out the motion of the water below: seas quiet but regular, tons of water smashing rhythmically into the stone.

'A long way down.'

'Not for merrows,' said Cumara cheerfully. 'Not for you, while you are in our charge. But no human could survive such a dive unaided.' He pointed to a place a score of yards below them, where waited a few more of his race. 'We will manage all.'

'I could shapeshift, and put such a change upon the others as well – '

'Nay, you would not know how to manage in a form like to ours, and there is no time for it anyway. Look, the pursuit is more than halfway down . . . Stay you as you are, Gwydion, it will be very well.'

A flurry of laser bolts turned the air bright blue around them, and Cumara tugged at Gwydion's arm.

'Now!'

Gwydion closed his eyes and launched himself outward. Almost simultaneously two gleaming dark red bodies were beside him in the air. With a swift practised move, one fitted a red cowl over Gwydion's face even as they fell, and then they speared the water.

To Gwydion's astonishment, he found that, deep under the cold black sea, he was not drowned; the red cowl-like thing appeared to be a sort of artificial gill, a selectively permeable membrane that enabled him to breathe and see and hear as a marine creature. Through the inky water, other shapes appeared to be moving nearby; as his human sight, outraged at first, grew accustomed to this new vision, he could see by the faint phosphor glow of underwater his companions, cowled and attended by merrows even as he himself, all swimming slowly along the foot of the cliffs, down along the coast to the southwest.

Ten miles down the coast from Caerdroia, they staggered up out of the surf at last, on the soft yielding sand of a beach on the lee shore of a tiny island.

Gwydion, coughing and gasping for air, stumbled across the beach up to the thick warm sea-grass of the machair that ran down to the edge of the sand. Here he collapsed, hearing through a great ringing in his ears the sounds of the others coming to shore. *We sound like a herd of sea-pigs*, he thought, *and noise carries so by water . . . I hope no one is near enough to hear*. But his muscles that had been shrieking with the strain of the long swim were already beginning to quiet themselves in the warmth of the sand and shaggy grass, and he could not – would not – have moved if Jaun Akhera himself had come marching up the beach.

As if he had sensed Gwydion's concern, Cumara flopped bonelessly beside him, earning the other's bitter envy: The gruelling swim had troubled the merrow not at all, and he looked as fresh as a flower.

'This place is safe entirely,' said Cumara. 'It is Morrich-mor, Sea-plain, an old dancing-ground of our folk, and no one else comes here. But where would you go now?'

'Off-planet, if I can manage it.' Even the simple effort of speech cost Gwydion more breath than he had to spare; as for his new-found freedom, he knew it in his mind, but the knowledge had yet to come real to the rest of him.

Cumara looked doubtful. 'We would be of little help there,' he said. 'Though we could get you to the Kyles of

127

Ra easily enough. It is said that some of the Fianna and Dragon Kin are there in hiding, but I do not know the truth of that word. Even with the help of the current, it would be two days' swim at the least; more, for that you are unused to it.'

*Two days* . . . Gwydion wanted only to burrow into the sea-grass and sleep for a week, but –

'Aye, then,' he said, dragging himself to a sitting position. 'Let us begin at once, though. If we rest here too long we will not be able to – '

He broke off. Cumara, beside him, was staring out to sea with wonder in his look. Gwydion was on his feet at once, his eyes following the direction of the merrow's gaze, all his weariness vanished in the face of new and possible peril.

Something was coming towards them over the wave-tops, gliding across the face of the waters with the same serene power with which the *Firedrake* moved across the stars. It glowed like phosphor in the dark, and it left a trail of dancing fire behind it, and it made not the smallest whisper of sound.

'What craft is that?' asked Helwen Drummond. Slim and shivering in her wet black camouflage suit, she had come up to stand with Gwydion and the merrow.

Gwydion shook his head. 'I know not, lass.' His eyes were fixed on the unknown vessel. *She must have a shallow draught indeed, to come so far inshore* . . . Then the shock of it ran over him like seawater, though colder far than the water had been: The ship had crossed the shoals, and the breaker line, and now was coming at them straight over the sands, and she was made all of crystal.

Helwen took a step backward that brought her up against Gwydion, and he put a comforting arm around her shoulders, though he never took his gaze from the ship. And still the craft came on, in an eerie silence and the same faint water-elf glow, until she sailed the machair itself, coming smoothly to a halt not ten yards away above the waving sea-grass.

'This is a fell thing,' said Cumara. 'Some druidry of fith-fath, no proper ship at all. Where is her captain, her crew?'

Gwydion lifted his hand a little, and Cumara was silent. Then, upon the railed deck of the glittering ship, a tall figure moved out of the shadow of the mast – a mast to which no sail did cling. Stepping to the high carved prow, the stranger threw back the hood of his red cloak.

'Well met, kinsman!'

The voice was no less well remembered by Gwydion than the face: Allyn son of Midna, that lord of the Sidhe who had been guide to the Prince of Dôn in the deeps of Dún Aengus, who had spoken for him before the throne of Gwyn son of Nudd, King of the Shining Folk, what time Gwydion had had a perilous errand to that king, in the days before Caerdroia fell . . .

'You!' The astonished laughter and recognition in Gwydion's own voice and face caused the others to turn and stare. But he was already running to the ship's side, a smile upon his face such as none of them had seen from him for long.

'Allyn Midna's son,' he said, looking up at the Sidhe lord, 'I had not looked to see one of your folk in such a place; or indeed in any place apart from your dúns.'

'We live not always in our palaces, King of Keltia.' Allyn's fair face was alight with gaiety. 'Any road, I have been bidden by Gwyn to bring you this ship in your need. It is Manaan's own, and is named *Aonnbarr* – Wavesweeper – and as you see, it can sail both sea and stone. It will take you and your company to the Kyles of Ra, or anywhere else you may wish to go on the face of

129

the planet.' He beckoned to the others. 'Come now; Wavesweeper longs to be gone.'

They vaulted aboard, some more willingly than others, but Gwydion first of all. Then Allyn laid his hand lightly upon the mast – there was no helm that any could see, nor any rudder either – and the ship stirred beneath them, gliding back down to the sea.

All that night *Aonnbarr* skimmed the waves soundlessly southwestward, holding her course to the Kyles of Ra with no more guide or conning than that one touch of Allyn's hand. Gwydion stood with the Sidhe lord in the bows; the others, human and merrow alike, clustered together amidships, seeking physical warmth as much as psychic comfort, for the wind that streamed over the prow was strong and cold, and the strange light like cloudy ice that rose up from the deck beneath their feet was unsettling. Even the merrows were ill at ease aboard the crystal ship: The Shining One known as Manaan Sealord was a demigod to the Moruadha, ruler of tides, Wavewalker and Stormbringer; the white-capped waves of a choppy sea were his horses, in harness to his silver sea-chariot; to know that he had sent his own ship to save them was a thing almost passing belief.

As grey dawn began to break over grey ocean, and the Spearhead faded in the growing light, *Aonnbarr* raised the most northerly of the scattered islands that made up the Kyles of Ra. That region was as much sea with land between as land with sea between, as if some fist from heaven had in time past smote the earth, shattering it into a million patchwork pieces of grey and green and brown that the silver sea had stitched together.

*Aonnbarr* slackened her pace, and Allyn turned to Gwydion. 'I must leave you here, kinsman,' he said; his face, vivid still, was graver now in the morning light. 'Manaan's ship is not a craft to be seen by everyone; he has done much in granting you its use, and he calls it back now to its haven. And I too am called back; but we shall meet soon again – has it not been promised?' He held out his hand, and without an instant's hesitation, and with many words of thanks, Gwydion clasped Allyn's forearm with his own.

Now *Aonnbarr* moved up the beach and rode over the low grassy hillocks of the little islet. She hovered briefly, as a well-trained horse will stand for its rider to dismount at leisure, and her passengers jumped to the ground; then she sailed on across the hills and vanished into the morning mist.

They watched her go, then turned thoughtfully away. Gwydion rubbed a hand over his face, for he felt on the point of collapse, and spoke to Cumara.

'Once more I would ask you to be our friend at need. You heard rightly, as you told me earlier: Some of the Dragon Kin and the Fianna have indeed gone to ground here in the Kyles, and Prince Declan, the Ard-rían's brother, leads them. Can he be found, and we brought to him?'

The merrow nodded, awe still shining deep behind the mother-of-pearl eyes. 'Leave it to us, lord,' he said. 'If he is in these waters, we shall find him.'

Cumara proved as good as his word, and before nightfall, Gwydion and Declan were embracing each other in the surf that edged a grim granite-fanged island some way to the south. Beyond hope, the merrows had succeeded in locating Declan and his warriors in their hidden stronghold. Still more miraculously, they had managed to convince the prince of their incredible tale, so that he had given them a lonna and strong boatmen to ferry the exhausted humans the last little distance.

Reeling up the rocky shingle, sun red in the west

behind him, Gwydion was nearly knocked off his feet by the surge of a powerful breaker, then nearly knocked over again as Declan, knee-deep in the swirling water, swept him up in an exuberant embrace.

'Braud! Brother! The sea-folk told us you had escaped; even so, I hardly dared hope – ' Declan's delight, unbounded at seeing his brother-in-law, redoubled as he saw and recognized the others. 'Ah, Cameron! Sabia, Grelun – is that young Helwen? – well met, all of you. Cumara, my debt to you, as I said before, and my duty to the Morar-mhara Faruane. My sister will thank you herself, in good time.'

'She will,' said Cumara confidently. 'How could it be otherwise?'

'It would have been very much otherwise without your help and your folk's in this,' said Gwydion. 'I owe a debt of my own for life and freedom both to the Moruadha, and I shall not forget it.'

'There is no debt,' said the merrow. 'Did not Manaan Sea-lord save us all alike? Only drive out the Marbh-draoi, Gwydion, and bring Aeron home again. Shall you still go off-planet, then?'

Gwydion nodded, and even that small motion set him swaying on his feet, so weary was he by now with his long flight.

'I will try to get to Gwynedd, to raise my own troops there and bring them back to Tara.'

Declan shot him a sideways glance. 'To Gwynedd? Is that wise?'

'Maybe not wise, but surely necessary . . . Though not for a few days yet, please gods. I would rest a little before I go.'

'And that will start now.' Declan put an arm around his friend for support, gesturing the boatman to draw up the lonna into the concealment of a nearby beach-cave, and then the little party went up into the island's interior, where in the hidden stronghold waited many to welcome them.

But behind them, in the last red light across the waves, the merrows, their bodies like fire in the slanting glow, slipped once more into the sea and were gone.

Haco Grex was seated at the round table in his quarters. The debris of dinner had been cleared away and replaced by neat sheafs of reports by the time his two consuls came in to join him. They greeted him with personal warmth and professional curiosity, and took their seats at his right and left at the table.

He studied them covertly as they read the reports he had already seen. He knew them both well, of course: Thomas de Valadon, the junior of the two, was tall, blond and athletic, possessed of the blunt imperiousness of the aristocrat or the spoiled brat – both of which he was. But he was also a scholar, and the scion of a family that had made a profession of diplomacy for a thousand years, and a good deal had apparently rubbed off on him through mere exposure.

His other consul – Grex flushed scarlet as she glanced up at him and down again at her papers, but he did not stop watching her. In that one darkly trenchant glance, Deonora Maronchuk had probably catalogued the entire situation; such was the scope of her talent as a psychic alienist.

*And Mother of God*, thought Grex, not without piety, *how I can use that talent now* . . . He rattled his own papers, and the other two looked up at him, eyes wide.

'Have you read enough for us to discuss this?'

Deonora glanced quickly at Thomas, then nodded. 'I was sorry to learn of Captain Haruko's death,' she began. 'I know he was a dear friend of yours . . . From all that I have heard, and from what I read in Admiralty records, he was an exceptional officer. Certainly he died nobly enough.'

Grex nodded, face impassive. He had wept when he read of Theo's death, though that was not for his consuls or the rest of his staff to know, and he had forced himself to put his grief aside for a more appropriate time. Theo would have understood, and that was all that mattered.

'Did you speak to the surviving members of the mission?' he asked, looking down at his notes for the names. 'Lieutenant Warren Hathaway and Ensign Athenée Mikhailova?'

'We both did,' said Valadon. 'An extraordinary tale they had to tell, Grex, and some parts of it extraordinarily unpleasant. The part played by the late Lieutenant Hugh Tindal, for instance: disgraceful behaviour. The Admiralty will have a good deal to say about that.'

'No doubt,' said Grex drily. 'What do you make of their report on Keltia?'

Deonora shrugged, pushing back dark bangs. 'A stable civilization,' she offered. 'Quirky, but stable. Extremely sophisticated as to technology and weapons, sociologically solid, and very wealthy indeed. Their outward trade is varied and substantial, and we should be able to deal with them quite profitably. I'm no judge of military matters, but I should think they'd make a formidable ally – or enemy.'

'And their ruler? This Queen Aeron?'

'I would say she has already proved herself a friend to us,' said Valadon. 'Did she not get herself into a war simply by trying to make alliance?'

'Well, yes and no. There's a lot more going on there than just that . . . What did Mikhailova and Hathaway have to say about her?'

'They were very impressed with her,' said Deonora. 'Possibly because Captain Haruko had come to be her close friend, and they themselves were also close to her. And the other lieutenant, Sarah O'Reilly, actually chose to stay there in Keltia – clean against regulations, though it seems Queen Aeron did submit a request to the Admiralty to have both her and Captain Haruko seconded there.'

'Haven't you talked to the Keltic ambassadors, Grex?' asked Thomas, surprised. 'They've been waiting to be summoned aboard the *Argo*.'

'I know.' Grex stood up, and though he was not the tallest person in that room he was the most commanding. 'Shall we go and meet them?'

# Chapter Nine

The crash, when it came, was not a bad one, but it was jarring. Morwen redistributed herself painfully in her blastchair – her impact into the restraint field had all but cut off her air – and threw Aeron an evil look.

'Was that the soft landing you promised? Then gods spare me from a real jolt.'

'My sorrow for the uncivil ride; *Retaliator* seldom sets down so roughly. Did the shuttle crash where we plotted its course?'

Morwen checked some readouts on her console, nodded with satisfaction. 'And so completely and ruinously that no one will ever be able to tell that we were not aboard it. That was not such a bad idea, to divert them on a false trail, though if ever we have need of the shuttle we shall be in sore shift indeed.'

'Well, the left hand goes not into the right gauntlet . . . So this then is Fomor. Let us get out and have a look at it.'

The sail to Fomor from the Morimaruse had not been entirely without incident. They had approached the enemy planet unchallenged, but once within the outmost moon's orbit they had been picked up by ground installations. Several patrol ships had been sent after them, and only *Retaliator*'s enormous speed and manoeuvrability, and Aeron's piloting skills, had allowed them to evade the pursuit. Aeron had thought to take them down into subspace, as she had done once before in need, but Morwen balked at the idea, thinking it far too risky, and unnecessary besides.

*And most likely Wenna had been right*, thought Aeron, unsealing the door and casting carefully around with every sense at full stretch. *I was lucky once to have sailed subspace; two times would have been to press it hard.*

They emerged into a wide field full of wiry salt-scrub that faded into morning mist. The smell of the sea was heavy in the summer air, and the scent of nearby pines. Morwen looked around her, breathing deeply and delightedly.

'It smells like Duneidyn! This is a fine place – even though it be on Fomor . . . What are you doing?'

Aeron had pulled their packs – heavier now with gold counters and Fomori garb – from the ship, vanished the door and was now setting a control in the ship's nose.

'Come; we must be at least a few score feet away.'

From the edge of the scrub-pine wood they watched as the air around *Retaliator* suddenly brightened as if from within and began to dance. Only a moment; then the ship was gone, and the little twisted pines seemed to grow where she had stood.

'Name of Dâna – what did you *do*?'

'The ship must be hidden while we are gone from her; therefore did I put the tirr upon her. It is a thing Rhain and Elharn worked up between them, a kind of cloaking effect; no other ship in our starfleet has it, not even *Firedrake*. It can be useful enough at need.'

'I would say so! Will it hold, though you are not here to keep it active?'

Aeron nodded, shouldering her pack. 'It is sorcery, Wenna,' she said with a smile. 'Well, mostly so. But it will hold until I turn it off. There is a beacon in the ship's hull keyed to lithfaens that I have placed in each of our packs, and using those we can find the ship again without having to run up slap against her. Though of course if someone else should chance to run up against her, the

137

game is well and truly up . . . But this area seems deserted enough to take that chance.'

Morwen picked up her own pack and looked around. They had set down in large part where they had been forced to, pursued by the Fomori cutters, and not by choice or policy of their own. Only chance and luck – *neither of which Aeron believed in*, thought Morwen with exasperation – had sited their landing place here in the southern hemisphere, in a clement, uninhabited region perhaps ten leagues from a sizable city. They would head there; indeed, there was no other place they could go. *But Mighty Mother, I do not love the idea, and I can sense disaster not far distant . . .*

'Well, Taoiseach?' Standing a few yards off, Aeron was smiling at her. 'Shall we slog?'

Alone in the black darkness, Morwen halted, suddenly unsure. She could hear surf rushing up a stony shore, now distant, now uncomfortably near. The sea-wind on her face was welcome after the closeness of the woods in which she had been wandering, but there was a daunting sense of something enormous close by, out there where black sky swagged seamlessly into black ocean. It was as if a lid had been set down over the world, like the cover on a dish of meat, and out there at the edge of sight the world came to an end in a cloudy wall. Then there came to her, out of the darkness, a line of deeper darkness, a movement that she could best see from the corner of her eye. It rolled smoothly towards her, then edged itself with white: the breaker line. She was closer to the water than she had thought.

All at once Morwen was paralysed with causeless terror: the true Panic that can drop from nowhere upon those caught out alone in the wild, the unreasoning primitive terror of the waste places. Something big and elemental and very much not for mortals was close by, somewhere out in that breathing seamless dark: the sea itself, recharging its power in the night.

But at least she knew now which way it was she must go, to get back to even the doubtful safety of the forest, and she turned her back on the unseen ocean. It was one of the bravest things she had ever done outside the heat of battle, to walk away so with her back to the water; but she forced herself to one step after another, and not to run, and presently she came again to the edge of the woods.

*If Aeron –*

But she broke off that thought at once, with the speed and finality of a heel coming down on a dry stick, though it would have to be fairly faced, and sooner rather than later. The moon came out from behind the clouds as she struck a wide smooth path through the trees. *This region showed all empty of folk to our scanners – who would make a path here through such desolate woods, and to what purpose?*

It was warmer under the eaves of the forest, after the cold wind that had come blasting off the water, and as Morwen walked deeper in, rain began to drip from the leaves, pattering on the forest floor: the only sound in all that midnight wood, a hushed and private sound, soft and comforting, while above and outside the storm renewed its rage.

After an hour's march she came to a rocky outcrop out of the wind's eye. She was exhausted by now, drenched and hungry, depressed beyond belief; and there was not even a cave or cleft in the rockface in which she could find shelter as she had hoped, to sleep in some poor safety through the remainder of the night.

Morwen stood irresolutely in the middle of the clearing. No longer could she put off acknowledging the calamity that had weighed all day upon her: When the storm had begun, some ten hours ago, she and Aeron had lost each other in the wood.

They had been following a rough heading towards the city they had noted on their way in, thirty miles to the west of where they had hidden *Retaliator*; had taken refuge under the trees as the cyclonic fierceness of the storm had come crashing down upon them. It had been the kind of storm the Kelts called cam-anfa, 'crooked storm' – a black funnel of devastation, and winds no other kind of tempest could match: soon over, but deadly while it lasted, and they had been helpless beneath it.

Staggering through the lashing underbrush in the blinding rain that had followed in the funnel's wake. Morwen had realized with sudden horror that Aeron was not with her. She had hunted for hours in the aftermath of the storm, but had found no trace of her friend. At last, her frantic fear for Aeron dulled into something very near hopelessness, she had reluctantly resumed her course for the city, or as near as she could make it. Presumably Aeron would be doing the same: if she was still alive, and if she was able.

Morwen leaned heavily against the trunk of a giant leathertree, then slid slowly and deliberately down the shiny wet bark to the tangle of roots just above the moss. She was giving up. She was finished and she knew it and she did not care one crossic. She was lost and cold and tired, and Aeron was probably dead or captured, or at the very least just as lost and helpless as she; and this was the end of everything.

All at once she felt perversely cheerful. Even the thought of her husband and daughter could not turn her will to survival; Fergus and Arwenna would do perfectly well without her, Clann Douglas and the royal family

140

would see to that. The image of her dead brother Roderick drifted before her fading sight. *I must greet him from Aeron, unless she is with him before me . . .*

Wrapping her cloak around her, blond braids inside the sodden hood, she settled herself with her back to the tree-trunk and her face to the wind. Presently she smiled, and her eyes fluttered closed and her thought pulled away into the citadel of her spirit.

So she never heard the rustling, and she never felt the feather-soft fingers upon her face, never heard the tiny concerned whispers. And when the forest came alive around her, she was not awake to see it.


Many miles away, on the other side of the forest, Aeron sat in the concealment of a fernbrake at the top of a little hill, looking warily down at the walled city. Large enough to be a district or provincial capital, it was Zennor, the town she and Morwen had been making for when they became separated in the storm two days ago. Aeron closed her eyes in sudden pain: She had searched for her friend when the storm's fury had abated, and found no sign of her. In the Ban-draoi way, she had turned the negative thought on itself, though it had cost her much to do so, repeating it to herself like a rann: Morwen was well and safe, she was on her way back to *Retaliator*, she would wait there for Aeron's return.

*I may say it, and I may pray it; but do I believe it?* She shifted her position among the ferns, taking care not to let herself be seen against the sky. Be that as it must, she would return to the ship herself, as soon as she had the information she so desperately needed. This town would surely have libraries and other information centres, though how she might come by access to those she had not the smallest idea. But that was another fret for another time . . .

She cast a professional eye over the obstacles to her even getting into the city at all. There was a castle on the high place at the city's centre; what looked to be a fane or temple of some sort; a cluster of governmental-seeming buildings bordering a central square; and what was certainly a garrison of some strength. The city's fortifications were impressive even to an eye accustomed to the hundred-yard-thick walls of Caerdroia; and she had long since noted the complement of wall-guards and gate-guards – and their patrol patterns.

At last she sat back on her heels to consider her options. It would be impossible to slip into the city clandestinely; not only were there the guards, but there would be devices as well, maybe droids or even trained beasts. Yet enter she must; she had food for no more than another two or three days at most, and her clothing, though Fomorian, was unsuitable for the local climate. Cloaked and hooded, she should be able to get through the main gates unremarked, if she was extremely careful and spoke only as was needful. There had been a steady stream of people, afoot and ahorse and in all manner of vehicle, through the gates in both directions ever since sunrise; not hard to lose herself in the midst of such.

*Well, nothing wagered, nothing won . . .*

Luck was with her through the Zennor gates; no one took any notice of her at all. Once within, she melted into the throngs of idle pedestrians that crowded the streets, then began to walk with casual purpose towards the central market square. In a very few minutes she was in possession of suitable clothing that, though of good quality and workmanship, gave no overt indications of wealth or rank; the mercer who sold her the garb accepted her gold trading tablets incuriously, weighing them out and giving her proper Fomorian coin in return.

In a clean comfortable room at a small inn off the main square, Aeron changed into the new clothing: the loose trousers, drawn in at the ankles and tucked into soft leather boots, the billowing short chiton favoured by Fomori women of all stations, and the long rectangular maphorion or head-veil that could be drawn at need across her face; her own cloak would serve well enough for outer garment. She would not pass for Fomori herself, of course – red hair and pale skin were uncommon on this world, and her height too was beyond the usual – but that did not concern her overmuch. This place seemed not unaccustomed to offworld visitors, many of whom adopted native dress on a new planet, as a courtesy, or for convenience, or simply out of love of dressing up. Any road, the more she appeared as everyone else, the better it would be for her; also the looseness of the clothing would conceal the glaive that hung at her hip. She had hesitated before making the decision to wear the laser sword – no citizen she had yet seen had carried a weapon of any sort, except of course the guards – but to go about unarmed would be madness, and in the end she had buckled the sword-belt around her waist under the chiton.

She sat now cross-legged upon the bed, eating some of the food the inn servant had brought up for her: cold meat, a thick hot stew of seafood and vegetables, a small gold cheese, bread and fruit and butter and honey. For drink there was what she had asked for: plain fresh water. She drank half the jug and leaned back against the wooden bedstead, feeling the wind that sprang up at sunset blow in at the windows and across her face.

For the first time in the four days since she had landed on Fomor Aeron allowed despair to take her. She was alone here, in perhaps the greatest danger of her life, danger that was growing worse every hour, possibly already identified and hunted even now; Morwen was just as alone, in just as much peril, injured or perhaps even dead; and she had no idea in the worlds of how to accomplish her quest. If Arthur had come to Fomor, as the Coranian captain had claimed, he might have gone anywhere on the planet. His errand had been to rescue captive Kelts, and – if one could trust Taliesin's account – he had succeeded in so doing. Doubtless there would be records of such an event, but she had not yet worked out a way to come at them. On Fomor, learning was jealously guarded by the learned; the masses, with few exceptions, were not encouraged in study. Strangers were not encouraged at all.

Aeron sighed and activated the farviewer screen, hoping to see something of use to her, fearing to see an alert on herself or Morwen. She could do no more tonight, save to fret herself into the dubhachas – that evil mood known to its victims as the 'Keltic blacks' – over Morwen's plight and her own; better it would be to get as much rest as she could, while she could. Tomorrow would begin in earnest the search for Arthur.

Even so, her thought went out into the night to Morwen, wherever she might be, and farther still: to Gwydion and to Rohan and to all those others she had left so very far behind her.

Disaster did not overtake her until her third day in Zennor. Perhaps the folk at the inn had gossiped overmuch, perhaps someone in authority had grown curious about the tall veiled offworlder with the gold currency-counters making inquiries about library access, perhaps even some alarm had been set off in some data bourse by the inquiries themselves; but that afternoon Aeron heard what she had dreaded to hear ever since her arrival on the planet: the step of soldiers behind her, and the brusque command to halt.

Even then she tried to brazen it out, turning to face the captain of the four-man patrol and speaking in Lakhaz as fluent and colloquial as if that speech had been her native tongue. But he twitched aside her maphorion, his face hardening at the sight of the fair skin and green eyes, though after a few questions he permitted her to go on her way.

She fled straight back to the inn and the comparative safety of her room, locking the door behind her and leaning back against it, her heart racing. She had never been safe here, of course, but now she would have to get out of the city as soon as she could; this very night if possible. Or perhaps it would be wiser to leave this inn, where they had surely traced her, and go elsewhere, even stay in the streets all night, and slip out the gates in the morning? Her thoughts spun round like a wheel-brooch, and she could find no footing for her fears.

She was lying on her bed, indecisive, nerve-taut, her right hand on the hilt of her glaive concealed under the pillows, when a soft knock came at the door. It was no doubt only the servant with her nightmeal; but – Her grip closed upon her sword-hilt.

'Enter.'

The door opened silently and a uniformed man stepped swiftly inside, his blastgun levelled at her before she could move. After a small tense pause, she took her hand from her sword and flipped the pillow off the bed, so that the weapon lay in plain view.

'Greeting to Your Keltic Majesty,' said the intruder. He stepped forward into the light, and Aeron sat up with a gasp of recognition. It was Borvos, the captain who, back on Tara, had allowed her and Morwen to ride

145

unpursued through the Pass of the Arrows, on their way to Keverango and escape.

She laughed, shaking her head. 'And to you, Captain Borvos. May I offer you this – ' She extended the glaive to him, hilt first, and he took it with a formal bow. His bearing was much as it had been on Tara: briskly military, though now his brown hair was half-hidden under a crested helm, and he was clad not in battle-dress but in a quilted breastplate of gilded leather and a soft padded tunic beneath it.

'I am sorry to see Your Majesty in such straits.'

'I am sorrier to be the object of your pity . . . But what do you do here, Captain? I thought you attached to King Elathan's guard.'

'And so I am,' said Borvos, dropping into a chair and setting aside both gun and sword. 'Promoted Commander, in fact. But my wife's brother is military governor of this district, and when he had word of an alien starship – Keltic by her configuration and *Retaliator* by her looks – crash-landing in his territory, and traces of fugitives heading in this direction, he very naturally contacted me about it. And I – very naturally – mentioned it to the King.'

'Who – just as naturally – sent you here to look for Aeron Aoibhell.'

Borvos nodded, smiling. 'A long way from Bwlch-y-Saethau, Aeron . . . Well, the King wishes to greet you in person, and I am to escort you to Tory. There is a further escort waiting outside,' he added, 'in the event you chose not to accept His Majesty's invitation all so readily.'

'Yes, I am sure there is.' Aeron sounded amused. 'So you had heard only rumours, then, that I was here, and here alone?'

He nodded again. 'Though no one knew for sure; we

146

have not found *Retaliator*, and that wrecked shuttle was a clever piece of work to set us off your track.'

'It would seem, not clever enough.'

'No, well, perhaps not; but you did not come here alone, surely?'

But Aeron remained silent, and after a moment Borvos laughed and questioned her no more.

She was lodged for the night in the castle on the city's high place, in a tower room as palatial as to be a royal guestchamber rather than a cell for a prisoner. But the windows that overlooked the city were paned with vitriglass – the same crystalline substance used in the viewports of starships – and the double doors were fashioned of a metal only a little less hard than findruinna. Aeron had expected nothing less by way of security measures, and something very much worse by way of quarters, so on the whole she was grateful.

Still, captivity however gilded was captivity all the same – as Gwydion had also learned – and her mind was busy with what the morning might bring. By now Elathan had surely been informed of her presence on his throneworld, and Borvos, who was no fool, would certainly have passed on his suspicions as to Morwen's being at large on Fomor as well. After all, he was himself the one who had made possible their escape from Tara; he would assume that they had continued their flight together, and he would be correct in that assumption. But the longer she could keep Morwen's presence a secret, or at the least uncertain, the longer Morwen would remain safe and free – given that she was still alive to be so.

*Oh, Wenna, stay away*, she thought desperately, leaning her forehead against the icy vitriglass. *Do not come looking for me; get back to the ship and get off the planet, do not tarry for me . . .*

She turned from the window, noting the spy-eye set in plain view above the door. Borvos was taking no chances; there would be no chivalrous gestures this time. The situation was utterly altered: This was his homeworld, he a servant of his King; and Aeron, queen though she be, was not an unauthorized offworlder but the chiefest enemy of Fomor, destroyer of Bellator and slayer of Bres.

No, the only mystery remaining was what Elathan had planned for her. And that she would know, will she or nill she, in a few hours' time. To fret about it beforetime was less than stupid, more than futile; she would rest instead.

Someone had brought her pack from the room at the inn; with imperial disregard for whoever might be watching at the spy-eye, she stripped off her Fomori disguise and dressed once more as a Kelt. Feeling strangely happier, she lay down upon the bed, and forgot her fears and hopes alike.

# Chapter Ten

Elathan was sitting with Camissa in the conservatory, discussing plans for their wedding – though in truth the plans had long since been forgotten, and the two were rather talking idly and intimately, laughing softly together – when his sister, Rauni, came hurrying into the big glass-walled room. Her golden hair was tousled as always, but her face was uncharacteristically sombre.

Giving the briefest, most distracted of greetings to Camissa, with whom she was on the best of terms, Rauni knelt beside Elathan's chair to whisper urgently into his ear. To her astonishment, he did not appear at all surprised, but nodded, and withdrawing his hand from his lady's, got lazily to his feet.

'Who told you this?'

'Treic,' said Rauni, staring at her brother's calm face. 'Borvos sent him on ahead from the landing-field. He – Treic – had neither eaten nor slept, otherwise he would have come to report to you himself. So I sent him to do both, and told him I would bring you the news.'

'Good. Tell Borvos, when he comes, to conduct her to the Small Presence Chamber. I will come directly.'

When Rauni had gone again, Camissa reached forward and gave a pointed tug to Elathan's sleeve.

'"*Her*"?'

He stared at the sound of her voice; in the mass of speculations roused by his sister's message, he had completely forgotten Camissa's presence.

'Her indeed: Aeron Aoibhell.'

'The Keltic queen! What of her?'

149

'She has elected to pay us a visit, it seems. I did not tell you, but there were reports that *Retaliator* had been seen to land here, and I sent Borvos south to the Mirregaith to look into it. Late last night he informed me that he had captured her in Zennor. He is bringing her now to Tory; the aircar has just landed.' He shook his head in bewilderment. 'But why, with all the galaxy to flee into, and safer places by far, does she choose to come *here* – '

'But you knew she had escaped from Jaun Akhera.'

'Yes, and Morwen Douglas with her – Borvos told me when we came back from Tara of his part in their escape. He was so honourable about it, thinking I would at the very least banish him.' Elathan laughed, recalling his officer's speech. 'He was astounded when I promoted him to commander of my guard because of it . . . But to come here herself! She must be mad; or else she had some plan in mind.'

'A plan that miscarried.'

'Has it? Has it really?' He held out a hand to her, and she rose obediently, twining her fingers with his. 'Well, we'll know soon enough. Come: I would have the future Queen of Fomor meet the present Queen of Kelts.'

*She is so tall*! was Camissa's first thought, as she and Elathan entered the private presence chamber used for receiving friends and family, where Aeron now waited under heavy guard. So tall, and with all that pretty hair; and in spite of her travel-stained clothing, she looked much more like a royal guest on a state visit than a friendless prisoner . . .

Elathan crossed the room to stand within a pace of Aeron, who had been watching him with wary amusement ever since his entrance. Neither of them paid the slightest attention to the others in the chamber.

'So it *is* you.'

Aeron inclined her head. 'Your Grace of Fomor.'

'Why are you here, Aeron?'

Her laugh was soft and full of irony, as at a private desperate jest. 'To look for someone.'

'Is Morwen with you?'

'Elathan,' she said, still smiling, 'I am very tired, and very hungry, and I have been dragged a very long way in a very uncomfortable craft with some very dour folk for company. May I be shut up now? I have no intention of answering your questions if you keep me standing here all night.'

They had spoken quietly, to be heard by each other alone. Now he looked for a long moment into the clear green eyes six inches below his own, then nodded.

'Conduct the Queen of Kelts to her chambers, and see that she has all that is necessary to her comfort. I will join her there presently.'

Aeron smiled again, but said no other word, and went out with Borvos and the guards. Alone in the chamber, Elathan stared after her, unmoving, unseeing even, until Camissa came up beside him.

'So that is the Hammer of the Stars.' She used the epithet deliberately; it had been given to Aeron by the Fomori in the aftermath of Bellator, and not out of admiration. It gave her some satisfaction to see Elathan flush and turn away.

'I suppose she is that, all right,' he agreed after a moment. 'The same one the Coranians call the She-wolf of Keltia; and no whelp of Fionnbarr's litter is more dangerous.'

'And you will keep her here?'

'Certainly I will keep her here, until I find out why she came to Fomor and what she planned to do here and where she was headed afterwards. But as a guest, not as a prisoner.'

'And what then – for this *guest*?'

Elathan's glance flew to her face; there had been a strange note in her voice that had sounded like jealousy, though that seemed hardly possible. He was amazed to see that the waspish snap had been genuine: A tiny flame of hurt and possessiveness flickered in Camissa's dark-blue eyes.

'Cami, surely you do not think – '

'I do not know, Your Grace, what I *should* think.' She tried to pull away from him, but he caught her and drew her to him, and held her until she stood, rigid with protest, and gave over her struggle to escape.

'My love, I have told you my dream of friendship with Aeron and with Keltia; what better time than now for it to begin?'

'She killed your own father.'

Elathan spun her to face him, rare anger showing now in his eyes. 'Yes, and my father killed her father, and many others besides. We shall never have an end to it if we do not make one now. You and I have spoken of this before; I thought you of all people surely understood. You cannot wish this to go on forever?'

'I don't know,' she said in a low, troubled voice. 'I do not know.'

He pulled her close again, and this time she did not struggle but clung to him as if he were her last hope of escape from a burning land.

'Then trust me, Cami; only trust me, for I think I do.'


The chambers to which Aeron had been escorted were even more luxurious than the ones she had occupied the previous night in Zennor. When the doors closed after her guards, she ran a quick glance over the room, more out of habit than in any real hope of escape. *There will be no way out of here but Elathan's way . . .*

She went to the windows that looked down a thousand feet over Tory, and after a moment put out a fingertip to touch the pane. Immediately the finger went cold and numb in the grip of the forcefield that guarded the window, and she smiled and turned back to the room.

An elaborate meal had been set out for her on silver dishes, but she did not touch it, and instead placed a deep-cushioned chair so that she could see the sky through the arched casements. Seating herself, she closed her eyes and composed herself to pray.

When Aeron prayed in earnest, she called as the High Atlandeans had done upon the Shepherd of Heaven, Artzan Janco, that god who is above the gods. *For surely no lesser deity can aid me here* . . . She felt the peace take hold upon her, sending her spirit into that familiar fugue state of prayer, a moment almost of dissolution, curiously caught out of time and place and body.

She was called back into herself by the sound of the door opening behind her. Without turning her head, she spoke to the one who had entered.

'Greeting to you, Elathan.'

Elathan grinned involuntarily with appreciation of the gambit and dropped into the facing chair.

'And to you, Aeron,' he said easily. 'Though a trick like that would surely get you burned for witchery among some of the more superstitious of my people . . . I see you have not, despite your claim of hunger, either eaten or drunk; do you fear death in the cup?'

For answer she picked up a gold goblet from the table, filled it with wine from a gold decanter and drank it down in one swallow.

'Ought I to fear it?' she asked mockingly. 'I think not; nor on the plate either. I will eat a little later, when we have talked.'

'Did you rest well, at least, last night in Zennor Castle?'

'Very well indeed: the best rest I have yet had on your world. We slept rough enough before that.'

His brows arched a little. '"We"?'

'We the Queen of Kelts,' she said smoothly. But that was not what she had meant, and she was annoyed with herself for the slip, knowing that he had caught it.

'Whatever.' He appeared to lose interest in her evasion. 'What were you doing in Zennor? I would not have thought that, having come here at all, you would risk venturing within walls.'

'I had no choice; as I told you, I was looking for something.'

'What thing?'

'Knowledge.'

'A misfortunate looking.'

Aeron shrugged, and picking up a purple-skinned fruit from the dish on the table bit into it.

'As you say. It ended in my being brought here; misfortune enough.'

'Yet surely your art would not fail you, even on a foreign world? You could have put a – fith-fath, I think you call it – upon yourself, and so avoided the chance of being recognized and captured.'

'I could have done,' conceded Aeron. 'But real magic demands care and strength; it is not that you wave your fingers and it is accomplished. The laws that rule magic are different on different worlds; what works in Keltia might work to the opposite on Fomor, or might not work at all. Nor can one sustain two spells at a time, unless they are small pishogues or cantrips. How if while I was wearing a fith-fath I had sudden need of another, greater magic? Besides, any reasonably competent sorcerer – even a Fomori one – can see through any ordinary glamourie in an eyeblink. To cast an illusion that is itself proof against magic, or to work a change that *is* change and not mere phantasm, takes time and effort indeed. I had not the time, and dared not risk the effort.'

'Lucky for me, then.' Elathan was silent a while, watching her openly. Aware of his scrutiny, Aeron continued calmly eating her fruit: People had been looking at her since the day she was born; she had long since inured herself to stares.

Elathan envied her that ease. Though he too had all his life been the subject of public curiosity, he had never been able to grow accustomed to it, and even now, even as King, he still grew uncomfortable at the thought of eyetracks upon him . . .

'What do you think must happen now?'

Aeron looked genuinely surprised. 'Surely there is no uncertainty about that? I had assumed that if I should be caught, either would I be made an end of right here or else be packed off to Strephon like a stray parcel, to be used as a counter against Jaun Akhera's safety on Tara. Are there other possibilities?'

He drew his glance away from hers with an effort, stared down at the marble floor. 'You will not be aware of this, but my late father and I did not agree on many matters of high policy. That matter upon which we differed most violently was his policy towards Keltia and the House of Aoibhell.'

'And so?'

'And so I did my best to change his mind about joining Jaun Akhera in the invasion. He did not listen, of course, and many people – my half-brother Talorcan among them – condemned me for my wishes.' He leaned forward in his chair, eyes fixed now on her face. 'But now I am King of Fomor, and I may make my policy to fit my wishes. And my wish above all other wishes is truce and friendship between Keltia and Fomor; between House Aoibhell and House Corserine; between Aeron and Elathan.'

More than Aeron's eyes had been watching Elathan while he spoke: Ever since his first words about the differences he had had with Bres, she had been kenning him closely, and she had realized almost immediately that he spoke the truth.

'You mean this,' she said softly, incredulously. 'You are serious.'

'I do. I am. And you?'

Aeron laughed, throwing her hands outward with a shrug. 'I am confounded. After all that has been, can such a thing be?'

'If you and I choose to make it be. In the end it will be up to Your Keltic Majesty. I have said what I would do, and I have spoken of it, even, to my councillors.'

'By the gods, did you! And what did they have to say?'

'They were not precisely delighted with the prospect, for various reasons; but they could not deny the logic and the merit of it, and in the end they came to agree. There has been hatred long enough between our Houses; I would be a friend to the Aoibhell, yet how can I, if the Aoibhell will not meet me halfway?'

Aeron held herself to utter stillness. Well, and was he not right? Had it not gone on long enough, and too long? So many had died so hard for it down the years: his father, her father; her mother and her lord and her friends; her first Terran friend, Haruko; Elathan's younger brother, Tharic, dead among the other thousands on Bellator; Bres's elder brother Budic, almost forgotten now, who should have been King of Fomor and who had instead perished under the guns of her great-uncle Elharn's warships, in an out-Wall clash when Aeron and Elathan had been years yet unborn; and Elharn too had died for it in his turn . . .

'Long past time,' she said softly. But still some small hard knot in her soul held fast to the old distrust. Would she, could she, truly hold out her hand to Fomor in friendship? Or, for all her pretentions to enlightenment, was she merely just another marauder-monarch, a vengeful royal brigand no whit better than Bres or Jaun Akhera? She had flattered herself that it would be Aeron of Keltia who should lead her kingdom back into the world beyond the Pale; yet it had been Elathan of Fomor – *Fomor*! – who had had the vision and the courage to make the first proffer of peace. All her instincts were bidding her trust and accept, she knew Gwydion himself would bid her do so; yet still –

'Ah well, perhaps I am not yet so farsighted as yourself,' she heard herself saying, the old defensive bite back in her voice. 'Or even as I might like to think . . . But then, now I mind me of it, no more are you; I was informed by a Fomori prisoner on Tara that scarce had I slain your father than you had sworn further vengeance – the first thing you did as king – upon me and upon Keltia.'

He smiled gently, shaking his head. 'That is not true, Aeron. There was no oath, no swearing, no wish for revenge. The first thing I did as king was order my armies home, for that I wished to fight no more with Keltia or with you. Jaun Akhera himself heard me give the order; he would attest to it, for he was furious with me for doing so. If we reckon it purely loss for loss, you have suffered more at Fomor's hands than I at Keltia's, and have therefore the more to forgive; but I have always believed that the more enlightened the spirit the more that *can* be forgiven.'

'Very flattering, for all it sounds much too much like the teaching of the Christers for my taste. But have you forgiven – or forgotten – Bellator?' It was she who smiled now, though the smile was glacial. 'Nay, Elathan, I think

157

I must remain your "guest". That other – well, that other is beyond me.'

'I do not accept that answer,' he said, rising to leave. 'And to prove my faith, I tell you now that you are no prisoner, but truly a guest. You will be neither guarded nor spied upon; you will be free of the palace and the city; your weapons shall be returned to you. I shall give orders that you receive whatever help you require to find whatever you came here to learn, and Morwen Douglas – I know, I know, she was never even with you – shall be found and brought here in safety also. I would have you believe that I am your friend, and I would have that friendship returned. Think on it.'

Aeron looked up into the earnest dark eyes and away again. 'It seems I shall have time for little else.'

Of all those in Elathan's confidence as to his intentions towards the Keltic queen, only Talorcan had gone so far as to do somewhat on his own about them. Although he had had no further direct contact with the Coranian operatives since that brief meeting after his brother's coronation, he had busied himself over the past weeks with making sure of his arrangements on Fomor and with the Phalanx and with Helior; now that Aeron Aoibhell had so obligingly entered the picture, he began to put his plans into action.

Like all the rest of the kingdom by now, Talorcan had heard that Aeron had been found in the south and had been brought to the capital. So much, and no more, was the general knowledge. And, like all the others in the palace, the first Talorcan saw of her, despite his best efforts, was that night at dinner.

Elathan had ordered a state banquet, a thing unusual for him; still more unusual, he had kept his guests waiting on his arrival a full fifteen minutes.

When at last he arrived at the banqueting hall, the company at the long table rose as one, and as one they caught back their astonishment with civilized little gasps, for on Elathan's arm was Aeron.

*She looks singularly good for a prisoner*, thought Camissa with dismay renewed, watching Aeron take the guest-place of honour on Elathan's right at table. The Keltic queen was attired in Fomorian fashion, in draped and cross-girdled silk the colour of topaz, and topazes sparkled at ears and wrists and throat. Her hair was drawn smoothly into one thick plait bound round her head like a coronet and, once seated, she gave a gracious half-bow to the silent table.

'My lords and ladies,' said Elathan, face solemn though his eyes held a look of amusement that was almost defiance. 'I have the honour to present Her Majesty Aeron Queen of Kelts, who is to be our guest here in Tory for as long as it pleases her to be. Shall we dine now?'

Talorcan had slipped away after dinner all unnoticed, while the others, more obedient than he to palace etiquette, remained in the state drawing-room, watching Elathan and Aeron with varying degrees of interest and horror. But Talorcan had muffled himself in a dark cloak over his splendid red silk feast-garb, and left the palace by a side gate, moving quickly through the empty streets.

After perhaps a half-hour, he came to a small house in the maze of wynds that huddled like a nest of snakes at the foot of the castle rock. The house, neat and well-kept, showed no lights at its tightly shuttered windows; but Talorcan knocked once, twice, then bared his palm to a scanner. There came a whirr and a click, and the door-gates slid aside for him.

Within, he headed confidently, as one who had been

there often before, to an upstairs room away from the street; its windows opened onto a garden tucked under the huge buttresses of rock that, a thousand feet above, were crowned by the palace. The room seemed deliberately chosen, even as the house itself, for security's sake: Facing into the cliff as it did, it could not be overlooked from above, nor from any of its neighbours in the little wynd.

Talorcan carefully snibbed the door behind him, and within the chamber's softly lighted confines, a dozen men rose to their feet at his entrance. Nodding to them to resume their seats, he took his own accustomed place at the round table that filled most of the centre of the room; all in silence. All their movements had the feel of habit, as if this dark stealth were something they had practised often before, and would again; and when at last Talorcan spoke this was confirmed.

'Any difficulties getting here tonight?'

A small ripple of denial ran round the table: shaken heads, low negative murmurs. None had been followed, and these were all men who would surely know it if they had.

'Good.' Talorcan leaned his hands upon the table in front of him, his lean face suffused with urgency. 'I am quite sure that by now all of you have heard of Aeron Aoibhell's arrival on this planet, and of Elathan's avowed intentions towards her.'

'We've heard, all right,' said the man who seemed to be senior and spokesman among them, one Dargato by name. He was a well-known general, as were a number of the others; men of power and command and influence in the armies and starfleets of Fomor; and, because wars need money to fuel them, a merchant prince or two; but all of them without exception disaffected and disgusted to the point of this present treason with Elathan and his policy towards Keltia. They had mistrusted it when he was yet only Crown Prince; now that he had become King, they actively detested it, and they had resolved, all of them, to do somewhat about it. So that Talorcan, choosing tools for his deadly purposes with deadlier care, had found in them a ready weapon to his hand; and they for their part had found in him the point that they had needed for their own treasonous lance.

'When you told us Elathan wished alliance and friend ship with Keltia,' continued Dargato, 'we – to be frank, my lord – found it almost impossible to believe, what with Bres dead barely hours and that at the hand of Keltia's queen. But we had heard such talk from others, long before; and since then we have of course come to see for ourselves the truth of it. For now Aeron Aoibhell is here at Tory, as Elathan's honoured guest, no prisoner at all, even though she came here as an unlawful fugitive.'

Talorcan studied the fine-grained wood under his tapping fingers. 'Incredible, is it not . . . We are fortunate only in that so far Aeron herself has apparently proved reluctant to accept Elathan's overtures of friendship. You can see that she longs to do so, but she is still mistrustful, and it will take her some time to decide what her course will be.'

'What will she decide in the end, do you think?' asked a bearded blond man from across the table.

'Oh, no question but that she will make peace with my brother.'

'How if she does not live long enough to make that peace?' asked one of the other commanders. 'Assassination has an ancient history as a political tool.'

'And Fomor would take the blame for her death,' said Talorcan. 'Have you thought what Prince Gwydion would do, once he heard of it? Or her brother Rohan? Bellator would be a happy memory by comparison . . . No,' he continued, 'this way is best for us. The deeper Elathan goes in friendship with Keltia, the easier it will be to unseat him from his throne. Aeron's coming has given us a lever without price. More than that: Afterwards, she will make a useful consideration in any arrangement we might wish to effect with Strephon, say, or even with Gwydion, should he succeed in taking Keltia back from Jaun Akhera; the which she would not if she were dead.'

'If she allies with Elathan before we can strike, we shall be hard put to it to break them.'

'Then we strike before that can happen, and strike hard. *Can* we do so?' Talorcan shot suddenly at the blond man who had spoken earlier.

'We have strength to topple Elathan, certainly,' he replied; he was Salenn, who had been one of Bres's chief war-leaders in the fighting on Tara. 'So long as it comes as a surprise to him, I say we shall manage handily. Those in this room command loyal troops, and sufficient ones, and – most crucial of all – unquestioningly obedient ones. Overthrowing your brother, lord, and putting you in his place is more than possible.'

'But?'

'But we shall need that promised aid from the disaffected Phalanx leaders, and, most especially, from the Imperium, to keep you there. What says the Princess Helior?'

Talorcan smiled for the first time since his arrival. 'All that is well in hand. In fact, Her Serenity herself shall arrange things with those Phalanx lords you speak of, Salenn. And, of course, after she has helped us, then we shall help her – as was the bargain. We need not worry on that account: She will keep her promise to us to save her son's position . . . and his life.'

'I am glad to hear it,' said Dargato bluntly, and there was a bass counterpoint of agreement. 'We joined your plan, my lord, because we as generals of Fomor liked not to see our King making common cause with our enemy. To ally peacefully was not what we had it in mind to do to the murderer of your father. If Aeron is not to be killed, then she must be used to the utmost as a means against Elathan; if Elathan cannot be dissuaded from this course of appeasement – as it seems that he cannot – then he must be removed, and you as the only other male heir must be installed in his place. This is what all we here are prepared to do – what we have sworn to do.'

Talorcan nodded gravely. 'And put your lives and ranks and futures in peril to do so . . . None knows this better than I, my friends, for I have likewise pledged mine to you. Go carefully home.'

# Chapter Eleven

On board the *Argo*, the Terran ambassador and his two consuls waited in the gallery of the shuttle bay for the craft carrying their Keltic counterparts from the *Sword* to finish docking manoeuvres.

'Hathaway and Mikhailova are with them,' remarked Valadon, and his chief nodded, eyes on the shuttle settling to the deck in the grip of the tractor fields. Beside him, Deonora stood still as a statue, but, Grex well knew, with every sense alert to the scene.

The big spacedoors closed ponderously; air flooded the bay and doorseals opened all over the hangar. Grex crossed the floor to stand a little distance from the shuttle's main hatch, Valadon and Deonora flanking him a few steps behind.

The hatchway opened, and first out were Hathaway and Mikhailova, in formal uniform. Saluting Grex, they took up positions of attention, facing inward, on either side of the door. After a moment, a very young, very pretty woman emerged and looked around her; then, seeing Grex and the others waiting, she smiled and came forward. Right behind her was a man, much older, much taller, his rawboned frame alert for any suspicious movement, keen pale eyes in a gaunt face searching the demeanour of the Terrans. His bearing held authority, and wariness, and a great paternal protectiveness towards the girl who had preceded him off the ship.

They were followed by a tall black-clad man who carried himself like a warrior, and another man all in dark blue, whose face reflected cool interest and a kind of detached, almost critical amusement.

Grex stepped forward. 'The greetings of Earth to you and to Keltia,' he said. 'I am Haco Grex, Ambassador to the Court of Aeron Queen of Kelts.'

The crag-featured man bowed in return. 'Gavin, Earl of Straloch,' he said. 'Sent by Her Majesty as envoy to Earth. May I present Your Excellency to Her Highness the Princess Fionnuala.'

Grex kissed the slim outstretched hand, but said no word. It was for royalty to speak first, even to ambassadors.

Apparently Fionnuala remembered this only belatedly. 'It is my privilege to bring you the greetings of my sister the Ard-rían of Keltia,' she said, blushing slightly, then breaking into a delightful smile that melted into almost a giggle. 'I pray you forgive me, my lord Grex; I am not at all practised at this sort of thing.'

Grex smiled in return; princess she might be, but Aeron's sister looked no more than a charming child.

'And no more do you need to be, Your Highness. May I present my consuls, Sieur Thomas de Valadon' – Valadon bowed over Fionnuala's hand with even more panache than Grex – 'and Mistress and Doctor Deonora Maronchuk.' Deonora curtsied briefly, and Fionnuala smiled at them both, a little uncertainly. 'Now that we have met at last,' continued Grex, 'I wonder if perhaps we might not begin our talks at once. I know I am not mistaken that the last word we had from Queen Aeron was that she would send no embassy to Earth until we ourselves had arrived at Caerdroia.'

Straloch's face was grim. 'Things have rather altered themselves since then, lord. You already know most of it, but by all means let us speak without delay.'

\* \* \*

The room Grex conducted them to was a richly appointed one, a long boat-shaped table in the centre and computer-pads inlaid at each place. Grex seated Fionnuala on his right and Straloch on his left; Valadon and Deonora took their own places a little way down the table, with the other two Kelts – Morgan Cairbre and Emrys Penmarc'h, as Grex had by now learned; one was a bard, the other a Dragon, and both of them were certainly spies – and Hathaway and Mikhailova still farther along. The only others present were the *Argo*'s captain, Grex's secretary and his personal aide.

Straloch had given the Terrans a terse, unemotional account of the events that had struck Keltia since the arrival of the *Sword*, an account that was at certain points corroborated by Mikhailova or Hathaway or both. Grex had made no sign or reaction to the tale of betrayal and invasion and treachery and desperate exile, but he had begun to flick his seal ring around and around on his finger, as he always did in moments of stress. Beyond Straloch he could see Deonora; she was in her functioning mode as psychic alienist, and she was recording mnemonically every nuance of word and voice and expression for later recall – she would not participate in the discussion lest it prejudice her observations.

Grex cut his glance to the other side, past Fionnuala's red-blond head and lovely lowered profile. Valadon was watching Straloch with an expression of entirely reserved judgement, as if he were perfectly prepared to accept or reject with equal aplomb anything the Kelt might say.

'So Queen Aeron and the First Minister have fled, and Prince Gwydion is hostage, and Jaun Akhera controls your throneworld.' Grex drew his fingers over his silver beard. 'None of that is good news, of course; yet your military position seems otherwise satisfactory.'

'It seems so,' said Straloch carefully. 'But you understand, lord, that we have ourselves only just heard all this. Aeron sent us off in the *Sword* not three hours after the breaking of the Curtain Wall, and it was not until we came out of hypersleep, and were able to review the various transmissions that had reached us while we slept, that we learned of what has happened in Keltia since we left. The last report in the combanks was that our fleets had cleared the Imperials out of all systems save Tara and Kymry. Jaun Akhera himself seems confined to the Throneworld, and Rohan, the Ard-rían's brother and heir, who leads the main fleet, is strong enough to keep them there.'

'Buying time for your Queen's return,' remarked Valadon. 'Just where has she wandered off to, anyway?'

Fionnuala's head snapped up at that, and the cool violet eyes flashed with something of Aeron's own fire.

'My sister the Ard-rían – ' she began with considerable heat, then stopped as Straloch, across from her, cleared his throat softly. 'Very well. I am reminded that you as ambassador, my lord Grex, and these your officers as well, have the right and the need to know . . . Aeron has gone in search of certain – weapons; weapons that she hopes shall carry the day for us when she brings them back again to Keltia. Morwen Douglas, our Taoiseach, is with her on this errand; and Gwydion himself saw to it that they fled. So, at least, we have been informed.'

She dropped her head, struggling for self-control. Fionnuala had wakened from coldsleep only a few hours since, to be told of the peril into which her sister and Morwen had gone, the peril in which Gwydion remained, the treachery wrought by Arianeira that had caused that peril and the treachery against Jaun Akhera that had atoned for it. Though it was plain that the true Aoibhell steel was there in full measure, as it was with her

167

brothers and sisters, Fionnuala was not yet of an age and experience easily to mask her feelings, and no one at that table thought any the less of her for it. Grex, who had himself wept for his friend Theo not very long before, now kept sympathetic silence until she had once again mastered herself.

'Highness,' he said then, 'and my lord Straloch, what do you ask of us? You know that no formal treaty has been concluded – far from it – but intent both legal and binding has been declared by your Queen and our Prime Minister, and that is a bond certainly sufficient to enable you to call upon our help in this matter. Shall I send a message to Earth to mobilize a force?' From the tail of his eye, he saw Valadon's start of surprise, instantly checked.

Straloch glanced across the table to Cairbre and Pen-marc'h. The two Kelts spoke no word aloud, but even Grex could sense the wordless negatives sent back to the Earl.

'I thank you for that offer,' said Straloch. 'But I think it best held in reserve; Aeron wishes it so, for one thing, and there may well be a time coming when it will be needed more sorely than now. For the moment, I put it to you that we remain here, and confer upon the terms of the treaty.'

'That is acceptable,' said Grex, rising and offering Straloch his hand. After a momentary hesitation, the Kelt grasped it in both of his, and Fionnuala did likewise in turn.

After the Kelts had gone, escorted by the other Terrans to new and far more comfortable quarters aboard the embassy ship itself, Grex slid his glance over to Deonora, who sat very still, palms flat upon the table before her.

'First assessment, consul?'

'They have not told us everything.'

Valadon snorted. 'Of course they haven't! Did you think they would, straightaway?'

'No, Thomas, of course I didn't,' she returned peaceably. 'But there is a good deal more to this war, and to this queen, and to her quarrel with Bres and Strephon, than we have yet heard.'

'And just how long do you think it'll take them to tell us?' asked Valadon.

Grex turned a cool stare on him. 'After three thousand years,' he said, 'I think a few weeks more or less will make extremely little difference one way or another. And I also think that, in the end, they *will* tell us everything. All we have to do is wait. And time, for the moment anyway, is on our side.'

Deonora's smile was a little bitter. 'It is surely not on theirs.'


'You are determined, then, to do this?'

The Abbess Indec studied O'Reilly's face with eyes that saw much more than surface images; but her own face showed only doubt and loving concern for the girl who stood so tensely before her.

The Terran nodded. 'If I cannot find Desmond or Rohan,' she said, 'I promise I shall come back here to Glassary, and you will hear no more complaints. But, Mother, I *must* go. There has been no news for weeks, just rumour; and terrible rumour at that.'

Indec looked still more apprehensive. Rumour had indeed been fearful: that Gwydion had escaped from Caerdroia by diving off the cliffs and had died in the attempt, that Rohan had killed Jaun Akhera, or that Jaun Akhera had killed Rohan, or that both had killed each other in a parley over terms of surrender; and other tales worse still. And now O'Reilly chafed to leave the safety of sanctuary to go out to see for herself.

'You are lawfully my charge,' said Indec in a thoughtful tone. 'By the Ard-rían's own order.'

O'Reilly fidgeted under the steady gaze. 'Well, yes, I suppose that's sort of true.'

'And she will be very angry with me when she finds out that I allowed you to leave here – as will Prince Desmond.'

O'Reilly cast away all pretence of pride. 'Abbess-mother, I must see him! It has been so long . . . Please, give me your blessing, and then let me go. If you don't, I'll steal a ship and sneak off-planet first chance I get; but I would so much rather go with your good will.'

Indec laughed unwillingly. 'That is no way to plead your case, lass, but to get yourself locked in your room.' Once again she searched the thin eager face, the hazel eyes fixed so imploringly on hers, then glanced down at the heavy seal ring on O'Reilly's hand, with Desmond's device of the black bull.

'Ah well,' she said with a sigh. 'Aeron will simply have to understand.'

That night, having made her farewells to the Sisters and received Indec's blessing, O'Reilly sat herself down in the cockpit of a small singleship belonging to the convent. She ran her hands appreciatively over the controls: It was such a long time since she had been in a ship, and this one was particularly fine . . . Indec had in fact seen to it that O'Reilly was provided with the best and safest ship that could be obtained on such short notice – the thinking being that if the girl must go, at least she should go in the greatest safety that could be managed. The craft, though small, looked very fast, and carried combat-weight shields and gun consoles that would have sufficed to arm a ship twice the size.

O'Reilly activated the autohelm, and launch data began

to flow across the screens. Easy enough to get off Vannin; the problem was where she would go once she *was* off-planet. Desmond would undoubtedly be on board *Firedrake* with Rohan; but she did not even in her most optimistic mood think she could manage to locate the flagship within the enormous stellar reaches of the Bawn. If she found *Firedrake* at all, it would be by luck – or dán – alone.

She called to mind Indec's recounting of the rumour that Gwydion had succeeded in escaping from Caerdroia. With the exceptions of Desmond and Aeron herself, there was no one else in all Keltia with whom O'Reilly would feel safer. She did not for an instant believe that he had been killed in the escape attempt; lesser folk, maybe, but not Gwydion. And where would be the most logical, most secure place for the Prince of Dôn to go upon his escape?

Only one answer to that . . . With a smile, O'Reilly punched into the astrogational computer the coordinates for the planet Gwynedd.


Little news more had come to Alphor in the weeks following the Emperor's confrontation with his daughter. Strephon had held fast to his policy that Jaun Akhera should receive no more help than he had to hand already; Helior, too proud and too angry to ask again, had kept to herself and made plans of her own. And when at last she felt herself ready to act upon those plans, she approached an unlikely associate indeed . . .

In the room behind the grillework windows, Tinao stared at Helior, unable – and unwilling – to believe she had heard correctly.

'To set aside your Imperial father?' the girl whispered at last. 'Madam, you cannot mean to do this!'

Helior's amber eyes glowed feral yellow. 'I would do

much more than that to ensure that my son gets the help he needs – and deserves.' She paused a moment. 'Do you recall the visit last month of the king of Felire?'

Tinao nodded, now totally bewildered by the rapid shifts of subject and emphasis.

'Well,' continued Helior, 'my father knew it not – for all his much-vaunted network of spies – but Laharan of Felire came to Escal-dun at *my* bidding. And before he went home again, he and I came to an understanding. You may have heard that several of the Phalanx overlords have been, to say the least, something foot-slow in the confirmation of Elathan of Fomor as Archon of the Phalanx in his father's place, and Felire is leader of those.'

'I did hear.'

'So. Laharan and I compacted that, if I as Regent for my son were to help the Phalanx – or at least that part of the Phalanx that answers to Felire and his friends – put down Elathan in favour of his half-brother Talorcan, which plot is already well under way on Fomor, they would then help me to aid Jaun Akhera in Keltia. It seems a reasonable bargain, all things considered – and believe me when I say I have considered *all* things; and most especially now that Elathan seems to have embarked upon friendship with Aeron Aoibhell.'

Tinao chose her words carefully. 'But to do this thing, madam, you would first have to *be* Imperial Regent. Your father would have to be – removed.'

'He would have to be killed,' said Helior bluntly. 'There would be no other safe way. I should need help in such an undertaking: help I could trust completely, from someone who shares my goals and plans and hopes. My father,' she added, with a vicious twist to the word, 'is failing of his judgement in his age. If he will not choose to help his own chosen heir in need, then he must be swept away.'

'And you ask me to help you do this.'

'If you love my son as you say, why would you not wish to?'

Tinao turned away, pressing her gold-tipped fingers to her lips. To kill the Emperor – a fearful deed for any Coranian, no matter the motivation: regicide. But for Helior, not merely regicide but patricide as well . . .

'It is all for Akhi's sake,' said Helior, her voice soft now as hydromel in the shadows of the room. 'Does that not make it something easier to contemplate: a thing that would also make it easier for you yourself to become – well, for your relationship with my son to take on, let us say, more regularized overtones. As Regent and Empress-Mother, I would be able to make certain demands of my son; demands which he would be by no means reluctant to meet . . . once he had learned what you had done for him. Perhaps the crown-matrimonial is not out of the question after all.'

The persuasion in the cool little voice was almost irresistible; but Tinao did not see the flushed face and glittering gold eyes – if she had, she might well have fled and would surely have hesitated – nor the intensity with which the Princess focused on her, as if willing the girl to obey.

'I will do as you bid me, Serenity,' said Tinao at last, turning around to give Helior an elegant subsidence of a curtsy, head bent and hands clasped in front of her. 'But for Akhi only, not for the promise of gain for myself.'

Helior smiled down at her. 'I swear by all our gods you shall not regret it.'


When the Princess had gone, exultant in her victory, Tinao curled up in the window seat and stared out at the willows that lined the riverbank behind the marble quays. The sun slid down the sky, the blue afternoon shadows lengthened, and still she did not move.

'Young mistress?'

Tinao looked up at the sound of the well-known voice, then smiled and stretched herself. In the door stood a figure that would have been alarming indeed, were not the face so cheerful – and so loved by her.

'Indarrak! I did not summon you?'

'You did not. But I saw the Princess Helior leave some time ago; and when you did not come out, or ring for me, I thought to see if all was well with you.'

He came forward into the room: a giant of a man, bald save for the carefully tended braid at the crown of his head; powerfully built, clad in the immaculate pleated yellow linen worn by male servants of free rank within the Imperial palace.

'What is it, innaga? Tell me and be easy.'

Tinao felt as she had felt so often as a little girl: tiny, frightened, unable to influence her own immediate world with anything other than her small fists and her budding mind. She had been an unhappy child, living in the Imperial compound with her parents, Coranian nobility in attendance on Strephon and the late Empress Azaco. Sensitive, moody, creative, she had been often alone and always lonely – part of the bond she had with Jaun Akhera came from that, their childhoods had been much alike – and the giant eunuch who had cared for her and her brother had filled all the functions of a loving parent; far oftener, and far better, than had her true parents. She was suddenly sullen, though he knew well it had nothing to do with him.

'I do not wish to drag you into this as well,' she said in a small tight voice.

Indarrak looked surprised. 'If you are in it, child, then

already I am in it. Can you think I would stand by and let you entangle yourself in such plans as our Princess's?'

She gave him a long level look. 'And what would you know of Her Serenity's plans?'

'Only that, whatever they are, there is little serene about them: she is not the one for that. Their direction is not hard to fathom: Her interest is her son's interests. And his are yours, and yours are mine. And my interest above all others is to see you happy, and it appears you will only be so with that young lord of yours. So he too then becomes my interest – '

'I will never be his empress.'

'That remains to be seen. I did not think you wished to; but if Helior can help you to what you wish, then I will do my utmost to help her to that which she does wish. Now tell me.'

Since Gwydion's escape, few had dared go unsummoned into Jaun Akhera's presence; and those whom he himself sent for went before him shaking more than somewhat in their boots. When the news had first been brought to him that Gwydion had managed to spirit himself away seemingly before their very eyes, Jaun Akhera had been possessed of such a fury as none of his companions had ever seen before; and all the more terrifying for that it was so cold. They would have far preferred shouts and curses and thrown crockery and even blows to this controlled icy blaze.

Only to Sanchoniathon did he allow himself the luxury of an emotional unburdening. Ever since their childhood, Jaun Akhera had always turned to his younger brother; and, later, Tinao: the only ones to cheer or soothe or buffer him; the only ones who loved him; the only ones who did not fear him; and he turned to his younger brother now.

'How? *How*, Sancho? Tell me that! It should not have been possible, yet there it is. Oh, the She-wolf has found herself a fit mate in *that* one. Bres damned him for a sorcerous cozener, and *I* laughed . . . Yet it cannot have been by sorcery, for surely I would have known – '

'Simply a very clever plan, then; engineered and executed from within the palace itself?' Sanchoniathon had seldom felt so helpless, and the suggestion was one of desperation.

But his brother halted in his pacing as if a rope had been flung round him from behind.

'He would certainly have had help. But whose? Just as certainly, whoever helped him is not here now, any more than Gwydion is.' He returned to his seat behind Aeron's desk, his face a little calmer. 'Where would he make for, do you think?'

Sanchoniathon sank with some relief into his usual chair, swung one leg over the upholstered arm. 'Gwynedd? No, of course not; much too obvious, much too dangerous.'

'Yet Gwynedd is the base of his personal power: household troops, wealth, folk unswervingly loyal to him, places he could hide in for years in safety . . .' Jaun Akhera sat back, fingers steepled under his chin; then a look of hushed certainty lighted his hawk's face. 'Dyved. He will go to Dyved.'

'But that is Powell's princedom – '

'And Powell was Gwydion's father's foster-brother; and so, according to the Kelts' own tiresome custom, he is Gwydion's nearest male kin. No less is he a prince near as powerful as Gwydion himself, with access to all those things I just now mentioned. As a hunted fugitive, to whom else could Gwydion turn?' The certainty became smiling satisfaction. 'And to whom else will Powell turn when Gwydion does so – but to me. And who else is on Dyved as our liaison to Powell but Kynon ap Accolon – '

'You managed that very well, Akhi.'

Jaun Akhera caught the note of veiled disapproval. 'So? You have some difficulty with that, Prince Sanchoniathon?'

Before the Keltic campaign, Sanchoniathon would have been, not fearful, but reluctant to speak so to his brother; but in the past months he had begun to emerge from Jaun Akhera's eclipsing shadow, to stand in his own light, according to his own lights, and now he did not hesitate to voice his criticism, or respond to the implicit challenge.

'Yes, I do! I liked it not at all when you attempted to suborn the merrows, Akhi, and the seal-folk with them; and I liked it still less when you began to play at tossing sops to such Kelts as were treasonous enough, and greedy enough, to snap them up.'

'Yes, so you said at the time.' Jaun Akhera was silent a moment. 'Well, I cannot say I am sorry, Sancho, for I am not. I would do far more, and far worse, to put down Aeron.'

'If she still lives.'

'Oh, she lives, right enough. This matter between us is not yet settled. She will not permit herself the low road until it is.'

# Chapter Twelve

Aeron had been at Tory for nearly a fortnight. Despite the best efforts of many searchers, no trace had been found of Morwen, though even yet Aeron maintained the fiction that she had come to Fomor alone and uncompanioned. For still there was the considerable chance that everything Elathan had said and sworn and promised was a lie: that as soon as he had both of them securely to hand, he would turn right about and kill them, or sell them to Strephon, or devise for them some other fate equally unpleasant. For herself Aeron could do nothing, and cared less than nothing; but if there was still a chance for Morwen, then by the gods she should have it, and Aeron would do nothing to jeopardize that chance for her friend.

Then again, there was the equally considerable possibility that Elathan did *not* lie, that he meant all he had so convincingly warranted: to be her friend, and Keltia's ally; to put an end to the enmity between her House and his. And she wanted desperately to believe him; and yet, and yet . . .

They had fallen into the pleasant habit of spending the late afternoons in Aeron's chambers, for easy discussions over wine or the fragrant steaming brown brew called by Haruko's people chai – she remembered how proudly and formally he had served it to her, many times, at Turusachan, in an ancient and elegant ceremony as stylized as a dance.

That afternoon Elathan had been less than unfailing of his patience, and Aeron did not blame him, for she was in a mood to be as perverse as even she could be; and at last his temper had snapped.

'My gods, Aeron, but you are a pest of hell! How if I did, then, what everyone from my Prime Minister to my bootmaker is begging me to do, and put an end to you right here on Fomor?'

She shrugged, and poured another cup of the comforting chai. 'Then gods save the Ard-rígh Rohan.'

Elathan, in his irritation, could not forbear the taunt. 'Say if he is dead, and the rest of your brothers and sisters with him?'

'Then the election could turn up anyone from a King Revelin or King Deian to a Queen Melangell or Queen Slaine.' She laughed, struck by the idea. 'You'd be much worse off with Queen Slaine than with Queen Aeron, I promise you. My cousin Slaine, dearly though I love her, is far less reasonable than I.'

Having heard some campfire tales about Slaine of Ralland, only daughter of Elharn Ironbrow, Elathan believed it. Still –

'My advisors have pressed me hard,' he said slowly, 'and with most excellent arguments, to hand you over to Strephon. Either as surety for Jaun Akhera, or for pure vengeance's sake; and your sentence to the block still stands.'

Aeron shrugged again. 'My death, however pleasing Jaun Akhera might find it, would bring him peace of mind both brief and small, and mean very little in the end. As I have said, there are first of all my five brothers and sisters, each one of them fully capable of ruling Keltia to his detriment. After them come some very warlike aunts and uncles and a great many bellicose cousins. All of whom would avenge me upon Jaun Akhera – and upon you – until the gaurans come home. I think you would tarry long before you would choose to pull

179

that down upon your head. But any road it makes no differ, for no soul in all of Abred goes out five minutes before the time its dán has set it . . .'

He glanced up, caught by a strange change in her voice; it had lacked its usual bright brittle edge of mockery and defensiveness, had sounded all at once wistful, reflective, very young. She was not looking at him now, but out at the golden afternoon. All her guards seemed down: She had lost that look of strength-in-reserve that was her usual mask, and suddenly seemed far too fragile to be the adversary that deeds and rumour had made her. As if for the first time, he saw how delicate her frame was; for all her height and strength, he could snap the bones of her wrists with little effort.

And, thinking all this, Elathan was astonished by the wish, the urge, even, to protect her that came over him. Despite his personal inclinations, she was still held to be the sworn enemy of his people and his House. To most of those people, and most of that House, there was but one thing that should content the King of Fomor where the Queen of Kelts was concerned. Instead, there was this troubling new feeling . . .

But was it in truth so new after all? He turned his mind back to Rath na Ríogh, in memory seeing Aeron again for the first time, on a cold sunlit morning, sitting her black horse in the midst of her friends, her hair like fire down the back of her purple cloak –

She had turned, and was watching him – had been for some moments – with a kind of alert half-smile upon her face, as if she knew his thought. But she had been remembering, too: her shock at seeing Elathan upon that same morning, that same place upon the plain. She had not known him then by sight, and when her friend Dafydd Drummond had told her who he was, she had been surprised and unaccountably resentful: so beautiful a face

– dark blond hair, features as hard and proud and sculptured as Gwydion's – and her undisputed enemy, the son of her parents' killer.

Neither of them could ever remember afterwards which of them took the first step towards the other, who first pulled the other into the embrace that suddenly seemed so inevitable to both, whose mouth first came down upon whose.

When they parted at last, Elathan stared down into Aeron's face. She seemed as shocked as he, the green eyes veiled with puzzlement.

'Where did that come from?' he heard himself asking, his voice unsteady with the very attempt to keep it even.

She looked up straight into his eyes, seeing her own astonishment reflected there.

'I did not mean for that to happen,' she said, 'though I thought it not unlikely that it might.'

'Did you indeed!'

'Oh, come, you knew it just as well yourself! How could it not, and how could there be any more to it than that?'

He moved deliberately away from her. 'Explain it to me, then.'

Aeron gave a little shrug, the gesture more in her face than in her shoulders. 'Curiosity. Tension. Testing. Confusion. An attraction we both felt, I think, since that morning at Rath na Ríogh. I certainly felt it – Morwen noticed, and maybe others did too – and the fact that you felt it seems to have been common knowledge among your army.'

He did not trouble to deny it. 'It could have been more,' he said after a while.

'Easily,' she answered, her voice as frank and bare of artifice as his had been. 'Had other things been other wise . . . But it will not – not now, not ever that way, and if we forgot that just now, two others there are who are surer, and who will not forget. But maybe this was no bad thing: It has freed us, I think, to go on.'

'To what?'

'What this has been all about: to be friends or adversaries. That choice can be delayed no longer.'

Elathan came back the little distance. 'I have made that choice already, Aeron; and you know what I chose.'

Her eyes changed, fell, and when she raised them to his again they glittered like emeralds; not with the hot battle-light that so often ignited them, but with a sparkling overlay of unshed tears.

'Then I choose likewise,' she said, breathing a laugh that was more shiver than mirth. 'Though it ended rather differently the last time I faced a king of Fomor.'

' – who had himself once faced another ruler of Kelts . . . Nay, Aeron, all that is done with now. Let it be.' He kissed her fingers with the grace of a courtier, and she closed her hand around his.

'Mar a bha, mar a tha,' she murmured. '*As it was, as it is*' – words from the Keltic funeral rite; appropriate for the death of the old way. 'Well then,' she said, and felt the past swing closed behind her, 'Fomor and Keltia have much to say to each other that has never been said before. Let us make, at least, a beginning.'


Night again, a night of low heavy cloud and sullen wind. In the peaked-roof house below the castle rock, Talorcan called to order the last meeting of the conspirators before their move was made.

An undercurrent of excitement was almost palpable, thrumming like a musical note just below, or just above, the level of human hearing; but the men in that upper room were too disciplined to permit it to affect their mood or their minds.

Talorcan too was aware of it, as he took his usual place and glanced around at the faces turned expectantly towards him.

'As some of you already know,' he began, 'this will be the last time we shall meet here. When next we are all assembled, it shall be in the throneroom itself, and we shall be there by right of conquest.'

'Is it so, then?' asked one of the junior generals. 'You have heard from Helior?'

Talorcan nodded. 'She has engineered a pact with our Phalanx colleague Laharan of Felire – and he acting on behalf of a sufficient number of other Phalanx worlds to suit us – that will provide us with back-up troops and arms from Imperium and Phalanx both. In return, of course, for the promise of our future support of Jaun Akhera, once Elathan is removed – which promise we were pleased to give Her Serenity. Dargato, what report have you?'

'Troops loyal to us are even now moving into key positions around the city. There will be a good deal of resistance, of course, but on balance Elathan will have no real chance. Say the word, my prince, and by dawn I shall be calling you my king.'

Talorcan smiled. 'In two days' time that word shall be said. Until then, my lords – and my friends.'

'Until then,' came the eager response. But Talorcan was gone.

Camissa paused outside the door of Aeron's chambers and raised a hand as if to knock; then, angry at her own timidity, she straightened to a more regal posture and flung wide the door.

Aeron, as usual at that hour, was reading in a chair near the windows. Though her eyes had lifted briefly when the door opened, she gave no other sign that she had even noticed Camissa's presence.

'Good day,' said Camissa, when the silence had grown ridiculous – but a little uncertainly all the same. Should she say 'Majesty'? But Aeron, queen though she was, was not queen *here* . . . Still, to call her 'Aeron', as Elathan did in private, seemed not only curt but dangerously familiar; to call her nothing, the least rude of the choices.

'And to you, Lady Camissa,' said Aeron, immediately closing her book. 'Is there somewhat I may do for you?'

Camissa flushed scarlet, then paled again; then it came out all in one rush, her voice sounding hurt and childlike even to her own ears.

'What is my lord Elathan to you, madam, and you to him?'

'Ah. I wondered when you should come to ask me that. Let us walk a little and discuss it.' In silence they went out through the tall doors into the gardens. It was an afternoon of golden sunlight and strong winds: Spring was by now well entrenched in Tory, though the trees and shrubs were as yet only a thought more green than brown.

'Well, there is nothing between Elathan and me, Camissa,' said Aeron then. 'That I say before the Goddess. But I cannot say that there has not been something.'

In the blind wave of feeling that swamped her then – pain and fear and anger and jealousy all mixed – Camissa still managed to keep her voice cool and her face calm.

'So it was the truth I have been told. Truth, even though it came from – '

'From Talorcan? I would wager much that Elathan told you first himself.' Aeron reached out and caught Camissa's hand in hers. 'I swear by that by which my people swear,' she said slowly and distinctly, 'as Queen of Kelts to Queen of Fomor, that there is now nothing, nor has there been, nor shall there be, between Elathan and myself; save only what there was.' She released the younger woman's hand and absently rubbed the bare place on her midfinger where she was used to wear the Great Seal of Keltia; then, realizing what she did, she laced her fingers deliberately together in front of her.

'True it is we were drawn somewhat to each other,' she continued. 'As I doubt not he himself has told you; and true also that we permitted ourselves to act somewhat upon that attraction. But that is all there was, and all there was ever meant to be.'

'You said just now you found each other attractive.' Camissa's voice, small and strangled, came from a few yards away, where she had retreated so that Aeron should not see her face.

'Aye, but both of us also saw why that should have been: for curiosity, for strangeness, for the strain of the situation; for sympathy's sake, even. But we saw even more swiftly than that why more should never be: for you, and for Gwydion; and for the sake of what is between you and Elathan, and between my lord and me. That was the end of it right then. No more.'

'But Talorcan said – '

'Oh aye, I can well imagine what he said: suggestions that Elathan's hope of alliance with Keltia had more to it than politics only.' Camissa's silence confirmed it, and Aeron nodded grimly. 'I thought as much . . . But you must also know how much it is in Talorcan's interest to cast a shadow between the King of Fomor and his future queen. That it should be my shadow he strives to cast works still more to his interest.'

Camissa had composed herself, and now came round to stand before Aeron, bewilderment plain in her eyes. 'Why would that be?'

'Why, for that Talorcan wishes to prevent friendship between Fomor and Keltia, for one; and wishes also to have you to his own lady, not wife to his brother.' Aeron had spoken matter-of-factly, but seeing the shock and revulsion on the other's face, she asked more gently, 'You had known that, surely?'

Camissa dropped her head, then nodded. 'I had hoped not to *have* to know it; and had desperately hoped that no other knew.'

'I think that all the palace must know it,' said Aeron, still gently. 'Most certainly Elathan does.'

'No, he must not! He cannot! If he did, surely he would have – '

'This can make but little differ. What matter now if Talorcan casts his eyes on you in vain?'

Camissa looked troubled. 'I do not know,' she said after a long pause. 'Except I feel, somehow, some way, he is planning something – to do my lord a mischief. And if he can do so through me . . .'

She met Aeron's sympathetic gaze full on, with a warm, incredulous shock of feeling. Suddenly – she could not say how, and doubted the other could either – between one breath and the next Aeron had become a friend. Camissa felt it beyond any doubt, and she saw that Aeron felt it too.

'Forgive me, Aeron. I am sorry that I spoke so, and felt so. If I had thought a little more, and felt a little less – '

'Nay, my sorrow that I gave you cause.'

The moment was all: They sat on together, relaxed now, wearied by the intensity of the emotion-freighted moment they had shared; but their silence now was also shared, a peaceful companionate silence that overset all barriers of strain and doubt.

'What shall you do now?'

'I must find Morwen,' said Aeron. She glanced sideways and laughed at the expression on Camissa's face. 'Aye, I know; not even to Elathan did I admit that Morwen had come with me on this voyage. But she did, and she was lost when we were parted in a storm, and I have been filled with fear for her ever since.'

'If she were injured, she would have been taken to a healing-house,' said Camissa encouragingly. 'We should have had word of her long ago, even if the news were not good.'

'And if she is dead, or lost in the great forest? Would word have come of her then?' Camissa did not answer, and after a moment Aeron gave her an apologetic smile. 'Nay, it is no fault of Fomor's; only mine, for that I brought her with me on what may well be a doomed quest and a fool's errand. She is well enough, I can feel it.'

Camissa looked a question, then lowered her eyes, feeling suddenly shy – prying, almost – in this new-born fragile friendship.

'Then you shall find her, Aeron, and soon.'

Aeron smiled again, this time in gratitude as shy as Camissa's reticence had been.

'Do you know, I believe that you are right . . . But the sun has gone, and that is a cold wind. Let us go back in.'


The coup was struck in darkness. The first Elathan knew of it was the sound of bitter fighting outside his chambers, the shouts of his guards and the clash of several different sorts of weapons. He was still fully dressed, not yet having retired for the night, and he was reaching to arm himself when the doors burst open and Talorcan's minions streamed into the room.

He was dragged down the corridor to a windowless

strongroom and flung inside. When his head cleared, he saw that the person kneeling beside him was Camissa.

'Are you all right, Cami?' He tried to sit up, but the movement drew a black star-sparked curtain over his sight.

She nodded, fury fighting with tears on her face, and carefully helped him to a sitting position.

'They took us all in the dark.' She gestured to the far corner of the room, where Basilea huddled, seemingly in shock, her arms around her daughter Rauni.

Before Elathan could speak again, the door opened and Aeron was shoved unceremoniously through. She was clad in the Keltic garb in which she had arrived at Tory; the garments were torn and disarrayed, as though she had resisted her assailants.

'They were too many,' she said as if in apology. 'What place is this?' She was taking quick inventory of the room, noting Basilea, Rauni and Camissa almost cursorily.

'An old strongroom,' said Elathan. 'There is no way out.'

She seemed almost cheerful. 'There is always a way out. We have only to wait.'

Elathan stretched his long legs out in front of him and leaned back against the wall.

'Well, now that we seem to have the leisure for it,' he said, 'perhaps you might like to tell us all, Aeron, exactly what happened on Tara after I left, and why you came to Fomor, and who it was came with you – Morwen, I believe – and what you were planning to do next.'

Aeron's mouth curved in a slow smile. 'That may take long.'

'Ah well, to pass the time, then.'

\* \* \*

Aeron's tale had got *Retaliator* to the space off Fomor when a soft noise came at the door. In fluid unison she and Elathan, no word spoken, leapt to stand each side of the entrance. Another furtive scratching, then the door opened. Aeron, who had moved instinctively to strike, found her upraised arm caught from behind by Camissa. She did not know the woman with the long grey-silver braid who entered, but Elathan embraced her, and Camissa exclaimed with joy to see her.

'The Lady Thona,' said Basilea in Aeron's ear – the first words she had uttered since their imprisonment in the vault – and Aeron nodded.

Thona cast a quick anxious glance at each of them. 'You are all well? – Good, you must come quickly. Borvos has arranged an escape for us.'

She continued to speak as they readied themselves for flight. 'It must be now, while things are still in turmoil within the palace. Your troops, Elathan, are giving fierce resistance, more than apparently was counted on. But they cannot hold out much longer, and Borvos – '

'Do not trust her, my son!' snapped Basilea. 'It is *her* son who has made this treason.'

For the first time in his life, Elathan turned on his mother in anger. 'Not only do I trust her, mother, but *you* shall trust her, and thank her and ask her pardon should we all come safely through this . . . Madam' – this to Thona – 'we are deep in your debt whether we escape or no. Where to?'

'There is an aircar standing ready on the tower pad in the southern wing; the rebels led by – my son have not taken that area. Borvos and two of his officers hold the lift to the tower roof. If we can reach the courtyard, we are safe.'

'Unarmed?' That was Aeron.

Thona shook her head. 'At the foot of the stairs – I

gathered up all the weapons I could find. Quickly now, there is very little time.'

The pursuit caught up with them coming across the courtyard, the only exposed part of their flight. Through an archway in the tower's base-court, Borvos waved frantically for them to hasten; he had seen, as so far they had not, the soldiers pounding grimly after.

Aeron, who had taken upon herself the position of rearguard, glanced behind her and turned at the bend of the corridor.

'Get them into the lift, Elathan. I will delay these a little.'

'Not alone you will not.'

Aeron smiled, but did not take her eyes from the archway where the pursuing troopers would have to show themselves.

'None of this is ever alone – did you not know? Besides, they will use their swords, not blastguns, for fear of the bolts flying wild in so tight a space.'

Elathan, about to protest again, bit back his words. *Well*, he thought, a little bitterly, *who better than she with a sword*? He saw in her eyes that she had read his thought.

She chose not to remark on it, but flexed her wrist instead, looking with interest at the interlaced steel ribbons that formed the hilt of her sword.

'Never have I fought with such a blade as this; it is hilted like a withy-basket.'

'And therefore do we call it a basket-hilt.'

She laughed. 'Very logical. We shall see what may be done with it. Elathan, I beg you, get them away now; and do you not return yourself, either. Easier for me if the only one I must ward is myself . . . Send the lift down again for me and I will come directly.'

He hesitated, then hurried to obey. But after bundling the four women into the lift manned by Borvos's officer Treic, he heard the sound of combat behind him; and as soon as the lift had rocketed up to the landing pad, he raced back to Aeron.

When Elathan came round the corner of the tower, Talorcan, with five or six of his guards behind him, stood in the centre of the archway facing Aeron. She had apparently slain two guards already, for they lay between her and Talorcan, and they did not move.

She dared not glance at Elathan as he came up beside her, but she allowed her annoyance to show.

'I told you not to come back for me.'

'The King of Fomor still commands in his own palace; or is that no longer so? Talorcan? What do you say?'

'You may give order, my brother, to your heart's content. But who will obey you? You heard the siege lasers – the walls are breached. My forces hold the palace and the city; very soon now, the planet. And I hold the throne.' Talorcan spared a contemptuous glance for Aeron. 'And all by grace of the Queen of Kelts; it is your alliance and friendship with her that killed our father that has undone you. Will you now let her fight for you as well?'

Elathan stepped forward in unthinking anger, but Aeron moved to bar his path.

'Stand away, Elathan; you will not shed your family's blood if I can hinder it. As for you, Talorcan – I have killed one king of Fomor, as you have just reminded us. I would think less than nothing of killing his successor's usurper.'

'In unhappy time, Aeron, draw you a sword.' Talorcan leapt forward unexpectedly, aiming a vicious two-handed swipe at the pair who stood in his way. Aeron raised her own weapon to counter the blow, and the sparks flew blue where the metal met.

But if his late father Bres had been some match against Aeron, Talorcan was none, and in four passes she had disarmed him and laid open his cheek. She had raised her blade for a killing lunge, but inexplicably she hesitated; and in that moment of hesitation an explosion rocked the tower – a direct hit from the siege lasers outside the walls, sending smoke and stonedust billowing along the corridor.

Half-concussed, unable to see through the thick smoke, Aeron felt Elathan pull her away and down the hall to the lift. All but choking on the dust, they emerged seconds later on the landing-pad a few yards from the hovering aircar. Borvos dashed forward to grab Aeron, his officer Ralia caught Elathan, and together they half-dragged, half-carried them into the ship.

'My gods, Elathan, we thought you'd never get here!' Borvos, so far unstrung with relief and the terror that had gone before it as to forget his formality in his love for his King, slammed the doorseals behind them as Treic lifted off the tower at full throttle.

Even as the craft became airborne, the tower crumbled away beneath, as a second, and greater, explosion disintegrated it into dust and flame and roar.

# Chapter Thirteen

Gwydion had remained with Declan and his Fians on the island in the Kyles of Ra for nearly a month, recovering his spirits and his strength. Then he had left detailed messages for such kin and friends and officers as Declan might chance to find or who might make their way to him, and taking one of the precious starships he had headed out for Kymry.

In so small a ship, the trip took longer than he was used to – *Retaliator*, or his own ship *Seren-alarch*, 'Star-swan', would have made nothing of the distance – but Gwydion was glad of the time thus afforded him for thought. Once safe in hyperspace, he put the ship on autohelm and, for the first time in months, dropped all of the guards he had so rigorously maintained.

His chiefest problem at the moment was the matter of an immediate destination. Gwynedd, of course, was his first thought, and his heart yearned for it, and for his mother and brother, whose fates he had not yet been able to learn; but he put the temptation firmly aside. Jaun Akhera would have ordered to Gwyneddan space every ship he could reasonably, or unreasonably, spare, in hopes of intercepting his escaped prisoner: in which case a nest of piasts would be a safer place by far for Gwynedd's Prince than his own planet.

Or he could try to find *Firedrake*, and Rohan; but that might take long, and this ship had neither range nor resources for a prolonged sail. Caledon, where Aeron's brother Kieran dwelled at Inver, and where Ríoghnach and Niall and many others had fled to, was still farther beyond his reach.

But there was one place, closer by many star-miles, where Gwydion could count on help and friends and shelter. He had not been there for many years; but then he remembered his rights of fosterage, and his doubts vanished.

With confidence he keyed a sequence into the autohelm. *Dyved it is, then: Caer Carrig Cennan.*

Far away, O'Reilly too was sailing blind, hoping for a safe harbour. Her first instinct had been to seek Desmond, but she had quickly realized the impossibility of such a quest. So she had headed for Gwynedd, having heard like everyone else the rumour of Gwydion's escape from Caerdroia, and thinking that even if he did not himself go to Gwynedd, his brother Elved was there, and many others loyal to their Prince, who would, she hoped, welcome one both he and Aeron had honoured with the name of friend.

Gwynedd was a flat silver disc below her when she called the inboard computers into play. Gwydion's seat of Caer Dathyl was only a half-hour's sailing time to the north of her orbital entry position, and she used the minutes of the descent to rehearse what she should say, for Gwydion was sure to be cross with her for not having stayed in sanctuary as Aeron had ordered.

When the ship touched down at last, O'Reilly emerged onto the landing-field into small rain from an overcast sky. In the mist and drizzle, she could see nothing to identify the place for her, and she peered uncertainly through the gloom. *This* has *to be Caer Dathyl*, she thought fiercely, *the coordinates all checked out –*

Then she whirled around, as a squad of cloaked Fians came towards her over the wet paved surface of the field.

She sagged a little with relief: Fians would surely know Desmond – probably they were in Elved's service – and she herself was wearing Fian brown . . .

Her smile turned quickly to a puzzled frown as senses that the Ban-draoi had sharpened came into play. That man who stood off to one side . . . There was something very familiar about him, and very nasty; and the way he hid his right arm beneath his cloak –

O'Reilly turned to flee back to the ship, but they had cut her off neatly and efficiently, and she stood unmoving as the man in the cloak came forward. As he drew his shrunken and withered arm from the cloak's concealment, she knew him without a doubt, and all her hopelessness showed on her face.

'Lieutenant O'Reilly,' said Kynon ap Accolon pleasantly, 'welcome to Gwynedd.'

'It was no easy victory,' he informed her a little later, sitting at his ease in a lavishly appointed tent below the walls of the enormous grey stone citadel of Caer Dathyl. 'Elved is almost as talented in war as his detestable brother.'

'I'm surprised to hear you call it victory,' said O'Reilly, glancing around. 'It seems to me you haven't won until you've broken the defences or taken Elved. It certainly looked like siege – or rather, standoff – to me. And where *is* Elved, anyway? In the castle? No? Ah; somewhere else, perhaps?'

Kynon bridled at the sarcasm in her voice, though her face bore only the most innocent of inquiring expressions. 'You Earthers know little of our manner of making war.'

'No doubt that would explain it,' agreed O'Reilly mockingly. 'But tell me, how did you end up here? The last I heard of you was that the Cremave had taken exception to your little fable about Arianeira and who had led whom into treason, and that Aeron had banished you as daer-fudir. But here you are.'

Kynon scowled at the mention of the Cremave, and his right hand twitched inside the specially tailored pouched pocket where it rested against his chest.

'Aye, and where is *she*?' he snapped. 'But to satisfy your curiosity . . . Jaun Akhera himself appointed me here as his personal lieutenant – in reward for my services – and as liaison to the lords of Dyved.'

'Very nice for you, I'm sure. But I'm afraid I won't be of much help to you.'

'You think not?' Kynon leaned back in the chair, studying her. 'Jaun Akhera has offered a reward for you: not so high as that which he would give for Aeron or Gwydion or Morwen, of course, but an extremely respectable sum all the same. I know not what use he might have for you, but that is no concern of mine.'

O'Reilly pushed her fear out of her mind. 'You will send me to Tara?'

After a moment he shook his head. 'Not just yet. My immediate masters have already ordered that you be sent first to them. Later on, it may well be that they will decide to pack you over to Jaun Akhera, but that is for them to say.'

'Who might these masters of yours be?'

'The Prince of Dyved, my lord Powell; and his son Pryderi, who is lord of Caradigion.' He made a question of it, but O'Reilly shook her head blankly. 'Ah well, they know *you*; and you will come to know them well enough before long. They will be pleased to see you, and pleased still more with me for having found you. Shall we go, then?'

O'Reilly stood up and straightened her cloak. 'Where to?'

'To Powell and Pryderi; where else?'

'Gwydion!' Pryderi stood in the Great Hall of Caer Carrig Cennan, eyes fixed on the man who now approached him.

'Long time since Caer Artos, Pryderi.' Gwydion grasped the other man by the arms in salute. After the briefest of hesitations, Pryderi returned the clasp of friendship, and, weary as he was, Gwydion did not notice the infinitesimal reluctance.

'Long time indeed, my old friend. How came you here? All Keltia thought you a prisoner in Turusachan under the Marbh-draoi's hand; when you called just now for permission to land, I could not believe it was truly you.'

'Myself, right enough; though up until four weeks or so ago I was indeed Jaun Akhera's unwilling guest.' Fatigue overcame him, and he put a hand on the back of a chair to steady himself. 'But may the tale wait until I have eaten, and perhaps rested a while? I did not think to have to remind a friend of the rules of hospitality.'

Again the tiny hesitation, and again Gwydion did not see; then a bright smile, and Pryderi's arm was flung across Gwydion's shoulders.

'And nor did I ever think to need such reminding! Come, Gwydion; you shall bathe and eat and rest as is proper, and later we shall talk, you and I, and my father when he is home from the hunt.'

'You are certain he suspects nothing?' Powell flung his cloak on to a bench by the wall and advanced upon Pryderi, who raised a hand and shook his head in exasperated denial.

'Nay, he has no thoughts of betrayal; why should he have? He came here for sanctuary, to his own boyhood friend and his father's foster-brother.'

'If I remember aright, his own sister gave him excellent reason to suspect any kin-bonds, be they of blood or of fostering.' Powell was stripping off his everyday tunic as he spoke, changing into clothing more appropriate for a feast. 'As for Arawn, he has been dead these twelve years, and in all that time neither of his sons has consulted me thrice on matters either state or personal.'

'Aye, well, what *of* Elved? If he gets wind of our plan for his brother – '

'He will do what? Gwynedd was badly hit by the Imperial fleets, and Caer Dathyl is still under siege – a siege led, I need not remind you, by our faithful servant Kynon. Elved has at present far too much in hand to trouble himself with vague rumours of Gwydion's whereabouts.'

'And the Terran woman, Sorcha ní Reille?'

'Most completely uncooperative. I have had Kynon take her to Caer Sidi; let her cool her heels, and her temper, in Carcair awhile. That prison has loosened the tongues of even the most resolutely silent; sea and isolation often have that effect. Very like, it will see Gwydion too as a guest, before long.'

Pryderi looked startled. 'Gwydion in Carcair? You do not mean to send him to Jaun Akhera? Such an act would assure the Coranian of your good faith beyond all possible doubt; the only thing to gain greater favour would be to turn over Aeron herself.'

'I have not said Gwydion will *not* be returning to Caerdroia,' replied Powell, buckling a jewelled belt around his hips and fixing a formal dirk upon the hanger. 'Only that he will be remaining here on Dyved for a time – until such an hour as I think it most to our advantage to return him. But let us not keep him waiting.'

\* \* \*

When Gwydion came down from the guestchamber, all was ready for the nightmeal in the Great Hall. Though Rohan's warning had not been forgotten, just now it was not at the forefront of his awareness: Powell and Pryderi were friends and family, why should he suspect those two? Later he would wonder that he had had no smallest inkling of what was to follow, but just now he sensed only friendship and sympathy surrounding him; and when he entered the hall, the two Dyvetian lords rose eagerly to greet him.

'Ah, Gwydion! My sorrow I was not here to meet you when you came, but glad am I to see you safe!' Powell embraced him, then held him away at arm's length. 'You have grown to favour your father, lad . . . But come; let us eat and talk.' Taking the seat at the head of the long table, he gestured Gwydion to the chair upon his left against the wall, and Pryderi took his usual place at his father's right.

Over the meal Gwydion recounted to them the events leading to the siege of Caerdroia and the city's fall. Aeron's flight with Morwen, his own escape and his present desperate need to make contact with Rohan. And all through the meal Powell smiled and listened, nodded and smiled, keeping his guest's winecup filled and his ale mether unemptied.

The wine and ale together must have muddled his weary senses, and his memories of boyhood trust lowered his guard, for only too late did Gwydion see in the faces of his hosts a shadow-reflection of their intent. As his othersight confirmed the treachery, he rose so swiftly that his chair was knocked over backward, but the wall behind him opened silently and secretly, and eight of Powell's guards were already through into the room; warrior though he was, Gwydion was soon overmastered.

'My sorrow, Gwynedd, that it must be so.' Powell's

face, for one vivid instant, registered real regret; then it fled, withered beneath Gwydion's blazing grey stare.

'I see it was true, then, what Rohan had heard from Shane: that certain opportunistic Keltic lords had treasonously sold themselves to the Marbh-draoi. Never in a million lifetimes, though, would I have dreamt that Powell of Dyved could be among those.'

'Who knows what he would do, given the choices? Recall you how your own sister chose? Even you, Gwydion, might have done as I have done, did you stand in my place.'

'I think not!' Gwydion, calmer now, though no whit less angry, caught Powell's gaze and held it. 'I make no boasts or threats, Powell, of future vengeance; but I call you to remember that you have betrayed a guest under your roof, and he of your own fostering. You, Dyved, and you also, Caradigion, have shattered the law of the coire ainsec; for which transgression, if harm be meant to a guest, the punishment is death. For the past love that was between us, and between you and my father, I hope that I may not be called upon to be the means of your punishment; but I confess I shall not mind overmuch if so I am.'

Powell's face had remained unchanged through Gwydion's speech, though Pryderi had gone very white. Then Powell: 'Dán shall decide that, Prince of Gwynedd. In the meantime, you shall lodge under another roof than this one, where you will have the company of someone very well known to you.'

'Who, then?' asked Gwydion, as possibilities each more dreadful than the last volleyed through his mind.

But Powell only smiled, and motioned the guards to take him from the room.

* * *

Aboard the *Firedrake*, the officers' common-room was filled with people, in and out of uniform, all in various stages of disarray and disorientation. Among them, Desmond stood apart, his hands hugging his arms under his cloak, and none troubled his silence with ill-timed questions. Across the room, a haunted-eyed Fergus was being urgently talked to by Gwennan Chynoweth, with Aeron's soul-healer cousin, Melangell, hovering nearby.

There came a stir at the door, and Rohan hurried in, clad only in trews and a hastily donned cloak. In all that throng, he saw but one person.

'Desmond – '

Desmond broke then from his glassy stillness, and every eye was on him as he slowly crossed the room. Halting before Rohan, he bowed deeply before his cousin and friend.

'Ard-rígh,' he said then, in a voice that sounded as if the word were dragged from him under torture, and around the room ran a sharp intake of breath, as at a sudden blow. 'My sorrow to announce to you the reported death of the Ard-rían Aeron in an escape attempt on the planet of Fomor. Morwen Douglas, Taoiseach of Keltia – I am sorry, Fergus – and Elathan, King of Fomor, among others, are said to have perished also.'

Then in that worst of all evil moments Rohan laughed. 'They are none of them dead, Desmond, not one; and this is the best word we have had in many weeks.'

'Rohan, we had certain word of it.'

'From *Fomor*? Oh, come! Since what time have we accepted any word from there as truth? Did they tell me stone was hard I would use a rock for pillow.'

There was a rustling among his hearers as his words – and above all, his cheerful everyday attitude – began to work upon their own doubts. Desmond saw it happening, felt it in himself.

'Well, the word comes – through several mouths, I admit – from Talorcan, now calling himself King of Fomor in the stead of his brother Elathan. He says that Aeron landed in secret on Fomor; instead of executing her out of hand, Elathan rather sought her friendship and an alliance with Keltia. Claiming he but followed the wishes of the Fomorian people, Talorcan then overthrew his brother by means of a coup backed by certain disaffected military elements – and, no doubt, with covert Imperial support. He now claims the Iron Crown for his, by right, as Bres's only remaining male heir; so the Princess Rauni's rights, too, have been set at naught. Any road, Elathan fled Tory with Aeron, Morwen and some others; and – again according to Talorcan – they were all killed when their ship was fired upon and destroyed.'

Rohan shook his head impatiently. 'Lies all, and now I am certain of it. They may have gone to Fomor, right enough, but I'll wager any stake you choose and give odds beside that they succeeded in that escape. Elathan too, most like; and Talorcan is no more King of Fomor than I am King of Kelts.'

'Then you will not accept the Ard-ríghachtas?'

'Not only do I not accept it, but I do not accept even the mandate to rule in Aeron's absence. I may be Tanist; but while Aeron lives the only king in Keltia is Gwydion. And that I uphold, until such time as we might have proof incontrovertible that the reality is – is other wise.'

Desmond's face showed despair renewed. 'There is news of him too, Rohan – and of O'Reilly.'

O'Reilly lounged unhappily on the low couch recessed into the stone wall of her cell. By her own tally, she had been stuck here in this godawful prison-castle for a fortnight – a standard two weeks of her own estimation, since she had no idea what a local week was; since she had no idea what planet she was on.

Kynon had brought her here from Gwynedd, to this little island – Caer Sidi, she had been let to know – and then others had escorted her to this castle that stood, an island unto itself, in the cold sea to the north, linked to the larger island only by a single causeway covered completely by water, save for a few minutes a day at low tide.

She kicked listlessly at the thick woven blankets piled at the couch's foot. So far, at least, she had not been ill-treated in the slightest. There had been a few sessions of almost perfunctory questioning, but not the smallest of hint of physical abuse, not the whisper of a hint of a threat. It was all very strange. Her training had of course included many strategies to cope with just this sort of situation, but she could not summon up the energy to try any of them. *Maybe that's just exactly what they want*, she thought idly: to drive her mad by inaction. If so, it was certainly working; all she wanted to do was just lie around and watch the patterns of the sunblink off the sea, reflecting on the plain stone of the ceiling.

But faces kept getting in the way; Rohan's, cheerful under his rumpled red-brown thatch; Desmond's – oh God, Desmond – that impossibly black hair and those impossibly blue eyes; Aeron's, so pale that one could see the veins running blue under the white skin; Gwydion's, eyes grey as the winter sea beyond the windows, lowered as he played the harp . . .

So real were their faces that almost O'Reilly could smell Aeron's sea-rose perfume, almost could hear that crystal shower of notes from the little gold telyn under Gwydion's hands –

With one electrified move O'Reilly sat up, so fast that she hit her head on the couch's overhang. That was no

203

fantasy: The sound of the harp still poured in at her window, and surely there was only one person anywhere who played like that . . . Rubbing her forehead where it had cracked against the stone, O'Reilly pressed herself along the restraint-field that guarded the window and called softly across the little courtyard.

'Gwydion?'

At once the music ceased. She tried again, a little more desperately. 'Gwydion, it's me, O'Reilly – it's Sorcha.'

The harp began again, and she collapsed against the wall in defeat. Then she stiffened with amazement, for it seemed to her that now there was a voice in the music; yet no voice spoke, and she realized that the voice was within her mind, and the voice was Gwydion's own.

'It *is* you, Sorcha; I was afraid to try, lest it be some trick. Nay' – the thought came swiftly as she began to speak – 'say nothing. I have but little time for this before they sense it. Powell and Pryderi – I went to them for help, but they betrayed me; they have sold themselves to Jaun Akhera. But how came *you* here? Think it to me, and I will know.'

O'Reilly closed her eyes and concentrated, and in a moment Gwydion's mind-voice spoke again.

'So, Kynon still lives . . .' The texture of his thought suddenly altered. 'I must leave you now. But I will speak with you again, and soon; we shall make a plan, you and I.'

No sound came now from any quarter, and O'Reilly, still leaning against the wall in staggered disbelief, wondered if the whole thing had not been an illusion. Certainly it had had all the flavour of hallucination . . . But in the night, as she lay awake on her bed, watching the moonlight on the floor and pondering the day's events, she heard the harp again.

# Chapter Fourteen

With Borvos at the controls, the aircar shot away from the palace, streaking like a meteor low over Tory, then arrowing upwards and out over the surrounding mountains, its flight so swift and unexpected that Talorcan's watchposts were taken by surprise, too laggard and too lax even to track its passing.

In the passenger cabin, there was silence taut as an overstrung bow. Elathan was staring out the viewport beside his blastchair, and even Camissa did not intrude upon his mood. On the cabin's other side, Aeron slumped back into the high curved contour of her chair, her eyes closed and her hands resting on the seat's padded arms. She had distanced herself in a light trance, to try to regain some degree of calm after the stresses of the escape, which calm her instincts told her would be soon and sorely needed; but she retained enough everyday awareness to hear what passed around her.

The silence was broken at last by Basilea. 'Where do we go to now?'

Elathan never took his gaze from the planet below him. 'Ask rather the Queen of Kelts.'

Aeron spoke without opening her eyes. 'My ship is hidden near the town where Borvos found me. With the help of the gods, Morwen, who came here with me, is by now safely back there. *Retaliator* can overmatch any craft Talorcan might send against her; and she can carry more passengers away from Fomor than she did bring to it.' She paused a moment to take mental tally: with Morwen and herself, ten people. That would make a not inconsiderable freight even for *Retaliator*, but she knew the ship could easily manage it.

'A generous offer, lady,' said Borvos, who had come into the cabin while she was speaking. 'And indeed we had expected as much, from you, but other arrangements have been made. Only the King shall go with you, by your courtesy; for he will now be hunted as hard on this world as were you on yours when Jaun Akhera took Caerdroia. The rest of us will remain here, in a place that has been prepared against just such a need.'

Thona seemed to stiffen in her seat. 'Then you knew my son was planning treason?'

'Never,' said Borvos fervently. 'But enough of us noticed enough things to make us nervous, and we thought to arrange a safe retreat for the King and his near kin if some emergency should arise. Unfortunately, the emergency came on before we were ready to repulse it. But, with Treic and Ralia, I had at least secured a refuge for us with the dûhín.'

'The dûhín!' Elathan was startled out of his study. 'They do not concern themselves with the affairs of men.'

A strange wistfulness flickered over Aeron's face. 'Once before have I heard that claimed,' she said, so softly as to be speaking more to herself than to the rest of them. 'It proved not so upon my own world, and it is in my mind that it will be not so here as well.''

'Oh Borvos, do you think they will really hide us?' asked Camissa, as she sat with one arm around Rauni's shoulders; Elathan's young sister had said not ten words in all the hours since Talorcan's guards had thrown her into the strongroom prison with the others, and only Camissa seemed able to give her any comfort.

'It is the only hope we have,' he said evenly. 'But yes, I think they will help as they have promised.' He turned to re-enter the command cabin. 'One word more: We have a long flight ahead of us, for I dare not take a more direct route to the southern forests than the one we travel at present, and even so we are sure to pick up some pursuit sooner or later. May I suggest to Your Majesties and your ladyships that you get some rest while you can; if you can. I will see that you are awakened in good time to ready yourselves for the march.' Saluting Elathan, he closed the door after him.

Aeron stretched palug-like, one limb at a time, and sat up straight. The tensions that had been rising in the cabin ever since the predawn departure from Tory were beginning to reach an unimaginable intensity, as complex and interfretted a lattice as any piece of Keltic knotwork. And, as with the knotwork, each strand could be followed under and above and around and behind the others, without break or flaw in the pattern: tension as palpable as a blow, and as dangerous. Without doubt the explosion, when it came at last, would be of a nature and a magnitude none of them would soon forget; or, possibly, forgive. Sleep would be the quickest and easiest way out of it, though a coward's way, and even so she longed all the same to take it; but there was another thing needed more urgently to be done –

She slid from her chair and crossed the aisle to the seat beside Elathan. She knew precisely how he felt at this moment, as no one else in that cabin, in all of Fomor, could know: She too had had to flee her throne to save her life. That it was for them both but a temporary abdication – for she refused to consider any other possibility, and knew he felt the same – made it no jot easier. She put a hand on his arm in sympathy, but he pulled away from the light touch.

'What then?' she said. 'Do you think *I* do not know? Say it out and do not fear.'

'You know already,' he muttered, deeply angry: with himself, Aeron knew, not with her. 'And know it better than anyone: A king should not shy from adversity like some half-broke colt.'

'Well, and neither should he intemperately invite it,' returned Aeron. 'Discretion and caution are no bad underpinning for a crown.'

Elathan burst out laughing in spite of himself, and felt better at once. '*You* say this? I am sorry to laugh, but since what time has Aeron Aoibhell grown such a model of queenly restraint?'

Aeron had the grace to blush. 'I confess I am myself but half-broke to royal harness; though perhaps I have learned somewhat of moderation in the past weeks, however against my will. All the same, that is nothing to do with this.'

'Oh, is it not! Come, Aeron; I invite you to consider your activities since leaving Tara – which I think we have still not got to the bottom of – and then I defy you to speak to me of discretion and of caution. Was it for those you spared Talorcan's life, back there in the tower passage?'

She shook her head. 'For lack of time, rather, to do the job properly . . . Nay, that is not true either: I hesitated for that he is still your brother, and I for one have seen enough of kin-slaughter.'

'Yes, I thought that might be it. But in spite of everything, I cannot say I am sorry you did not kill him.'

'You knew how he hated you, and that he plotted to have Camissa for his own queen, after your overthrow?'

'Oh yes,' said Elathan simply. 'I knew.'

'You knew!' Camissa rose in her seat behind them, a tide of dismay washing over her, feeling hurt and deceived. 'And it made no difference?'

'A very great difference. Had he attempted openly to

take either my crown or my lady I should have put an end to him with my own bare hands. And no hesitation for kinship's sake would have held me back. But for all that, he is my father's son and Thona's, and to take his life . . . Even you, Aeron, forgave Gwydion's sister her treasons. With cause as great as yours, should my clemency be any less?'

'As to my actions, you do not know the half of the reasons for them.'

He turned in his seat to face her full on. 'That is true: I do not. And before I commit myself beyond my ability to pull back' – and here his eyes grew cold indeed – 'I must ask you a thing. Tell us, Aeron, of Bellator.'

It seemed that this time the silence in the cabin would never break. Even Thona and Basilea, who had been maintaining all this while between them a tacit truce, glanced at each other in shared apprehension. Camissa had nearly nerved herself to say something, anything, when Aeron spoke at last.

'Bellator was a lesson and a warning. For *me*, Fomor: not for you nor your father nor even yet your folk. You paid for your ambush, for that you violated all laws of safe and free passage in high space; but I too paid – paid so that I might learn – and the price of that learning is not yet full-reckoned.'

'And did you learn?'

Aeron nodded slowly. 'Oh aye.'

'But how?' Camissa burst out. She was feeling torn two ways at least: It had been only a few days since she and Aeron had come to find each other as friends, and now already this fragile new relationship was being put severely to the test. Yet, try as she might, Camissa could not reconcile the woman she had come to know and like and even begin to admire with the creature who had, alone and unbelievably, killed without mercy a Fomorian planet. 'How could you do it? Not how might you bring yourself to do it – that I think I can understand – but how could such a thing even be done, how *did* you – '

'How!' repeated Aeron bitterly. 'How was the least of it. But true it is that you must know. A spell, then; a spell that never is taught, but that all the same is often learned: by the overcurious or the overconfident or the overvengeful. It is a simple thing – though no simple matter – for a sorcerer, any adept of the Ban-draoi or the Dragons or the Druids, even a Cabiri . . . I could teach it to any of you here. It has any number of uses. It has even been used on me: My foster-sister Arianeira used it to break the Curtain Wall and let the Imperial armadas into the Bawn of Keltia.' She stretched out her left arm, and suddenly the air in the cabin had gone freezing cold. 'Reach out, then; your arm is many thousands of star-miles long, your hand a glove of light with the power of a sun. Close your fingers around that which you would destroy – an eggshell in a mailed fist – then pull back your hand, and the heart of the planet comes with it. Feel how easily it is done. I could do it now, with the world that lies below us.'

Camissa felt as if handful of her guts had been ripped out through the unbroken skin of her belly, and her face must have been as grey as she saw Elathan's to be. Beside her, Rauni was trembling like a puppy against her arm.

Then Aeron released them as abruptly as she had seized them, and the unearthly cold was gone, and her face softened as she looked at each of them in turn.

'But I *would* not do it,' she said. 'Not ever again, not though the fate of Keltia, or Fomor, or the galaxy itself, rode upon my choice. I do not ask you to accept my word; but I give it all the same. You wanted to know, and I have told you.'

*And now we know*, thought Camissa. She forced herself

to speech. 'That was a hard thing for you; harder for you to say, I think, than for us to hear. But I am glad we have been told, and I for one will take that word of yours.'

Aeron, who had been sitting with head bent, hair hiding her face, looked up at the Fomorian woman; then gratitude and surprise came over her countenance, and she turned hastily away as her control started to slip.

But that had been only one strand of the knotwork . . . Queen Basilea had risen from her chair, and was standing now beside Thona.

'There are some other matters of equal difficulty that must be spoken of, and this is the time for those also.'

She looked down at Thona, then, with tremendous precision and a rigid control, dipped and rose again in a court curtsy before her rival.

'My everlasting thanks to you, my lady, for the lives of my son and my daughter and my daughter-to-be, and for my life too, that you saw fit to save at the cost of incurring your own son's hatred. There may never be love between us – after all that has been, I do not know if that ever can be; but surely there might no longer be open warfare?'

At Basilea's first words, Thona's fine eyes had filled with tears, and now thay spilled down her cheek. 'Majesty,' she began, 'madam, there is no need to speak of this.'

Basilea shook her head. 'I have not yet said all that I must say . . . You wished to know, Aeron, why Bres hated your father so? Camissa, I know you too did wonder; well, now all of you shall hear.'

'No, she shall not, nor any of us!' That was Thona, fierce and quick and oddly protective. 'Basilea, I say you will not speak of it.'

'If the Queen of Kelts can find the courage to speak of Bellator, then surely the Queen of Fomor can find strength likewise to speak of Ganaster.' Her voice wavered on the name.

Thona's expression showed only pity. 'There is no need to torture yourself further – what you have done already, in thanking me, is more than enough. You said yourself some past things are best left in the past. Leave it now.'

'If I choose the pain, it is *my* choice; and this truth has long been owed its hour.' Basilea paused by Aeron's chair, then reached down to brush a gentle finger over the younger woman's cheek. 'How fair you are, child; such a look of your father to you.'

Aeron had gone stone-pale and stone-hard at Basilea's touch and the mention of her father alike. 'In such affection was my father held by your late lord, Majesty, that in the end both of them died of it.'

The clear dark eyes that Elathan had inherited met hers steadily. 'And did you never ask yourself, Aeron, what the cause was of that feud? Yes, I am certain that you did. Well, it is not a pleasant tale. Elathan, Rauni, I am sorry you must hear this, and hear it now, but the sooner it is told the better for all. My lord Bres did hate Fionnbarr of Keltia because Fionnbarr and I, together, betrayed him. It was long before you, Aeron, or you, Elathan, were even born; before Fionnbarr wedded Emer, before he had even met her. A very long time ago – even before I had wedded Bres.'

She dared a quick fearing glance at her son's frozen face, at Aeron's white drawn expression, for each of them had seen at once where Basilea's words were leading.

'Yes, we were lovers then on Ganaster, your father and I, Aeron,' she went on, in a voice of iron utterly at odds with the emotion of the words. 'And Bres found us out. A strange thought, is it not, and a supreme irony:

that had things fallen out only a little differently, you two might have been brother and sister.'

As Basilea spoke, a hammer had begun to pound slow blows somewhere deep within Aeron's head; at every stroke, her whole body seemed to resonate with a pain she could not yet feel. *Somehow this is a thing I have long known; why does she trouble me now, with this* . . . It seemed a thing they had all known, without knowing they knew it: a thing that had needed only to be put into words, and the words were the least of it. But Elathan said nothing, and looked at no one; Rauni huddled closer to Camissa; and Aeron, when at last Basilea ceased to speak and looked tentatively at her for reaction or reply, kept her own voice cool and neutral, forming her words with care around the hammering in her head.

'Even given this tale is true, Bres carried his great hatred down the years, pulling Fomor, and the Phalanx, and in the end the Imperium, into the feud with him. There must have been more to it than this alone.'

'There was,' said Thona. 'Princes' squabbles, political vendettas . . . In brief, there was a dispute between Bres and your father, Aeron, over a planetary system each kingdom claimed under the terms of a treaty made by the High Queen Aoife many years before. Probably neither kingdom had the right to annex it, but that does not matter now. Against all advice, even that of his own father King Budic, Bres conducted the case before the Justiciary on Ganaster, and his betrothed was with him.' She glanced up at Basilea's haunted face, and faltered. But the Queen nodded once, and with a sigh Thona continued. 'Fionnbarr won, embarrassing Bres before Budic, and before Fionnbarr's father the High King Lasairían and the Phalanx overlords and even Strephon's father, the Emperor Errazill-jauna who died the following year. Bres never forgave Fionnbarr for it. But even so, that was nōt the true ground of Bres's hatred.'

'No,' said Aeron. 'The cause of *that* was other where . . . Did you love my father, madam?' she snapped suddenly at Basilea, in a voice that was no longer either cool or neutral, a voice like a tiger's leap.

Basilea flinched at the violence implicit in that voice, as had many others before her, but she answered at once. 'I did, Aeron. From the first moment I saw him on Ganaster, at the time Thona spoke of; I loved him, and he me. I did not know then that he was heir to Keltia, not until after; no more did he know I was affianced of Bres. We did not need to know such things, though when at last we came to learn the truth of it, it was the death of our time together. Even then he asked me to leave Bres and come with him, that he would make me Queen of Keltia, but I lacked the courage, and after that he did not ask again. Then he met Emer, and chose her for his queen; I knew he loved her dearly and had put me from his mind. But I loved him on Ganaster, and I loved him when I stood with Bres to be married, and gods forgive me but I love him still.'

'And Bres? What of your royal husband?'

'Over the years I came to respect him,' said Basilea in a steady voice. 'And to admire him as a king. I gave him three excellent and beautiful children, and I lived with him as a loyal wife and queen and partner, sharing his throne and his duties. But never did I love him, and he knew it. And in part to punish me for it, he kept to Thona for all the worlds to see . . . You spoke before of prices paid, Aeron; well, this is the price that I have paid, down all the years, for that time on Ganaster. And until four years ago, I counted the cost well spent. Then Bres attacked the embassy ship – What do you imagine I felt then, when I heard that Fionnbarr was dead, and

Emer, and your Roderick and all those others? That too was part of the price for what we had done; Fionnbarr paid, and I paid, and now Bres too has paid.'

'A very great pity, Queen Basilea, that the last crossic of that price has not yet been counted out.' Aeron's voice had the cold curl of An-Lasca, the Whip-wind itself, to it now. 'True it is that I myself exacted from Bres that price you speak of, as éraic for my kin; but I have paid a price of my own to this rechtair vengeance, and so now has your son. And your son as well, Thona, will be made to pay dearly in days not so far off now, for his share in this debt; be very sure of that. My compliments to Basilea: Few women of Fomor, or indeed anywhere else, can have exacted so great a fee for their favours.'

'Aeron – ' began Thona.

'Nay, madam, leave off – though it must be said, Lady Thona, that you were loyal indeed to your Queen. All these years you kept her secret, better than many friends might have done, and you all the time her detested rival . . . For *that*' – here the coldness became freezing flame, and even Elathan, who was scarcely less angry than she, flinched at it – 'for that, Bres set kingdom against kingdom, held hatred alive for decades, took enmity to his marriage-bed, turned the Phalanx against Keltia, allied with the Imperium for sheer malice's sake. For that, he bloodied his hands with treacherous murder, caused me to use my art in vengeance, himself died under my sword and came within a blade's thickness of compassing my own death. And in the end his acts did cause his rightful heir to be overthrown and hunted into exile by his other son. I do not – cannot – hold my own father free of blame in this, but when I see where love may lead I begin to lose hope.'

'Love?' asked Elathan. 'Would you call it so?'

Aeron looked over at him for one unguarded moment,

and for all his own pain, his heart nearly failed him at what he saw in her face.

'I must, else I must call it – well, no matter. It is long over, and I must put it aside as others have done before me. But I mind me of first causes, and also of a thing Gwydion said to me once . . .'

Without another glance at any of them. Aeron turned to the window, setting her back at them and her face to the cloudy dark.

# Chapter Fifteen

It remained so in the cabin for some hours: Aeron wearing cold anger like a cloak; Elathan in a state of mind only a little less turbulent than hers; Camissa and Rauni huddled together, the dark head of the one drooping as she dozed, the other curled up on the seat beside her, as neatly asleep as a golden kitten; Thona and Basilea, each consumed with her own thoughts and hurts and memories, and those were the same thoughts and hurts and memories.

But it was Aeron and Elathan who had been wounded deepest by Basilea's confession; and all understood, themselves not least, that they were best left alone just now, to allow to work the alchemy of reason upon emotion.

In Elathan at least, that process was already well advanced. In the first moments of his shock, he had felt much the same feeling as had Aeron: rage – at Bres, at Fionnbarr, at Basilea; revulsion that such a feud had been permitted to grow so monstrously; revulsion too that it had had so base an origin. But then, little by little, his reason began to prevail, and his temper cooled, and he stole a quick glance across at Aeron. Her face was still rigorously averted, so that all he could see was a veil of coppery hair, but even with her back turned her posture seemed eloquent of fury.

He sighed and looked once more out the viewport, though by now it was night again and nothing could be seen of the surface of his Throneworld far below. He could perfectly well understand her anger and pain, for he shared most of it: her father, his mother – it seemed almost beyond comprehension, and still more so than that, the answer Bres had made to the problem. Inappropriate, the alienists would say, for Bres to have responded so. But he had, and in so doing he had changed galactic history and altered the course of many lives; not least of those his own heir's. *Yet how can I blame either of them, when I myself entertained much the same feeling – however briefly – for Fionnbarr's daughter* . . .

And then there was Thona. Elathan almost groaned aloud at the thought of her. In the heat and hurry of escape, her sacrifice had gone unnoticed and unappreciated: In electing to free them from their prison she had set her own son against her; she had chosen Elathan over Talorcan, as she had done so often before, letting love override the claim of birth. *And this time Talorcan would never forgive*, thought Elathan, *neither her nor me* . . .

But such emotion cannot long endure at such a pitch: By the time the cabin door opened once again, to admit Ralia – an officer of Elathan's guard who had been assigned months before to protect Camissa – the mood in the cabin had moderated to something more bearable of intensity, though no less deeply felt.

Even Ralia sensed it; she paused beside Elathan's chair, spoke tersely and swiftly, then vanished back forward with an air of intense relief. Elathan rubbed his tired eyes and swung about in his chair.

'We shall be landing in a few moments: Borvos tells us to use the restraint fields on our chairs.' He suited action to words, and the others followed his example, Aeron last of all.

The aircar landed without incident; outside it was full dark, and as they were making ready for the march, Borvos and his two officers came to assist them.

'As near as we can make it,' he said to Elathan, 'this is within ten miles of where the Queen of Kelts is thought to have landed her ship. There would be more accurate information, but the Queen hid the craft too well for us to find it.'

'Aye, well, let us hope that *I* can find it.' They turned in surprise, for the voice was Aeron's. She had spoken no word for hours, not since Basilea's disclosure, and had spent the time since in a mood compounded of rage, heartsickness and her struggles to master both, or either: For in truth she did not know with whom she was angriest – Bres, Basilea, her father or herself. *Though I am a fine one to judge*, she thought bitterly. Fionnbarr and Basilea, or Aeron and Elathan – was there any difference at all; and if there was, was that difference only in degree, and not in kind? True, she and Elathan had acted only minimally on what they had felt, had recognized it and rejected it as their parents had not done; but that she had felt it at all now made up a not inconsiderable part of her inner turmoil, and it had taken much to quell it.

But she had succeeded so far in that now a kind of blank weariness was all she felt, and, rising from her seat, she ran an indifferent look over the others who now watched her so closely. In her new mood, their unease seemed to her almost comic. *But what do they expect me to do*? she thought. To rail at the choices of the past was a fairly futile exercise; one wove the best and most serviceable cloak one could from what threads one had to hand. What wool had been sheared to spin those threads was no choice of one's own; only the pattern, the weave and weight itself . . . and even that was dictated by dán, by the ever-changing weather of one's fate.

'I have means of locating *Retaliator*, of course,' she added aloud. 'But there is a tirr – an unlight, a cloaking effect – over it, and that is always chancy.'

'And Morwen?' asked Elathan.

Aeron let a moment pass. 'She will have found her way back to the ship by now.'

'And if she has not?'

'Question me less, King of Fomor, and furnish me instead with a few more answers! We are still upon *your* throneworld!' Aeron saw Rauni shrink back against the cabin wall, and was instantly remorseful. 'I am sorry to snap, but you *press* me so, Elathan . . . Are there no folk who live in the forest, that she might have taken refuge with?'

'None to speak of,' said Elathan, slinging a pack onto his shoulders and helping Camissa with hers. 'Save for the dûhín; and, no matter the arrangements made by Borvos, they fear humans. I doubt if they would come to the aid of a stranger lost in the wood.'

His head jerked sharply upwards, as a sudden sound came to his keen ear, and a new wariness crossed his face. Aeron's gaze met his in shared concern, for she too had identified the sound: the muffled whine of pursuing aircars, flying low.

Two hours later, Borvos allowed them to rest briefly from their strenuous nightmarch in a little clearing, its floor plush with moss, bisected by a chattering stream. Aeron lay down beside its banks and scooped up clear water in both hands to drink, then lowered her flushed face into the welcome coolness. Beside her, Rauni sank cross-legged into the ferns, a little timid still, but the warmth of Aeron's smile gave her heart.

'I have a sister of my own who is about your age,' said Aeron as if in explanation. 'And I wonder where she is now . . . please gods, in a better place than are we.'

Rauni bent to drink from the stream, holding her blond plaits away from the water. 'Do you think they can track us here?'

Aeron shook her head. 'Not by night, not from the air; even their nightsight devices would be thwarted, for there are many beasts in the wood, and we should look much the same as they on any scanner's board. But certainly they have followed us thus far, to where we set down in the aircar, and I fear it will go hard with us if we have not found *Retaliator* before the sun is well up; or, if not that, then at least some place of shelter to wait out the sun again, for we dare not travel by day. Whatever, we must not linger overlong in one place . . . How does your mother?' added Aeron in a lower voice. 'And the Lady Thona?'

Rauni turned her head away from the others, and spoke as low. 'Not very well. They make a brave effort, but they are not accustomed to such activity.'

'No more, I think, are you, alanna . . . Well, perhaps Borvos can find us a place to spend the daylight hours. Where is your brother?'

Elathan was sitting alone on the other side of the clearing, one hand trailing in the waters of the stream. He greeted Aeron with a tired smile; there seemed to be peace again between them, and as if by tacit consent each avoided mention of the day's revelations.

'No ground pursuit?'

'None that I can detect,' she said. 'Still, Treic and I have covered our trail as best we can. When day comes they might put land-trackers, or hounds even, upon our traces. It cannot be far now to *Retaliator*, and my lithfaen seems in good order, but to – ' She broke off, flinging up a warning hand to the others.

Her caution proved unnecessary. With a sigh and a smile, Borvos stood up, palms turned outwards and empty, and spoke to the rustling wood around them in a soft-voiced bubbling language.

And he was answered from the trees. His weary and

bewildered charges thought at first *by* the trees, and in their exhausted stupor they could have accepted even that. But then the underbrush parted, and they saw who it was that had spoken.

Aeron woke to cool golden dawnlight and a strange rushing sound like many waters. After a moment, she realized that the rushing sibilance was not water but wind through the branches of trees in full leaf, and that the shelter she lay in was woven of living saplings. She turned her memory back to bring her to this place: There had been a long dark march in the night behind unseen guides, then welcome warmth, and food, and sleep. She sat up cautiously. Beyond her, Rauni lay curled up under the same light nubby blankets that swathed Aeron; on her other side slept Elathan and Camissa. The rest of the little party lay on the far side of the leaf-thatched shelter; all were deep asleep.

Sensing someone's attention on her, Aeron snapped her head round to the doorway. Within the woven curtain, hazy in the morning sun, stood three figures, one a little in advance of the others. She stared at them in wonder, for these were the dûhín, and she had barely glimpsed them the night before.

Small they were, of only the stature of a ten years' child among the Kelts, and delicately built, with six thin elegant fingers, two of them thumbs, on each hand; they were green-skinned like the tiny jade-coloured treesnake, with hair of a darker green, and no visible ears. Their clothing, what there was of it, appeared to be woven of the same slubbed fibre as the blankets; they were clothed in treestuff. They wore no shoes or boots, and the six toes on each foot were prehensile; but where their eyes should have been was only the same feathery fur that covered the rest of their bodies.

'You cannot see!' she gasped unthinkingly, with the tactless bluntness of a child, then apologized at once. 'My sorrow to speak so – I will be less rude when I am less weary.'

The foremost figure smiled; or rather, the feeling that emanated from it was the feeling of a smile, though far more than any smile of the mouth could ever be. It spoke to her then, and its voice was strangely tuneful, as if a stream were to speak; her ear caught the rhythms of the bubbling language Borvos had used in the clearing in the night.

'It is true that the dûhín have not eyes as you do know them; but we see well enough even so. You, lady: You are tall and slender, and crowned with red like a rowan-tree in autumn, and you have the knowledge of the trees. What tree is your own? Think us the picture of it, and say its name, and we shall know if you say true.'

'Saille,' she breathed in the Gaeloch, the picture already forming in her mind: the grey-green bark of the furrowed trunk, the silvery sword-edged leaves.

'Ah, you have the willow-wisdom: wide-spreading, firm-rooted, sheltering many, yielding in time of great storms. Nor are you a stranger to speech without speaking, or Sight that needs not eyes. And there is one beside you – he is not here in the body, but I see him all the same – your lord, I think. Very tall he is, and straight as an ash-spear, with a hand to draw music from the singing wood. What tree is to him?'

'Derwyth,' said Aeron, still softly, and the strength of the oak in her mind stiffened her back.

'The Door-tree of the Universe; oak and willow, a good combination – strength with flexibility. A fated pairing, to make one soul of two. This is strong magic.' The wild thing came forward, and Aeron sat very still. 'I am called Ta-vecher,' it said. 'These my brothers are

Cho-runya and Vi-khansa. You are welcome to the home of the dûhín.'

Aeron bowed with as much dignity as the blankets and her disarray allowed. 'I am called Aeron,' she said. 'But you will have known that already.'

A wave of amusement rippled from the dûhín. 'That and more,' said the one called Vi-khansa. 'We have given you our help, as was agreed, for the sake of our King; but also we have been harbouring another stranger for some days now – someone that you, Aeron, will be glad to see again.'

The curtains at the door rustled in the rising breeze; a hand caught them back, and, against all hope or logic, Morwen stepped inside.

Aeron was across the room in one move, hugging her, laughing and weeping and cursing and talking, and Morwen was doing all those same things back, and now the others had sat up, wakened by the sound of reunion.

Over the morning meal, tales were exchanged. Morwen listened with horror and fascination to Aeron and Elathan, but when pressed to recount her own adventures, only shrugged.

'Little enough to tell,' she said through a mouthful of cheese and bread. 'When the cam-anfa had passed over, Aeron, I looked long and hard for you, but I could not find you in the wood. I wandered in the forest until nearly dawn, and then I lay down both hoping and expecting never to wake up again on this side of this life. But when I opened my eyes, these were all around me.' She indicated the dûhín. 'They took me to a village of theirs not far from here, and fed me, and made me supremely comfortable, and gave me such news as they could. But they had heard no word of you, Aeron, not until Borvos came here a week ago to make his final arrangements for sanctuary. They did not tell him that I was here, but he told the dûhín chiefs that things were unsettled in Tory, and like to grow more so, and looked not good for Elathan; and then he spoke of Aeron, and of her friend that went missing. Ta-vecher passed all this on to me, and that' – she shrugged again, this time smiling – 'is all my tale. I came here only just now with some folk from the village I have been staying in – At-valki and Ni-laro, a few others.'

Aeron shook her head. 'So all this time you have been living in this fair place, with these most wonderful folk, while I have been shut up in Tory fretting for your safety.' The smile on her face belied the mock severity. 'Fergus would have committed regicide and kin-slaughter both upon me, had I returned to Keltia without you.'

'And if we speak of returning – ' Morwen paused.

'Oh, we have no secrets here any longer,' said Aeron. 'Elathan comes with us on *Retaliator*. The others remain with the dûhín, until such time as we return from our errand.'

'But why did you come to Fomor at all?' asked Ta-vecher. 'An enemy planet, and you in flight for your lives – '

'We came here because Arthur came here. He was King of Kelts long ago, and fought the Fomori, among many others. He was known to offworlders – and to us too, after, for the device he bore – as the Red Dragon.'

'The Red Dragon!' said Elathan, as astonished as the others of his countrymen. 'Why did you not say so sooner? Everyone on Fomor has heard tales of him: how he outfoxed the Vellamians, and stole a march on our own King Nanteos, and courted the warrior-queen of the Yamazai; and many more tales besides. But he did not remain here very long, Aeron; only long enough to make a rescue of the fewscore Kelts we had taken in the raid on Clero. He freed them, and then he was gone, and they with him.'

She nodded. 'This we know, though little more. Any road, we seek the wreck of his flagship *Prydwen*; on board that ship, we hope to find the Thirteen Treasures, vanished from Keltia these fifteen hundred years.'

'What are these Treasures?' asked Rauni.

'No one knows for certain,' admitted Morwen. 'There have been goleor of lists in song and story; many of the Treasures may well be mythical, or even mystical. It is said they were thirteen in number, but tallies vary as to what they were: such things as a halter that could tame even a falair; a dagger that could draw blood from the wind; a chariot that could run on land or sea; a cloak of invisibility; a drinking-horn and food-wallet that could never be emptied no matter how many were given to eat and drink; and other things beside. But all accounts agree on four objects most sacred of all: a sword of light that can cut through any substance no matter how thick; a spear that never fails to find and destroy its target; a cauldron that can heal any wound and even death itself; and a stone that can bring death for a mile round to any who look upon it unprotected. These are said to have come with the Danaans of old when they fled Atland and came to Ireland, from the holy cities – or they might have been planets – Falias, Findias, Murias and Gorias.'

No one spoke for a little, then Camissa looked up. 'How do you know that these things – if they exist – are on the ship you seek?'

'We do not know,' said Aeron. 'Gwydion was merely bidden to tell me to seek for *Prydwen* and the lost Treasures, and I decided that this should be my path. I may well be mistaken; but without that word I should certainly have remained on Tara.'

'Where by now – just as certainly – you would be dead

at Jaun Akhera's hand, you and Gwydion and Morwen all three,' said Elathan. 'And, for you would not then have come to Fomor, I and my kin likewise at Talorcan's. I owe a debt to whoever gave Gwydion that word. When we come to Tara I shall thank that one myself.'

Aeron gave him a long thoughtful look, but said nothing.

'But where shall you go now? Children?' Thona had understood little of the conversation, but had been fretting silently over the immediate future of the three who would be remaining.

'I do not know, lady,' answered Morwen. 'The words we were following led us here, and no farther. Unless Aeron has managed to glean some new knowledge from the poem in her time since?'

'I have not, though not for lack of trying; I had much leisure at Tory for scholarship.'

Basilea, silent all this while, spoke up suddenly, as an old, half-forgotten tale that had been tugging at her memory came clear at last.

'This Arthur – whom we call the Red Dragon – he went on, did he not, Aeron, to his final resting place?'

'He did: a land called Afallinn.'

'I know, I have heard some of your hero-tales – but that is its name among its own folk. Offworlders know that place as Kholco.'

Aeron sat up so violently that she scattered the crockery on the low table. 'Kholco! That is the volcano planet – is it close by?'

'Not far,' said Borvos. 'But it is a terrible place. The only ones who live there are the Salamandri, the Firefolk. It is not a world for humans.'

'But humans could survive there?'

'For a time, in the more stable areas. It is said that the Salamandri themselves dwell in the very fire-mountains. You did not know of this?'

Aeron shook her head, her mind plainly racing. 'All know in Keltia that Arthur's long home was in the island Afallinn, but I would guess that if any ever knew at all that such a place was a planet, the knowledge was lost with the raising of the Curtain Wall. Not even the bards have a record that Afallinn is Kholco. I am grateful to the Queen Basilea; this information has surely saved us time and trouble, and may save us all in the end.'

'No thanks owed to me,' said Basilea quietly. 'It was Fionnbarr who first told to me those tales; only long afterwards did I learn that the two places were in truth the same. You will go there?'

'I must, and at once,' said Aeron, looking not at her but at Elathan. 'For I give my promise that, if we come to find the Treasures, they go first to Fomor to win back Elathan's throne for him, before we take them home to Keltia to regain my own.' She placed her hand over her heart in pledge of the oath, and Elathan inclined his head in acknowledgement and acceptance.'

'And I go with you,' he reminded her. 'As we agreed.'

'If he, then I,' said Camissa a little defiantly, as if she feared Aeron would deny her the journey, and leave her behind with the others among the dûhín.

But Aeron only gave her a level look, then nodded assent; and Camissa was too surprised at the ease with which she had apparently obtained permission – and too grateful that it had been given – to pursue any reasons.

'We will leave for *Retaliator* tonight,' said Aeron then, 'when it is dark enough for safety. In the meantime – ' She rose from the low table. 'Elathan, I know you have business of state to settle with Borvos and with your mother and sister; I leave you to it. As for myself' – she smiled down at the dûhín still seated upon the cushions – 'I shall speak with Ta-vecher and his kin, if it is their pleasure, concerning the knowledge of the trees.'

# Chapter Sixteen

'You sent for me, father?' Helior entered the fountain-room, her slippered feet silent on the marble floor, and made the sketchiest of obeisances before approaching the Emperor's chair.

'That I did,' said Strephon after a rather long pause. He looked up at her with an unreadable expression, then down at a computer billet that rested in his lap. 'There has been some news.'

Helior kept herself to utter stillness, only her hands clenching and unclenching in the silken folds of her skirts betraying her effort.

'Has there?'

Strephon began to laugh – a convulsive silent chuckle – and his voice was a purr. 'Oh, *very* good! A most convincing display of disinterest – I'd not have thought you had it in you . . . Well, it seems that apparently I have loyal servants in occupied Keltia after all, who are capable of getting a simple message to me in spite of the Kelts' best efforts to the contrary.'

'My son – '

The purr became a throbbing snarl. 'Your son, madam, seems more and more *in*capable, however simple the task! I wonder now that I ever thought him able to win me Keltia, let alone fill my throne after me.' He flung the billet at her; she made no move to catch it, and it fell to lie half-concealed by the hem of her skirt. 'Not only could he not keep Aeron Aoibhell safely imprisoned in a fallen and garrisoned city, he could not even manage to hold on to the one valuable hostage he *was* left with – the Prince of Gwynedd, or, as I suppose I must now call him, the King-consort of Keltia.'

'Gwydion has escaped?'

'He has. Is Jaun Akhera deaf and blind as well as careless, to let his only bargaining asset stroll out of Turusachan, and not lift a finger to prevent it?'

Helior flushed. 'From what I have heard of Gwydion – '

Strephon cut her off with a wave of his hand. 'Yes, yes, no doubt. Still, the fact remains that your son had him and now he has lost him.'

Helior's fingers tightened until the jewelled nail-tips drew blood from the ball of her thumb. 'May I ask how this message came to you? I had thought communications into and out of Keltia were mostly jammed by the Kelts.'

'Ah, now that *was* clever. A smallship broke through the blockade and got far enough outside the Curtain Wall long enough to get a message off to me. They were detected by the Kelts, of course, and destroyed, but the transmission was already safely sent.'

There was silence in the room for a few moments, broken only by the plashing of the fountain.

Then Helior: 'What will you do now?'

Again Strephon paused before he answered. 'I have thought much on this,' he said then, and a tide of dread lapped around her at the implicit pity in his tone. 'I warned you this might happen . . . My only recourse now is to remove Jaun Akhera as my heir-designate. I entrusted him with the most critical, delicate and desperate military operation we have ever undertaken, and he has made of it only a shambles. The gains he did make now crumble daily under his fingers, but his grasp on Keltia was a feeble one from the first. Doubtless he was overmatched against Aeron after all . . . Since I had informed him before he left that he would get no further assistance from me, I can hardly use that now as either

230

threat or punishment. So this is my only alternative, and I do not choose it lightly, or willingly, or gladly. But according to our law the heirship, the etcheko-primu, is mine to bestow as I please. Any Coranian has this right, the head of any house, be he Emperor or goatherd; and I truly thought I had chosen well.' He looked up at her. 'I am sorry, Helya, that it must be so.'

Helior bowed her head, keeping her face carefully empty of what she was feeling. 'I understand and accept, my father, though you know as well as I how little I like it . . . Well, give you good night, then. Perhaps the morning will bring better news, or new counsel.' She bent over him, brushed a cool kiss on the seamed cheek and was gone.

Strephon stared after her. That was never like her, to take such a blow as that so mildly and so calmly. His fingers moved mechanically, stroking the long fur of the little dog he held in his lap. Helior had coveted the Imperial heirship for Jaun Akhera too long and too fiercely to allow it to be snatched away now; she had even relinquished her own rights and expectations in the succession to be the surer of the coronet, and the greater crown to come, for her eldest. She would not now sit tamely by and watch the prize go to another – one of her brother's neckless brood, it would have to be, for Sanchoniathon, loyal to perhaps a fault, would never accept the heirship over his elder brother. No, Helior would not allow Akhi to be so dispossessed and displaced; she would sooner kill him, Strephon, first.

*And that being so* . . . Strephon set the little dog carefully on the floor and leaned back in his chair. Well, flesh of his flesh though she be, *that* he could not run the risk of. Since Helior could no longer be trusted to put her father's life above all other values, she herself could no longer be trusted to live.

231

Strephon permitted himself a pang of remorse at the decision. The woman was, after all, his own and only daughter; she had been his dead wife's pet. But even Azaco would have understood Imperial necessity as it applied here. It was a pity to have to decide so, but pity mattered not a whit: If he allowed pity to hold back his hand, Helior would surely strike him down first.

'A pity all the same,' he said aloud, and snapped his fingers for the little dog to come to him.

When the summons came from the Princess Helior, delivered by an impassive maidservant, Tinao did not obey at once, but nodded a mechanical acceptance and some words of reply. Though she did not know what in her panic she had said, it must have made at least some sense, for the servant bowed and went away again.

Tinao sat staring into the mirror of her dressing-table, seeing not even her own exquisite reflection. Something must have happened, then, something fairly terrible, for the Princess had few reasons to send for her son's mistress . . . If it had been something to do with Jaun Akhera, by now the news would have been all over the palace. Therefore it must be the other thing: Helior was ready to move against her father the Emperor, for the sake of her son the Emperor's heir; and now she summoned Tinao to fulfil her promise.

*So it begins*, thought Tinao, fresh panic rising at the imminence of the thing. *And I gave my word to her that I would aid her. I cannot withdraw now even if I would. Death to break that word, and perhaps death as well to keep it* . . . With bleak resolve, she pinned up her streaming hair and left the room.

Since the interview with her father in his fountain-room, Helior had not been idle, neither of thought nor of deed.

Plans had been made, messages sent far afield – to Talorcan, to Laharan, to other planets and other places where favours were owed her and deference due. It had not been easy, as she had known it would not be, to decide upon her father's death as her only sure way of keeping the Cabiri Throne for Jaun Akhera. But she was not only her father's daughter but her son's mother: Once that death had been determined upon, it remained only to find the best and the easiest way to accomplish it. Strephon was wary with years and nature, and more than a few overreachers – her own late husband among them – had tried in years past to achieve what she sought now. They had tried, and they had failed, and they had perished very painfully for it.

*I must* not *fail*, she thought passionately, fingering the gold collar at her throat. *For Akhi's sake I must not* . . .

But plots take time to arrange, for suspicion must be avoided and traces concealed, and some weeks passed uneventfully by in the palace at Escal-dun before any move was made.

For all that time, Helior had been the very model of a dutiful daughter. Though she was careful not to overstep her habit and so rouse her father's suspicions, nevertheless she was equally careful to be seen with him by others in the palace as often as might be, and never in anything other than a merry or a loving mood. She walked a fine line and she walked it well, for when at last the night came that she had staked all upon, Strephon was not expecting it.

Which was not to say that he had become careless, lulled or gulled into fatuity or trust by Helior's machinations; nor had he repented of his own intentions towards her. It was only that – well, he was old, and he was tired, and it was surprisingly pleasant to sit with his daughter of an evening, and with his old friend Tenjin's pretty child, the one Akhi was so fond of; and listen to them sing, or play the cithere, or let them beat him in a game of senet for stakes of a bracelet or a biscuit . . . It was a habit they had fallen into during the months that Akhi and Sancho had been away at the war; nothing new there, and so nothing to suspect.

So when the guards outside the anteroom to his chambers admitted Helior that warm spring night, accompanied as usual by Tinao and that eunuch who was never far from her side, Strephon did not think to think ill of it. That that lack of thought might perhaps prove fatal, never even crossed his mind.

It had, however, crossed the minds of some others. Earlier that night, there had been a scene in Tinao's rooms . . .

'I cannot do it! I cannot do as she asks!' Tinao, face blotched with tears, black hair ragged where her fingers had torn in distraction at its smooth coils, looked wildly up at Indarrak. 'I thought I could, for Akhi's sake, and so I promised. But it is impossible, 'Darrak, and what shall I do now?'

*'Darrak*, he thought. *She has not called me that since she was a child; but she is still a child, and no child should be made to play such odious games* . . .

'What has she asked, innaga?'

Tinao laughed, a silvery note of hysteria in the usually sweet sound. 'What has she not! I have just spent three hours with her – three hours of unbearably complicated plots to do with powders in rings and potions in wines; there was even some talk of a retro-poison to be baked into the breadcrumbs he feeds to his goldfish!'

'Which will she attempt?'

'She had not decided when I left her,' said Tinao with

a tired shrug. 'Neither the means nor the time has yet been fixed on; though not for any daughterly softening of heart, I can assure you. She grows colder and harder and more like Strephon every hour – almost I cannot believe that Akhi is her son.'

Indarrak had lowered his eyes and kept his face a noncommittal mask. Not for all the worlds would he have insulted Tinao by saying so, but she was probably the only person in the Imperium ever to call Jaun Akhera's heredity into question – particularly his maternal antecedents: So patently was he his mother's son, and she her father's daughter, that sometimes it took one's breath away to watch them all together.

Yet it hurt him to think that his young mistress needed to think of putting her hand to the same Imperial muck . . . 'Do not worry,' he said at last. 'You will not have to obey Helior's command. You will not disobey her either, but you will not need to do anything you do not wish to. Trust me.'

Tinao looked up at him through long dark lashes that tears had spiked together. 'You have said that ever since I was a little girl – "Trust me."'

'And you did.'

'And I did, and was never once sorry for it.'

'Then do so still. You will not be sorry now either. Ready yourself to go to the Princess; it is nearly time for her to make her nightly visit to her father, and he will expect you there as usual.'

Always that voice and that face had meant security and love and trust for her; inconceivable that it should now be otherwise . . . Presently Tinao began to repair the damages done to her hair and eye-paint, and Indarrak withdrew to wait upon her finishing.

\* \* \*

'See, father, Tinao is here to play for you.' Helior took her customary place on one of the silk-draped couches that ringed the carp-pool, reclining on one elbow, the fingers of her other hand trailing in the cool waters of the fountain. A few hungry carp came up, nibbling at her fingers for their usual breadcrumb meal, and she repressed a shudder and the sudden mad longing to bat them out of the water, like a bear seeking his supper.

She threw a glance across the pool at her father. *He seems old tonight*, she thought. Older, and tired, and yes, bored with things. Perhaps it was boredom at the root of creation: the real force behind the universe, the true face of entropy, the natural state of existence; and all deeds that ever were done were only vain struggles to not be bored . . . She saw her father's gaze begin to swing around to her, and she forced herself to stare idly at the glittering fall of the fountain's water amid the exotic water-plants. The sound of Tinao's little cithere mingled with the noise of the falling water, and Helior tried to relax. Another dull domestic evening, the Imperial family at home – but another cornerstone in the edifice of normality she was constructing brick by dull laborious brick, so that some night soon, one night neither dull nor normal . . .

With a shock colder than the iced drink she sipped, Helior felt Strephon's attention upon her; he looked neither old nor tired, and most assuredly he did not look the least bit bored. The citrine eyes were blazing, and triumph was scrawled across the furrowed face.

'So, I have caught you out at last, my daughter . . . No, do not trouble to deny it; I knew you should grow careless sooner or later. You hid your thoughts well all these weeks; almost I believed – well, no matter now what I believed. But the Plexari have long been skilled at reading each other's thought: You are my child, I am your father; how could we not know what the other is thinking? But I will tell you all the same: You planned to kill me to secure the crown – *my* crown – for Jaun Akhera, and I planned to kill you before you could do so. The question now is, who has been the swifter to plan – and to act?'

But before Helior could draw breath to answer him, before the denial that would never have convinced the stupidest slave in the palace was even formed in her frantic brain, Indarrak had moved from his place along the wall – implacable, huge, silent, strong. Indarrak, who had come tonight as attendant to Tinao according to his custom and duty; who had stood in the shadows, again as was his custom, noticed by Strephon no more than a piece of furniture; Indarrak, who now plucked the Cabiri Emperor from his golden chair; who – expressionlessly, silently, without even the sound of a splash to alert the guards beyond the doors – pitched the old man down into the tiled carp-pool, and, with all his giant's strength, held him under the surface of the water.

The carp fled in panic from the billowing white linen, the thrashing limbs; then suddenly there was no more movement, no more bubbles rising from below, and Indarrak's glance came up to meet Helior's in perfect understanding.

'That's finished, then,' he said.

And still Tinao sat frozen upon her pillow, her fingers continuing to pick out the Emperor Strephon's favourite melody, like some ghastly and inappropriate dirge, upon the little cithere.

Helior swung her gold-slippered feet to the floor and padded around the pool's circumference. No question but that it was finished: Her father's body floated face down, limp and lifeless, among the lilies and water-acanth and bright-striped amylle. *Better sure than sorry* . . . She arched one slim leg over the pool's rim, and with the point of one of the gold slippers gave Strephon's floating form a vigorous shove. The body bobbed gently in the water, and Helior turned away in satisfaction.

'You have done well, Indarrak,' she said then. 'Superbly well, and I shall not forget it. Tinao, do not stop your playing, my dear. We must all remain here a while longer; the thing must seem to be an accident when the servants come to my father at his usual time of retiring.' She laughed, a little feverishly, and her eyes glittered in the low light. 'Though tonight he has retired perhaps a little earlier than he might have wished to – '

'A good story to tell the guards and the servants, Serenity,' suggested Indarrak. 'That the Emperor wishes not to be disturbed until morning: it will buy us a little more time.'

'Yes – yes, that is well thought of. I shall give orders to the guards when we leave. It is even true enough, in a way.'

'There will be questions,' said Indarrak, as one who states a simple fact.

'Certainly there will be questions. But who shall dare ask them of the Princess-Regent, mother of the new Emperor?' Helior's face assumed a mocking sorrow. 'A tragic accident, was it not? In attending to the feeding of his fishy pets, my father slipped on the marble floor and fell into the pool, hitting his head and drowning. Alas that no one attended him at the time, else he might have been saved; though by merest chance and ill luck, his loving daughter and his heir's consort and her loyal servant had all left him only moments before. A sad story; but it has happened before, to old and careless folk far less lofty than emperors, and it will happen again . . . as accidents do.'

'I am sorry, madam,' said Tinao in a low voice; a string snapped then on her cithere, and she started at the sound.

'Sorry! For what? Your Indarrak has spared me a most disagreeable task.' Helior looked at Indarrak, who was now looming protectively behind Tinao. 'I know your long loyalty to Tinao-anderë, Indarrak, and I will see to it that my son knows it too. You shall have for reward anything the House of Plexari can give. Only name it; it is yours.'

But the eunuch shook his head. 'Reward enough, if my young mistress and her lord be happy together.'

'Well, they shall be, now,' said Helior with emphasis. 'In the morning I take order that my son gets the aid he has been so long denied. In his name I will rally the levies and call up armies and fleets alike. Before the month is out – say, by the time the late Emperor Strephon is lying in the splendid tomb in the Valley of Kings that his grieving daughter shall build for him – those fleets shall be in Keltia. But long before that, Akhi shall know that he is Emperor.'

'How can he know?' asked Tinao, wondering. 'Keltia is both besieged and blockaded; no message gets in or out.'

'That's the least of my problems. Ways will surely be found after tonight, now that the old lion no longer lies in my path.'

'One reward I would ask of you, Serenity.' Indarrak, having carefully rubbed dry his bare wet legs and mopped the water from the floor, now bowed ponderously before Helior. 'That I might go with the fleet to Keltia? I should like to strike a true blow for the new Emperor.'

'No blow could ever be better struck than the one you struck tonight. But I grant this happily, and more reward to come. What is more, I myself shall go to Keltia.'

'Oh, and I too!' Tinao rose from the pillows, the cithere

forgotten in one hand. 'Please – I have not seen him for so long.'

Helior did not answer immediately, and Tinao began to panic at the implied refusal. Then the Princess smiled, and lifted the girl's chin with one gold-tipped finger.

'Nor has he seen you,' she said. 'Though how he could forget such a sight . . . Well, perhaps a closer sight might put the thought of Aeron Aoibhell back into proper perspective for our Akhi. However he may think of her, he thinks of her too much, and I want her out of his mind altogether. But first steps first, and we must leave now with caution.' She began to move towards the doors, raising her voice so that the guards might hear, her tone clear and merry. 'I shall do as you bid, my father, and command the servants that you wish not to be disturbed. Good night and a sound sleep to you.'

She passed through the little anteroom with Tinao and Indarrak behind her, and the golden doors closed after them. Within, in the tiled pool in the centre of the empty room, the golden fish swam unconcernedly about.

'I confess, Straloch, I found your story astonishing, and a good deal more complex than I imagined.'

'Or than you could have imagined?' Straloch allowed himself a small smile and relaxed in his chair. He had dined that night as the guest of Haco Grex; there had been no others present at table, which was not usually the case – the Kelts had dined with the Terrans almost every night of the weeks they had spent in link, and invariably the guest list had been more extensive, drawn from the ship's officers and embassy staff personnel aboard the *Argo*. To exclude the Princess Fionnuala, particularly, was unheard of. Perhaps there was some special thing that the Earth ambassador wished to discuss in private with the Keltic ambassador?

It seemed that there was. 'Her Highness and the others will join us later,' said Grex casually. 'It was only that I wanted some time for us to speak of matters among ourselves alone.'

'Aye so?'

'The Princess Fionnuala – '

' – is the ceremonial head of this embassage,' said Straloch carefully. 'But the Ard-rían Aeron has commissioned me her negotiator-general, invested with all due and royal authority to bargain as might be needful.'

'And what is your Ard-rían's idea of what may be needful?'

Straloch's rare smile warmed his craggy features. 'For now? Earth's promise only, as I said to you in our first discussion. Later, maybe, that promise might be called in.'

'Military assistance, then. That is certainly possible, and within the bounds my Prime Minister has set – although, as you have said, it might not be needed. From what you have told me, your forces managed to beat off the combined power of the Imperium and the Fomori; cleared their fleets – after a surprise attack, too – out of all your star systems save two, and even those two you keep for the most part blockaded. What help could we give you? Surely you will regain Tara in a very little time, once the Queen has returned.'

'Gods willing,' said Straloch. 'But Aeron has given me very specific instructions, and I must obey her commands.'

'She has already agreed to a protocol of intent, and I anticipated working out the terms of a treaty with her myself. Those are in fact my own instructions from the Prime Minister and the Council of Worlds.'

'And so you would have done,' said Straloch, 'had not Jaun Akhera and Bres of Fomor altered the arrangement . . . No, what Aeron wishes now from Earth is only that

241

you wait and watch; she has her own plan, as has been explained.'

'Yes, so you said.' Grex tilted the cut-glass decanter: an antique, as priceless as the port it contained. 'These Treasures she has gone to seek – I think you also said that the Queen did not know where they might be, or even if they existed? Well, let us for discussion's sake assume they do exist, and she does in fact find them and bring them safely back to Keltia. What can she do with them then?'

'More than even she thinks, very like. They are magic things, and I am no Druid to call down the moon or bid the sun stand still.'

Grex frowned slightly. Magic: a fairly imponderable factor. He himself was no materialist to belittle or reject such things – mindpowers had been developed too long, and demonstrated too convincingly too often, for there to be many scoffers left – but to stake an interstellar kingdom on so ephemeral a weapon seemed, to say the least, quixotic.

'A hard thing to prove,' he heard himself say after a while.

'Or to disprove. It is more than magic, though, Grex. It is our own particular science, the knowledge that raised the Hanging Dance – Stonehenge – and the Great Pyramids and many other great works beside. Those works still stand upon your world; they were made once, and then never again; the secrets of their raising were lost to you forever, and for all these centuries you Terrans have wondered why. The answer is that we took the knowledge with us when we left Earth: it was our heritage from Atland, given to the Keltoi of Earth by their Danaan ancestors – and to the Coranians also, my sorrow to say, by their own Atlandean forebears, the Telchines. We – and they – have expanded and refined that knowledge

242

–

many times since. The Treasures Aeron seeks are part of it, and if Aeron says that they will serve her purpose, then believe that it is so.'

'I do believe it,' said Deonora, after Grex had run the tapes of the talk with Straloch for his consuls to comment upon. 'He so clearly does not approve, yet he shows utter conviction. Oh, she is a clever one, that Queen. She knew that someone like Straloch would plead her case far better than someone who was more in sympathy with her methods. I look forward to meeting her.'

'Thomas?'

Thomas de Valadon yawned. 'Either way, it costs us extremely little,' he remarked. 'He says his Queen does not ask for military aid at this time; no problem there, we issue a statement of solidarity – Keltia has Earth's full sympathy and support. If she fails in her bid with these sorcerous toys of hers, and asks for our help in more concrete terms, most likely it will already be too late for any help of ours to do her any good; and we issue a sad, shocked statement deploring the Imperium's aggression and annexation of Keltia. No problem there either. After all, Grex, it is only politics.'

*True enough*, thought Grex, appalled at his consul's brutal pragmatism, but only too well aware that Valadon, however cynical, was unfortunately correct in his assessment.

'Well,' he said, 'draft something for me to send home, then, and notify the captain to resume course. Only' – he turned in the doorway – 'inform him also that it need not be full speed ahead.'

'To Keltia?' asked Deonora.

'Where else? Oh, and the *Sword* will come with us. There is no point in their going on to Earth while the war's outcome is still in doubt.'

243

But as Grex walked down the passageway towards his own quarters, he found himself ashamed of his hope that, whatever was about to befall Keltia, Terra would get there too late to be able to do much about it. *I don't even know them*, he thought, *but I do know they deserve better than that.*

# Chapter Seventeen

Under Aeron's hand, *Retaliator* had fled Fomor like a spurred falair. They had been chased all across the system by ships of Talorcan's that had been lying in wait for them, but the pursuit had been little match for either *Retaliator* or her pilot: though heavily fired upon, Aeron had returned not a single round in defence, relying instead on evasive action, and had winked her ship into the safety of hyperspace the instant it was possible to do so.

Then she had left Morwen to ensure that they had indeed got safe away, and gone to the ship's common-room to relax a little; she had been nearly four hours at the controls, under fire and pursuit, and she was exhausted.

She was sitting on the upholstered bench by the room's main port, chin resting on her folded arms, staring out at the unfamiliar stars, when Elathan came in behind her.

'Crossic for them,' he offered.

'My thoughts? They are worth not half so much.'

'Not true, Aeron, for I know very well you are thinking of Gwydion. Would you set so low a valuation on him?'

'The half of my kingdom would not be price enough.' She spoke lightly, as had Elathan, but he saw the solemnity of the feeling that lay behind the jest.

'He was alive and well when we left Fomor,' he volunteered, feeling helpless that he could not give more substantial reassurance, knowing how he himself must feel if Cami had not been safe only a few cabins away but back in Fomor as a hostage. 'I had word only a short time ago from the Imperial ambassadors posted to Tory that Jaun Akhera still held Caerdroia and that Gwydion was still prisoner there – prisoner, but safe, Aeron; that must be some comfort.'

'Better comfort I would think it to hear of his escape.'

'*Could* he escape?'

Aeron gave a short laugh. 'From Turusachan? Guarded night and day by the Marbh-draoi's minions? Not likely! By force of arms it would be impossible, and by magic also impossible. Trickery would be his only hope, and even then he would not be able to manage it alone. He would need at least *some* help – and help will not be thick upon the ground.'

'Perhaps the palace folk – ?'

'I ordered them out of the City with the troops. As for the folk of Caerdroia themselves, I should think very few remain, and those who do probably cooperate to save themselves; or at least I hope.' She turned to stare once more out the port. 'Gwydion stayed to keep Keltia for me, and tricked me into flight; sooner would I have fled with him into exile, or stayed with him in prison, or stood with him on the scaffold. Where would not have mattered, so long as we had been together.' She cast him a sidewise glance. 'Is that not why Camissa came with you? She could have stayed in Tory in pomp and safety as queen to your usurping brother; but she accompanied you into peril, for love, and for faith in your return.'

'And in yours,' he said smiling. 'She is very impressed by you and Morwen.'

Aeron looked away, acutely embarrassed. 'That's as may be,' she muttered. 'But I still think she had been better left like the others with the dûhín.'

'Yes, she wondered quite a lot about that: why you so readily let her come – Not, of course,' he added quickly, 'that we are arguing the decision. But we both expected a good deal more resistance than you gave.'

'No mystery there,' said Aeron. 'I but thought of how I had felt, having to leave Gwydion behind. In spite of the danger for her, I did not wish to be the cause of such pain for another.'

Elathan sat down across from her and cast desperately about for a change of subject, for he saw that Aeron was very near to tears.

'This planet we sail to – what will it be like?'

'Kholco? Harsh beyond belief. I have been studying tapes – ' Grateful for the diversion, she touched a button on a nearby panel, and the wallscreen filled with views of a blasted world: obsidian plains, rivers of frozen stone, giant conical mountains robed in smoke and crowned with fire; on that world no green thing grew. In a silence more eloquent than speech, Aeron switched off the screen and looked inquiringly at her companion.

'What like are these Salamandri?' he asked at length.

'Reptiloids, who by all accounts can live in the fire itself, as Borvos told us. But by preference they dwell on the slopes near the active volcanic ranges, where they mine all manner of rare earths and metals for offworld trading. We – the Kelts – have even dealt with them in the past, or so the data-tapes say: long centuries before the raising of the Curtain Wall. I did not know that. Perhaps, if they remember, that link of old may serve us now.'

'And if not?'

Aeron shrugged. 'They are a neutral planet, protected by treaty but unaligned and unarmed. All they can do is forbid us the search.'

'And if they do?'

'Are all kings of Fomor so full of questions? Chriesta tighearna! If they do – well, if they do, then we will think of something else. Now let me consider in peace a little while more. Go and plague Morwen.'

247

When Elathan had left, very pleased with himself for teasing his friend a little from her sombre mood, Aeron rose from her seat, and going to the viewport slowly drew her fingertips over the vitriglass pane. Over there – in the far top corner of the window – there lay Keltia. Her fingers paused, pressed harder to the glass as her heart reached out to the stars she knew so well and could not even see. *Easier it would be to see the back of my own head . . . oh, Gwydion . . .*

She began dispassionately to review the events of the past months, herself sitting in judgement upon herself, and the verdict of the Queen's hearing-court was severe. She would not be surprised, when she returned to Keltia (*if* she returned to Keltia) if the Kelts should vote to depose her for cause. She had half-expected it after Bellator: They would not have been to blame, then, had they refused to sanction her as Ard-rían. But they had been in shock as deep and grief as devastating as her own, and her actions had seemed to them good and right, the only answer that honour could have made to Fomor.

And now she had taken that same Fomor by the hand in friendship. *Nay*, not *the same; for then it was Bres, and now it is Elathan* . . . Aeron laughed aloud, and the laughter had the brittle edge of derangement to it. Well, the Kelts would simply have to accept it, as would the Fomori; and she and Elathan were the only ones who could teach them.

The planet below them grew larger as Aeron brought *Retaliator* in to land. Kholco, the volcano planet, was a place unscaled for men. Though most of the tales told of it were not true – the seas did not boil there, for the simple reason that there *were* no more seas, only dry oceans of what had once been liquid rock – it was a place both bleak and dramatic. They flew for hours over flat plains and broken hill country, ash deserts and smoking chemical lakes; and all the time they saw never a sign of life, and nothing grew in all that waste.

At last Aeron set down in a place the data-tapes had indicated, near the edge of a great lava plain that rose gradually to a ring of encircling mountains, their rose-red peaks as sharp as knives. For all the seeming desolation, though, it was indeed a place where people dwelt, for by the time the travellers emerged from the ship, a crowd of perhaps a hundred had gathered to meet them.

Standing forward of the other two, Aeron and Elathan undertook to speak for their party. Though the Salamandri were a technological race, they were not themselves spacefarers; neither were they inclined to warfare, and on all the planet there was not so much as a sword or spear or blastgun. The visitors had therefore laid aside their own weapons, and they stood before the Salamandri now unarmed.

Aeron regarded the Firefolk with open interest. They were an ophidian race of middling height, in build something like to the merrows of Keltia, though thicker and less attenuated-looking, with an aura of strength and iron endurance – both of which they would surely stand in need of, living as they did on so harsh a world. For on Kholco, evolution had taken a different turning: Here it had been the reptile races, best equipped for the savage environment, that evolved to intelligence; and the weaker mammalian species – what few of them there were – that remained mere beasts. But the Salamandri were dominant: Their features were humanoid, though adapted, with nostrils and ears that could be sealed against the omnipresent volcanic dust, and a thin inner eyelid to protect their sight. Their skin was scaled and leathery, ranging in colour from silver-blue to almost black; the humans would later learn that skin colour among the Salamandri varied according to the region each tribe inhabited: lava plain, ash hills, high desert.

The one who seemed pre-eminent among them stepped out from the rest and bowed to his visitors stiffly from the waist.

'Welcome, friends from far.' The voice was sibilant and strangely high-pitched, but the tongue was fluent Englic.

Aeron answered in the same language. 'And greeting to you, my masters. We seek in peace and ask your help. I am called Aeron.' She pushed back her hood, so that her hair fell down around her, gleaming golden-red in the dusty light, and tensed suddenly as a ripple of consternation passed over the Salamandri.

Their chief silenced them with a curious gesture, and turned again to Aeron. 'And I am Sargus,' he said. 'Father to those of our folk who dwell here on the Morann. If I can help you, I will.'

'I do not know, lord, if you can,' replied Aeron. 'But I thank you whether so or no. The others who are with me on this errand – ' Swiftly she introduced Morwen, Elathan and Camissa, and Sargus saluted each with the same grave courtesy.

'Where would you go on our world?' asked Sargus at last. 'We are seldom visited by outworlders these days, but when they do come, they have as a rule a definite destination in mind.'

'That is just our trouble,' answered Elathan. 'We do not know where we must go, only what we are looking for – and whom.'

Sargus exchanged a quick glance with members of his company. 'And what – or whom – might that be?'

Elathan shook his head and gestured towards Aeron. 'This lady began the search, and she must tell you what there is to tell.'

250

Sargus and Aeron contemplated each other for a long moment. 'Then perhaps she had best do so,' he said. 'But in more comfort than here. Can you all manage riding-beasts? – Good; then come with us to the Ras of Salhi. We will speak there of this errand of yours, and of how it may work upon the Salamandri.'

He turned his back on them and began to walk towards the cliff-face, and after a moment's hesitation they followed.

In the shadows of the lava bluffs stood a number of small horses, riderless, their wide reins thrown over their heads and dragging on the ground; the beasts were trained to stand thus for many minutes, waiting on their masters.

Morwen, whose racing stables were famous all over Keltia, exclaimed with delight, for she had never seen such a breed before. The horses of the Salamandri were small compared to the big-boned chargers of the Kelts, with slim elegant legs heavily feathered above the hoofs; they carried delicately modelled heads on powerful necks, their manes fell past the points of their shoulders and their arched tails swept the ground.

'They are stronger than they look,' said Sargus, noting her attention. 'And bred to the weathers of this world – even as ourselves. Mount and ride.'

He marked the ease with which his alien guests swung into the high-cantled saddles – *horsemen born*, he thought, *all of them* – and moved his own beast out. The rest of the company fell into line behind him, six of his own folk bringing up the rear.

Aeron spent a few minutes learning the paces of her horse, then sent him into the long rolling trot, so easy to sit to, and came up beside Sargus.

'Where do we ride to?'

He pointed ahead to a low dark line on the horizon.

'To the Ras of Salhi, as I have said. It is perhaps half a day's ride. That is our chief settlement in these regions, so near to the – ' He fell silent, and would say no more.

*So near to the what?* Aeron stood in the round leather stirrups and looked out across the plain. Streaked grey and brown and ochre, marbled sands hard and waterless stretched for miles, shading to scarlet as the ground lifted to the needle-sharp red mountains that ringed the horizon. Off to one side in that far range stood a peak so huge and fair of form that she could not stop staring at it.

'That volcano – ' she began, then faltered, disconcerted, as the same low dismayed muttering as before went up from the Salamandri nearby. Sargus glanced at her from around the edge of his hood.

'I think it best if we do not speak of such just yet,' he said, and his voice if not hostile was certainly not cordial.

Aeron bowed her head and moved her horse out a few lengths from Sargus's side. The others had not heard the exchange, but they marked the attitude, and rode for the most part alone and in silence.

Toward midday, they came to a seemingly endless lava plain, glassy black ropes and swirls and lacings as if spilt from some drunken giant's pudding-ladle. Black grit stung their cheeks and crunched in their teeth and blurred their eyes to tears. They pulled their cowls up over their noses and mouths; already they were finding it hard to breathe in the hot rising wind.

'Not long now,' said a Salamand with satisfaction, to Elathan who rode beside him. 'Soon home.'

Elathan looked around him with disbelief. The lands before the lava came had been the bed of a vanished ocean; even now, the low brown hills with their scrubby brush and twisted trees – the only vegetation he had yet seen – seemed not to belong under heaven, and Elathan

252

could not imagine how long it had been since they had drunk rain.

'It rains seldom in these parts,' said Sargus, who seemed to possess an uncanny ability to read alien thought. 'There are but two seasons here: short, cold and wet; and long, hot and dry. I know not which an outworlder would deem worse.'

On his other side, Aeron drooped forward along the neck of her horse. Though there seemed to be no lack of water in the capacious saddle pockets, she was afflicted with an intolerable thirst, and the waves of heat rippling up from the lava ground struck her like whips in the face. Her skin burned where the sun could reach it, though beneath the hooded cloak she shivered as with fever.

Sargus saw this too, and cursed to himself. Not clever to have brought them this way, though he had done so in the interests of speed; but it was scarcely the first time offworlders from a place of cool northern mists had been nearly grilled alive beneath the fierce Kholcan sun. All four strangers were suffering cruelly from the dryness and heat, but the two Kelts seemed afflicted most, and worst.

'Only hold on until we reach those cliffs,' he said encouragingly. 'That is our home, the Ras of Salhi, and there will be coolness and shade and all the water you could wish.'

By the time the cliffs threw their welcome shade over the riders, the four visitors were so ill of the heat and dust that the Salamandri had to help them down from their horses. Sargus gave quiet commands, and more of his folk came out from the great cavern-gate set into the cliff, two to each stranger, helping them up the sloping path that led back into the mountain's hollow depths.

'Take these to the guest-place, as quick as you can,'

he said, himself half-carrying Camissa. 'Wrap them in waterblankets and see that they stay quiet until the sun is fully down.'

In the air-cooled dimness within the rock, Aeron felt the burning tightness leave her skin, and she had only to lift a hand to find another keeve of cold water standing ready. As the light withdrew from the high window, and cool violet twilight took its place, she sat up, feeling her old self again, and saw with a smile that the others looked equally restored.

Before any of them thought of sending word, Sargus came in, followed by others of his folk bearing enormous copper trays laden with food.

Greeting each of his guests by name, he gestured them to join him upon the pillows and carpets, in Salamandri fashion, and the trays were set down in the midst of the circle of pillows.

'How is it with you, now?'

'We were feeling forspent indeed,' said Morwen. 'But no more.'

'You were sun-touched; it is a common ill for offworlders. I am sorry to have had to subject you to it, but I thought to bring you here by the quickest and shortest way, and dared not wait for nightfall.'

'What need of haste?' asked Elathan, setting down an empty water bowl; it was refilled before he had taken his hand from it. 'And if there *was* such need, why ride? Our ship could have brought us all both quicker and easier.'

'That, I fear, would not have been permitted,' said Sargus; and though they could not read his expression, they sensed concealment. 'No ship may come into this country, not now.'

But Aeron had caught a faint note of something else. '"Not now", you say; *was* there once a ship that came to this place?'

Unlidded silver eyes were turned upon her, not Sargus's only but those of every Salamand in the room, and it took all Aeron's training to endure those stabbing alien glances. She decided to risk all on one throw.

'I think there was a ship,' she went on boldly. 'I think a ship from the outworld came here many lives ago, and I think it is here even now. What say you, Sargus? Is this not true?'

No mistaking the reaction this time: not the low muttering she had evoked from the Firefolk twice already that day, but a full-throated accusing shout. The Salamandri, save for Sargus, had all leapt to their feet and were staring hard at Aeron. She rose more slowly to her own feet, indulging herself in one passionate regret that they had come unarmed, and fell almost instinctively into a Fianna combat posture, the one used 'for random hazard', when the one attacked does not know from what quarter attack will come.

Sargus barked a command to his people in their own tongue; still whispering menacingly among themselves, they melted away into the shadows. He himself had not stirred from his own place upon the pillows, and now he indicated that Aeron should resume her seat beside him.

'Sit, lady. When you have heard, you will know why you have so alarmed my folk. *Sit*; I cannot talk to you when you loom above me like a fire-mount.'

Aeron hesitated, then obeyed, setting one leg behind the other and folding herself down upon the carpets like a roosting heron. 'Tell us, then, if you can, and what you may. Better it will be for all of us if all is known.'

The Salamand chieftain nodded. 'I think so too. Well, this ship you seem to know of, it came indeed to Kholco, and it landed not far from here – though it came from a long way away before that, and you would know from where better than I. It set down upon the Holy Mountain, the Firehorn – ' Again there came angry hisses from the shadows, and he waved his people to stillness with the odd chopping gesture he had used before. 'Indeed, it landed in the fire itself. But it did not burn, and it did not melt; and after much discussion we pulled it from the fire and brought it to a secret resting-place, where it remains to this day.'

'Did you look inside, to see if any folk yet lived?'

'We knew from our scans that all aboard were dead,' said Sargus. 'But those who took the ship from the fire opened it up to be certain of it. You understand that all this happened many hundreds of years ago . . . But they found none alive within, and they were grieved to find it so, for the warriors of the stranger ship looked brave and high of heart, and their leader highest and bravest of all.' He paused, for Aeron had drawn herself up, with a look of desperate urgency on her face. 'No, they had not suffered; they had not died of the fire, nor of the crash either, but were dead when they came to it. They looked asleep; in fact, those who first entered the ship thought they *were* asleep, not dead at all. But there is more.' Now it was Sargus who drew himself up, his silver eyes fixed on Aeron's green ones. 'There is a price set on the knowledge you seek, and before I may give you that knowledge, that price must be paid: to me, and to my folk, and to those that will come after. It is no price of coin or bartering, but one of courage and faith. Will you do so?'

Morwen cut in swiftly. 'That shall be seen when the price is told!'

He ignored her, still watching Aeron. '"Let he who is a leader be a bridge" – so it is said among my people, and so it shall be proved. Which of you, then; for it is you and you' – he nodded in turn to Aeron and Elathan – 'who are bridges to your folk, not so? Which of you?'

256

'I,' said Aeron, before Elathan could speak. 'Any of us, if heart should count for all. But I for that this journey of seeking had origin in my need, and so the risk rightly must fall upon myself.' She lifted a hand to silence the protests of her companions. 'Nay, my lions, gainsay me not. This is the Gabha-Bheil, the trial by Beli. It is what I have come here for; not to venture it now were vain indeed.' She turned again to Sargus. 'When?'

'Tonight?'

She nodded. 'No more delay; the swifter it is done, the swifter I shall know.'

When Sargus had gone from the chamber, and the rest of his folk with him, Morwen turned on her friend and Queen, and Elathan and Camissa were not slow behind her.

'My soul to the mountain, Aeron, and all my kin's with it! Sometimes I think Straloch has the right of it, and you are every bit as thrawn as he would have you! Or is it just that your brain was cooked too long in the sun today? You do not even know what is this trial he speaks of – '

Aeron let them scold, calmly sipping all the while at still another waterbowl – it seemed that never again could she drink her fill. Then she lay back on the pillows and looked up at the rock-hewn ceiling not many feet above their heads.

'It matters not at all what is the trial,' she said quietly. 'Whatever it is, it must be met, and mine it is to meet it. Any road, I do not wish to speak another word of it now. I want to rest for a little, and you should do the same. They will come for us when they are ready.'

# Chapter Eighteen

It was full dark when Aeron stepped out of the mountain-cave's high door, to stand beside her friends under the great blue vault of the Kholcan sky. No moon circled that world, so that the stars held sway unchallenged in the dark. A cool breeze fingered her hair, and stirred the embroidered sleeves of the black robe she had been given to wear.

Sargus, coming up to them, bowed formally, then led them in silence down a path like a long flight of wide and shallow steps, its uneven length lighted by alum torches stuck into the ground at regular intervals. As they walked, they could see in the torchlight that the path was lined by Salamandri robed and hooded, four and five deep in places. Elathan reached for Camissa's hand, squeezed it briefly to give her encouragement; her answering clasp drove his coronation ring into his fingers.

After perhaps five minutes' walk, they came to an open place, where a glow rose up as if from many torches, or a great lowe or giant quartz-hearth. They could sense tremendous heat not far away; every now and again the ground trembled beneath their feet, and there came a faint far-off rumble.

Sargus halted where the path came to an end, and turning to Aeron he drew her forward; the others came cautiously after.

They were standing on the lip of what appeared at first glance to be a river, rolling slow and dark in its own wide channel. Then their perspective shifted, and they realized, with a jolt of sickening horror, that it was no river but a stream of lava, many feet across and near as many thick, a flume of molten stone running between banks of harder stone. It moved slowly along the edges, eddying and backing much as a true stream might do; in its centre there seemed to be swifter currents, tidestrings where the blazing stone raced like water under a thin crackling crust.

Morwen was seized with ambiguous dread. 'Aeron – '

'What is this place, Sargus?'

'It is our holy place, the Kasulathra, our place of testing here at the Ras of Salhi. It is said that only truth can live in flame, and whoso would speak the truth and be believed must be willing to put it to the fire. The folk have been told that you claim a right to the knowledge we spoke of earlier, and now they demand that you prove that right. For you see it is not your doom alone, and this is the price of your quest.'

'This is reasonable,' said Aeron at once. 'I accept.'

'Will you not wait one moment, Aeron!' snapped Elathan in a savage undertone, then aloud to Sargus: 'If we refuse to allow this?'

'Then all your lives are forfeit,' said Sargus. 'That is the penalty for sacrilege and blasphemy.'

'And if I fail?' asked Aeron, though already she knew the answer.

But Sargus said nothing.

'What is permitted to me?' she asked after a while. 'What means may I use; what is it, exactly, that is asked of me?'

'You must walk the fire,' said Sargus. 'Our priests will do so first, to show that it can be done, and that there is no trickery about it. Then you must do the same, if you can. If you succeed, you will earn the answers that you seek. If you fail – '

'Aye so.' Aeron was silent a moment. 'What of magic?'

259

The Salamand studied her face. 'You may call upon whatever power you wish, your gods' or your own, if you think your magic may obtain here or your gods will hear you. That is certainly lawful. But do not forget that we have here gods – and magic – of our own, and I do not know how such a calling would be received.' As Aeron seemed lost in her own thought, Sargus bowed and stepped away. 'When the priests have crossed to the other side of the fire, then you must make your own crossing. The flame shall determine of the truth.'

One by one, five priests, their hoods pulled low over their eyes, came to the edge of the lava stream, poured plain water over their bare feet, and then, in single file, moved smoothly across the ghastly river to the stone ledge at the far side. When all were assembled, they thrust their hands inside their wide sleeves and settled expectantly into a posture of waiting judgement.

Aeron stared until her sight blurred to tears with the heat rising off the molten stone. *No haste*, she told herself. *Those priests will wait forever* . . . The fact that the priests had successfully crossed the fire-river gave her no smallest mind's-ease: had not Borvos said that the Salamandri could actually *live* in the flame? If so, then merely strolling across it were no great hardship for them; but it might be rather different for a human. But then she turned to her friends, and what she saw in their faces made her heart shake within her: hopefulness, fear, concern – all overlaid with a blind confident terrifying trust that she could, and would, succeed in this ordeal. *Ah gods, would I were myself so sure* . . .

She stepped forward to the edge of the channel. A few feet away from her, the stream of lava was dark and clinkered on its surface; it certainly looked solid enough to support her weight, and indeed had already borne up the five priests, who weighted far more. All across its width ran streaks and cracks through which glowed white liquid fire, like seawater ebbing down the strand where a wave has broken. Yet this was not water but a river of rock, come straight and bubbling up from Earth-heart.

She would have to do it, and now, before she lost her courage altogether. *Another fíor-comlainn; but I had sooner face ten Bresses as face that flame* . . . She was, like everyone else, already barefoot in the holy place, and now she bent down and poured warm water over her feet to ritually cleanse them, as the priests had done. But the water served only to purify, and would give absolutely no protection to her crossing the fire. *Do it now, then; no more tarrying.*

Aeron lifted her arms in the Ban-draoi attitude of prayer, her othersight turning inward, then out on a rising plane. Immediately she sensed the presence of a Power, to whom all other powers were subject in this place. Yet she could also sense that it was not totally alien, nor was it inimical to her presence. The touch of its huge immortal attention was upon her; she had plucked the sleeve of deity, and now that deity was turning to see who it was that had called.

She felt as a child that has tugged its mother's skirts and is now abashed at its own temerity, to trouble that vast eternal being. And that was maybe no bad comparison, for this goddess of the Salamandri was herself also the Mother; though in a strange and alien garb, surely even so She would recognize Her servant –

Those who watched so closely saw Aeron's face, flushed till now with the heat of the lava, go pearl-pale, and then a look of real awe mounted like a tide into her face. She laid fist to heart in salute, and spoke words in a tongue no one knew to One whom she alone could see.

'She is afraid after all,' muttered Illach, a kinsman of

261

Sargus who stood beside him. 'She will fail as I have predicted.'

'Not she. Look now.' Sargus leaned forward, and Morwen who stood on his other side caught her lip between her teeth.

Aeron had lowered her arms now, holding them sloping downwards, extended from very straight shoulders, wrists slightly lowered in an attitude of unconscious elegance. Her posture was that of a dancer, perfectly balanced within herself, and her expression was that of a swordsman, alert for the slightest flaw in enemy defences. Her fingers were spread wide apart, and blue fire flickered from tip to tip.

'That is no magic of the Salamandri,' said Illach, voice touched with reluctant admiration.

'No . . . who was it, do you think, that she spoke to?'

'How can we know? She might have called upon the Dark Ones to help her; aye, Sargus, *they* would have been pleased to interfere.'

Sargus glanced at him contemptuously. 'Since when have the Dark Ones held any sway here? Well you know whose place this is, and She keeps it well defended. If the outworld witch has power here, it is by Her consent. Now watch and be silent, and see the truth.'

That last injunction was strictly unnecessary: In all the vast throng, none had taken his eyes from the scene before them. And now Aeron, moving slowly and stiffly, as if she walked in dreams or deep water, came to the edge of the lava.

She never hesitated but set her bare foot down upon the molten stone as if it had been cold marble. Her foot showed unearthly white against the shifting colours of the lava, and it left a clear print behind when she lifted it to take the next step, and the next and the next and the next after that, all in the same stately stride.

Elathan caught a long shuddering breath. The soles Aeron exposed as she moved across the face of the lava were unblistered, unburned, as healthy and whole as they had ever been.

And still that dreadful pacing continued, ceremonious and terrible. They knew they were witnessing something magical; but Aeron moved on, steadily, deliberately, unaware of the many watchers, her eyes fixed on something a few yards in front of her that those watchers could not see.

Reaching the far bank, she stepped back onto firm rocky ground where the priests awaited her. Still exalted, still half-entranced, she smiled at them from all the divine distance of her remove, and as one they threw themselves to the ground before her.

That broke her distance; she looked around helplessly. Such prostrations were unknown in Keltia, and the idea disturbed her peace. She was rescued by Sargus, who had crossed the lava stream by an arching bridge, and who now gently shooed the priests away.

'Look at your feet.'

Fighting reluctance, Aeron obeyed. But except for a dusting of fine black ash, almost invisible, and a few tiny pieces of gritstone clinging to the arches of her feet, nothing marred the smooth skin.

Then Morwen and Elathan and Camissa were upon her, gleeful and triumphant, all talking at once. More practically, they had brought her boots with them, and now she sat on a rock spur to pull them on. Reaction had set in, and she was feeling drained in body – though, paradoxically, unbelievably elated by the experience. As for her feet, there was not even a tenderness or soreness to them. She rubbed her hands over her face and looked up at Sargus, who stood beside her, his slate-coloured face, so alien, so vividly concerned.

'Do you always prove your guests with such an antic? Small wonder then that the Firefolk have so few visitors.' But her smile showed no sting was housed in the words, and he smiled in answer.

'Not always; but any who came on such an errand as yours would have been so tested. It is a matter far graver and deeper than you know.'

'Is it permitted to ask of this?'

Sargus nodded. 'That you earned when you walked upon the fire.'

'Did you see what happened?' she asked, pitching her voice away from those who pressed around them. 'Did you see what I did see?'

'This night, no; but I felt it, and I can guess – and other times, even, I have been fortunate enough and favoured enough to have seen. Did She speak to you?'

Aeron nodded, eyes hazy with memory and wonder. Then the green eyes suddenly sharpened into focus again. 'She said – Well, She did not *say*, just so; rather did She look, and somehow I did know. First of all She did promise me I would not be burned by the flame; and then – '

But Sargus suddenly grave laid light fingers upon her lips, so that she was silent. 'Speak not of it here,' he said. 'As I have promised, you have won by this night's work the right to know all, and your companions with you. But not here, and not now. In the morning. In the morning you shall know.'

But when morning came, Sargus was not to be found. After a light breakfast, Aeron and the others were conducted by respectfully silent Salamandri to the cavern entrance, where their horses stood saddled and bridled, each with laden panniers; and still no word was spoken.

After a swift-paced journey of perhaps an hour, guided

264

by Firefolk outriders, they came to a place where the land fell sharply away before them. On the far side of the broad defile thus formed, the terrain began to climb again, rising in the distance to the range of mountains Aeron had noted the previous day.

In the shadow of the cliff wall, Sargus stood waiting for them, and when they rode up, he bowed in greeting and gestured that they should dismount. 'We must go on foot from here.' But where it was that they were going, or how long it would take to get there, he did not say.

After they had taken the packs from the saddles and shouldered them securely, Sargus led them up a narrow valley that cut through to the other side of the great ridge, its uneven floor choked with fallen rocks and drifts of dust. The valley debouched at its far end onto a vista unparalleled: Across the hard dry plain of the Morann, low cinder hills ringed the giant volcano that they had seen on their ride to the Ras of Salhi. Today it was in eruption, a towering pillar of cloud rising from its cratered peak.

Sargus pointed. 'That is where we are going.'

'To the volcano?' exclaimed Camissa. 'But why? Surely it is not safe.'

But Aeron and Morwen exchanged swift glances, and their thought was the same thought: This was what they had come to Kholco to find.

'Not to the peak itself,' Sargus was saying reassuringly to Camissa. 'But close enough; though the mountain has played a part of its own in this matter.'

'What is it called?' asked Elathan, shading his eyes against the glare and shimmer of the sun on the arid plain.

Though he made no move of the body, Sargus's whole being seemed to reach outward to the burning peak.

'That is the Firehorn,' he said then. 'Mount Terror.'

Hours later, the little party plodded wearily to the crest of a low volcanic ridge that rose out of the dust of the plain like the back of a whale. Grateful for the halt however brief, the offworlders flung themselves to the stony ground, to find what ease and coolness they could. Elathan poured a cup of water for Camissa, who was tired but whose cheerful spirits had not flagged all day. Leaning against a rock nearby and eating some of the provisions the pack had contained, Morwen closed her eyes and blessed the comparative chill that the cloud had brought to the lands beneath.

Aeron sat cross-legged a little apart from the rest, strangely drawn by the huge volcano. For miles they had seen it as they walked, half-slipping, half-limping, behind Sargus as he picked his path unerringly through the black-glass desolation.

From this angle, the volcano had a massive outline: Its great shoulders rose some ten thousand feet in two tumbled levels, the central perfect cone rearing itself up another three thousand. All of it was dwarfed by the colossal billow of flame-shot cloud pouring upward from its summit. They were near enough now to see the scoriac streams that crept down the mountain's torn flank. The eruption had begun last night, Sargus had told them; indeed, the tremors heralding its onset had been those felt as Aeron came to face her firewalk – and among the Salamandri, the feeling, again as Sargus had told them, was that the two events were not unrelated.

*Be that as it may*, thought Aeron, *Arthur came here once; and if he, once or still, so now I . . .*

Morwen had come up beside her, eyes on the same awesome sight. 'Mount Terror – '

'We are intruders here,' said Aeron. 'This is where

worlds begin. This is Earth-soul and Fire-heart, the Forge of Heaven, the Goddess's Anvil. We look upon the flame that is Forever.'

They watched in silence as the mountain tore itself apart with a new convulsion, opening a gaping earth split. Fire hung like mist in the air, fire ran like water over the ground, fire danced yelling in the mountain's throat. The ground shuddered continuously, and across the miles of air came a low growl as of prisoned thunder. After a while, Morwen touched her friend's shoulder. 'Aeron, come away.'

Aeron shook her head. 'It will not harm us,' she said, still staring rapt across the rifted valley.

'Come,' said Sargus, and his word unlike Morwen's was command. 'The time is now that you have waited for.'

The ridge they followed now led them up onto the slopes of an extinct crater, dead and elder twin to the labouring Terror. High up the gentle swell of the mountain's side, a great cleft yawned upon darkness. Yet not entirely darkness: As she climbed steadily nearer, Aeron could discern a glow from within, not that of flame but a luminous werelight that somehow reminded her of something, she could not say just what . . . She turned to look over her shoulder at the glowing Firehorn, and then she understood.

'The horns of light,' she breathed, and in front of her Morwen stiffened. '"Before the portals of Uffern, the horns of light shall burn . . ." Sargus, when did this mountain last give fire?'

He did not slow in his stride, but they heard the changed note in his voice: a teacher's pleasure at a clever pupil's reading of some obscure text.

'When the ship you seek came to this world, both this

mountain and its sister blazed like beacons to light all the Morann. Then the fire died here in Scarva, and now only the Firehorn is still alight, though that but seldom. But you are right, Aeron: This is the place your poet named Uffern, and we are here.'

They followed Sargus in at the mouth of the cavern: An underground vault vast in area, its soaring ceilings were lighted by a steady phosphorescence coming off the rock formations that rose from the floor and reached downward from the roof.

'You have won the right to enter for yourself and your friends, Aeron,' said Sargus then. 'You will find in this place that which you have lost.'

'Arthur?' asked Morwen, her voice quick and questioning. 'Is Arthur here?'

But Sargus, his eyes fixed on Aeron, made no answer. Then Camissa, who had run ahead a little in her eagerness, turned and called, her clear voice echoing hollowly in the huge stone spaces.

'Aeron? Aeron, come and see. There are pictures on the walls.'

She looked where Camissa was pointing, and could not keep back a gasp. Upon the living rock of the cavern walls, where the stone had been melted and made smooth, prepared like a canvas for the artist's hand, pictures were carved and coloured, in wide panels like tapestries of stone. Strange beasts and stranger people – if people they could in truth be called – scenes of mystery and unknown import, all lighted by the weird glow of phosphorescence. But the panel Camissa stood before –

'How came this here?' Aeron heard herself asking. 'Sargus? How can this be?' She drew her fingertips wonderingly over the carved and inlaid stone: a picture of the Ras of Salhi, and the Kasulathra, and the river of fire she had walked only the night before. On one side of the painted river stood a figure she somehow knew represented Arthur; and on the other –

'It is I,' she said in a small voice. 'But I do *not* understand.'

Sargus traced reverently the image of a woman all in black whose red hair fell around her to her knees, like the fires of Terror itself; above whose head hung a crescent and ring of stars; beneath whose feet was a cross-quartered circle: Keltic signs, Ban-draoi signs, signs that no Salamand could hope to know . . .

And, farther along the cave wall, scenes of utter and inconceivable devastation: walls of fire, tides of lava, the planet itself cracking open along its seams like an overripe fruit . . .

'This is what She told me of, last night, when I was crossing the fire,' whispered Aeron, and Sargus bent his head.

'What more did She let you to know?'

'She showed me that my coming was as the herald of the End for all the Firefolk,' said Aeron with some difficulty. 'That your people must now prepare for – ' She used a word in the tongue of the Salamandri that she did not know even as she spoke it. 'Is it so? Was I told aright?'

'You were, and that is why when you first stepped from your ship and greeted us, my folk were so dismayed to see you. Not because you were an unexpected offworlder, but because you were the living image of this' – he touched the stone again – 'and the second sign of our ending.'

'Sargus – '

'Do not grieve for us, Aeron. We have long known that it must come, and we welcome it.'

'Aye, but though Kholco must die, surely the Salamandri need not die with it? There are goleor of other worlds you might go to – uninhabited ones that you could mould to suit your needs and likings – green and clement planets, where you would not have to live as dwellers in the dust.'

'That is true enough; but you see that we were made to fit this world, in spirit no less than in body. Its fate and ours are linked, and when time comes for it to change its life, then so too shall we. Think of it, if it frets you less, as transformation, not as ending. But I need hardly teach *you* how death is no ending: Did you not tell me only last night of the beliefs of your people, and the faith they put in fate – dán, you called it. Well, this then is the dán of the Salamandri. You are a forerunner of our end, but you are not the cause. Neither blame nor shame in it.'

When she did not answer, he smiled and put a hand under her elbow to lead her forward, and after an instant's resistance she allowed herself to be led.

Beyond the anteroom cavern, the stalactite roof, running down to meet the floor, opened upon a much vaster cavern, the far walls of which were lost in darkness. The entire centre of the mountain was hollow as a gourd. Hollow it might be, Aeron saw at once, but it was far from empty: In the centre of the wide smooth floor stood a starship.

Bigger it was than *Retaliator*, though still less big than some craft: a long, lean ship, graceful of line and scarred with battle, its hull of dark green metal eerily lighted by the phosphor-lichen growing on the cavern walls.

Aeron never knew afterwards how long it was that she stood there, unable to accept the moment now that it had come at last: the implications, the depth and breadth and scope of it. This, then, was the end of her searching; and whatever that ship might hold, it held her dán, and the dán of all Keltia beside . . .

'How did you ever get it here?' That was Elathan, trying to master his awe with pragmatism; he and the

270

other two had come up quietly behind Aeron and Sargus as they stood.

'Not easily,' admitted the Salamand. 'As I told you last night, it crashed upon the Firehorn, many cordoan of ori ago – hundreds and hundreds of years, in your reckoning. We believe, judging by eyewitness accounts and records of such things as speed in air and trajectory and changes of course, that it crashed not by accident, but was deliberately flown into the Firehorn by its pilot, on a course he did not live to see completed. We had already determined that none lived within, so we did not rush to pull it from its resting place; and when, eventually, we did, we brought it here. As to the pictures on the outer walls of this cavern, they were made later, after the ship was placed as you now see it; for models we used things that had been seen within it, the one time it was opened, and also things that were shown to us by other means – We touched nothing and no one,' he added. 'All is as it was, and your kinsmen have slept in peace.'

But Aeron was no longer listening. She had walked forward, as one in the grip of the mightiest of magics, and stopped now before the ship's main door. *Prydwen* . . . She reached out a trembling hand to touch the green metal hull, her thought veering back to the Coranian ship, that first *Marro*, as remote and alone in the Morimaruse as was *Prydwen* here, each in its last littlest harbour, each sheltering its gallant ghosts: *Prydwen* moored in earth and fire, as the *Marro* was moored amid darkness and stars.

Elathan touched her arm, and she started violently. 'Will you go in now, Aeron? As Sargus says, this is what you have been seeking.'

She lifted haunted eyes to search his face. '*Have* I been seeking?' she asked quietly. 'Or rather have I been sought?'

271

'I do not know the answer to that,' he said as quietly. 'In the end, is there so great a difference? Is there even a difference at all?'

Aeron's eyes shuttered briefly, as if a lamp had gone out behind them. 'Nay,' she said then. 'Very like no difference that would *make* a difference; and perhaps the seeking was the true test, and not the finding . . . Let us all go in, King of Fomor. This is all our seeking.'

# Chapter Nineteen

Elathan and Camissa stood very close together, watching as Aeron vanished within the ancient hulk. *It has been almost too strange*, he thought: Aeron's coming to Fomor in the first instance, and the friendship that had been so delicately wrought between them, and then the hammer-blow of Talorcan's betrayal and usurpation – all the things and more beside that had combined to bring them to this place. He knew very well what Aeron hoped to find here, and he understood the desperation that had sent her on such a search, understood even what she must be feeling at this moment, for the Red Dragon was as much a legend on Fomor as on Tara. *But what now? There is surely more to this quest than mere discovery* . . . He felt Camissa's hand pulling at his, knew that she had spoken to him and he had not responded.

'Aeron is calling us,' she said, and gave another tug to his hand. 'Did you not hear?'

When they came up to her, Aeron was standing a few yards inside the door of the dead ship. She had found the light-board, and now a dim green glow illuminated the long corridor that opened up behind her. She said nothing, but gathered them all together with her eyes and moved carefully along the passageway, her boots stirring up dust as she went.

She headed first for the command cabin, remembering how it had been aboard the *Marro* – Jaun-Zuria, dead in his captain's chair – and thinking that perhaps Arthur would have done likewise. But when she stepped through onto the bridge, she saw in the low green light that the room was empty, and she turned away again.

'In the cabins, then?' asked Morwen, voice hushed.

Indeed, in the cabins: As they moved through the corridors, what they glimpsed beyond several half-open doors gave evidence of how those of *Prydwen* had bestowed themselves at the last; and behind those doors that had not sprung ajar over the centuries it was much the same.

Within the cabins, they lay upon blast-couches and improvised pallets, like warriors in a royal barrow-mound or chambered tomb, their hands still folded around the hilts of their weapons, torcs still gleaming dully at their throats, heraldic devices on their shields and cloaks and tunics still decipherable even now. Without tears Morwen beheld several who bore the black Douglas lion, and Aeron the wolf's head of Aoibhell, and nor was the gold-antlered stag of Gwynedd's princes absent from that place.

Yet still after many minutes' searching they had not found the one they sought, and also dreaded to find; not until they came upon a chamber opening off an alcove somewhat removed from the others, to deosil and aft of the ship. Two guards still sat flanking its door, their backs set against the metal wall, eternally vigilant against who now knew what looked-for enemy; their hands still gripped the hilts of their naked swords.

Aeron halted, putting out her hand to Morwen, whose return clutch was painful in its pressure. This was the end of their search, here, behind that door, the answer to a question that Keltia had asked for fifteen centuries. She had only to step through for all to be made known. Even so, it took more than a few moments for her to gather herself to pass between the seated guards, to put her hand to the door-stud; there came a faint whine of metal

274

moving over metal, and then the cabin stood open before her.

It was larger than she would have thought to find on a starship of that era: a chamber of perhaps a score of feet on a side, its ceiling of quilted metal some ten feet above the black solenized floor. No dust lay in here – the room had been sealed too well for that – but the ubiquitous green lights burned here too, and their glow fell upon the low couch, and on the man who lay there.

Tall he had been, Aeron saw, taller even than Gwydion: his hair and beard a chestnut brown streaked with grey; strong bones and square hands, though the fingers were unexpectedly graceful – hands for harp and sword and pen alike; and though the lids were decently closed, Aeron knew that the eyes behind them had been dark as peatwater.

But the face astonished her. Death had not diminished, nor had the centuries taken away; and whatever torment of body or of spirit may have attended this man's going out, it had not marked his countenance, for he had not allowed it to do so. Strong was that face, and wise, and gentle, and implacable, and somehow merry, as if he knew something more true than he would tell. Aeron moved forward as if drawn by the hand, and when she reached the bedside she went instinctively and unselfconsciously to one knee.

'Hail King of Kelts,' she whispered, and, taking Arthur's hand in both of hers, kissed it in the age-old gesture of fealty. She glanced up at the others, saw Morwen's face streaming, though her features were fixed as iron; Elathan's, pity and respect both alike upon it, and she could not tell which was meant for her and which for Arthur; Camissa's, open with all the sweetness of her nature; beyond them, Sargus's, and almost it seemed that she could decipher the alien countenance a little, and that he too was not unmoved.

She rose and stood looking down at the dead king, aware as if from a great distance of the others quietly quitting the chamber, leaving her alone with Arthur. It seemed that she could stand there forever, that this was the centrepoint of all her days, the still spiral's core, from which spun off like a triskele in all directions the rest of her life and Keltia's together.

She had thought she would be focusing on Arthur only. Instead, she found her mind turning inexorably back to that time three years ago, that time standing out from Bellator when time had stood still for her then as it did now, when she had knelt beside another dead King of Kelts upon another dead ship. Memories came crowding back like hungry ghosts, and she reached blindly behind her for the cabin wall, leaned back against it as her senses reeled, present and doubled past becoming all one, and all pain . . .

Ah, better it had been if they had been blasted to atoms, bright particles to dance through frozen space forever. But that had not been the way of it. Upon Rohan's giving her the ghastly tidings, she had left Caer-droia without a word, had taken her ship and gone straight to the place of the disaster. She had walked upon the crippled embassy ship, had seen the broken bodies of her parents lying in each other's arms; the poor twisted shells of the crew, the other members of the diplomatic party – all of whom she had known and many of whom had been friends.

And then, worse still, the destroyer that bobbed disabled a few score lai away, Rhodri dead with the others upon the bridge, his bright hair dulled with dust and blood. She had knelt beside his body, her face a mask, her eyes wide and dry and stony as bones, no tears, no visible emotion even; and that too had become part of the legend. But that had not been it at all. She had not wept because tears were ridiculously not enough for what she was feeling; in the white-hot heart of grief, that motionless blaze at the core of her being, a fury was forming that would destroy a world.

She had put her grief by then, choosing instead to nourish her vengeance; then later there had been very nearly madness and death, and no time to mourn but only to try to survive, and even that only by grace of her cousin Melangell's devoted efforts. But all of it came back upon her now, no longer to be denied; and now she did not put it by but let it break over her, throwing wide the gates of her soul to let it in. And, alone in the cabin, just Aeron and Arthur together, she dropped slowly to her knees, and, burying her face in the King's cloak, she began to weep; wept now for all those times she had not dared to weep: for Rhodri, for Fionnbarr and Emer, for Elharn, for Theo, for Arthur himself . . .

When she could cry no more, Aeron rocked back onto her heels and stood up again, brushing tear-dampened hair off her face, unspeakably weary but incalculably glad. A kingdom's long search had been ended here, but also a woman's long burden had been lifted, and both by Arthur's hand.

Emerging again into the corridor, she saw the others standing a little way away. They looked relieved to see her, if somewhat subdued, and Elathan gave her an unsmiling glance that was like a handclasp of support and affectionate approval.

'It is well then, Aeron?' asked Morwen, who had sensed something of her friend's feeling, and had been the one to shepherd the others from the cabin, to leave Aeron alone with the dead king.

'It is extremely well.'

'We have been all through the rest of the ship,' said Sargus. 'And everywhere it is as we saw earlier, your folk all peacefully asleep in their cabins. They do not seem to have suffered.'

'They did not,' said Elathan. 'We found a log of sorts in the command cabin. They came here because at first they hoped to find materials with which to repair their battle damage; but before they even reached the planet, they realized they were finished and could never make it home. The ship's first officer, one Bedwyr, reports in the log that they managed to get seven of their number – all they could save in their only operable lifeboat – off on a pretext, and then they deliberately sent the ship into the volcano's heart. They were dead by the time that happened, of course.'

'"Three times the fullness of Prydwen were we that went with Arthur,"' murmured Morwen. '"Except seven, none returned from Caer Coronach" – All that way through so much, only to end here, even though they be with Arthur.'

'Better to sleep in Arthur's bosom here in Afallinn than to rest in the Valley of Kings.' Aeron found that she could not convey in words or even in kenning what she had felt back there in the cabin; it had been too much hers for her to share. *A matter for princes as well as for people*, she thought, *for am I not Queen of Kelts but by Arthur's grace?*

'There is a thing we must do now,' she said presently. 'Little enough do I like to do it, now that I have seen; but it is that for which we came here.'

'The Treasures,' said Camissa, and Aeron nodded.

'They are within, in a chest at the bed's foot; I sensed them as soon as I entered the ship.'

Yet when she knelt at last in front of the ancient iron-oak chest, her hands resting lightly upon its carved top,

Aeron was gripped by a paralysing reluctance to raise the lid. It was not that she felt unworthy to do so, or that her action would profane that which lay within, for she knew she was both cleansed for it and bidden to it; but rather it was that very sense of inevitability which daunted her, a feeling of being moved by dán and not by will, as one piece in a great game of fidchell that had been laid out upon a cosmic board long before she had been born in any life; and too, a sulky ridiculous resentment at being so used. She shook off rebelliousness and reluctance alike. *These within, however sacred, are still but tools to my hand; and I a tool to – whose? And if it is fidchell, better to be a queen than a pawn* . . . She took a deep breath and lifted the lid of the chest.

Within, thick folds of some stiff and metallic fabric covered the contents. Forcing herself to a fine semblance of outward tranquillity, Aeron turned back the fabric with a hand that shook only a little. Beneath the cloth, a glittering tangle of objects lay exposed, shining in the room's green light with all the glamour of the Sidhe.

'The Thirteen Treasures,' breathed Morwen.

Aeron's face had an expression upon it before which the others, even Sargus, looked away. Then she stretched her hands, as if in blessing, over the jumble within the chest, seeing shapes now: a sword-blade jutting out at an angle, a round bowl or quaich wrapped in a dusty mantle, other things she could not as yet discern.

'With these,' said Aeron, in a voice not even Morwen had ever heard her use before, 'with these the Danaans won Ireland, and Brendan won Tara, and Arthur won Keltia back again for us all.'

She closed her hand over the hilt of the sword, feeling it leap to the touch, vibrating beneath her fingers as she drew it slowly clear of the chest. It was a broadsword, long and heavy, of the kind used in Keltia since the earliest days. Its hilt was two intertwined serpents: In the mouth of the golden one was an emerald, in the silver's clear rock crystal. Their eyes were rubies, and each scale of them was separately etched. A plain leather scabbard, worn with age and use, concealed the blade, but Aeron did not draw the sword from the sheath.

She smiled at the surprise on their faces. 'This is Fragarach, the Retaliator for which my ship was named. It is the sword of light Taliesin speaks of; to draw it now, in curiosity only and not in need, were death for all. It will be needed dearly enough later on.' She set it carefully aside, looking up the length of the couch at the King's face. *Nay*, she thought, with a feeling that was the inner equivalent of a smile, *you do not begrudge me your weapons, my lord; for it is your dán as much as it is my own: mine to come, yours to wait till that I came; and also it is Elathan's, and Sargus's, and I cannot say how many others'; all bound alike into a sword-knot that has been a thousand years and more in the making . . .* She reached again into the chest and removed a long, thin object, perhaps as long as a tall man was high, tightly wrapped in folds of silver silk.

'And that?' asked Camissa.

'The Spear Birgha.' Aeron could feel the power in it; it tugged at her hands like a horse at the bit, straining to be away and about its work. 'It is said that never has it missed its mark nor failed to slay. It kindles fire from the air with the speed of its flight, and when it strikes home in righteousness, it roars.'

Elathan felt the small hairs on his nape suddenly stand on end. When Aeron had first confided in him of her search for the sacred things of her people, he had acquiesced in her hunt, for he had no better plan of his own and of force must go along with hers; but also because it had seemed no bad idea, and too, she had taken oath

280

that his throne would be won back by those Treasures, even before her own. And he had believed her, and still did. But this had grown now to something so far beyond anything he had ever anticipated, consciously or no . . . Beside him, Camissa made a little flinching movement and a small sound, and he put an arm around her, feeling her fear. *I too, my love*, he thought grimly, *and, I would bet, for all her confidence, even Aeron*

Aeron, had she been aware of Elathan's mental wager, would not have taken it for any coin: she *was* afraid, and did not deceive herself about it, though she took care to conceal it from the others. *Even so, Wenna doubtless knows* . . . She put the thought aside, and bent again to take something from the chest. Her wrists almost snapped with the unexpected weight of it, and Morwen leapt to help her hold it.

But she too was surprised, and taking it from Aeron carefully balanced the thing in her hands. Astoundingly heavy for its size, beneath its still-supple covering of gilded leather it felt smooth and round and hard. Morwen began unthinkingly to unfasten the jewelled clasp.

'Do not so, Lochcarron.' Aeron's voice was softly pitched, so as not to alarm, but it carried command like the bite of a whip. Morwen set the thing down hastily at Aeron's feet, for she was suddenly afraid.

'What is that, Aeron?'

'I think it can be only one thing: the Eye of Balor, called latterly the Stone of Fál.'

The names meant nothing to the Fomorians or to Sargus, but Morwen stared fearfully at the leather-covered globe, the size of a man's head. If only half its deeds had been done that were sung or spoken of – a tenth part – then this stone was one of the mightiest weapons the worlds had ever seen, and one of the most destructive. It was said that the Danaans had captured it from their earth enemies the Fomori, when first they battled for possession of the land of Ireland. The tales told that none could look upon its unshielded gaze and live, that it could bring burning death to anyone and anything for a league around; and in that moment Morwen believed it all.

'Which is?'

'A stone of power; kin, maybe, to the crystals whose wrongful use caused the sinking of Atland. It is a fearsome weapon, and a fearful thing to think to use, even in self-defence.' Aeron had in her hands now the bowl-thing she had noticed first of all when she opened the chest. 'And this is the last of the four chief Treasures: Pair Dadeni, the Cauldron of Rebirth.' She drew off the gold-embroidered silk mantle, itself a Treasure, that had wrapped it, revealing a fair silver bowl set with pearls in the band of knotwork around its rim. 'It has the power – or so, again, it is said – to restore even the dead to life, so that they are laid within it.'

'It is but a quaich!' protested Morwen. 'Scarce of a size to fit a hand!'

'As to that,' said Aeron, shrouding the bowl once more in the cloak, 'it is in my mind that not always is it as we see it here. It is the original of all crochans and saining-pools; if it did not exist, no more could they, for it is from this' – she held it up in both hands – 'that they take their power. You and I, Wenna, of all those here know most truly how such a thing might be.'

Morwen, as clearly and vividly as if she had been teleported there, found herself back at Tomnahara that terrible night when Gwydion had dared to fashion a crochan for Aeron's own healing, without which she had surely died. And this, then, was the source of the power upon which he had called, the reality of which she herself had felt, and so could not deny . . .

'If I understand you rightly,' said Sargus, who had said no word since they re-entered Arthur's chamber, 'these things you have come so far to find have more to them than what we see here.'

'Truly,' said Aeron. 'They are both symbol and reality, operating upon more planes than we know, or can know. They are relics, right enough, but they are also tools, meant to be used. And by the gods I do mean to use them; much work for them to do, and they have lain idle long enough.'

'And Arthur?' asked Sargus. 'You will take the holy things of your people back to their home; will you not take the Red Dragon and his folk home again as well?'

Aeron shook her head, surprising all but Morwen, and began putting the sacred objects back into the chest. 'Nay, that would be to fly in the face of dán. It was written that the King should sleep at the last in the island Afallinn, with his companions about him. Here they shall remain.'

'It was also written, if I am not mistaken,' remarked Elathan, 'that he should come again when Keltia had need of him.'

'Well, and has he not? Not in his own living person, perhaps, but certainly as he is here, and in his spirit, and in the weapons he has put into our hands; and in the long truth of his ending, which is a greater weapon than most. What need is there of more return than that? We shall take his spirit home with us; so will his dán be accomplished. That, maybe, is the real meaning of the legend.'

Even in her deepest soul Aeron did not voice the hope she cherished as future reality: that, perhaps, some time years yet to come, there might be a child of hers and Gwydion's, a child of Arthur's spirit – and that child would be the true return of the Red Dragon. Such a

283

hope, however, if not the height of traha and vainglory, and even if possible by the laws of dán, would be many years away from fulfilment; and perhaps Arthur was already reborn, anyway, and would make himself known in a new life in a new and different manner.

'Nid myned a ddel eilwaith,' she said aloud. '"What comes again has not gone" . . . But tonight we shall make a fitting farewell to the King of Kelts.'

That night, as the sunset glow was fading from the sky and another, eerier, glow grew brighter from the peak of Mount Terror, a long skein of torches stretched like a string of fire-pearls along the ridgeback from the cavern entrance: the Salamandri of the Ras of Salhi, called to this place by their leader Sargus, and their outworld guests, all come to lay the Red Dragon to an honoured rest.

Aeron stood flanked by her friends as the great inner cavern filled with Salamandri: the same folk that had watched the previous night as she walked the fire; and even when they were all assembled inside the cavern, they filled but a small corner of that enormous space.

There was more in the air than ritual: The Salamandri had come to do honour to Arthur, and also to Aeron, who as chief priestess of Keltia would deliver that honour to him, and who had won as much for herself. But beyond even that, there was a sense almost of mourning, a kind of palpable autumnal feeling, that seemed to cloak the Firefolk in its aura. It caught at Aeron's soul like a cold hand, and she turned to Sargus with pain and query in her face.

'We have talked of this before, you and I,' he said gently, for he knew that she was feeling: guilt, responsibility and other things besides. 'It is that the people accept that you are in truth the second messenger, as the

Red Dragon was the first; and the third messenger, the Herald of our Change, is not so far off now, though I think few of us now alive shall live to see it. You spoke only a little while ago of the legend of Arthur and his rebirth; and you have faith in your own life after this life – well, the death of Afallinn will be no less a rebirth, for it and for us, and that is why we do not fear it. We can sorrow for it, but we are not afraid. No,' he added swiftly, to forestall Aeron's protest, 'nothing was made to last forever in this world; not a people, not a planet, not a galaxy. This you know; and it is no burden of yours – no, nor ours either.'

Aeron kenned in his words and in what lay behind them how very right he was; though her sadness remained, it was not all sadness now, and when she turned to face *Prydwen* her head was high and her countenance unclouded.

The ship stood as she had done for centuries; within the now-sealed doors, the Sleepers lay as they had passed into slumber so many lifetimes ago. Arthur himself had not been disturbed, though the carved chest was gone now from the foot of his bed. One thing only was there that he would not have known were he suddenly to awaken: Aeron, liking not to take and leave nothing in return, had placed on the hand that had once wielded Fragarach the black and silver signet of the House of Aoibhell, that had come down to her from Brendan Mór, first of her family to wear the Copper Crown. She touched the white indentation on her finger where the ring had been, looked up to meet Morwen's sympathetic gaze.

'Did I do right, to put the ring where it now is?'

'Leave it there, so,' said her friend. 'It is very well bestowed, and not even Brendan Mór himself would say otherwise.'

After a moment Aeron nodded. *It* is *well bestowed,*

285

*though now my hands are bare indeed* . . . First the Great Seal had gone from her finger, the big carved emerald of unknown antiquity signifying the governance of Keltia, which she had left in Caerdroia under a fearful guardianship; and now the Unicorn Seal as well. Still, bare her hands might be, but scarcely empty: Weapons had been given into them, and those weapons the wonders of the earths. And that, surely, could be no bad bargain . . .

The cavern was filled now. The light of the torches in the hands of the Firefolk went up and up, throwing the dripstone icicles of the ceiling into sharp relief, casting black and fantastical shadows over *Prydwen* and onto the cave floor beyond.

Aeron stepped forward, and profound quiet settled over the watching throng. 'With the ebb, with the flow,' she said in a clear carrying voice, beginning the litany of the Keltic death rites. Behind her, Morwen, who had also instructed Elathan and Camissa, gave the response with the others.

'Mar a bha, mar a tha, mar a bhitheas vyth go bragh.'
*'So it was, so it is, so it shall be forever'* . . .

As the ceremony proceeded, Elathan found himself paying more heed to Aeron herself than to the ritual. *She has changed*, he thought. There had been a strange forging here in this forge-planet; a forging of soul. There seemed something in her now that had only been possible before: possible as the sword-blade is possible in the rough length of findruinna, before the smith's hand is set to it in earnest, before it is heated in the fires of the smithy. And if the strength be not there, or if a flaw furrow the metal, then all the smithcraft in all the universe cannot draw that power forth, nor make shift to work round that flaw . . .

Morwen too found her attention wandering from the prayers to the priestess. Self-confident Aeron had ever been, like almost all her family; at times spectacularly so. Though the war and its sequels had badly shaken that confidence, now all the swithering uncertainty Morwen knew her friend had been plagued with of late seemed to have vanished. In its place was a quiet new assurance – nothing vaunting or boastful, just a calm confidence, fixed and solid, as if it had its roots in something more enduring than the earth of this world.

*Something happened in that cabin*, thought Morwen. Something between Aeron and Arthur; some secret exchanged between soul and soul in a fated hour. What it was she did not know, and doubted if even Aeron herself yet did; but, whatever it might be, it was of such a nature as would not for long stay hid . . .

The rite was not a long one; quite a few minutes before Elathan would have thought to grow restless, it was over. Aeron spoke the Last Prayer, with a silent farewell of her own, and traced the sign of the circled cross in the air before her. Where her hand passed, the outline of the sign glowed silver-blue in momentary afterimage, then faded, and Aeron turned again to her friends.

'An unnecessary speeding, most like – doubtless they have all long been gone from here, and been reborn many times over – but a thing that cannot hurt; and besides, one never knows.' She flexed shoulders and neck in a stretch. 'Gods but I am tired; and we have still to get back to *Retaliator*.'

Morwen's heart sank at the thought of the long punishing ride back to the ship, but Sargus smiled and shook his head.

'That at least we can spare you. Your ship has been brought here; it awaits you at the foot of the hill.'

Elathan stared. 'But I thought – '

'You thought we had no such technology,' said Sargus matter-of-factly. 'Well, we are not so simple as we appear,

287

and mean to appear, to offworlders. You will recall, Aeron, how I said your ship could not come into this part of our world; and that was true enough, then. There was a srith laid upon us: a sacred ban, a proscription – '

'A geis, in our tongue,' said Morwen.

Sargus nodded. 'Well, in brief,' he continued, 'we were forbidden to allow any ship to come here because *this* ship was already here. But what was done at the Kasulathra, and equally here tonight, has caused that ban to be lifted, and so your ship has been brought.'

'With this secret technology you did not wish to display,' said Camissa.

Sargus shrugged, a marvellously human mannerism. 'No great wonders,' he said. 'Tractor fields, antigravity floats; simple enough means. But now you must leave the Firefolk and their world. Your choqa – your journey of seeking – is done, and I and my folk must now begin to prepare for a choqa of our own, the greatest and last.' He took Aeron's hand in both of his, touching it to his forehead in the style of leavetaking used by the Salamandri when the farewell was permanent.

'I cannot thank you and your people, Sargus, as is fitting and right,' she said. 'If there is anything I can do, or might be permitted to do – '

'There is: You must come safe home, and set to rights that which must be settled. That is all you are meant to do. Go now.'

The last sight any of them had of the Firefolk was Sargus standing alone in the mouth of the great cavern. Aeron, looking once over her shoulder as she pulled herself up into *Retaliator*, saw him raise his arms in farewell, and as she lifted her own arm to return the salute he was gone. She sealed the doors behind her and went forward to take the helm.

The last sight they had of that planet was the fire-mist

hanging like a golden nimbus around the head of Mount Terror; then *Retaliator* rose up through atmosphere, and Kholco – Afallinn – went dark beneath them. Aeron never saw that world again.

# Chapter Twenty

Sanchoniathon knocked once on the gilded door and went into the state salon that Jaun Akhera had long since commandeered for use as a bedchamber. Mindful of other times he had been summoned so, he was apprehensive; more so still on finding the chamber empty, illuminated by only a low-set crystal lamp on the chest beside the silk-hung bed.

*If Akhi means to make me nervous, he is doing a fine job of it. Waking me up and commanding me here . . . where can he be, and what does he want?*

His first question was answered almost at once, as Jaun Akhera stepped back into the room from the terrace beyond the windows. He had apparently been himself on point of retiring, perhaps had even been asleep as had Sanchoniathon, for he was clad only in a gold silk chamber-robe; his dark hair was disarrayed, and his feet were bare. Closing the glassed door behind him, he motioned Sanchoniathon to a chair near the hearth and himself took the facing chair.

'I know you are cross with me, Sancho, for calling you here at this hour, but I think you will forgive me when you hear.'

Jaun Akhera's voice was strangely vibrant, and his face seemed to be concealing some great happiness, so that Sanchoniathon bent upon him a puzzled look that changed into expectation as Jaun Akhera spoke: *Here is my second question about to be answered . . .*

'I wish you to know first of anyone here in Keltia,' continued Jaun Akhera, 'save only the one who brought me the message: Our grandfather, upon whom be the peace of Seti, is dead. I am now Emperor of the Cabiri. Our mother, who has taken up rule in my name as Princess-Regent, contrived to get this word to me; a smallship managed to break through Rohan's blockade and land here on Tara. So we learn also that we are not so tightly sealed off as we had thought . . . But the news is absolute. She has given order that the main force of our starfleets be sent to relieve us here on Tara, and she herself will be coming with the fleet.'

Sanchoniathon had risen to his feet during his brother's speech, and now he crossed the hearth-space in one stride, his eyes shining. Going to one knee, he took his brother's hand and kissed it.

'Majesty,' he said, and rising again threw his arms around his brother in a warm embrace.

Jaun Akhera returned the hug, face animated as Sanchoniathon had not seen it for too many days. 'Sit here and talk to me – there is much to do before Mother arrives with the fleets. Will you help me, Sancho? I know I have not been easy to be around these last months, but all that will be different now, I promise.'

'Akhi, you are my brother and my friend. You have no need either to ask or to apologize. And now that you are also my Emperor, you have no need to do anything but command.'

'But I would not command *you*,' said Jaun Akhera, his fine-featured face oddly intense. 'Not you, nor Hanno, nor Garallaz, nor any of my true friends . . . I must tell them presently of what has happened,' he added. 'But there is more news yet.'

Sanchoniathon smiled. 'What news could be of any importance beside this?'

'You shall decide. I have heard word from Dyved. My new friend and loyal collaborator, Powell, Prince of that planet, has managed to come by the company – the extremely unwilling company, to be sure – of Lieutenant Sarah O'Reilly. She was detained on Gwynedd by our old friend Kynon ap Accolon.'

Sanchoniathon frowned, faintly unsettled. Kynon was hardly the surest of auxiliars: He had been the lone survivor of the plot that Jaun Akhera had made with Gwydion's treasonous sister, Arianeira, and her accomplice the Terran lieutenant Hugh Tindal. For his sins, Tindal had been beheaded by his own captain; Arianeira, after arranging Aeron and Morwen's escape, had taken her own life in atonement. But Kynon had somehow managed to survive it all, though at Aeron's order he had been subjected to the ordeal of truth by clearing-stone. In his attempt to lie to the Cremave, Kynon had been terribly maimed, and Aeron had declared him kin-wrecked and clann-broken. All of which had served only to increase his bitter hatred of the House of Aoibhell and all its friends and allies; Jaun Akhera, finding him wandering in banishment after the fall of Caerdroia, had rewarded him by making him Imperial liaison to Powell of Dyved, and had sent him to Gwynedd in command of the forces besieging Caer Dathyl.

'How comes it that she was on Gwynedd?' he asked presently.

Jaun Akhera shrugged. 'She will not say, and it does not matter anyway; though undoubtedly she was searching for Gwydion. It is a great earnest of Powell's good faith that he offers to send her to us. I have little use for her at present, now that Aeron and Gwydion are both beyond my reach and impossible to sway by concern for the safety of their Terran friend. But she may be able to give us some information about Earth itself, and the part it may play in the impending alliance against our Imperium.'

'Your Imperium.'

'*My* – ' Jaun Akhera looked thunderstruck, then remembered, and smiled. 'Yes . . . I must declare a period of mourning for Strephon.'

'Did Mother tell you how he died?' asked Sanchoniathon with a certain hesitation, running his finger along the chair's carved gilt arm. His brother noted the hesitancy, and spoke to it as though he had already noted and addressed it in himself.

'Her message said only that there was an accident; that he drowned in his pool, having slipped on the stone when he leaned too far over.'

'And you believe her?'

'She *is* our mother, Sancho . . . Well. I believe that Strephon did indeed meet such an end as she describes – mostly; I would not be her son if I believed that that was all there was to it.'

Sanchoniathon nodded distantly. He loved Helior, but he harboured no illusions as to what she might not do to keep the Cabiri Throne for her firstborn, and he set resolutely aside the picture that his mind had conjured up.

'When do you think the fleet may arrive?'

'Any time now. The ship that brought the message had to go very cautiously to evade the Keltic blockade, and that took some days. Her captain tells me that Rohan keeps the *Firedrake* lying out beyond the Criosanna like a spider, and the chief part of their starfleet seems now to be deployed between this system and Kymry.'

'The only places where we have still any strength.'

'For the moment,' said Jaun Akhera, touching clasped hands to his chin. A smile came over his face, wiping away cares and years alike. 'At least until Mother gets here.'

\* \* \*

'Emperor!' repeated O'Reilly in utter disbelief. 'You're lying, Pryderi.'

Pryderi shook his head, enjoying her discomfiture. He had arrived at Caer Sidi that afternoon from Caer Carrig Cennan, to bring the news to his two unwilling guests.

'Jaun Akhera himself sent word to my father late last night. It appears that Strephon has been dead for some little time now, and the Princess Helior rules as regent in her son's name.' When O'Reilly remained doggedly silent, he continued, 'She has raised the Imperial fleets and called up levies from the vassal systems; it is said she will be leading them here herself. Or, at least, she will be on board the ranking ship; I doubt she is quite so skilled in war as other royal ladies I might name. Rohan will be hard put to it, if she comes in any force. And as for the odds now on Aeron's return – ' His shrug was eloquent, and infuriating.

O'Reilly turned her back on him. *God* but she would like to scratch his eyes out and then dance on his bloody face . . .

'Why do you and your father hate Aeron so?' she asked instead. 'What can she ever have done to you? And Gwydion – he's your father's foster-nephew; he was your friend too.'

Pryderi shrugged again, tapping on the table with the bronze cuff he had taken from his left wrist. 'I have no real grafaun to grind against Gwydion,' he admitted. 'Though my father feels slighted that Gwydion never came to him for advice after Arawn died . . . and perhaps he is also a little put out at Gwydion's rise to royal power and influence.'

'And you, of course, are not?'

He laughed, his father's short fox's bark. 'As a failed suitor of Aeron's, I might have greater cause for grievance than my father – and more cause to be envious of Gwydion's success in that quarter.'

'You are a pig-dog,' said O'Reilly evenly, 'and not fit to clean Gwydion's muddy boots.'

'Nay, Sorcha, no indignation here; though it does you much credit, I am sure. Well, I'll tell you. When Aeron came to the throne, my father made petition to her over a trifling matter. It was denied, and she had not even the grace or common courtesy to do it herself.'

'That does not sound like Aeron,' said O'Reilly. 'She has always seemed the soul of courtesy; but I'll bet it was no trifling matter either, what Powell asked her to do. Was your father sure of this?'

'Ah well, the words of refusal may not have come from her own mouth, but they were certainly said with her full knowledge. When Turusachan speaks, the other worlds obey, and there's an end on it.'

O'Reilly leaned her elbows on the window-ledge, wondering what Gwydion was doing right now, if he could by some magical means be hearing any of this . . .

'Did you come here just to annoy me? Or is there more?'

With her back to him, O'Reilly did not see Pryderi's eyes go hard and narrow and colder than a piast's. 'Oh aye,' he said softly. 'My sorrow that it seemed to slip my mind. There was also word from Fomor, in the name of his new majesty King Talorcan.'

O'Reilly whirled to face him. 'Talorcan king! Since when?'

'Since the death of his brother Elathan in an escape attempt – with Aeron.'

O'Reilly went rigid. 'Are you telling me Aeron is dead?'

He nodded, his face a mask of malice. 'So we have heard, and so we like to think. Morwen too, and a few ladies of the Fomori royal family; all shot down in an attempt to flee the planet after Talorcan's coup. But Talorcan has taken his brother's crown, and, it would appear, his brother's life as well. To take Aeron's too is a happy extra.'

'And you expect me to believe this?'

'As you wish, of course.' Pryderi slipped the bronze cuff back on his wrist and stood up, and suddenly she was afraid of him, as she had not been before. 'But another small matter slipped my mind until just now: My father has also had word from Jaun Akhera as to you. We told him you were guesting with us here in Carcair, and now the new Emperor wishes to offer his own poor hospitality back at Caerdroia. We are sorry to lose so charming a guest, of course, but who dares gainsay an emperor? You will be back at Turusachan within the week.'

'And Gwydion?'

' – remains here for now.'

O'Reilly smiled triumphantly. 'And how if I tell the new Emperor of the Cabiri that his loyal ally Powell keeps back a prisoner far more important than one Terran lieutenant?'

'Then Gwydion dies within an hour of your saying so . . . As you see, Sorcha, it is not so simple after all.'

*By God, it never is . . .* O'Reilly did not look up as the door closed and locked behind him. Back to Turusachan – unbidden, a flood of memories came over her with such force that her knees gave way, and she sat down hard on the bed. Not for one minute did she believe Pryderi's preposterous twaddle about Aeron being dead – why would she have gone to Fomor, of all places, to begin with – but the rest of the tale sounded plausible enough.

Jaun Akhera emperor, and wanting her at Turusachan. He would not be asking for her if he did not need information, he and Sanchoniathon and their hired sword

Hanno. Bar that, her only value would be as a hostage; and with Aeron and Gwydion both gone, there was no one with whom Jaun Akhera could use her to bargain.

*Well – information, is it? Let him ask. Maybe he'll get some answers he hadn't counted on.*

In the stonewalled chamber across the courtyard from where O'Reilly had confronted Pryderi, Gwydion too had had an unwelcome visitor, and at that same moment was trying to restore himself to calm after his visitor's departure.

Kynon ap Accolon had accompanied Pryderi, and he had been unable to resist the impulse to steal a march on his master and taunt the Prince of Gwynedd face to face; it had taken all of Gwydion's self-control not to let the Kymro see his angry loathing. This, after all, was the creature who had dragged Gwydion's sister into treason, by playing cunningly upon her insecurities and doubts of herself and her jealousies of Aeron – of Aeron as Ardrían, of Aeron as Gwydion's lover. If not for Kynon, Ari might be still alive, Keltia still inviolate, Aeron still beside him . . . So Gwydion had held himself to white silence, and at last Kynon, angered by his inability to break that armour, had flung his most malicious spear.

'And I not even a sorcerer! How say you now, Gwynedd; has not my curse come home upon you and Aeron in full measure? So much for the justice of the Cremave; and you, for all your wizardry, did not even know that she was dead.'

Gwydion had turned slowly round to him at that, and Kynon shrank back at the look upon his face. But his voice had held only polite interest when at last he spoke.

'What news is this: that Aeron is dead?'

Kynon had backed towards the door as he answered. 'A message from Fomor, Jaun Akhera told Powell . . . it is said that Aeron died with Elathan of Fomor, Morwen too – ' In his sudden panic he had begun to gabble, and then had slipped through the door and slammed it behind him.

Gwydion, leaning against the wall now in a kind of relief, felt also a kind of triumph – that Kynon had left the chamber alive. *That hell-wrought curse*, he thought passionately. Every word was cut into his memory as if with a laser-pen, and now unflinchingly he called it up: 'The stars' wandering between you, Aeron, and the brother of the one who betrayed me. Your crown from your head, your lord from your bed, and may the Shining Ones themselves ride forth to war before you return again as queen to Caerdroia.'

He believed not one syllable of Kynon's story – some tarradiddle concocted by Jaun Akhera, or Powell, or both of them together; but a complete untruth, whatever. If she were dead, he would know; his magic would not fail him there, and that was all there was to that. Yet oddly enough, Kynon's claim about Fomor and Elathan carried real conviction; he had kenned it. Could it be that she had gone there after all?

*Ah, Aeronwy, I have failed you*, he thought in sudden, and uncharacteristic, despair. *I have failed to keep Keltia safe for you, failed even to keep myself safe*. Many had died to get him out of Caerdroia; the merrows had managed a daring escape for him; the King of the Sidhe himself had sent one of his great lords to his aid with Manaan's own ship; Aeron's brother Declan had given him a starship and his blessing and seen him safe off-planet. Yet Gwydion had allowed himself to trust where no trust was merited, and had ended up again a prisoner. Worse still, the little gold horn that had been given to him by Gwyn, that he had carried with such care out of Caerdroia, had been lost; thrown by Powell into the sea surrounding this island prison, when first Gwydion had been brought here from Caer Carrig Cennan.

But for all that, still they had not found the Great Seal of Keltia – he closed his fist over the massive emerald, hidden by his magic from the sight of any save he alone. This he would keep for Aeron despite all; they would have to take his hand off to come by it.

*Still, what matter if I have the Seal, if neither Aeron nor Keltia be here to make it reality* . . . Gwydion threw himself down upon the bed and covered his eyes with one bent arm, then sat as suddenly up again. The veriest amadaun he had been, not to have thought of it sooner . . . His elation blazed, and he instantly damped it down, lest it be somehow sensed by his captors.

But the excitement remained alight, like the groundfire that runs through the peat-hags just below the surface. If those who held him here were of any merit or mettle as sorcerers, he reminded himself, his plan were all in vain. But he knew that they were not, though for a while he had forgotten; and upon that lack of facility all his newborn hopes were pinned. He lay down again, and behind his strongest shields his plan began to form, and he began to smile.

'Serenity? You did send for me?'

Helior turned; upon seeing who stood there, she made a little obeisance – more than a nod, less than a bow – and a look of unaccustomed deference came over her face.

'Greeting, Irin Magé,' she said. 'You come most promptly upon my summoning. Please, seat yourself.'

The chief priest of the Cabiri order silently took the proffered chair, settled his hands inside the sleeves of his orange silk robe and bent a keen dark glance on his Emperor's – and star pupil's – mother. To his sight, the deed was plain, despite Helior's by no means unskilled attempt to conceal it.

*So, it is as I suspected*, he thought. *Her hand, in the end, may not have struck down her father, but her mind surely directed another's hand to do it, and she would not have hesitated to do so herself if it had proved necessary* . . . For all that, what of it? If one were to indict for patricide or other exotic forms of murder, legal or no, all the Plexari who stood guilty of such, the Imperium would have to find itself a new royal house. All this passed through Irin Magé's mind in an eyeblink, and he waited now for the Princess to come to her point.

Helior came to it with speed and bluntness. 'You know we sail for Keltia in less than a fortnight, to come to the aid of my son. What I wish to know from you, Irin Magé, is what difficulties magic may present to us once we come to Tara.'

*So that is it* . . . 'What difficulties has it presented heretofore?' he said carefully. 'Aeron Aoibhell did not choose, for whatever reasons, to avail herself of her own sorcerous powers – which are agreed by most judges of such matters to be considerable, both in depth and scope – and, unless I am much mistaken, it was by sorcery that your son brought down Caerdroia. He seemed to have little enough difficulty there.'

'Oh, play not coy with me, priestling!' snapped Helior. 'You know perfectly well just how Akhi managed that, since it was you yourself who taught him. Also it was you advised him, before he left for Keltia, to refrain from magic altogether. Since he did not – for whatever reasons – I want to know what complications may arise from his actions.'

'Difficult to say, madam.' Irin Magé's look was cool and measuring, as if he were assessing what level of truth she was fit to hear. 'Well then, when your son used magic in his war on the Kelts, he opened the door for magic to be used on him. Aeron would never have been the first to do so, not after her experience at Bellator; your son, by the use of his art, raised the tenor of the war from that of the purely material to a level involving much, much more. If he wins, in the end, he shall win on an earthly plane only; but if he loses – '

'If – '

'If he loses, he shall lose a good deal more than a war, or even his life.'

Helior was silent for a while. Then: 'Because of Aeron's sorcery?'

'Because of his own. But also because of what she may now have as weapons. I have by my art seen things I like not at all: shapes and powers each more dreadful than the last, and all of them as swords in Aeron's hands and hosts at her back.'

'Then you must stop her,' said Helior evenly. 'And I promise before the goddess Selk that you shall rue it if you do not. You shall come with us to Keltia, bringing whoever you may need – priests, qizars, whatever – such as will best serve my son.'

'Your son will need more than that, I fear,' replied the priest. 'I trained him myself in the ways of the Cabiri, as Strephon was trained, and Errazill-jauna, and their fathers before them. But it is in my mind that Jaun Akhera may fail, and, failing, he shall fall. What I have seen coming could sunder the Imperium itself. I have seen a hand holding a sword of light, and a silver cup out of which wounded warriors rise up whole; an army of trees; an old woman washing bloody shirts; a huntsman in grey who courses a pack of red-eared, white-coated dogs . . .' He gave a convulsive shudder, and ran a hand over his eyes. 'No more,' he whispered, as if in pleading protest to one who could spare him further visions.

301

Helior looked at him, herself suddenly cold with a nameless dread; to her eyes he seemed to have somehow withdrawn, to be receding from her even as she watched, moving away from her like a retrograde moon.

Irin Magé took visible control of himself. 'My priests and I will be at your command, Serenity,' he said formally. 'But as to promises . . . well, that is not the way of magic. Jaun Akhera knows that as well as any; and Aeron Aoibhell knows it better than most.'

# Chapter Twenty-One

When Caerdroia fell to Jaun Akhera's magic, the rest of the Aoibhell family had long been gone, by Aeron's express command. Some of them had gone into places or perils just as uncertain: Rohan to *Firedrake*; Fionnuala on the embassy to Earth with Gavin Straloch; Declan to the Kyles of Ra, where Gwydion had found him after making his own escape from the City.

But many of the other members of the royal family, and others who were friends and courtiers and close to the Crown, had headed for the planet Caledon, and the castle of Inver, where Declan's twin, Kieran, was lord of the district surrounding. No Imperial forces had penetrated to Caledon, thanks to the crack system navy and the support of the main starfleet, and Inver, tucked away in the wilds of the Decies Country, was a haven both safe and remote.

Among the very last to leave Caerdroia had been Aeron's sister Ríoghnach, Princess of the Name and next eldest after Rohan, and her husband, Niall O Kerevan, Duke of Tir-connell, one of Aeron's most trusted generals. Kieran had welcomed his sister and brother-in-law, and all the others who had found their way to Inver, and the castle had soon become a nexus of information and planning and plotting, a clearing-house and nerve centre for the resistance movement that had sprung up almost of itself in the wake of Aeron's flight.

With a ferocious vigour almost akin to anger, Ríoghnach had tackled the colossal task of organizing and coordinating the masses of information, with Niall and

Kieran as military interpreters, and she kept in almost constant touch with Rohan, feeding information to him, receiving what he could tell her and passing it on to where it might do the most good. But the strain had taken a toll: When the rumour reached Inver of Aeron's and Morwen's alleged deaths on Fomor, Ríoghnach had suffered a nervous collapse – understandable, in the circumstances, but totally unacceptable to her; and now that she had recovered, she was pushing herself as hard as before, and harder still.

Sitting up late that night, poring over the newest data from Rohan, Ríoghnach heard three sharp barks below her window. The small white odd-eyed cat dozing in her lap stirred, gave a lazy hiss and fell asleep again. *Now that is a strange thing*, she thought. *Kieran keeps no hounds here* . . . Still, doubtless there were dogs belonging to others in the castle, or even curs wandering up from the nearby village. She scratched the cat soothingly under its silky chin, and had returned her attention to the reading-screen when the barks came again; louder and sharper now, almost annoyed and impatient in timbre. She frowned; then setting the protesting cat aside, she went to the window and opened it to the cold spring night.

The immense Caledonian moon was only two nights off the full, and Ríoghnach could see as clearly as if the scene had been floodlighted for her. Silver brilliance poured down over the low hills that fell away from the castle on the east; to the fortress's other side was a thick wood, then gardens and the sea. The barking came again, triumphant now, and then her sight was caught by movement off to her left.

A huge wolf was playing like a puppy in the moonlight, dancing and leaping and flirting with his shadow on the grass. Ríoghnach stood very still, for though she had seen him only once before, there was no way she would not have known him again: the Faol-mór, the great spirit-wolf that was the clann guardian of the Aoibhells. Seldom did he show himself to the family he protected – even Aeron, who besides being Queen was also clann chieftain, had seen him only a few times – and never but for some tremendous reason.

*Has something happened to my sister, then*? Cold came over her that was not the cold of the air; but no, had there been disaster to warn of, the beast would be howling the caoine, the lament. Instead, he was disporting himself like a delirious cub, wild with joy and seemingly heedless of who saw him; he had even barked to attract Ríoghnach's attention, so plainly did he wish to be seen. But what as yet unknown event did he celebrate?

She watched for many minutes, and the wolf below her never tired of his dance. She could sense the joy of him, how strong and glad he was; and she knew that he meant her to feel it. Behind her in the room, the door opened, and Niall came in.

'Ríona?' he said, surprised. 'Do you wake so late?'

She lifted a hand to silence him, then beckoned him to the window. He stood behind her, taller by more than a foot – in a family of tall redheaded siblings and cousins, Ríoghnach was the odd one out, small and dark-haired and delicate like her great-grandmother Fíona of Aros – and peered obediently out into the night.

'What do you watch, anwylyd?'

She breathed an incredulous laugh. 'See you nothing, down there – there, where the trees pull back from the lawns?'

'Nay, love, nothing but grass in moonlight. Come away, it is unhealthy cold.'

*Look how he goes*, thought Ríoghnach, her heart leaping even as the wolf leapt, one last tremendous

305

spring, straight up, clean as a sword or a salmon, turning tip for tail and landing on his paws again without a sound. Then he shook himself all over, turned his shaggy head to stare up at her window – for an instant she saw his eyes, like green fires where they caught the moon – and then he was gone.

'But what do you think it may mean?' asked Niall at last, when she had finished telling him of what he had not been permitted to see. 'Is it some portent, do you think? Has some ill befallen Aeron, gods forbid, or Rohan?'

'A portent to do with Aeron, certainly,' said Ríoghnach, her dark eyes thoughtful. 'But not, I think, something baneful.'


At Caer Sidi far away, that dawn brought more than portent. Gwydion had had no unearthly visitor in the night, nor had he had any sleep either, but instead had spent all his time in the marana trance, fashioning what he prayed to every god that ever was would be escape for him and O'Reilly. He had wasted a little time at first berating himself for a fool: This was not like Turusachan, where he had had to depend on the courage and cleverness of others. Here at least he could rely upon himself, on his own skills and daring and resources, for the first time since the breaking of the Wolf Gate, and that knowledge cheered him as nothing else had in months.

Turusachan had been stiff with Coranian sorcerers – not least among them Jaun Akhera himself – who would not only have detected Gwydion's magic but could have thwarted it, parrying it with spells of their own. But Powell and Pryderi were both of them untrained and unlettered in the art; and, with the unease which those who eschewed magic often felt in magic's presence, they kept no sorcerer of any rank here at their prison-fortress – not Dragon nor Druid nor even a bard. Within the walls of Carcair there was no person who could even detect Gwydion's labours that night, far less halt or hinder him; and in the grey-gold dawn, as his working came confidently to an end, he spared a part of his attention to reach out to touch O'Reilly's mind.

It was the sound of shouts and pounding footsteps that waked her first. O'Reilly leapt from the bed and ran to the eastern window. What she saw stopped her breath: An armada seemed coming to Caer Sidi by sea and by air, sleek armoured longships shadowed by craft that looked like falcons, rolling like thunderheads out of the dawn. The sea was hidden by the findruinna hulls, and the sun by the black wings, and the shouts of warriors came faint but clear to her ears.

She stared entranced, a wild hope beginning to blossom: Aeron, Rohan, Desmond, coming to rescue her and Gwydion; and then a voice spoke in her mind, a voice to which she paid close heed. Presently she nodded, and dressed herself quickly and quietly, braiding her hair and looping it above the collar of her cloak to afford no purchase for an enemy's grip. Then she waited in readiness just inside the door.

Outside, the soldiers of the prison garrison were still racing in panic to repel the coming invaders. O'Reilly could hear them shouting and cursing on the battlements above, in their unavailing struggles to bring the laser turret guns to bear on the incoming aircraft; but the guns were fixed and could not be turned around. She smiled with delight, hugging herself under the cloak; then Gwydion's voice came clear and urgent through the door.

'Sorcha? Are you there?'

'Gwydion! Yes! Is it all right?'

'Very right. Stand away now from the door.'

O'Reilly moved hastily back into the centre of the

307

room, and a few seconds later the thick oak door burst inwards into a million splinters. Beyond, in the corridor, stood Gwydion, in his hands a blastgun he had taken from a dead guard.

'Come, we must be quick.' He grabbed her hand and pulled her along the corridor.

'How did you do it?' she asked, puffing a little with the speed of their passage.

'Do what? Ah, the "invasion". Well, it is of course a fith-fath, a glamourie; naught real to it.'

'Yes, but those ships and aircraft give a solid reading to scanners; otherwise nobody would be fooled, and they wouldn't be breaking their necks up there to get the laser cannon shifted. There must be more to it than illusion.'

Gwydion's rare smile flashed as he turned to her. 'I see your months with the Ban-draoi were well spent . . . Well, this is not the time for a lesson in sorcery, but aye, there *is* rather more to it than that, and I shall tell you all about it soon enough. Now we must get off this island, and quickly, before they find out all those forces are but sham.'

They had reached the ground floor of the castle, and now ventured warily into a deserted guardroom. O'Reilly took advantage of the moment to grab up some weapons from the piles left on the tables: a glaive, a blastgun, a pair of sgians.

Opening the small postern, Gwydion reached out with all his senses. No one near; all the guards were concentrating on the 'invasion' now nearing land on the castle's other side. He beckoned to O'Reilly, who dashed up to crouch beside him under a stone buttress.

'How *are* we going to get off the island?' she whispered. 'The only ships are at the landing field across the tide-race; we can't swim it, not with weapons, and the current is too strong anyway.'

308

'We shall have good help.' He leapt down the path that led to the rocks at the water's edge, and O'Reilly followed close behind.

Down on this sheltered side of the island, the tumult up at the castle could not be heard, and the beetling granite cliffs shielded the fugitives from view. Standing on the seaweed-covered rocks, Gwydion allowed himself to relax a little, and the face he turned to O'Reilly was years younger.

'I was a fool to have let us languish there so long,' he said ruefully. 'But having had to keep my mind from magic for so many weeks, I was slow to think of a magical way out for us. Also,' he continued, his voice lower, 'it seemed somehow dishonour to take such a way, an unfair advantage. Which makes me even more the fool, for certainly no such scruple constrained Powell or Pryderi – the which I shall settle with them on a day not too far off now. But come stand with me, Sorcha, and see our help come to us.'

He leaned out over the rocks, the moving water no more than a length below him, dark and cold. O'Reilly gazed out over the surging tide-strait with despair in her heart.

Then Gwydion began to sing, softly at first, then in a voice of power that gathered power to it as he sang. *Any who heard that voice would want to do nothing but obey his summons*, thought O'Reilly; but to whom did he sing?

As she stared out to sea, she became gradually aware of four small dark heads bobbing towards them over the roughening water. She stiffened to wary attention, glanced sideways at Gwydion, who had not ceased to sing, his strong voice carrying a rhythm like the waves' own. She was caught up in it, heard in the deep-mouthed chanting echoes of a strange life and a wild, far below the surface of the rolling ocean: life under a green glassy roof, with floors of gold sand and fantastic castles of pearl and crystal, with the lacy red weed flickering up to the light like underwater flame.

With an effort O'Reilly cleared her mind of the dizzying images; Gwydion, whose song had ended, threw her a reassuring smile.

'It is the seal-singing,' he said, knowing her confusion. 'The effect will leave you in a moment. I have called the Sluagh-rón to our aid. Wait now.'

The bobbing heads were very near now; one of them raised up out of the waves and turned to look at them. It was sleek, round, dark-furred, with long delicate whiskers; big dark eyes regarded them critically, and with an alarming degree of intelligence. Then the creature spoke, and O'Reilly jumped.

'You called us, lord,' it said in a voice of haunting timbre. 'What would you of the Sluagh-rón?'

Quickly Gwydion introduced himself and O'Reilly, with a formality of manner that much gratified the seal-folk, and explained their plight. When he was done, the silkie he had addressed dived without a word, and the other three heads followed him underwater. They seemed to be gone a long time, and above, the two humans waited in tense expectation. Then, in a fountain of foam, the four silkies exploded up out of the sea, in a curve so full of grace that O'Reilly exclaimed in wordless delight, to stand beside them on the weed-slick rocks.

'I have spoken to my brothers,' said the silkie who appeared to be spokesman for the little group. 'We will help Gwydion Prince of Dôn in whatever way we can.'

As Gwydion thanked the creatures, O'Reilly tried not to stare, but she was frankly fascinated. Unlike the merrows, the silkies of Keltia were not humanoid in form, but retained most of the physical characteristics of their

310

phocine ancestors. She could not imagine at what distant moment in the past the gifts of speech and reason had been passed to the Sluagh-rón, or by whom, though Slaine had once told her that the silkies had come with the Kelts from Earth in the first great immrama, and even those long-ago Kelts had believed there was human blood among the seal-folk – and vice versa. She suppressed a desire to stroke the thick shining fur of the one that stood nearest her; then it looked up at her out of brimming limpid eyes, and ducked its head against her knee, and with shy delight she drew a gentle hand along the line of its neck.

But Gwydion was gesturing her to join him lower down on the rocks. 'The Sluagh-rón will help us cross the tide-race,' he said when she stood beside him with the sea swirling around their boots. 'On the other side of that promontory is a small landing-field, and if I cannot manage to steal us a ship then I deserve to be Dyved's guest. Are you ready?'

Before she could reply, the chief silkie chattered something in his own tongue to one of the others, who held out to Gwydion a small leather pouch that looked as if it had been for a long time in cold deep seawater.

'That, I think, belongs to you, lord. We found it some time ago, and have held it for you since.'

Scarcely daring to believe it was in truth what he thought, Gwydion opened the little pouch. Inside, sealed in waterproof oiled silk, was the small horn of dull gold that had been given to him in Dún Aengus by Gwyn ap Nudd, King of the Shining Folk.

'I had not expected ever to see this again,' he said quietly. 'I thank you for its return; it may mean more than you or I shall ever know.'

Wrapping the horn again in its silk covering and fastening it to his belt, he turned to O'Reilly. 'Let us go; the

311

tide will soon be against us, and my illusion cannot hold very much longer.' He slid into the freezing water, a warm seal body on either side of him for support, and looked up at O'Reilly, who stood hesitating on the rocks. 'Come, Sorcha; it is not the first escape I have made by water. Jump!'

O'Reilly closed her eyes and leapt.

# Chapter Twenty-Two

The sail back from Kholco to Fomor had been a swift one. Aeron had pushed *Retaliator* as never before – even Morwen had been surprised – and though the voyage had not been exactly a merry one, it had been replete with unspoken satisfactions.

On the edge of the Fomorian system, Aeron hove the ship to, to the considerable mystification of Elathan, who was at that moment occupying the co-pilot's chair.

'We will remain here for a few hours,' she said, not looking at him. 'I must make some adjustments before we take *Retaliator* in to Fomor – adjustments to ready the ship for battle – and also I would discuss with you where we must go and what must be done when we get there.'

'I think first of all we must return to the dûhín, to see what Borvos and Treic may have been able to do in our absence,' said Elathan, more baffled than ever by her suddenly stiff demeanour. 'They will have been in contact with the forces that remain loyal to me, and perhaps they will have devised some plan that will march with ours. Beyond that, we can only hope for justice.'

Aeron's laugh was bitter. 'Justice! When folk say they wish for justice, what they usually mean is indulgence for themselves and punishment for everyone else . . . Well, maybe that is not such a bad thing either. You have been as sorely tried as I; still, you shall be King of Fomor again, and soon too. That is justice, if anything is.'

'And you shall soon again be Queen of Kelts,' he

offered, trying to help her, though he still did not understand her mood.

'Queen? I am a thrall. Once the Copper Crown has been set upon a sovereign's head, there is no release save death or the will of the people. I have some expectations of the one, but little hope of the other.'

'Aeron, I do not know what this mood is that is on you, but I wish you would speak honestly to me of your trouble. After all, you once bade me do the same, and I did, and was the lighter for it. Maybe I can help you in like manner.'

She ran a hand through her hair. 'Upon my soul, Fomor, I do not know *what* is on me . . . Only a selfish graceless carlin could find cause to complain. I am glad of the Treasures we did find, and glad too that we could speed Arthur with decency and honour, and excessively glad that we shall soon do to Talorcan as he so richly deserves. For the rest of it – ' She spread her hands in helplessness. 'Have you ever had a thing in your mind to do; then when it is all but done, and the fruit of all your labour in your grasp, have held back from it as if from very poison? I can put no other words to it. Can you believe that almost I wish *not* to return to Keltia – to leave you and Camissa and Morwen on Fomor, to take *Retaliator* and keep sailing on across the galaxy, until I die, or the ship dies, or the galaxy dies.'

Full of sympathy, Elathan took her by the shoulders and shook her gently. 'I can believe you would *wish* to wish it – but no more than that. For one thing, it would be the wish of a weakling and a coward, and you are neither. You are only tired, and no wonder. Listen, I'll tell you something: When we have Fomor back from my pernicious brother, we shall first of all rest a little. Then we will formally declare our alliance; Cami and I shall be wed, with you and Morwen among the chief witnesses;

314

and then I will call the fleets to assemble and we shall sail.'

A spark of colour seemed to return to her drawn face. 'For Keltia?'

'For Keltia.'

'Shall we, do you think?'

'Yes. If you are right about the powers of the Treasures. They must win Fomor back for us first.'

The warmth had reached Aeron's eyes. 'Oh, aye,' she said. 'Of that, at least, I *am* sure. As to what power they may have against Jaun Akhera, that shall be seen. He is a formidable sorcerer, and it is in my mind, I cannot say how, that he will be stronger than we know when we do come to Keltia.'

'You speak of him almost to praise him.'

'It is only the craven belittles a foe. I think I have not yet grown so abject with ill haps that I cannot praise a worthy opponent.'

'And my brother?'

'Ah, he. Well, kinship is no guarantee of anything, as Gwydion would be swift enough to tell you. Of all us here, you know Talorcan's mind best. What do you think his plan will be?'

Elathan shrugged, looking out at the familiar space of his home system. 'That will depend on what control he has over the armies and starfleets. We cannot know that until we contact Borvos and Treic.'

'Which we shall do,' Aeron assured him, pausing in the hatchway, 'before another day dawns over Tory. Stay at the helm while I am gone.'

Alone in *Retaliator*'s command cabin, Elathan contemplated the stars a while longer, then reached out to punch up military frequencies on the ship's long-range transcom. It would all be coded, of course, and old signals for the most part this far out in the system, but perhaps he could pick up something that would be of use or interest.

*Ah, Talorcan*, he thought, *I would not be in your boots today for all the gold in Fomor. Did Aeron say kinship was no guarantee? True enough; for kinship would not now keep my hand from your blood were you twenty times my brother . . .*

*It has been almost too easy*, thought Morwen five days later. *And that of itself should make me most mistrustful . . .* Instead, she felt only confidence. Which had, admittedly, a solid grounding in reality, for she stood at that moment in the palace courtyard at Tory, while all around her the attacking waves of loyalist soldiery routed the last of Talorcan's mercenary rabble.

*It is almost as if the way has been smoothed before us. But perhaps there is a tide in these matters after all, and having run against us for so long, now the current bears us with it . . .* Whether that was so or no, they had landed undetected on Fomor, by dint of a brilliant bit of piloting by Aeron. There had followed an emotional reunion with those they had left behind among the dûhín: Thona, Basilea and Rauni; and a reunion more martial and purposeful in nature with Borvos and Treic, who had reassured Elathan of his strength among the armies and the populace at large. Talorcan, not surprisingly, was regarded as little better than a regicide, and his brutal policies had made him few friends.

They had gathered forces as they went north to Tory; Elathan had declared himself on the second day, and news of his return had spread within hours to all the worlds of that system. Only on the plain below Tory had they encountered resistance of any strength – Talorcan prudently opting to concentrate his forces around the city rather than engage his brother in the open – but Aeron

316

had told Elathan to move back his armies, and standing forth from the lines she had unlidded the Eye of Balor.

Even now, two days later, Morwen shuddered at the memory: that long leaping lance of fire, sweeping across Talorcan's ranks like an arm across a fidchell board, leaving smoking destruction in its wake. After that, Talorcan had pulled his forces back into the city proper, where Aeron dared not use the Eye; and for a day and a night and a day again the fighting had raged through the streets, until now it swirled like a bloody tide around the foot of the castle rock and up into the palace precincts. But it was a losing action; the Eye had turned the balance for Elathan, and very soon the castle's fall would signal the end of the usurpation.

Morwen rubbed her knee absently as she waited. It had not gone entirely smoothly, of course; almost no one was without an injury – she had hurt her knee, Elathan had sustained several serious cuts and a few bruises, Camissa had torn some rib cartilage, and Aeron – Morwen shuddered anew as she thought of it: As Aeron had been shuttering the Eye, a laser flain fired from Talorcan's lines had struck her in the throat. Luckily, it had been nearly spent and had glanced off her gorget, causing her little more than a deep scratch. But her friends had had a bad turn . . .

A series of muffled thumps came from Morwen's left; laser culverins, she knew, set in position by the first wave of the assault, to knock a passage through the fortress walls. She lifted her blastgun, and, with Treic, entered the outer bawn.

In the thick of the tumult, Elathan striding through the palace's ground floor met Aeron and Borvos running towards him from the opposite direction.

'Talorcan?' he husked, his voice cracking from the smoke and dust.

Aeron rubbed the back of a rather grimy hand across her cheek and shook her head. 'Not that we could find,' she said. 'And we quartered the palace for him.'

Elathan broke into an unwilling, and unamused, grin. 'Three things are equally unlikely to my mind: that the Coranians had no hand in this brawl; that the Salt Lakes turn to usqueba' – Aeron and Morwen had introduced him to the Keltic liquor, with great success – 'and that I may be in the same place with my half-brother, both of us sword in hand.'

'Perhaps not so unlikely,' said Aeron. 'Have we no one to ask?'

Elathan brightened. 'We have taken several who were with Talorcan in the plot. Let us see what they have to say for themselves.'

But when the prisoners – the general Bargoit, second-in-command to Talorcan's chief tool Dargato, and one Achivir, a starfleet commodore caught planetside when Elathan struck – were questioned, they proved something less than communicative.

Elathan looked up with annoyance – it had been a long and disagreeable session – as the door of the chamber opened, but his face changed when he saw Camissa and Aeron.

'I can get nothing out of them,' he said, coming over to them. 'They seem to be proof against drugs, and grosser forms of persuasion I think it scorn to try.'

'Let us see if they may be proof against me.' Aeron stretched out her right hand, the second and third fingers together, towards Bargoit; after a moment of rigid resistance, his head came slowly around to her.

'What did you do to him?' gasped Camissa.

'It is but a kenning,' said Aeron. Her voice held a certain distracted quality, like that of an archer who must make conversation and shoot to hit the gold at the same time. 'A telepathic probing, no pain in it. It does not even work on all subjects, and can be shielded against by those who are trained to it, but – ' She broke off, her gaze unfocusing, and stood very still. When she looked again at Elathan, her face was without expression. 'They have succeeded in getting off-planet,' she said, and her voice was as controlled as her face. 'Talorcan and his minions; they had Imperial help in the coup, and they have gone to Jaun Akhera.'

'In Keltia?'

She nodded once. 'In Keltia.'

Even given the unbounded delight of his people at his return, it took remarkably little time for Elathan to reassemble his government and reassert his control over his kingdom. Though Talorcan had executed those loyalists courageous enough to stand against the usurper – and unfortunate enough to be caught – very many of Elathan's trusted aides and ministers and advisors had managed to go into hiding, or to get off-planet, or otherwise simply to stay out of Talorcan's way. But now they flocked eagerly to Tory, to reaffirm their loyalty and love to their rightful King and resume their old duties.

And, rather less happily, to support that King's present policies: most specifically, the alliance with Keltia. For Aeron sat on Elathan's right at the council table, and though she chose not to remind the Fomorian councillors of her part in restoring Elathan to power, others were by no means so reticent, and did so loudly, frequently and at length: Camissa, Borvos and, especially and unexpectedly, the Dowager Queen Basilea.

It was not that the Council grudged Aeron the help

Elathan had promised her; like it or not, it was only by Aeron's grace that Elathan was even alive, much less restored to his throne and victorious over Talorcan with such comparative low cost; they owed her a debt, and they knew it. And it was not that they harboured anti-Keltic feelings and prejudices: None of them had been over-pleased to have had to support Bres's unholy war, and most would have liked to see an end to the hostilities long ago.

What the Council urged now upon their King was not default but prudent delay, until Fomor should be steadier and the strains placed on the Phalanx alliances should be eased – for if Fomor itself looked a little uneasily on the pact with Keltia, the Phalanx was thoroughly alarmed at the idea, and would take far longer to be placated and reconciled. And perhaps worse than that: Elathan was not the only one who had heard whispers of Phalanx involvement – the name most often mentioned was that of Laharan of Felire – and that involvement would have to be looked into. All this was political work that only Elathan could perform, and, his advisors argued most cogently, how was he to accomplish this if he was off leading fleets to Keltia to help Aeron destroy Jaun Akhera? Not that that was not a laudable and desirable goal, and one they would be proud to have Fomor assist in – some time in the near future, or not so near, when things were more settled . . .

Elathan listened to their arguments with a look on his face that was itself a challenge, letting them wear themselves out with their own rhetoric. He had expected resistance, of course, but his mind had long been made up as to his path of action; as he saw it, his only honourable and possible path. Still, it would be far easier for him, and for the Regent he intended to leave to rule in his absence, if his advisors could be cajoled or coerced into supporting him. Aeron would not speak, and that was probably a good idea, but . . . He glanced sideways at her; she saw the enquiry at once, and nodded almost imperceptibly towards Morwen. *An even better idea*, he thought. Reading permission in his face, Morwen seized the floor with practised confidence and began to address Elathan's Council.

Now Aeron had a ready wit and a quick tongue, if a sharp one, but Morwen was not called Honeymouth for nothing: Straloch had given her the sarcastic epithet one particularly stormy Council session at Turusachan, when she had sweet-talked him into agreeing with some pet position of hers much against his own mind. The ground of their dispute had been long since forgotten. But the name had clung.

*And why should Fomori be any more resistant to a golden tongue than Kelts*? thought Aeron, concealing a grin as she listened to her Taoiseach alternately charm, bludgeon, flatter and reason with the Fomorian councillors. It was a virtuoso performance; and indeed, by the time Morwen had finished with them, they had turned biddable as scolded children, only too happy to accede to whatever Elathan's wishes might be.

In the end, of course, his will prevailed, and he sat on with Aeron and some others after the Councillors had gone.

'But was it likely to end otherwise?' asked Borvos.

Elathan collected himself with a start. 'Not likely,' he said. 'In fact, never even in question; though I cannot say what I might not have agreed to, had Morwen turned her eloquence on me . . . But we wasted time and effort here, where we have neither to spare. There is much to settle before we can start for Tara.'

'One thing that troubles me,' said Aeron thoughtfully.

'Strephon. If, as those two traitors revealed to my kenning, Talorcan had Imperial assistance by connivance of the Princess Helior – '

'Then by now word must surely have reached Strephon of what has happened here,' said Basilea. 'And he will know that Elathan is restored, and that you, Aeron, are alive and on Fomor.'

If Aeron still harboured any of her previous resentment against Fomor's queen-dowager, it did not show now, for she nodded and weighed Basilea's words no differently than anyone else's.

'Or so, at least, we must presume. Unless Strephon is ignorant of his daughter's venture into interstellar meddling?'

Morwen shrugged. 'There seems not much he is ignorant of, though Helior might have managed it. But did not Talorcan go to her for sanctuary?'

'To her or to Jaun Akhera,' said Aeron. 'I could not tell from the kenning; both pictures were linked in the traitors' minds. In the end it makes little differ which, though I had thought Strephon did cut his grandson off from aid and reinforcements. On the other hand, Helior would not spare nor stint where her son is concerned . . . We may look to smite all three of them – Jaun Akhera, Helior *and* Talorcan – when we come again to Tara.'

'If I may say, Aeron,' ventured Camissa, 'they will try mightily to smite us first.'

'You may say,' agreed Aeron lightly, 'and they will try. But by the gods I promise them no joy of it.'

Events ran now in Tory at double-pace: the mustering of Fomor's forces, after a brief, brutal purge conducted by Borvos and Treic to remove any who had sided with Talorcan; and the arrangements for the King of Fomor's wedding, which had been advanced by some months, as

Elathan wished to solemnize his union with Camissa before his departure for Keltia.

The day before the fleets were to begin assembling, an emissary was announced to the King of Fomor and the Queen of Kelts. Elathan collected Camissa and Aeron, and went straight to the Presence Chamber, where the emissary in question was pacing up and down. When they entered the room, the pacing suddenly stopped.

'I bear greeting from Aojun, Majesties all,' said Panthissera of the Yamazai, which was not strictly correct, as Camissa would not be Queen of Fomor until the morrow. But the Yamazai had calculated the salutation to please and flatter, and it did.

Elathan returned courtesies, and then Aeron made her own duty to the envoy of the warrior-women's matriarchy. She had never met one of that fabled race before, and she was impressed: Panthissera cut a striking figure, dressed all in soft leathers stitched with beading and intricate embroidery, her black hair pulled smoothly back from a high forehead, in the centre of which a crescent moon tattoo rode blue above dark slanting eyes. But far more than any externals of appearance, she showed plain to Aeron's sight a grace of spirit, and a steel-true honour with it, that any Kelt in Aeron's kingdom would have been proud to claim.

'As you know, I am War-Leader of my people,' said Panthissera in excellent Lakhaz. 'And I am sent by Queen Tanaxio to offer the help of the Yamazai in this fight. We have our own small feud with the Prince of Alphor: You may not have known it, Queen of Kelts, but the Yamazai refused to join Jaun Akhera and Bres in their war upon you – as King Elathan will confirm – and we have suffered since for that refusal.'

'That I did know,' said Aeron sombrely. 'And for that

the Yamazai did pledge to lift no sword against me, I pledge to lift my own in aid of Aojun.'

Panthissera bent her head in acknowledgement. 'That is as Aeron Aoibhell was expected to reply. My Queen is glad of such a word, and she has a word for you in return: Aojun's need, as well as your own, can best be served at present by striking at Jaun Akhera, and this we would do alongside you. So Queen Tanaxio is sending such forces as can be spared here to Fomor, and has charged me ask that you allow us to sail with you to Keltia.'

Elathan clasped Panthissera's forearm in the manner common to his world and hers. 'We thank Queen Tanaxio, and you her War-Leader, for such an offer, and we accept gladly.'

'We too thank our sister Tanaxio,' said Aeron, using as Elathan had done the royal 'we', and putting fist to shoulder in salute. 'Tell her we shall meet when the battle is over, she and I, if the Mother allows it.'

'There is more news still,' said Panthissera. 'I doubt if Fomor's tracking stations have as yet logged their presence, but on our voyage here we passed near two ships in deep space. They were in link, and had apparently stopped to parley. One was a Terran ship bound homeward, Aeron, with your own ambassadors aboard her.'

Aeron's face lighted. 'Oh, the *Sword*! And the other?'

'An embassy ship from Earth; she is called the *Argo*, and she was on course for Keltia, with the Terran ambassador to your court.'

'Did you speak to them?' asked Camissa.

'Surely,' said the Yamazai, enjoying the impact her news appeared to be making. 'We conferred all three; and the upshot was that they are both following us here.

As the *Sword* is less swift than the other, they must hold back a little for her; and our cutter was faster and lighter than both, so we came here first. But, bar ill, they should arrive at Tory no later than the day after tomorrow.'

# Chapter Twenty-Three

As the shuttles descended like a shining flight of silver bees, Aeron, in a hastily run-up formal Keltic uniform, stood with King Elathan and Queen Camissa on the landing field; Morwen, Rauni, Borvos, Basilea and others of the royal party waited some yards behind them.

In spite of her outwardly calm demeanour, and her experience as Queen with such occasions, Aeron was in the grip of such an inner tremoring of anticipation as she thought must rock her entire body for all this foreign world to see. *Like a hare in the jaws of a hound*, she thought, *being thrashed to and fro – well, I care not if they do see. May I not be excited as they*?

In truth there was cause more than enough for excitement and stir. The day before, Aeron and Morwen had stood in the Great Hall of the palace, and watched with joy the joy of their friends, as Elathan set the crown of the queens of Fomor on Camissa's upswept dark hair.

Now came today the arrival of the Terrans, Fionnuala and Straloch with them; and as if that were not enough, there would be tomorrow a ceremony of solemnity and grandeur, at which would be publicly affirmed by Aeron as Ard-rían of Keltia and Elathan as King of Fomor a treaty of peace and friendship that would put an end forever to the bitternesses of the past. Both principals also hoped that the Terran ambassador would recognize the implicit possibilities for his nation in such an event, and would join with them to make a tripartite agreement. But that remained to be seen. For the moment, the moment was enough.

The shuttle from the *Sword* was first to land. First out

the door were Hathaway and Mikhailova, and Aeron's heart lifted at the sight of them. They saw her in the same instant, and ran halfway to her before they remembered their public manners and the context of this occasion.

Aeron demolished all protocol by herself dashing to meet them, embracing both before they could salute her.

'Oh Aeron – Ard-rían – ' Mikhailova was near to happy tears, and tears of memory too, and Aeron's own eyes were bright and brimming.

'Athwenna, Warren – did I not say we should meet soon again? Oh, but I am that glad to see you both . . .'

But then Fionnuala and Straloch came running, and formality was at an end. At last, after Morwen too had been greeted with hugs and tears, Aeron remembered herself enough to present all four to Elathan and Camissa.

Then the first craft from the *Argo* touched down, and they all turned to watch.

Haco Grex paused in the cutter's door for perhaps five seconds, as an ambassador should, then descended the steps to the field. Aeron and Elathan, gravely polite now, came forward to meet him; he looked from one to the other, then bowed deeply and deferentially.

'Your Majesty of Fomor, Your Majesty of Keltia: Haco Grex, ambassador to the court of Aeron Queen of Kelts. Madam, I had not looked to find you here, but you know better than I how that has come to pass.'

'I do so,' said Aeron, 'and you shall hear soon enough.' She slipped from Englic into the High Gaeloch. 'But for now we confirm Your Excellency all the same as the Federacy's representative to our presence and our Court.'

'And as our guest in Fomor,' added Elathan. 'My lord Grex, if you and your party would be pleased to accept hospitality here in Tory until plans may be made? There is much we must discuss, we three, for though you may not know it, you have come at a busy time.'

Grex nodded, grey-blue eyes suddenly keen. 'I rather thought I might have done . . . Well then, Majesties, let us do our jobs.'

Little more than a day later, Aeron, standing with Elathan and Grex in the palace's Great Hall, contemplated with immense satisfaction what the next few minutes would hold, and what the previous day had seen accomplished. *Chriesta tighearna, but that Terran ambassador is a neat-handed cogger; and that consul of his, that alienist, has a Sight on her any Ban-draoi would give much for . . .* They had been tough bargainers; still, she was rather more than pleased with the outcome of the negotiations. She ran it over briefly in her mind while Elathan spoke, addressing those few hundreds here in the Hall and all the watching billions: In only one day, she, Elathan and Haco Grex together had hammered out a preliminary treaty that, if all went according to plan in the coming battles, would put their three allied nations into such a position of galactic pre-eminence that not for the foreseeable future would Imperium or Phalanx or any other nascent and acquisitive superentity be able to challenge them.

*True, it is what my father said that I must never do; but it must be, Father, my sorrow but you were wrong, and I could have done far worse . . .* All in all, not a bad day's work; though in truth the bargaining had lasted nearly until dawn, and before it was done had involved not only the three of them but Camissa, Morwen, Straloch, Elathan's Prime Minister Svaros and the Terrans Valadon and Deonora.

She touched the hollow at the base of her throat. Not even a scar or a soreness there now, thanks to a Fomori medic's quick work with a skinfuser; and any road it had been not much more than a bad and bloody scratch. But gods, for an instant there she had thought that was the

328

end of it: Aeron Ard-rían, dead in battle on the planet Fomor, of an arrow in her throat. *It would have read very dashing in the histories, but I am better pleased still to be on life* . . .

Aeron was recalled to herself by Elathan's amused whisper. 'Are you *here*, Aeron? We must sign now.'

Haco Grex had done so already; now Elathan set his own signature to the treaty diptych, and pressed the Seal of Fomor into the matrix.

'You will have to be content for the present with my sign-manual only,' remarked Aeron with a smile, suiting action to word as she signed *Arigna Regina Celtarum* in her strong flowing script. 'But when I wear the Great Seal of Keltia once more upon my hand, then I will place that stamp beside Fomor's and Terra's.'

'I have a feeling,' said Grex with an answering smile, 'that that place upon the matrix will not remain empty for very long.'

All that past week the Fomori fleets had been assembling, lying to out beyond the comet clouds on the system's borders, waiting for the next day's sunrise on the distant throneworld before the sail to Keltia would begin.

At the spaceport that served Tory, a secret departure was being made under the light of the three moons. In a far corner of the field, a knot of people stood huddled anyhow, looking spectral and haggard in the light of shut-lanterns. The narrow beams fell on the glittering black hull of *Retaliator*, that stood ready and waiting to receive her passengers and her pilot.

Apart a little from the others, Elathan stood holding both of Camissa's hands in both of his, looking down into her eyes with love and apology.

'You cannot come, sweethearting. No matter both our wishes, you shall be safer here, and I shall feel better knowing you are so. Besides, you must be Regent in my absence, and that will take all your time and skill. Basilea and Rauni will be your sub-gerents, and you will have other good advisors, but you are sovereign of Fomor, and you act in my name and with my authority.'

'Plague on it. I want to go with you and Aeron – '

'Nay, my friend,' said Aeron, coming up to them in time to hear this last, from where she had been taking affectionate farewell of Borvos and Rauni. 'Elathan has the right of it, though I too could wish it otherwise. You have been a brave and a loyal companion through many hardships; but I am loath enough to endanger one monarch of Fomor in my fight for Keltia. To put two in peril would be insupportable. Stay then, and be Regent, and gods with you until next we meet – very soon, I promise.'

Camissa smiled, though tears stood on her face, and embraced Aeron fiercely. 'And with you as well. Take care of my lord, Aeron, and take care of yourself also.' She hugged Morwen, who stood near, then turned again to Elathan. 'Go, before I change my mind and stow away on *Retaliator*.'

Elathan kissed her tenderly, then turned hastily away to join Aeron on her way to the ship. The others who were to go on the faring to Keltia had already taken their places aboard, in the main cabin: Straloch, Fionnuala, Morgan Cairbre, the Dragon warrior Emrys; Hathaway and Mikhailova, who had begged long and hard to be allowed to go; and Haco Grex, who had surprised himself by the strength of his own wish to do so. So he had given permission to the two *Sword* officers, had put Valadon and Deonora in charge of the *Argo* and a small crew aboard the *Sword*, with instructions that both ships follow to Keltia with the Fomorian fleets, and now he was fastening himself into a blastchair's restraint field with a feeling of anticipation such as he had not had for years.

*No doubt it is extremely unprofessional*, he thought, with a smile behind the silver beard that was anything but

repentant, *but my Lord I am looking forward to this . . .*
He heard Aeron's voice in the command cabin, then
felt the ship start to rise, and gave himself up to the
motion. *Theo, my old friend, I will stand beside you soon
now . . .*

Below, alone on the field in the windy dark, Camissa
watched the black ship climb quickly into the summer
night sky. The blue ion-wake lay like a broad wavering
arrow, diminishing to a point as *Retaliator* stood off from
Fomor. Then came a sudden flash and golden smudge of
starlight, and Camissa knew that Aeron had sent the ship
into hyperspace, and they were already racing far ahead
of that farewell flash.

She looked up one last time. The heavens were clear
now, the ion-track vanished, and Camissa slowly returned
to her escort for the short trip back to Tory. And in all
that escort – Borvos, Rauni, Treic, five or six others –
not one person did not long to be heading to Keltia
rather than returning to his own city.

Once *Retaliator* was safely into hyperspace, Aeron turned
the helm over to Elathan, and, ignoring the merry chattering group in the common-room, disappeared aft into her
cabin. Morwen, exasperated as well as concerned – there
were, after all, certain duties even queens could not avoid
– gave her an hour alone and then went to the rear cabin
herself. When Aeron did not respond to her knock,
Morwen touched the door-stud and entered uninvited.

'In gods' name, Aeron, what is on you? Almost it
seems that the closer we come to home, the darker grows
your mood. What is your trouble?'

Her friend gave her a strange little smile. 'Today, in
Keltia, would be the observable day of Rhodri's death.'
There, she had said it, for only the second time in four
years to anyone other than Gwydion; his name was

331

spoken, and it seemed to fall dead at her feet even as it left her lips.

But once she had said it, she felt an overwhelming urge to go on speaking of him. It was true enough that both of them had been manoeuvred into the marriage by their parents, but that had been by no means the whole of it. She had adored Roderick Douglas since her childhood, with the total infatuation of a young girl for a hero warrior-poet some years her senior. Gwydion was as her own other hand, had ever been so and would ever be so, but Rhodri too had been special. She was blessed to have had two such.

'I know,' said Morwen, after a long dumbfounded silence. 'I thought you wished not to be minded of it – as ever.'

Aeron smiled, this time a radiant clear smile free of pain. 'Nay, Wenna, all that is done with now; four years' silence is silence enough, though it took Arthur himself to make me know it. There is much you and I have to say to each other, and now it can be all said. But I would be alone a little while longer, and perhaps sleep an hour or two. All is well; you may tell the others so.'

When Morwen had gone, Aeron drew herself up on the pillows and put her folded fingers to her mouth. This night four years since Rhodri had gone out forever: The Gate had opened for him and he was through, the shining spiral Path opening for him outwards and upwards. He had been called, and he had gone. For some pain-blinded time – could have been days, might have been weeks, she did not remember – she had thought to follow; but the same Power that had called him forth had called her back. *Not yet*, it had said to her, *and never like that*, and she had obeyed.

*Ah Rhodri*, she thought, the tears in her eyes turning the stars beyond the port into spinwheels of fire, though also she smiled, *I would not be thinking of you tonight if*

332

*you were not thinking of me. You do not grudge Gwydion
and me our love and life together, and now at last I can
believe that.*

She twisted around to look out of the port beside the
bed-head, out and down to that area of space where
Rhodri and her parents and so many others had met their
shared dán all unknowing; and beyond that, to where
Bellator once had spun around its white sun Alcluith.
*And that too is all part of the weaving . . .* But she had
never gone that way again, to pass that place among the
stars from which his spirit had fled. She had thought to,
more than once; but that same feeling of Presence that
had bidden her stay had halted her, pulling her from that
intention as a bit checks a captious horse: a hand upon
the reins of her soul, a tug strong yet gentle. And she had
bent her neck to it full willing; had felt, indeed, no
inclination even to balk, trusting that hand as the horse
will trust its rider's judgement, though its own instincts
say otherwise and it cannot fathom the rider's reasons for
those commands.

Aeron moved away from the port and leaned back
again upon the pillows. Her gaze fell upon the long
carved chest that stood over against the opposite wall:
the chest taken from *Prydwen*, within which rested the
Treasures that were the rightful inheritance of her people,
that had been sought so long and so hard.

*Even if I fall in the fight to come, and Gwydion with
me, and my friends every one of them, those here with me
now and those I have left behind me, still have I done one
thing that shall never be in vain, and shall never be
forgotten so long as one Kelt may live to sing of it: I have
brought the Spoils of Annwn back to Keltia. Set that
against all the rest, it can be no bad thing . . .*

She shifted restlessly upon the couch. All the laws of
courtesy demanded she rejoin the others: Social duties
indicated attention be given to Grex; sisterly affection

required still more, and deeper, to Fionnuala; and Hathaway and Mikhailova too had claims of friendship upon her – she had yet to tell them how Theo had met his end, even, though of course they knew that he had died. But it was a long voyage yet before they would sight the Curtain Wall, and there would be time enough for that and more besides.

For the moment, she would meditate a little, and in that contemplation she would remember Rhodri, and Arthur, and all the others who had helped her on this strangest and longest of quests: Sargus and his Firefolk, the dûhín of Fomor, Thona and Basilea, Borvos – all of them part of a pattern but dimly perceived and never to be wholly grasped. Strive though she might, it would forever remain just that last littlest most maddening glimpse, tantalizing, elusive as something seen at night from out of the corner of her eye, that, try as she would, she could never bring to focus.

Yet sometimes, as now, on that very verge between trance and sleep, it came briefly clear, standing revealed in almost mathematical strictness of form, a beauty and severity not to be admitted by the rejecting prosy eye of everyday. Seeing it, Aeron smiled; her weariness, taking advantage of the moment, blurred the boundaries of her trance, and, smiling, she slept.

Across the room, a faint white light spilled from between the cracks of the chest that housed the Treasures, like quicksilver through cupped fingers; bloomed, and was gone again. Aeron did not awaken.

# Chapter Twenty-Four

Aeron came back to Keltia on a wild, wet night of rain and spring winds. She had chosen a remote area of Caledon upon which to make planetfall: the Decies Country, a hilly region of lakes and upland forests bordering the sea, on the mains of Inver, the lordship of her brother Kieran.

*Retaliator* plummeted like a stooping falcon through atmosphere and touched down without a jar. Aeron shut down the systems, sat motionless for a moment, then rose and left the command cabin with no word to anyone. Elathan started to stand, thinking to follow, but Morwen put out a hand.

'Nay, let her be a little time alone. She is feeling much just now.'

'But could we not help – '

'Not we, and not now. But go and gather up your gear, and tell the others to do so as well. She will return when she is ready.'

Halfway down *Retaliator*'s length, Aeron stood in the corridor by the main hatchway. Her hand stretched out tentatively to the control-stud, then contracted into a fist and pulled back. Angry at her own hesitation, she punched the stud; the doorseal opened like a lens, without a sound, and through the opening flowed cool damp air.

The smell of wet green leaves, of the sea close by, of rain falling in darkness on peonies: Aeron stepped from the ship onto soaked emerald turf, and walking several paces forward buried her face in the flowers of a huge peony-tree. The petals were soft and fresh against her burning skin, and the fragrance rose up around her in the rain. She reeled against the trunk of the great rough-barked tree, clinging to it for support, unprepared for and overwhelmed by the wave of feeling that broke over her now. It was as if someone had suddenly sandbagged her, buckled her knees from behind; the smell of rain on new grass, the scent of sea and peonies borne on a freshening wind. It took her back twenty years between one heartbeat and the next, back to that spring night when first she had met Gwydion Prince of Gwynedd in the palace gardens at Caer Dathyl . . .

Above her head, the rain tapped insistently on the leaves; like an eerie counterpoint she could hear it hissing faintly on *Retaliator*'s still-hot hull plating. She pulled down a supple branch, let it spring sharply back, so that a shower of cold drops fell around her, and her fingertips brushed rain and tears across her cheek. She was home, she and her friends were safe. Already they had reclaimed one kingdom, and had the means with which to reclaim hers; had made an alliance that would hold like a schiltron even if all the galaxy should come against them in arms. What was it, then, this that hurt her so? Like an iron band around her chest – she could not breathe in for the pain of it . . . She tugged at the silk cord around her neck until a small silver medallion, warm from her body, came up into her hand. In the peripheral glow of the moon behind low cloud, it gleamed faintly in her palm: a dragon with wings raised, enclosed in a circle – sign and token of the Dragon Kinship. The little disc belonged to Gwydion, given him many years ago upon his acceptance into the Kinship; she had worn it nearly two years now, as he wore hers. More than ornaments, the dragon discs were weapons, protection and means of communication; it was no small matter to entrust them to another, for, psychically keyed as they were to their owners, they could command minds and even souls. She could speak through it now and he would hear her; she had only to call.

Aeron stared down at the silver medallion for a long time, her mind an incoherent iconoscope of memories and prescience, a palimpsest upon which was registered a rocketing volley of images of past and future, so braided and superimposed one upon the last upon the next that she could not separate what had already been from what was yet to come; only, she knew that what she saw, all of it, was the way her dán must go. She smiled then, and closing cold fingers over the still-warm silver, she sent her soul surging outwards through her hand.

In space standing off from Dyved, Gwydion swung the ship away from the planet, and beside him in the co-pilot's chair O'Reilly sighed with deep relief.

'All right, then . . . We *are* all right, aren't we?'

He nodded, smiling, and leaned back in his chair. 'If they are not after us by now, then they will never be, and we are safe away. I think, Sorcha, we must try first to find – '

He broke off abruptly, sitting bolt upright again, face ashen beneath its tan, his grey eyes clouded. O'Reilly, terrified, reached out a tentative hand to touch his.

Gwydion flinched as if she had slapped his face; then his colour flooded back, and warmth, and with both came a look of unutterable joy. 'Aeronwy – Aeron is back in Keltia. Just now I heard her call.'

'Aeron! But – '

'She is home. She is home, and not far away, and I know where we must go to find her.'

'Oh, Gwydion. I want to see her almost as much as you do, but are you sure?'

He laughed, a joyous, exultant sound she had never heard from him before. 'Never was I surer of anything in all my lives – could she call, and I not hear her? Sooner would the sun be black, or water dry . . . She is waiting for us, Sorcha; let us go and find her.'

Kieran woke, completely and instantly, from a dead sleep. Someone had called his name . . . But Eiluned lay peacefully beside him in the big bed. His thought reached farther, to touch their son; but the baby too slept untroubled. *Who, then?* He lay back on the pillows; then the call came again, stronger, and this time he knew.

Leaping from the bed, he pulled a tunic over his head and flung a cloak around him, and dashed barefoot through the silent castle to the postern gate. Fingers clumsy with haste and excitement, he overrode the security codes and threw the door open to the streaming night.

Aeron stood there, cloaked against the rain. He stared at her face in the folds of the hood, then swept her into his arms without a word. She let her head fall against him for a moment, then drew away a little to look straight up at him.

'Where is he? I did call him; he was *there*, Kieran, and then he was gone, and I could not find him again. I will blast Caerdroia down to bedrock if I must, to get him out of there.'

Kieran met her eyes steadily, and with pity. 'He escaped from Caerdroia, Aeron, and went to Declan in the Kyles of Ra.'

'*Where is he?*'

'He was betrayed by Powell and Pryderi, when he went to them for help. They have sold themselves to the Marbh-draoi; they are his creatures now, both of them. We heard that Gwydion was prisoner in Caer Sidi. There has been no word since.'

Aeron's face went white, so white the blood left even her lips, and Kieran caught her shoulders to steady her. 'Caer Sidi,' she whispered. '"Complete shall be the prison of Gweir . . ."' But before she could say more, Eiluned

338

came running into the gatehouse and threw herself upon her sister-in-law, babbling incoherently and joyfully.

Aeron staggered a little beneath the loving onslaught, recovering only when Eiluned caught sight of Morwen and Fionnuala and catapulted herself upon them in their turn.

But Kieran could not take his eyes from his sister's face. He was appalled by the ravages of change he saw in it, and wondered at the cause. *She has something of that same look Gwydion had*, he thought, *when he returned from his errand to the Hollow Mountains* . . . With a start he collected himself, and greeted Morwen as lovingly, if less boisterously, as Eiluned had done, and Fionnuala, his pet, as delicately as if she were made of crystal. Then he noticed the strangers who stood so quietly in the shadows just beyond the gate, watching this reunion of Aeron and her family with understanding smiles.

'Sister, what guests do you bring to Inver?'

Aeron drew them forward into the light. 'I have the honour to present the Prince Kieran and the Princess Eiluned to His Majesty King Elathan of Fomor – without whose help and friendship neither Morwen nor I should be here now – and His Excellency Haco Grex, Terran Ambassador to Keltia. We have all three of us come to an agreement that should stop even Strephon in his tracks.'

Kieran's face changed. 'But have none of you heard? Strephon is dead. Jaun Akhera is now Emperor, and his mother, Helior, rules as Regent.'

'By the gods, is he now.' Aeron seemed more amused than anything else. 'Well, I can see an evening ahead of us even a bard would be hard put to frame in words.'

Eiluned chose that moment to assert herself over guests, friends, kin and Queen. 'Aeron, do not keep them all out in the wind and the wet, standing on ceremony, sometimes you can be so – nay, come *in* then, *all* of you, and be welcome to our house. Where is Gwenvor? Come, lassie' – this to Mikhailova, who was shivering – 'you are as cold as a frog – Kieran, summon your man Llew for the King – oh Aeron, will you never come in – Wenna, up to the baths with you at *once*, I will not have you back from gods know where to take a chill on my doorstep – '

Elathan looked around helplessly, and Morwen, grinning, linked her arm through his. 'It is no use to oppose Luned under her own roof,' she said. 'Come inside now.'

'What will you do now, then?' asked Kieran.

It was well into middle-night; outside, the rain continued to fall steadily, as Aeron and the others recounted their tales to half the household of Inver. Ríoghnach and Niall too had been summoned from their bed by Aeron's telepathic call, arriving only moments after Kieran; others hearing the stir had naturally risen to inquire, and stayed to rejoice.

But no matter the urgency or drama, Keltic hospitality had come before all else. There had been the inevitable prelude of baths and clean dry clothing and food and drink, and only then talk. Much to say on all sides: Aeron had demanded a full account of how her kingdom had fared in her absence, and she had returned over and over to any scrap of news of Gwydion. But she had had to satisfy the others' curiosity as well; it had made a long tale, even with help from Morwen and Elathan and Grex, and her voice and mood had both begun to fail her well before it was ended.

'What will you do now, then?'

When she did not answer Kieran's question, Elathan threw her a quick look full of concern. 'Aeron? This need not be discussed tonight; we have a few days' time to plan. Let it be a while.'

But she shook her head. 'It is not that, though truly we

shall all plan far better after a day's sleep, and maybe more than a day's. Nay, it is but a care of my own, a private matter, and I think,' she finished with a rush, as if she must speak swiftly or tears would overtake her, 'I *think* I must deal with it alone, so go to sleep, all you, and we shall meet again tonight. Nay, Kieran, I said I must be *alone* – ' She brushed past him and ran, almost blindly, down the corridor and out into the gardens.

It was black dark, and her time-sense told her that it lacked perhaps four hours or so until dawn. A misty rain still fell, and water dripped from the trees, but a wind had come up, and at intervals the light of the old moon spilled through the rifts in the clouds.

Aeron had run out without even a cloak, but she felt neither the chill nor the rain, and there under the peony-trees she was again hit by the same causeless sorrow, far stronger now, that had so shaken her earlier that night. An unhappiness like a groundswelling wave spread out to enfold her in one great aching sadness, leaching away her strength until she thought she could scarcely continue to stand upright; her bones felt turned all to water, and the darkness pressed in upon her.

Then a deeper darkness seemed to form at the end of the alley of peony-trees; it moved, resolved into a tall shape as she looked up, straining her sight and her othersight through the mist. Even the rain seemed to hush, and then she was running through the dark, and the other was running too, and she flung herself into Gwydion's arms, and he caught her up against him under his cloak.

They did not kiss, not at first; what he felt, and knew she shared, was a feeling too huge and deep and solemn to be met with anything save silence and utter stillness, of body and of spirit. He held her close without a word spoken, and she leaned her head against his chest, and they did not move for many moments.

When at last he spoke, it seemed that his words were but a continuation, somehow, of something he had been saying to her forever, a speech that had never been interrupted and that had never been begun.

'They had told me you were dead, do you see; I did not feel it so, but after a while, alone there, times were when I did begin to wonder if they were not right. So even I lost courage in the end – '

'And even I, when I heard you were in Caer Sidi.' She drew back a little, looked up into his face. 'Just now – I did not think I could bear it.'

The rain had ended; the rising wind had torn the clouds apart, so that the moon now shone clear upon them. His countenance in the moonlight seemed suddenly strange; she had known it all her life, had loved it near as long, yet now the white light spilling over the planes of his face made all new: a country of unfamiliar contrasts and terrifying strengths, his skin blanched of all colour against the darkness of hair and beard, the grey eyes sparkling silver when the moon caught them, black under brow-shadow when he bent his head away.

What glyphs of change he read in her own face she did not know; surely he must see at least what Elathan saw, and Morwen, and Kieran, and doubtless far more than that. But he said no word of it, only drew one finger, callused from harp and sword-hilt both, down along her cheek and jaw and throat, and closing his hand over the neck-brooch of her tunic pulled her close against him once more.

'Keltia has been asleep without you,' he said into her hair. 'A troubled fitful doze full of evil dreams, and all we walking in our sleep. But now will come a fair waking.'

He felt her shiver once and grow still again. 'Better it might be if we stayed asleep, or slept forever,' she said quietly. 'I have brought such things with me, sacred as they are, as could be the engines of true nightmare. What

342

kind of day is that, for me to cause to dawn in Keltia – to make Tara into another Bellator? That would be no right awakening, but the worst of all dreams.'

'Then shall we all dream it together, and make an end of it.' She heard the confident loving certainty in his voice, burnishing its deepness; and it seemed that never had there been a time when that voice had not been the voice to her of all the strength and courage and conviction that she had at hand to call upon; not Rhodri's voice, not her father's, had ever held for her what this voice held that spoke now so quiet in her ear. She could lean against it, as a fixed rock that fails not though the planet crumble, and again she looked up into his face. He was not smiling, but the look in his eyes was a smile.

'Here is a thing I have kept for you,' he said then, and stretching her cold fingers across his palm slipped the Great Seal of Keltia back into its accustomed place. The huge flawed emerald had no colour under the moon, but deep in the heart of the stone a tiny twisting flame seemed to burn.

Aeron closed her hand at once to a fist; the ring was too big for the slimness of her finger, and for it to slip off now would be an ill omen indeed.

'Loose as ever,' she said lightly. 'I shall never manage to fit this thing, I think.' A look of bitter amusement came over her face. 'We might come out of this coil as emperor and empress ourselves,' she said, her voice both teasing and warning. 'Or come out of it not at all.'

'That is as it will be,' he answered after a while. 'When you found the Treasures, you altered the web of this matter as surely as did Jaun Akhera when he used magic to break the gates of Caerdroia. The final choice is still yours to make – but now, truly, are the buttons off the sword-points.'

\* \* \*

Aeron woke suddenly in the dawn, lay for a moment unmoving, her heart pounding, not knowing where she was or what danger might be near. Then she became aware of Gwydion beside her in the wide, carved-golden-wood bed of Inver's best guestchamber, his back to her and his face towards the door through which any danger must come. Her terror faded, and she fitted herself against him like one spoon to another, her breasts against the warmth of his back, her arm slipping under his to curve around his chest. In his sleep he sighed and murmured somewhat in Kymric, and clasped her hand; and comforted by his nearness and reality Aeron slept again.

Gwydion stirred as late-morning sunlight struck his closed eyes, and without opening them turned round to Aeron and kissed her bare shoulder. She smiled and nestled closer; but she had been lying awake for some time, watching the day advance across the ceiling, and thinking, and she said as much to him.

'Oh aye? And all before breakfast, too . . . Well, to what decision has this brought you?'

'Ah, strategy! Now that is for my First Lord of War to tell *me* . . . But I have thought, first of all, we must hold somewhat of a war council. Elathan's fleets are on their way, and we must learn what tally of our own can be sent to join them. Also I did a small piece of business with our new Terran ambassador that may be of help to us later, if we should need it. But the chief strike at Jaun Akhera I do wish to make myself. And, quite selfishly, I would dilute the pleasure of that strike as little as I must.'

They lay abed for some time discussing means and measures and news; and though they had talked far into the night, had talked near as hard as they had loved, always there was something one would remember that had not yet been told to the other, and must be imparted that instant. Then Gwydion upon rising discovered with some amusement that a lavish meal, half breakfast, half daymeal, had been discreetly left for them in the adjoining grianan. Aeron brushed out her hair, wrapped herself in a chamber-robe tremendously more elegant than those she was accustomed to wear in her own chambers – *Eiluned*'s, *surely*, she thought, very impressed – and joined him at the table. Suddenly she was famished, and this was the first food in months that had any savour for her.

'You said remarkably little last night about your stay in Caer Sidi,' she said after a while. 'Was that by policy, or did other matters rather drive it from your mind?'

He laughed. 'A little of both, I should think, though I do not recall hearing you ask for an account of it then . . . Well, though I told you not last night, I was not Powell's only guest-of-force. Sorcha ní Reille shared my condition.'

'Sorcha!' Aeron nearly dropped her ale-mether with very amazement. 'She was under strict orders to remain at Glassary; how came she into Powell's grasp?'

Gwydion related the events that had led to his discovering O'Reilly in the island prison, and Aeron's face grew sombre at the telling.

'I am grieved to hear this of Dyved,' she said when he had finished. 'He was ever a trimmer, but for all his failings, Powell was in the main a good friend to my father, and to know that he could be so readily seduced by Jaun Akhera is a bitter quaich to drink of. But,' she added, brightening, 'this news of Sorcha sits far better with me. I shall be very glad to see her again, even if she did disobey me. Where is she now?'

'Not far,' said Gwydion; he had kept as a surprise the news that the Terran had come with him from Dyved. 'She has proved herself a loyal Kelt; does not that merit reward from the Crown?'

'To reward O'Reilly? She gave up all to stay with us –

345

as did Theo – did you think I would *not* reward her, or him had he lived, insofar as is in my power? But Sorcha shall have, to answer your uncivil question, anything she wishes that I am able to bestow: a title, a precedence and position at Court, a maenor and a dúchas wherever she will. She is very dear to me.'

'Dear enough to become kin?' he asked, not looking at her; on the voyage to Inver, O'Reilly had, in a burst of candour, shyly and proudly confided in him of her love for Desmond, and his for her.

'Certainly!' snapped Aeron, in rather sharper a tone than she had intended, wondering why in all the hells Gwydion chose to pursue this now. 'Which of my brothers does she wish to wed? I'll approve the match this minute.'

'No brother,' said Gwydion, applying himself anew to fresh-baked bread and the excellent local ale. 'A cousin.'

She divined which cousin at once. 'Desmond! Oh, this is a *fine* piece of news! They shall be wed at Ni-maen, with ceremony, when all is right again. I will give them something substantial for tinnscra: a continent, or perhaps a small moon . . . When shall I see her again, do you think?'

# Chapter Twenty-Five

Upon her arrival with Gwydion at Inver the previous night, O'Reilly had been swept up jubilantly by Kieran and Morwen and the others, happily confounded by the presence of Mikhailova and Hathaway, plied with ale and pressed with questions. Though she had quickly learned the details of Aeron's adventures, she did not see her that night. Which was just fine, O'Reilly told herself hastily; Aeron was with Gwydion, and she would not have dreamed of intruding upon that reunion –

Only . . . she would so like to see her, just to reassure herself that Aeron was truly back, and truly safe, and that everything was all right. O'Reilly was honest enough to admit that she would probably feel a little less urgent about needing to see Aeron had Desmond been there; but that thought carried its own unease: In spite of all Desmond's assurances, how would Aeron really feel when she learned that Desmond and O'Reilly had agreed to wed, and all without the consent of the Ard-rían? More than that – what would she do?

Grey rainlight filtered through the tall narrow windows as Aeron entered the Great Hall. The big high-ceilinged room was deserted at this hour, the life of the castle all moved elsewhere, and it would not emerge from this curious suspension until the nightmeal, when light and colour and people and noise would once more bring it to life.

*Empty – but Gwydion told me to meet him here . . .* No, she saw then, there was someone at the far end of the room, someone cloaked and hooded standing by the cold hearth. *If that is Gwydion, he has lost over a foot in height since breakfast . . .*

'Who is that?' she said aloud, and the figure by the fireplace whipped so sharply around that the hood fell back, and Aeron saw in the light from the windows that it was O'Reilly.

For what seemed hours both women stood frozen, for Gwydion, wishing to surprise them both, had told neither whom she was really to meet in the Hall. Then O'Reilly was skimming up the room's length, heedless of protocol, certain of friendship's reception. Aeron held out her arms, and O'Reilly ran into them like a lost child home at last.

'Oh, Aeron – oh God, I thought we'd never see you again – and it was Gwydion all the time, in that terrible place – and I didn't even know it – and he got us out – the seal-people – and Pryderi – and they were right all along, they said you were on your way home, and here you are – '

Aeron disengaged herself gently from O'Reilly's frantic grip, and, putting her arm around the younger woman's shoulders, led her over to the window-seat.

'Softly, alanna,' she said smiling. 'Let me get a proper look at you in the light – Well, you seem not to have fared too badly. Though I have missed my esquire sorely these past months; still, that was no reason for her to bolt from sanctuary as she did, and I shall have a word with the Abbess Indec on that account; but who is this told you of my return?'

'Oh, you mustn't blame Indec, it wasn't her fault that I left . . . Well, as for the other thing, I'd forgotten it till now – but I was walking one afternoon, in the hills across the loch from the convent, and I met these – people. They were dressed sort of strangely, all in red, and they had the most amazing eyes – but I didn't think of that, somehow, when I was talking to them . . . Anyway, they seemed to know you, and Gwydion, and they seemed to know you'd be back soon. Then I left Vannin, and ended up in that castle on the island, thanks to Kynon. But *Gwydion*! He was *amazing*! He made this incredible magic – ships and warriors and aircars – and then he called the silkies to help us get away – there was a lot going on.'

'So I have heard,' said Aeron drily, though her face had clouded at the mention of Kynon. 'Desmond is on his way here this minute, with Rohan and Declan and Melangell and many others of our friends.'

'You know!' gasped O'Reilly, blushing furiously. 'Ard-rían, I never – '

'"Ard-rían"! What has become of "Aeron"? Nay, Sorcha, if we are to be kinswomen, you must learn to be easy with my name. After all, you will yourself be royal, with duties and obligations much the same as any other princess of Keltia. Surely you had thought of that?' she asked, sympathy replacing the teasing note in her voice as she saw the Terran girl's stunned expression.

O'Reilly stared back at her, astonished at her own obtuseness. 'No – no, I hadn't, really. Not like that – oh *God* no, I was just so worried about you: when would you be back, what would you think, would you even give us permission . . . I really do love him terribly, you know – he was so kind to me from the very first night I came to Keltia, and then after Theo's death . . . Well,' she finished, floundering a little, 'I just didn't think of it.'

'Naught to think of,' said Aeron, giving her hand an encouraging squeeze. 'For there is no difficulty . . . But for now, we have much to do, and the Ard-rían's esquire, no less than the Ard-rían, has been too long away from her duties.'

For all Aeron's words to O'Reilly, little work of real substance was done that day at Inver. Most of those who had come from Fomor took a quiet day of it, resting or reading or walking in the gardens. For Aeron, the hours were filled with reunions: In midafternoon arrived several of Keltia's chief generals and Council members – the Earl-Marischal, Lady Douglass Graham; Tanwen of Marsco, who had commanded all the foot-soldiery in the battles down the Great Glen; Grelun, Gwydion's Dragon lieutenant and rescuer, with Helwen Drummond; Helwen's elder brother Dafydd, Aeron's first lover and her friend for twenty years; Hollin Macdonald, the chariotry commander; family too – Aeron's grandmother Gwyneira; her favourite uncle Estyn, Emer's brother; and beyond all hope, Gwydion's mother Gwenedour and brother Elved, who had heard from Rohan of Aeron's return and Gwydion's escape and who had adventured an escape of their own from Gwynedd; and very many others.

And, far less welcome, came news of some who would not be returning: Denzil Cameron, killed in a space-raid off Droma; Maravaun of Cashel, supremely talented cavalry commander; Mahon, one of Aeron's Aoibhell cousins; Scota, a Kerrigan cousin; Wolf Graham, Douglass's brother, dead in the Fian raid that had freed Gwydion; and too many others.

Though the revelation of each new loss brought each its own measure of grief, Aeron set her sorrow aside for the present, to welcome the newcomers, to present them to Elathan and to Grex, to listen to their reports and accountings with as much grave attention as that with which they heard her own. But of all those she held most dear, still there was one person yet to come, and not until night had fallen again over Inver did his arrival make Aeron's homecoming complete.

The mood was sombre and sober at the nightmeal: thankfulness for what had been restored, but an awareness over all that in the morning the real work would begin, the task for which those now assembled had fought and waited and struggled to survive. As the Great Hall filled for the nightmeal, a tumult came outside the door; as all within turned to see the cause of the uproar, Rohan entered, with Declan and Desmond, Shane and Melangell, Fergus, Morwen's husband, and many others from *Firedrake*, which was now in orbit out beyond Caledon's moon.

Though everyone else that day had been rivers of query, Rohan had no question for his sister but one, and his eyes held hers as they made their way to each other through the crowd in the Hall, and came, a little breathless, face to face at last.

'Did you find what you did seek?'

She nodded, face solemn, but the light behind her eyes brimmed over into her face; and seeing the smile that broke then, Rohan swept her into his arms. Then Declan seized her, and Desmond; a few feet away, Morwen and Fergus were embracing, their joy the greater for the day's delay.

Though the nightmeal concluded with something better cheer than that which it had begun, still it was quickly over, for Aeron had called a council of war for early the next morning, and near all those present were commanded, and eager, to attend.


'Little time we have for preparing, and none to spend on private joys,' said Aeron, though her shining face gave that last the lie. 'We must lay our battle-plans quickly: I have called in our own forces, Elathan's fleets will be here within days, and I am told that my cousin Kerensa brings a small force from the Protectorates. Aojun too, by the word of Queen Tanaxio, has promised to send. Myself, I think it great shame if we cannot succeed with the help of such friends to throw out the Marbh-draoi and all his creatures, and to put a stop to whatever reinforcements the Princess Helior may be sending to help her son. The which, please gods, will not arrive too soon for us – But let us hear what our First Lord of War may say.'

'It has not gone all so ill in our absences, Ard-rían,' said Gwydion. 'But what must be done now is clear. All our fleetpower must assemble to beat back the incoming Imperial ships; as few as possible must reach Tara. We must land on the Throneworld whatever ground forces we can command: The catha of Tara, though dispersed after Caerdroia's fall, can be rallied quick enough to serve. We here, and any who can fight their way to us, must play at pig-i'-the-wood with Jaun Akhera, until the Fomori, at least, do arrive to join us.'

'You mean we must first lure him out of Caerdroia,' said Elathan.

Gwydion nodded, studying the hologram map of the Great Glen that filled the centre of the table. 'We need not be any great force to do so, for he will surely not refuse our challenge; though of course the greater our numbers the better our chances of an early victory. But he must be drawn out, and swiftly too, for any delay will favour him and not ourselves. Moreover, he knows full well that we would never countenance the destruction, accidental or otherwise, of the City. Some thousands of our own folk are still within, for one thing, and for another I do not think that even our magic could bring down its walls?' He glanced at Aeron, who shook her head but said no word. 'Well then, you have it, so.'

'I have heard much talk of force of arms,' said Haco Grex, and his unfamiliar voice and Terran-accented Gael-och caused heads to turn. Unruffled by the attention, he pursued his point. 'And that is of course a necessary thing. But I have heard no word of those – other means which Her Majesty endured so much to find and bring back to Keltia. Are not those weapons, just as much as swords and siege lasers, and why do we not speak of them here?'

'Little enough to say,' answered Aeron. 'They are here, and we shall certainly make full use of them when the time comes – when I say the time has come. I think it not wise to advertise their presence, or even to speculate overmuch, for as yet we do not know their full powers, or the price of that power.'

'Yet you risked your life and others' to bring them home,' said Thomas de Valadon from a corner of the room, where he stood with Hathaway. 'And you will stake the battle – indeed, the final outcome of this war – on these things, unproven and untried.'

'Without question,' said Aeron evenly. 'Do not forget, my lord, that these things, as you do call them, have been already proven in war many times over. When it comes that we need to know of their powers, it is in my heart that we shall know.'

Valadon sketched a bow. 'As you say, Ard-rían; though I do not understand, and I doubt the Emperor Jaun Akhera will even believe.'

'It is not required that you understand; nor even that you accept. It is not required even that I do so . . . The Treasures take no note of belief or unbelief, scorn or devotion; they simply are. As for Jaun Akhera, he may disbelieve all he likes; that will help him not at all when the Eye of Balor is glancing across his lines. We shall see how much he disbelieves then.' She turned once more to Gwydion. 'Let that tally be sent to Gwennan Chynoweth on *Firedrake*, of the ships she can expect to join her at the Roads of Grannos: their number, and kind, and complement of forces. A like tally has already been drawn up for the incoming Fomori fleet, by grace of Elathan.'

'Heard and ordered.' Gwydion looked around the

353

room. 'So, then. This for us is the Last Battle, Cymynedd, that shall win the world or lose it. There will be no midmeasures this time.'

'To lose the world or win it,' said Elathan. 'A fairly final prospect, either way.'

'If it be truly Cymynedd for us,' said Aeron, 'our task is only to fight it. What shall come of it in the end is not for us to rule.'

Elathan smiled. 'Dán again, Aeron?'

She matched his smile. 'As you say.'

Though begged to do so by almost everyone at Inver and many who were not, Aeron delayed for some days in announcing her return to the people. Those who knew that their Queen had come home had been told so only under the strictest oaths of secrecy, until such time as she thought it best to inform the rest of Keltia. When pressed for an explanation for her reluctance, she remarked only that she had her reasons, and Gwydion had more, and that would have to content them all.

Three days after the war council, Aeron and Gwydion, and others beside, could not be found at Inver; and Elathan and Grex were not alone in wondering what was afoot and where they were. The truth, had they known it, would perhaps have given them less comfort than their ignorance.

For a call had gone out the night before the convening of the council, a call that reached to every part of Keltia and was not hindered by either time or distance, a call that was heard only by those to whom it had been sent. It summoned them to a place they knew on Caledon, not very far from Inver as the hawk flies, a place called Pawn Shallow: a green plain that had once been the bed of a vanished loch, cleft for nearly a league where the rock had cracked and risen unevenly, pushed up from below by volcanism and down by glaciation from above. At one end of the great rift, a huge flat rock jutted out over the falling ground, like a natural platform or podium; and so it was used, for here at Pawn Shallow was the assembly-place of the Dragon Kinship.

They came now at Gwydion's own command, for this was one calling he would not entrust to his Summoner but had sent out himself; as many of the Ten Thousand as could respond. Many had been slain in the ongoing battles; some were too badly injured in body or in mind to answer his call; very many were unable to get to Caledon undetected; and many more were simply unable to get to Caledon at all.

But for all that, the plain below the rift was black with people as Gwydion stepped out onto the rock platform. Though few for secrecy's sake were robed in their usual panoply of black and purple, still at every neck gleamed the silver dragon disc, and upon every face upturned to the stone was written the same questioning expectation.

Any meeting of the Kinship was a solemn occasion, but this one, by context and purpose, was particularly so. *Perhaps*, thought Gwydion as he watched his foregathered Dragons, *the gravest and most desperately important that has ever been* . . .

A sudden alert stillness, like a collective breath being drawn and held, came over the assembly as Aeron joined Gwydion upon the great rock plinth. They were flanked by Shane and Melangell, both of whom had come down with Rohan from the *Firedrake*; Grelun, Helwen and others who had come from Inver stood a little below the rock.

Gwydion stepped forward and began to speak, and the rock overhang amplified his bard-voice, so that his words rolled out over the silent throng as clear and unstressed as everyday speech.

'My Kindred, I have called you here this night both to tell you a thing and to ask of you a thing. First the telling, though I know already that you do not need to be told: Aeron Queen of Kelts is once more home.' He held out his hand to Aeron, who took it and came forward to stand beside him.

'And it is I, by courtesy of the Pendragon of Lirias, who do the asking,' she said, still holding Gwydion's hand. 'Know then that with the help of many, Kelt and galláin both but all friends alike, I have brought home to Keltia the Treasures that were so long lost.' She paused a moment to allow the exultant murmur to die down again. 'Many of you, I know, will have felt their coming; and it is to the Kinship, founded in memory of the last King of Kelts who had the Treasures to his hand, that I thought to turn first. For they are not Treasures only; they are weapons, one of which I have already made use of in what I deemed a time of need. And I intend to use them all, as and if I must, to win back Keltia from the Marbhdraoi. Now, the power of the Treasures is of itself, and needs no aid of ours to be so; but they have lain a long time idle in a foreign place. Therefore I ask you to join now with Gwydion and with me in a rite of purification and reconsecration before the last battles; for weapons are most useful when cleansed and in best repair, and so also are souls. Jaun Akhera and I must face each other again, before all is over, and magic, not swords, shall decide the issue between us. I cannot know what form this fight may take, nor what power he may bring to it. Whatever, I must deny that power and win that fight, and I shall need not only the Treasures to my hand but the Kinship at my back. I may not command you in this matter: I am not Ard-rían here but Dragon only, under the authority of the Pendragon even as you yourselves. I may only ask.'

There was but one answer that could ever have been made to that, and they made it joyfully. Aeron's face lighted as she felt it, and when she turned to Gwydion she looked to his sight as a girl of seventeen again, all her years of learning and lore and power and responsibility somehow lifted, all the weight of queenship set aside.

He raised a hand, and, as had been arranged beforetimes, the four Treasures were brought out and set on a low altar at the edge of the lip of rock. First Helwen, carrying the Spear Birgha; then Grelun, with the Sword Fragarach; Melangell, who bore the Cup Pair Dadeni; and last Shane, in his hands the Stone of Fál. Though no visible signal was given, the four bearers stepped back as one, and Gwydion came forward alone.

'Even in this company we dare not remove the coverings from these holy things, save the Cup alone,' he said. 'To look upon the others in untimely hour is death, and we do not need to see them for them to be Seen.' As if in confirmation of his words, the same faint bloom of light that had come to the Treasures in Aeron's cabin aboard *Retaliator* began to gather around them now, like the Solas Sidhe or the tinna-galach, a ghostly flame that seemed to come out of the air itself.

Gwydion began the rite, but now he did not speak in words; those who were Kin to the Dragon were skilled in other means of communication, surer and clearer and altogether more tangible. As the rite progressed, it seemed that every soul upon that plain took fire from the Treasures' presence; but by the time it was done it seemed that the Treasures had drawn a fire of their own from the Kinship, a subtle reinforcement of their own matchless reality.

*They are realer than all of us*, thought Aeron, awed, as Gwydion concluded the ceremony and gave his parting blessing as Pendragon to the Kinship. *And tonight they have come alive again . . . They are alive again, the Spoils of Annwn themselves; and so are we – Keltia – for we and they are one. Let us never diminish ourselves again.*

\* \* \*

357

In the last hours on Caledon, most lay sleeping, gathering what rest they could before the dawn. In the morning Aeron would go to the *Firedrake*, there to announce her return to Keltia – and to Jaun Akhera. The strains of the last few days had been appalling: They had worked tirelessly, in the utmost secrecy that could be managed, and now the regrouped military might of Keltia was a grafaun poised to fall. For tonight, though, they slept, and their dreams were full.

Yet some still waked: In the great square room atop the keep, Kieran held his fretful son in his arms, soothing the outraged little squeaks with a murmuring bass rumble, and the baby soon quieted and fell asleep again.

In a spacious guest chamber, Desmond and O'Reilly stood watching the strange luminescence that burned far out upon the sea. Almost it seemed that creatures were dancing out there, by the light of those watery flames, dark slender shapes that arced and rose and leapt, wild with joy above the waves, and a high sweet singing came faintly to their ears.

And in the cool darkness beneath the peony-trees, Aeron spread her cloak upon the deep grasses and pulled Gwydion down with her, her arms closing around chest and back and shoulders as he lifted her beneath him, and his mouth came down on hers in the spring night.

# Chapter Twenty-Six

Jaun Akhera had been anything but idle in the weeks he had been Emperor. From the moment he had deciphered the message that his mother had contrived to send him, he had been as a man transformed, alive with a fierce fevered energy that crackled around him, like the blue sparks that leap from the fur of a cat in thundery weather. Though Sanchoniathon and Hanno, among many others, had counselled him to prudence – the forces Jaun Akhera was counting on were scarcely halfway on their sail from Alphor – he had redoubled his attacks on the Keltic raiders who had been making Imperial life at Caerdroia a hungry hell, had redeployed his remaining starfleet strength, which had been until now carefully, even grudgingly, husbanded, and – what was alarming his advisors most of all – had begun to strike back at the Keltic fleets beyond the boundaries of the Throneworld system.

Rohan, initially contemptuous, had quickly recognized in the altered tactics something more substantive than the all-out throws of a desperate general, and himself took the counsel of wariness that had been urged in vain upon Jaun Akhera. He had called in the main Keltic fleet to patrol those areas where the Imperials seemed to be concentrating their new raids; so that for the first time since the war had begun, the breach in the Curtain Wall was not so rigidly guarded as it had been. A ship from outside, perhaps, could even slip through unnoticed, if its pilot had great skill and its captain had need of passing the Wall, and if both alike were still more greatly daring . . .

Then suddenly Rohan was gone, and the *Firedrake* seemed to have vanished from the space around Tara.

'How can we lose track of a ship the size of a planetoid?'

Jaun Akhera's voice was full of all the irritation he felt. He did not really expect any answer, and he would have angrily dismissed any answer that his aides might have offered. But they knew better than to offer, and watched instead in prudent silence.

Leaning over the gallery rail in the Fianna War Room, Jaun Akhera stared at the huge two-storey hologram star display as if he could somehow reach into it and pluck out the *Firedrake* like a ripe plum. *Gods' curse upon you, Rohan,* he thought passionately, *you are very near as much trouble as your sister* . . . 'Tell the scout sloops to double their sweep range. We need more information and we need it now.'

'Majesty – ' began Hanno.

'Do it!' barked Jaun Akhera. 'I prefer my enemies where I can see their eyes; but if that is not possible then at least I want to know for sure if they are behind my back. Rohan is up to something, I can feel it.'

Sanchoniathon, coming at that moment into the War Room, looked around for his brother; then, seeing the lifted head and glance of greeting, joined him at the rail.

'You have word of *Firedrake*?'

He shook his head. 'No, Majesty; though there is certainly something going on we have yet to get to the bottom of. And we will,' he added hastily, forestalling Jaun Akhera's angry question, then lowered his voice for his brother's ear alone. 'For the moment, Akhi, there is other news – from Mardale.'

Jaun Akhera frowned. Mardale was the spaceport for Caerdroia, some five miles beyond the city gates in a small valley of the Loom. There seemed no reason why news should come from there – much less news important enough for Sancho to bring in person – since the port had been all but shut down since the fall of Caerdroia. All the same –

'What news?'

'I think it better told to you in private.' Sanchoniathon indicated the passageway leading back to the palace.

'Very well, Prince of Alphor.' Jaun Akhera swept a reinforcing glare over his generals. 'Gentlemen, I will leave you awhile. See that the new patrol patterns are devised by the time I return, and get out those scout sloops. I want to know where Rohan is, and I want to know quickly: I grow extremely weary of Aoibhells pouring like water through my fingers.'

'And now,' he said to Sanchoniathon, as they entered the passageway and the laserproof doors closed behind them, 'we are alone, so you may safely impart to me the nature of this news from Mardale.'

'Visitors,' said his brother tersely. 'Or perhaps I would do better to call them petitioners – or even beggars.'

'You would do best of all if you were to tell me who they are.'

'Well, there is Kynon ap Accolon; he arrived first, full of tales of a miraculous escape made by Gwydion and the Terran O'Reilly from – '

Jaun Akhera stopped dead in the corridor. 'Gwydion! Do you mean Kynon knew where he was and did not tell us?'

'Not quite; Kynon himself did not know until very recently; well, so at least he claims, and I believe him.'

'Do you! But you said "escape"; that generally implies *from* somewhere.'

Sanchoniathon took his brother's arm and gently urged him forward. 'You will not love this, Akhi,' he began. 'But you were right, you know, about where Gwydion would go, once he had escaped from Caerdroia.'

'*Powell*?' His eyes blazed like sunstones. 'Gwydion

went to Powell for sanctuary, and Powell kept that information from me?'

Sanchoniathon's silence confirmed it, and with an effort almost physical Jaun Akhera closed control over his rage.

'By the gods, but Dyved had better have an excellent reason for this,' he said at length in his usual voice. 'I suppose they are the new arrivals – Powell and Pryderi? Yes, they and Kynon, each hurrying to reach me first, to fill my ear with tales of the other . . . Well, I do not wish to see any of them, Sancho, not for at least three days and perhaps longer; attend to it. As for Gwydion, though it grates me that he is free and that I might have had him here again, it is of less import than it might have been, and maybe it matters not so much after all; not now that I am Emperor. Not now that Mother is bringing the fleet.'

'There is word of that too,' said Sanchoniathon eagerly, glad of being able to offer some good news against the tidings of Gwydion and his former captors. 'For some reason, the Curtain Wall seems not so tightly sealed as it has been of late; a cutter sent in advance of the main fleet has also landed at Mardale. Its captain is an officer of our mother's household, with news: The armada will be at the Curtain Wall in three days' local time, and here at Tara six days after that, if all goes well.'

The golden eyes took fire again, this time with exultation. 'Ah, now we shall see some real doings! We shall see, Aeron, who really holds Keltia for you: Rohan or I.'

As *Retaliator* rose up from below the orbit of Ruchdi, Caledon's moon, a gold glow seemed to come from the far side of the satellite, as if the sun were rising beyond that cold horizon. Then, with a suddenness that was startling even to those who were expecting it, a colossal spaceborne dragon seemed to be leaping at the black ship, claws outstretched to seize them. Grex actually flinched, and even Elathan shifted a little in his blastchair, as the *Firedrake* seemed to hang before them poised against the stars.

'I've never seen anything like it,' said Grex, recovering his composure, to O'Reilly who sat beside him.

'There isn't anything like it,' she replied happily. It had all come spinning back to her: her own first sight of that glorious golden ship, from the command cabin of the little *Sword*; how they had all felt, watching her grow ever huger across the star-miles, eating up the vast distances like some inexorable force of nature. Even the unavoidable thought of Theo that came with the memory, though no less sorrowful, somehow seemed less painful, linking her past with her present happiness. Glancing across the cabin, she met Desmond's understanding smile.

But already Aeron had brought *Retaliator* in to one of the flagship's many landing-bays, and was setting her down with a feather touch. When she emerged from the command cabin, they were already clustered at the main hatch, and she laughed to see the hopeful expectancy on their faces.

'All you look like children on Midwinter Eve, anxious for gifts in the morning . . . Come then, sillies; did you think I meant to lock you in the ship?'

Gwydion turned around as Aeron and the others came onto the upper level of the main bridge. He had himself gone up to the *Firedrake* from Inver some hours before Aeron's own departure, to ensure that all was in order on the flagship and that Aeron, when she came aboard, would have no trouble or fret about anything. But there had been new things in the meantime . . .

He saluted her formally as she came up to him, seeing the spark of amusement in her eyes as she returned the salute, for their parting four hours since had been anything but formal. But now was neither time nor place for a more affectionate greeting.

'Well, King of Keltia,' she said. 'You see that we are here.'

'Well, Ard-rían . . . Shall you speak now to the folk?'

Aeron nodded. 'If all is ready?'

'It is; we have blanketed all signals, and the Crann Tarith will be raised on all worlds. Only on Tara will that not be possible, but I doubt not Jaun Akhera will hear of your return without it.'

'And what a surprise for him.' She looked past him, at the activity of the bridge-well below. 'What is it you have not told me?'

'The Imperial fleets approach the Curtain Wall. They will be past the Barna-baoghaill, and well within the Bawn, before we can come to Tara ourselves.'

'What then could be the ill news,' said Aeron smiling, 'for surely that is good news in *my* ear.'

'Well then, it is all good. The Fomori fleets will be at the Wall before the Coranians. We are lowering a section – your cousin Rhain is overseeing the work – so that they may cut across the Bawn in hyperspace to join our own fleets and be waiting for Helior when she arrives. On Tara, as you did order, there are already many troops assembling; in secret, for we dare not challenge the Marbh-draoi openly just yet.'

Aeron's face lighted, and she exchanged a quick look with Elathan. 'Artzan Janco hear me, but Keltia and Fomor together shall give Alphor a welcome he will not soon forget. But first I must speak to my Kelts.'

On the Throneworld, no Crann Tarith had lifted its eerie banshee wail; yet all the same the people seemed somehow to know, and not a farviewer screen on all that planet lacked for watchers.

In Caerdroia, Jaun Akhera stood staring at the big screen in the War Room, rigid with shock at what he saw.

'*AERON* . . . By Seti, is it possible – '

'A trick?' suggested Hanno, though he knew as well as the rest of them that it was not.

'That is no trickery,' breathed Jaun Akhera, slowly shaking his head, never taking his eyes from the image before him: Aeron, seated at a table in what looked to be a starship common-room, Gwydion at her right and Elathan of Fomor on her left. Morwen sat next to Elathan, while beside Gwydion was a grey-bearded man of distinguished mien whom Jaun Akhera did not know. He was alarmed to see Elathan, annoyed to see Gwydion; but it was Aeron herself who commanded his full attention. She was speaking now, staring straight at him. She looked little the worse for her trials of the past half-year, whatever those might have been, but she did look different, and it bothered Jaun Akhera even more than the fact of her return that he could not decide what that difference was. Something about the eyes, perhaps, or was it the set of her mouth . . . With an effort he focused his attention on her words.

' – returned to Keltia by the help of His Majesty Elathan King of Fomor, and in company with His Excellency Haco Grex, Terran Ambassador to Keltia – and in alliance with both of their nations.'

A torrent of astonished angry comment broke out, drowning Aeron's next words, and Jaun Akhera hushed it with one raised warning hand.

' – since last I was with you. Though I can make no promise that the next days will not be more evil still, I am in the fairest hopes that they will not. No more time now for talk, though I do promise that if all goes as we wish it, then I shall tell you all my tale. But for me, and for the King of Keltia' – here her hand closed over Gwydion's – 'and for the King of Fomor' – her other hand covered Elathan's – 'for Terra and for Aojun of the Yamazai and for Keltia's Protectorates, we go now to Tara. Jaun Akhera, bide this tryst.'

The screen blurred to static, and all around Jaun Akhera a storm broke of which he was the unmoving eye. Sanchoniathon peered anxiously through the uproar at his brother's unnatural calm and untroubled face: Akhi seemed deep in thought, certainly, but neither stunned nor enraged by Aeron's dramatic announcement of her return. But why did he stand there so still? He *had* heard, surely?

'Shall we call in the fleets, Majesty?' said Hanno, and Jaun Akhera knew by the emphasis in Hanno's voice – a sort of exaggerated courtesy that was no courtesy at all – that his captain-general had asked the question at least once before.

'No, Captain-General, I think not. Let her come to Tara; she will in any event. But I want the fleets sent to the Curtain Wall with all speed. Elathan of Fomor is not with her merely for show, nor is he here in Keltia on some holiday jaunt. If he has come in alliance, as she has told us, then he does not come alone, and his fleets will not be far behind him. As for this Terran ambassador, who knows what strength he may bring with him, or have following; not to speak of the levies from the Keltic protectorate systems or those god-cursed Yamazai . . . I want our own forces to hold off the Fomori, at the very least, until my mother arrives with our reinforcements, and that will take some days.'

'And us?' asked Garallaz. 'What shall we do here on Tara?'

A slow smile touched Jaun Akhera's mouth. 'Why, we shall make ready to welcome the Queen of Kelts back to her Throneworld, my lords. What else should we do in such a case – and surely she will be expecting nothing less.'

* * *

366

There had never been any doubt from the first as to where Aeron intended to make her stand. If she had been at any time dismissive of Gwyn's word to Gwydion, she was not so now, and, aboard *Firedrake*, she headed straight for the vale of Nandruidion as obediently as if she had been ordered there.

Of all the narrow glens that came down out of the tangled massif of the Loom east of Caerdroia, Nandruidion, Valley of the Druids, was surely the bleakest. Threading off the northern slopes of Stratton Vow, where the saddle dipped and climbed again to the heights of Skirrid, Nandruidion ran down towards the Great Glen, bare at first, sombrely forested in its lower reaches. No window of croft or castle looked out upon the Valley of the Druids; the nearest habitation was the castle of Tomnahara, and that at the glen's very mouth.

But once a tall tower had stood a league or so up the glen, and there Edeyrn had dwelt when he had a mind to commune in silence with his own dark soul. The tower had been pulled down long ago, by Morgan Magistra herself, its very stones blasted to dust and scattered by the winds, and now only a low green mound showed where the tower had been.

Some thought it an evil omen, that Aeron should make this her ground of choice for her final confrontation with Jaun Akhera; others thought it eminently appropriate, even when they did not know – as in fact few yet did – the burden of Gwyn's prophecy. But when the doubters voiced their misgivings to Aeron, they found her more than usually obstinate.

'Gwyn said that he and Gwydion should meet again and that they should meet at Nandruidion; and that is that,' she said to Morwen, latest of those who had come to make known their fears to the Ard-rían. 'I am grown a fervent believer in any word of the Sidhe, since Gwyn's words did lead me to *Prydwen*, and to Arthur, and to the Treasures.'

But she well understood their uncertainties, and the inborn fears. She herself could scarcely credit Gwydion's own account of how Allyn son of Midna had come in Manaan's ship at Gwyn's behest, to aid Gwydion and his companions after the escape from Turusachan. In the past months, though, she had learned not to scorn help wherever it might be offered, and if the Sidhe deigned to offer – well, she had accepted aid before now from stranger quarters than that.

'Still and all, Aeron,' said Morwen severely, 'it is hardly the same. The dûhín and the Firefolk were one thing, the Terrans and Fomori and Yamazai are even as our own selves; but the Shining Ones are not – '

'Are not what?' challenged her friend. 'Are not human? What of that? No more were the Salamandri or the dûhín, and we did not scruple to take their help where it was given. Are not Kelts? Surely the Shining Ones are more Kelts than are the Fomori and those others, all of whose assistance we have not been too proud to accept.'

'Well, not mortal then! Aeron, they could be *gods*, and even if they are not, they – well, they are not like us, and the thought of it fears me.'

Aeron sighed and ran her fingers through her hair. If her own sister-in-law and Taoiseach had such difficulty with the idea of help from the Sidhe, what then would the rest of her people think, the most of whom held superstitions stronger by far, and ideas considerably less enlightened, about meddling with the folk of the dúns. But there really was no choice.

'Nay, they are not like us, that is true enough. But, Wenna, if they are gods, then they have power to grant prayerful petition, and that is well. And if they are not gods, why then, no more are we, and there is no problem.'

Morwen remained unimpressed. 'You have a clever

tongue, Aeron Aoibhell, like all your family, but fence
no words with me. And do not lie to me, either, not
about this. It is too important. Truly, now: Are you easy
about it?'

'Easy about it! Chriesta tighearna . . . Well, if by that
you mean do I have confidence in Gwyn and his word
that his folk will fight for Keltia, then aye, I am easy
about it indeed. If you mean rather do I take comfort
from the thought of possibly divine direct assistance, then
nay, I most certainly am not. But aye or nay, I welcome
Gwyn's aid when and where and how it shall come. And
if you have any respect left for my decisions, you will do
the same.'

Morwen stared at her, hurt showing plain in the blue
eyes. 'Aeron, after all that has befallen us since we fled
Tara, can you possibly *dream* I do not respect your
choices? You found Arthur, rescued the Treasures,
restored Elathan, allied with the Terrans . . . If you say
we go now to Nandruidion, and that the Sidhe will be for
us, then I am with you. How could I not be? Even did I
disapprove, could you think for one smallest minute that
I would let you go into this last alone?'

'Nay, Wenna, I never thought that,' said Aeron with a
tired smile. 'And I never will . . . But go now to Fergus.
He must leave us in the morning to rejoin his squadron,
and we must go down to Tara in *Retaliator* not very long
after.'

When Morwen had gone, Aeron sat down on the edge
of the blastcouch, looking around her quarters as if she
had never seen them before. *How long it seems since I
have been on* Firedrake – *last time, Elharn was with me
. . . and Theo . . .* But she had made her peace with that;
those losses had been healed for her forever, and other
losses too, when she had knelt by Arthur's side and
buried her face in his cloak.

She stood up again and went to look out the main port.

In the centre of the window, still a star and not yet a sun, burned Grían, the familiar yellow primary of the Throneworld system; two orbits out from her warmth and brilliance lay Tara, invisible from this distance. But before tomorrow was done, that sun would warm Aeron's face, and her feet would stand again on Tara's earth. And she and Jaun Akhera would meet once more in war, this time to be the last for one of them.

*If I, then I am ready for it*, she thought, and knew that it was true. And if he – well, that was a matter for him to settle in his own soul. But she knew that he waited for their meeting as eagerly as did she, and was every bit as ready. He too was a sorcerer; he could read the omens of the moment as well as could she, could discern as clearly the shadow of the Alterator come to change their worlds forever. The voice of Sargus echoed in her memory: 'Nothing was made to last forever; not a people, not a planet, not a galaxy.' True enough; and it was given to few indeed to see so clearly the moment of their change coming upon them. Sargus had been so blessed, and he had tried his best to make her see it too.

*And I do see it, now . . .* saw it rolling towards her as huge and inexorable and inescapable as that wave that rolled over Atland. And if that was indeed to be her fate, and Keltia's with her, well enough. She would fight until the wave pulled her under, and then let it carry her in peace to another shore. But if the wave came not for her but for Jaun Akhera, that too was well; though she would have to keep Keltia itself afloat in the backwash of that sea when it was raised at last, she had a new and certain knowledge that she could do so.

*I am a better swimmer than I was when last I saw Tara . . . Strange it is, though, that I should have learned to master such tides on a world that has no seas.*

* * *

Now in Tara, the word was war. However discomfited he may have been by Aeron's sudden reappearance, Jaun Akhera had rallied at once to the moment, seeming, to the eyes of his friends, almost to welcome it. Which observation was not so very far off the mark: As Emperor, Jaun Akhera had much to prove; as Aeron's adversary, still more.

But in the press of these more immediately crucial matters, he had held by his decision not to meet with Powell and Pryderi, though almost hourly they sent messages to him, alternately pleading and demanding, and ever more frantic, requesting an audience. The Dyvetian lords had been cooling their heels at Turusachan for almost a week before they were at last given access to the presence of the Cabiri Emperor, on the evening after Aeron's unexpected broadcast.

Jaun Akhera watched them with a certain detachment as they crossed the room to come to a halt before his desk. Apparently they had not as yet decided on the tack they thought best to try, for their manner was both servile and blustering. He allowed them to wait a long moment before even acknowledging their presence, and then peremptorily gestured them to sit.

'It was not well done, Prince of Dyved, to conceal from me Gwydion's presence at Caer Carrig Cennan,' he said at last, though his tone of voice was unaccountably mild, quite at variance with his demonstrated attitude. *Let them wonder why I am not angry* . . . 'But come, I forgive your lapse,' he said with an engaging smile. 'I regret that I could not receive you sooner, but you are of course aware that we are much taken up with preparations . . . I have asked you here to discuss what numbers you may bring to my meeting with Aeron. She will be landing on Tara any time now – there has already been heavy fighting as *Firedrake* approaches the planet – and I must meet her with what forces I have to hand and what other ones may reach me quickly.'

Powell, who had taken a deep breath to weather the Imperial wrath, let it out slowly and carefully. *So that is why he does not punish us for losing Gwydion – he kept us dangling around the palace to show his displeasure, but he has need of us now* . . .

'You know, of course, Majesty, that Dyved is at your service. It is in my interest now too to keep Aeron from regaining her kingdom. As to troops, Dyved is near enough to Tara that what forces I can call upon will be here perhaps even sooner than Aeron; certainly sooner than her Fomorian reinforcements.'

Jaun Akhera made a notation on the computer pad under his hand, then looked up again at Powell. 'They must be near indeed if they will arrive here before Aeron.'

Powell allowed himself a tiny smile. 'They are already within the Throneworld system. They will be landing on Tara in less than a day.' *And that's one for me, Coranian* . . .

Jaun Akhera's smile was even thinner than Powell's. 'You anticipate me. But all this can be conveyed later to Hanno and my other generals; and from them to our loyal servant Kynon ap Accolon, who is even now at Nandruidion with my assembling armies. Come with me now to Mardale; there is yet another new arrival, and I would have you meet.'

Escaping from Tory, his brother Elathan's forces close behind him, Talorcan had at first thought to find the Princess Helior and the Imperial armada that he knew she would by then be leading to Keltia. But his fellow escapees – Dargato, Salenn and some others – had succeeded in convincing him that it was madness to waste time in a search that had of necessity to cover nearly a quarter of a galactic sector; and unnecessary in any case,

as both Talorcan and Helior had a common destination –
the planet Tara. In the end, it had taken very little to
sway him, and he had ordered the ship to the Keltic
throneworld.

Though he had expected stiff resistance from the Keltic
fleets, for some reason Talorcan had found it a compara-
tively simple matter to slip through the gap that the
traitor Arianeira had made in the Curtain Wall; and once
within the Bawn, he had pressed the ship as fast as he
dared, for fear of pursuit or interception.

Now he looked out the viewport as the ship touched
down at Mardale. Yes, that was certainly Jaun Akhera
himself waiting to meet him, and his brother Sanchoniathon, who had been named Prince of Alphor and Imperial
heir-presumptive since Jaun Akhera's sudden elevation
to Emperor. *And I'd give a good few astari to know
exactly how* that *had come about*, thought Talorcan. *Then
again, maternal devotion can be a mighty power* . . . But
that only set his mind on his own mother, Thona, and
what she had done on Fomor, and that was a thing he
wished not to have to think of, at least not here and not
now. The Princess Helior, though, was another matter
altogether.

He remarked as much to Jaun Akhera, as they went
together back to the City, in company with several others:
Powell, Pryderi, Garallaz.

'Have you ever met my mother, Lord Talorcan?' asked
Jaun Akhera with an unreadable smile.

'I have not yet had that pleasure, Majesty.'

'Ah. Well, you will, no doubt. But as to family matters,
did you know that your brother the King of Fomor is
here?'

Talorcan's sudden sharp intake of breath told Jaun
Akhera that he had not. 'You are certain? He came with
Aeron, then?'

Jaun Akhera nodded. 'But do not entertain any rash

373

hopeful notion about a quick backtrack to Fomor.
Elathan has by all reports left it well and truly subdued to
his will, with his new queen as regent and his pet warlords
Borvos and Treic to give iron to her fist. I have had
certain information that he has seen fit to send a large
portion of the Fomori starfleet here to Keltia in Aeron's
need, and he comes to Tara with her on the *Firedrake*.'

'When will he – they – be here?'

'Perhaps even as we speak. The *Firedrake* holds in
orbit out beyond the Criosanna, and I do not think Aeron
will long remain aboard her.'

Twenty leagues to the east of Caerdroia, Aeron emerged
from *Retaliator* into the middle of a campment of war.
*Tara, again* . . . Caledon had been Keltia, of course, but
this world to her was truly home. She took a deep breath
and closed her eyes, letting the planet itself welcome her
back, then reluctantly returned her senses to the matter
at hand. *Rohan and Desmond did their mustering work
well*, she thought with satisfaction, looking around at the
enormous camp. *And Ríoghnach coordinated all perfectly*
. . . Already a vast army was assembled: Though not so
vast as the one that had met Jaun Akhera beside the Cliffs
of Fhola, still it should be sufficient for her purposes.

Shane, standing beside her, understood her emotion
and her thought. 'More forces are arriving each hour,
Aeron,' he offered. 'We are in better case than we had
feared.'

'And they are landing unhindered, those that come
from off-planet?'

'For the most part, though that is beginning to change
now that Helior's ships have penetrated the Bawn. But
our own fleets are keeping theirs too busy for them to
interfere overmuch with our landings.' They began to
walk down towards the centre of the camp, where above
an otherwise undistinguished tent the Royal Standard

flamed on the wind beside the Gwynedd stag. 'Two odd things, though. An unidentified cutter – Fomorian, by her markings – managed to land at Mardale some hours ago, and I had word just now from *Firedrake* that another small ship seems to have broken off from the Imperial fleet, and is headed here at speed. Shall I order it destroyed?'

Aeron considered a moment. 'Nay,' she said then. 'A minnow in a pool of fighting salmon – let it come. I have a thought as to who might be in that minnow, and in its predecessor with the Fomorian markings; and if I am right then we shall very soon have all our sword-guests within our reach. All the same, though,' she said reflectively, 'we shall still be outnumbered by the Marbh-draoi's forces.'

'Outnumbered, aye, but never overmatched.'

Aeron threw her cousin a grateful smile. 'That is not for us to say, Shane.'

'Nay, but for us to prove. Come, Ard-rían, you are waited for below.'

# Chapter Twenty-Seven

Had Aeron known for fact, though, who it was as passenger aboard the Coranian cutter, she might not have dismissed it so easily as a minnow, but instead have ordered *Firedrake*, that killer pike, to snap it up.

Even Jaun Akhera had no warning of the ship's arrival: not until his mother stood in the door of his chamber, Tinao and Indarrak behind her.

He was out of his chair in an instant, dashing across the room to sweep both women into his arms. 'But how did you come here?' he asked presently. 'I had not a word of your landing; Sancho and I and everyone else thought you still with the fleet.'

'And so I was,' said Helior, with an appraising, and approving, glance over the ornate room. 'But I decided that I had not come all those tedious star-miles to pace on the bridge of a second-class destroyer, and I wanted to see my sons, and I wished it kept secret to surprise them – particularly that son of mine who is Cabiri Emperor. As simple as that.'

Jaun Akhera smiled at her. 'And the Emperor's mother's secrets are surely kept . . . I cannot thank you properly, Mother, for your decision to send the fleets – and for bringing such travelling companions. Indarrak, it is good to see you again, especially so far from home; and as for you – ' He pulled Tinao close against him. 'It has been hell here, and sure to grow even more hellish now that Aeron has returned. But Auset knows how glad I am that you are come.'

'You will be gladder still when you hear what was done

for you,' said Helior. 'By Tinao and Indarrak both; you would not be Emperor without them.'

'I would not be your son, either, if I had not already a fairly good idea of what *you* have done, my mother . . . But such can wait until later. Let us take what time we have just to be happy together a while. In the morning, as you may know, we go out to meet Aeron. She has had too much time already to assemble her armies out at Nandruidion. We allowed her to do so unhindered only while waiting for you to arrive, though of course we have been moving our own legions to take up position against her. But now all is ready for our final victory.' He put an arm around each woman, nodded for Indarrak to follow. 'It is joy unlooked-for that you have come to share it. Let us go and find Sancho.'

In the Keltic camp at Nandruidion, Aeron stood in the doorway of her tent. Before her stretched the familiar sight of a battle-campment: all the tents and clochans, the horse-lines and chariot-ranks and rows of long-range lasers, the hundreds of thousands of warriors who had contrived against all odds to join her here, for perhaps the last, and surely the most decisive, battle Tara would ever see.

*And tomorrow is May Eve*, she thought, glancing up to judge the height of the sun. *Strange it is that all our most fated battles seem to fall out at Beltain – Brendan's first fight for Tara; and, on Earth, the fight of the Danaans against the Fomori for possession of Ireland, and later the Danaans' own fight to hold that land against the sons of Míl . . .* She let fall the tent flap, and turned again to those who had been watching her, knowing her mind, waiting in patience for her mood to alter.

'Well, my very dear,' she said smiling, 'that is a fine parcel of heroes below there.'

'Fine indeed,' said Desmond. 'But not so many as at

Rath na Ríogh, Aeron; and there we could not hold our ground against the Marbh-draoi.'

'That is so,' said Aeron unconcernedly. 'But we had not the Treasures then, and it is in my mind that those shall be all the army we may require. Also do not forget that other help has been promised, and I for one believe that it shall come.'

'All the same, Ard-rían,' said Gwydion, as she settled into a camp-chair beside him, 'we would do best of all to rely in chief upon ourselves. It is in *my* mind that the Treasures are so made as to give most freely, and most fully, to those who have already given all they have of their own; and that they have most power when they are least wielded.'

In the thoughtful quiet Gwydion's words produced, Elathan caught Aeron's eye, from where he sat over against the tent's outer wall, flanked by Rohan and Grex.

'And the Sidhe?' he asked. 'What shall they give?'

'That our need shall determine, and their grace confirm. We shall not know until their moment is at hand. But even so, perhaps – ' Aeron glanced across at Struan Cameron. 'Is there aught you can See for us, Cameron?' she asked with deference in her voice, for Struan was one of those Kelts gifted, or afflicted, with the an-da-shalla.

'The Hounds are on the track already, and the Washer goes even now to the fords,' said Struan after a while, in the dry toneless voice of prophecy. 'And they be not all: Comes the hungry grass, the Púca's bay, and a battle fought not with swords.'

'What more?' asked Gwydion softly.

'The way is dark, and darker grows. I see a white banner waving, and hear the sound of a horn . . .' He blinked, shook his head and spoke then in his normal voice. 'I could See no more, Aeron. I am sorry.'

'Nay, my friend, you saw quite enough. My thanks for it, for well I know that to force the Sight to order is no

378

easy or pleasant task.' Aeron pushed back her hair with sudden energy. 'Well, setting aside just now all such imponderables, we must of force meet the Marbh-draoi on unequal terms. Reckoned warrior for warrior, he has the greater army by many tens of thousands.'

'What if he does?' challenged Slaine instantly; Aeron's cousin had spent the months of her kinswoman's absence aboard the *Firedrake*, at the behest of her brother Desmond, where her very considerable healing talents had been put to good use. But now that it had come once more to fighting, Slaine had put aside her healer's tools for her sword; though the tools too would have their hour after. 'What if he does? We have right to our cause here; that counts more than mere numbers. Not so, Ard-rían?'

Aeron, who was looking at Gwydion, did not respond to her cousin's words, Slaine, however, was not one to let it bide.

'Sore disgrace to us all, Aeron Aoibhell, if you let yourself be daunted by a few Coranian sluglings the more or less. I for one had thought better of your courage.'

At that Aeron turned around, laughing. 'My gods, no question but that you are the most contentious Aoibhell who ever lived, and that is saying a great deal.' She gave her cousin an affectionate shove. 'Go, rattle your troops, Slaine nic Elharn; such a war-bent is wasted on us here.'

Slaine saluted exaggeratedly and left the tent, and Aeron looked after her with a smile still on her lips. 'I love her well,' she said, 'but sometimes I think I love her best of all at a distance.'

Elathan grinned. 'You are much to thank me after all, it seems, for sparing Keltia – and Fomor – the reign of the Ard-rían Slaine.'

A wave of easy laughter ran around the tent. 'Still,' said Aeron, pursuing her earlier thought, 'even though we be outnumbered, and even though most of the Fomori cannot get through to us on Tara to alter that, neither can most of Helior's forces get through to Jaun Akhera. Each of us must make do with what help is to hand. And though I tempt dán by saying so, I think that the weight will surely swing to us.'

'And may the Morrigu keep it there.' Gwydion looked up as one of the Fians on guard in the faha came into the tent. 'What is it, Linnhe?'

'There is a woman would speak with the Ard-rían, Pendragon,' she said. 'She will not give her name, but she shows this as token.' Linnhe held out an antique smallsword: hilted of silver, its scabbard inlaid with blue stones and in its pommel a sapphire the size of a walnut.

Aeron sat up with a glad cry. 'Ithell! Mighty Mother – but let her come in, Linnhe.'

The Fian shook her head. 'She asks that you come out to her, Aeron; she has somewhat to show you, she says, best seen first out of doors.'

'Well then, out of doors it is.' Aeron pulled on her boots. 'This is she I told you all of, this very Ithell, and Brioc her husband, who sheltered Morwen and me at Tintock, on our flight down the Dales to Keverango; healed me of the snow-sickness, and a raxed leg as well. For thanks, I bestowed upon her that sword.'

'And so she may demand of you?' Grex's tone was polite, if a little questioning.

'Demand as she pleases,' said Aeron with a matching coolness, 'for that she saved our lives.'

The sun had only just set, and the clear sky was lambent with afterglow as Aeron emerged into the faha; seeing what awaited her, she stopped so suddenly that Gwydion, close behind her, all but trod upon her heels. Then she was kneeling and almost flattened by the loving assault of her two great brindled wolfhounds, Cabal and Ardattin. Nor did Gwydion, Rohan or any of the other Kelts present escape their frantic greetings; and when at last the beasts were soothed and calmed, reassured that their mistress was not about to vanish yet again, Aeron turned with tears in her eyes to Ithell, who stood by, still holding in her hand the leather thong that had leashed the dogs.

'Once again I owe you thanks,' she said. 'But by what miracle did you manage to come by my hounds? Gwydion has told me that they ran away from Turusachan, some time after I had gone.'

'They came to us,' said Ithell. 'They must have tracked you over the Loom from Caerdroia and down through the Dales; a month or more after you and Morwen left Tintock, they arrived in a snowstorm. They were thin as withy-whips, the poor barebones; most like they had been hunting in your tracks all that time, sparing no time to hunt for themselves. But they seemed content enough to stay with us – we knew well whose dogs they were, and were more than happy to keep them safe against your return. They earned their keep, I will say that.'

Aeron smiled through her tears. 'Name what you will for reward, Mistress Ithell. But where is your man Brioc?'

'He is dead, lass. Your hounds were not the only creatures who followed you from Caerdroia.'

'The Marbh-draoi?' That was Gwydion. 'He came through the Dales in search of Aeron and Morwen?'

'Not himself,' said Ithell then, her face filling with pain at the memory, 'but a troop of his soldiers. They questioned us long and hard; Brioc had not been well, and he died soon after.'

Aeron's face had hardened. 'Say no more. You shall join my household as of this moment, and if it is your wish to return to Tintock, I will myself appoint a rechtair to help manage your affairs; or if you would prefer to dwell now elsewhere, you shall have one of the Crown maenors to hold, and your heirs after you.'

Ithell bowed her head to hide her own tears. 'You are

too generous, lassie,' she murmured, embarrassed. 'As I told you at Tintock, it was joy to serve you.'

'And now mine to reward such service. Go now with Linnhe, she will see you safe sheltered.' Aeron watched her go, her hand ruffling the soft ears of Ardattin, who was leaning happily against her legs. *Surely this is a portent of greatest good fortune*, she thought, *that my hounds have been restored to me: a portent of what else shall be restored, please gods* . . . She turned then to the others.

'I am a little foredone, I think; though more with good cheer than with fearfulness . . . Let us all take an early night, my friends, and rest well for the morning.'

When all had bidden them good night, Morwen and Fergus and Rohan last of all, Gwydion closed the tent flap behind them, spoke softly to the wolfhounds, who found their accustomed places at the inside door and collapsed into them with small contented sounds, and looked down at Aeron's face beside his shoulder. The green eyes were focused on nothing in the tent; yet even so she looked as if she saw something clear and plain and present before her that he could not see, something every bit as real as he himself, some thought or memory or imagining both signal and fair. What it was he could not say, and she chose not to; but he sensed its import, and he saw her smile.

'By the gods, beloved,' she said then, in the voice she used to him alone, turning to him and putting her arms around his neck, 'by all gods but I think we have won this fight already.'

As dawn came cool and brilliant to Strath Mór, Jaun Akhera and his party rode out from the commandeered castle where they had spent the night, taking the river road that led down to Nandruidion. A transport had conveyed them from Caerdroia the previous night, and now they were riding to join the forces that had been assembling for days, only a few miles away.

*A fine and fitting day for our last meeting, Aeron,* thought Jaun Akhera, as he led the little party at a canter through a straggling pinewood. Battle was imminent – indeed, both armies had been drawn up in attack order for some hours, now, waiting only upon their commanders' word – but the niceties of combat were worth observing, and he had had for some time now a wish to speak once more with the Keltic queen before their swords were drawn for the last time.

So he rode now to an unarranged and unannounced parley, not certain if Aeron would even be willing to meet him, but sure that he wished in any event to make the offer of speech. With him were Sanchoniathon, as always, and some of the lords of the household; Hanno and Garallaz and the other generals had gone ahead several days ago to the lines. With him also, guarded by a strong escort of his most trusted men-at-arms, rode Helior and Tinao.

As they cantered around a blind turn where the road ran through a fringe of thicker woodland, the horses shied suddenly and violently as one. Jaun Akhera, thrown onto his mount's neck, hauled himself back into the saddle, and, quicker than the others to control his horse, laughed scornfully to see what had so alarmed the beasts.

At a little ford, where a stream came out of the forest to cross the road over a bed of white stones, an old woman was kneeling and singing to herself. Beside her was a mound of stained linen shirts, the long, loose sort often worn by Kelts in battle, and on the other side, a heap of mail loricas; she was washing first one, then the other, in the water of the stream.

As he urged his unwilling horse nearer, puzzled at the animal's sweating terror, Jaun Akhera saw that the dark stains on the linen, which at first glance he had taken for soil, and the red ones upon the mail, that he had thought rust, were in truth blood, blood both dried and fresh, and as the washer scrubbed, the stains floated away, ominous streaks upon the surface of the water.

The woman – old, bent, her hair full of elf-locks, fox-grey and rough as goosegorse – did not look up once from her rhythmic washing, but continued her eerie croon unbroken, and the hair stood up on their necks as her words came clear at last.

'I am the Water Doleful One, O my sorrow; Bean-Nighe am I, the Washer at the Ford. I lodge in the green hills, the round hills. Come ye in, all you present. Soon shall we be dwellers together, thou and I; aye, dwellers alike, all in the same long land.'

Her voice was water dripping on iron, a sword drawn shrieking down the side of a breastplate. The horses panicked anew to hear it, and bolted screaming past her. But Jaun Akhera, looking back to the ford, saw only the stream flowing clean and untroubled over the white stones, and no one knelt beside it.


'I will not speak with him.'

Gwydion said patiently, 'It is warriors' courtesy, Aeronwy, as you perfectly well know. Even the lowliest galloglass would not deny any parley asked for under the white flag.'

'Now would he not! I am however no galloglass but the Queen of Kelts, and *I* say nay.' About to dismiss the Imperial envoy – not Garallaz this time but a lord called Amzallac, who had accompanied Helior and the rest from Escal-dun and who had been luckless enough to be elected Jaun Akhera's messenger – Aeron changed her mind with almost visible abruptness.

'Very well so,' she said. 'Let your master choose a place where I may see him, and I will join him there, each of us alone.'

'Majesty – '

'Alone, my lord, or there is no further discourse save at the sword's point. Tell him so, go.'

'He will never come, Aeron,' said Rohan, who stood by.

'He will come, right enough,' she said, looking out across the mouth of Nandruidion. 'Oh, but he will come.'

Jaun Akhera sat his horse at the top of a small rise in the land, halfway between his camp and the Keltic lines at the glen mouth. It was still very early in the morning, and he narrowed his eyes against the sunblink. *She has chosen ill ground this time*, he thought. *Little choice of ways to retreat – up into the confines of the glen on the one side, or into the Avon Dia on the other* . . . He shifted his weight in the saddle. Aeron did nothing without good reason, even if she was the only one who understood or even knew what that reason might be; and the suspicion that she had some hidden motive for her choice of battle-ground was growing hourly in his breast.

He sat up straighter, unconsciously shortening his reins, as he saw Aeron approaching at a gallop, on an unfamiliar grey horse with blue trappings. She did not slacken pace as she drew near, pulling up only at the last possible instant in a swirl of flying turf.

'Well, Marbh-draoi,' she said with a smile, 'have you no words of welcome for me? I have been long away.'

'Not long enough,' he said, returning the smile, though he had not meant to. 'Or perhaps too long: I have a grip on Keltia now you will find hard to break.'

'And I have a new way, or two or three, of loosening your fingers . . . What is it you would speak of, Jaun Akhera? I am in no mood to parley, and my soldiery are in no mood to wait battle on your words.'

'Then I shall speak both swift and plain. Your forces

385

are out-numbered and ill-equipped, your ground doubt-ful. Your spacefleets, even with the help of the Fomori, must contend with the armada my mother has brought. Yield Keltia to me now, Aeron, and I give you my royal word – my Imperial word – that you and Gwydion, and what kin and companions you choose, may go safely into exile.'

Aeron shook her head, smiling. 'My sorrow that we must always decline each other's suggestions . . . Well. As to that armada brought by your loving mother, I think you will find, if you communicate with its commanders, that there is by now but little of it left. As to the insufficiency of my army, or the inadequacy of their gear or the shortcomings of their position – I shall let the battle itself be judge of those. And so I will not bid you farewell just yet.' She gave him one last long sober stare, and spurred the grey horse back to the Keltic lines.

Jaun Akhera had barely regained the safety of his own lines before the chilling war-yell of the Kelts rising from across the valley – the barra-glaed that had struck terror into armies on the battlefields of many worlds – and the even more bloodcurdling wail of the war-pipes, in a banshee descant, signalled the beginning of the attack.

'Has she gone mad completely?' he demanded of Hanno, leaping down from his lathered horse. 'She is seriously outnumbered, as I told her just now.'

His captain-general nodded, attention nailed to his own advancing forces. 'Then she must be mad, for that seems not to matter to her. Look for yourself.'

'Then what? She cannot be relying on reinforcements from the Fomori; they are too busy engaging our own fleets – as *she* told *me* just now, and I want that looked into at once.'

'Something else, then,' said Garallaz.

'Yes . . .' Jaun Akhera paused a moment, standing

motionless, frowning a little, as if he strained to hear a faint voice in another room, a voice that spoke softly in a foreign tongue. 'I like this not – there is magic afoot.'

'A magic which you yourself gave Aeron licence to use.' The deep voice was not accusatory, but calm and almost pedantic, as if its owner were doing no more than stating an obvious, if unpalatable, fact.

Jaun Akhera turned at the sound of it. 'Irin Magé,' he said, real respect in his voice, and made a brief bow. 'My mother told me that you had accompanied her.'

The priest nodded. 'It is fitting that I should be here,' he said. 'But more even than that: There was compulsion upon me, that I be here to witness the ending.'

'The ending! You mean rather the triumph of Telchine over Danaan, of Cabiri over Draíochtas.'

Irin Magé's eyes remained distant. 'I mean the ending.'

Across the glen mouth, Aeron came to sudden alertness, feeling the touch of magical attention upon her, and sensing Jaun Akhera's personality in it. *Ah, Marbh-draoi, it matters not what strength you have with you – teacher, friend, kin, lover, whatever – before this fight is done, you and I must meet, and no other strength with us but our own.*

The battle continued for some hours then; the day grew warm with sun, though the wind stayed strong and cold out of the east. Aeron, who had fought among the knights of her guard, now watched through a field-glass, and, as Gwydion and Elathan came up behind her, turned to give each man a searching look.

'What word from the field?'

Gwydion met her gaze. 'No good word. In fact, it goes very ill just now. It seems we were perhaps a little overconfident as to our ability to hold off Jaun Akhera's force with force.'

'What then?'

'Go you both to the other side of the glen and wait there with Niall and Desmond. It is time to make a throw of desperation.'

She caught at his arm, suddenly fearing. 'What will you do? Gwydion – '

He smiled then, but the smile did not reach his eyes. 'Was there not a promise that you should have help unlooked-for in the last battle? Whatever that help might be, I go now to call it to us.'

In a while Aeron, standing with Niall and Elathan on a rise across the dale, heard the cry of a horn. High, bright, clear, ringing, it echoed from the rocks in a haunting shimmer of golden sound, bathing the whole valley in its call; yet it held no note of urgency, only a kind of sweet entreaty – coaxing, rather than command.

'Whom does the horn summon?' asked Niall, his voice hushed.

Aeron shook her head, equally hushed; for the sound of the horn had thrown sudden silence over the entire dale, and even the weary warring armies had paused where they stood.

'I know not, Niallán. Whosoever they may be, though, we stand in very desperate need of them.'

But across the valley, something strange was happening. The dark slopes of Nandruidion, clothed in iron-oak, silver ash, tall redpine, slender rowan, pale goldenbirch, all the other trees of an upland forest, were threshing violently back and forth as if in the grip of a high wind, though below the skirts of the wood the grasses were motionless.

Gwydion, who sat his horse midway down the valley floor, was thunderstruck to see moving towards him like a black wall the forest trees themselves. Then words were written upon his mind in letters of flame, burning in the air before his eyes, and he rose in his irons and began to chant.

> 'Sure is leaf, and heartwood sound.
> If my words be true ones,
> Come, trees, to battle array.
> I summon, stir, and call you up:
> A sword in the hand, a shield in the fight.'

And that was the first of the three ranns spoken by Gwydion Prince of Dôn at the Battle of the Trees . . .

The words of Gwydion's chant hung in the valley like the sound of the horn. And then, where the moving trees had been, stood warriors. Men and women both, some tall and dark and sombre as the oak; others lighter and lither of build, elegant as the bending birch; others again thicker and broader, sturdy as the sinewed pine. But all were of one grimness as they marched; their feet seemed to move through the earth, not upon it, and where they had passed the green turf remained unfurrowed and unbroken.

They quickly drew near to Gwydion, but he said a soft word and they halted; then he raised his arm and chanted again.

> 'Grass be sword to wound their feet,
> Leaf be shield to ward their blows.
> Needle of pine, be as arrows to the mark.
> Trees, in thy array strong chieftains of battle,
> Teach war to those who know it not.
> Pre-eminent thou in the field of blood.'

And that was the second of the three ranns spoken by Gwydion Prince of Dôn at the Battle of the Trees . . .

On the hillside, Aeron had been as awed as any as she watched the living trees become living fighters, and tolling dully through her brain, like some fateful harmonic to

Gwydion's chanting, rang the words of Gwyn: 'As to thee, Prince of Dôn, the very trees shall be thy warriors.'

*And these then are those promised warriors, given life by the horn – that strangest and most unexpected of hai attons . . .*

But now at Gwydion's rann of attack, the tree-warriors were pouring in a dark tide of slaughter over the Imperial lines. Jaun Akhera's troops had not waited for their commanders to call retreat, but at sight of the sorcerous army advancing upon them had broken and run, and Jaun Akhera himself did not blame them.

So did that fight begin which ever after was known as Câd Goddeu, the Battle of the Trees. For not all the Imperial forces fled, some standing their ground against even the terror of the trees; though not for long, and not victoriously, for wherever the trees overtook the enemy, very soon only the trees still moved.

Jaun Akhera watched impassively as a third or more of his warriors fell to the forest army, though his hand shook as it held the field-glass.

'Enough, Gwydion,' he said at last, and his voice too shook. 'In the name of all your gods, enough.'

He was not the only one who sickened of the unequal slaughter: Across the valley, Aeron closed her eyes as if she had heard her enemy's entreaty, and spoke to the air.

'Have done, King of Keltia,' she said softly. 'Make an end. Let there be clean battle in the morning.'

And Gwydion, standing on a rise at the glen mouth in the sunset light of Beltain, turned his head as if he had heard both pleas, and called home his strange forces from the fight.

'When the Shout is heard, the Cry above the Abyss,
Hope renewed, form altered, life changes.
From high twelve to ox-hour

Thou hast played in Lloughor.
Now sleep thou in purple.
There is hope for trees.'

And that was the third of the three ranns spoken by
Gwydion Prince of Dôn at the Battle of the Trees . . .

The dark tide now receded, the tree-warriors surging
in silence back up the valley, looking with every stride
less like warriors and more like trees; and by the time
they came again to their homeslopes they were all trees,
rooted once more in the forest mould as if they had never
left it.

In their wake they left a terrible stillness. Gwydion,
who had by this time returned to Aeron where she stood
with Elathan, threw his leg over his horse's neck and slid
to the ground, bone-weary. He was about to speak to her
when a sound came that turned their blood to sand.

A high despairing shout, a howl of grief and anguish
and helpless hopeless protest, rose up from the Coranian
side of the devastation wrought by the trees, hanging in
the valley like a ghastly echo of the horn-cry that had
earlier rung upon the air. Gwydion, his arm around
Aeron's shoulders, felt her catch her breath at the horror
of it, and knew as she did, the shout to be no cry uttered
by voice or throat, but a lamentation wrenched from
Jaun Akhera's very soul, imprinted upon the astral itself.

And forever after, on every May Eve, the echo of that
fearful cry was heard upon Tara, in every glen and forest,
on every loch and mountain, through every city and
village, over every hearth on all the Throneworld from
castle to farmstead; so was that battle never forgotten.

When the last keening echo had died away, Aeron
moved away from Gwydion's encircling arm, and stood
looking out across the glen, its horrors mercifully masked
by the growing darkness. Beyond the fateful trees, she
could see the pinpoints of light that were the Imperial

quartz-hearths. *Many fewer now than before*, she thought. *Though they be all my enemies, still had I not wished them such an end.*

She turned, intending to offer some word to Elathan. But the Fomorian king was looking at Gwydion; his face bore vivid traces of the shock and horror they all felt, but the chief emotion thereon just then was grim approval – and, not so strangely perhaps, a kind of pity.

Gwydion returned the look; then his eyes went to Aeron, and his mouth moved in what might have been either a stillborn smile or a flinch of sorrow.

'I did not know,' he said then. 'Upon my soul I did not. But had I known, I would have done no differently; that horn would still have sounded.'

'We do what we must,' she said, hearing the pain in his voice. 'But for now – ' Her mouth quivered as Gwydion's had done. 'It is Beltain; had you forgotten? Festival of summer and healing growth. Let the sacred fires be lighted.'

# Chapter Twenty-Eight

'I do not presume to instruct you, Aeron, in matters you know far more of than do I,' Elathan was saying carefully. 'But I think perhaps the time has come for you to use the Treasures.'

Aeron did not reply to this advice, instead studying her hand where the Great Seal of Keltia once more circled her finger; then she cast a look down and sidewise to where Gwydion reclined on a pile of furs, her hound Cabal lying across his knees. They were in Aeron's tent, where they had spent most of the evening; it was almost midnight now, end of a long and terrible day, and outside the Beltain fires still blazed upon the hills.

As was her duty by law, Aeron had made a brief public appearance some time earlier, to set alight the royal belfire from which all others in the campment would take their starting flame. But she had strangely scanted the rite, racing by rote through the prayers and almost flinging the ritual needfire onto the thirteen sacred woods. Ignoring worried friends and scandalized subjects alike, she had not even remained, as had been her custom and pleasure in years past, at the celebration that followed; for never in her life had she felt less renewed, and for once it seemed to her that her faith had failed to sustain her. "*Now at summer's coming,*" she thought bitterly, repeating to herself, like a rann against despair, a phrase from the prayers she had just recited. The bitterness rose: *This year at summer's coming, came death, not life; and I it was who did bid it come . . .*

Gwydion, well aware of her heaviness of spirit, and the reason for it, answered the question she had not yet summoned the strength to ask. 'Today's work reduced the Imperial forces by many thousands. But they still outnumber us by three warriors to two, and that is a margin must be narrowed as quickly as may be.'

'And that is why I think the Treasures must be used,' pursued Elathan, after a swift exchange of glances with Gwydion when Aeron still did not respond. All the same, he took pains to keep his tone one of pacification, for he was still, whether rightly or not, wary of her mercurial temper. 'You did not hesitate to use the Eye of Balor to win Tory for me, and that was Fomor. This is your own Keltia, and those warriors out there your own Kelts. What purpose to delay?'

He need not have feared her wrath this time; she looked over at him with a smile, thinking to herself that he had courage indeed to take her on just now, when many who could boast close kinship or long friendship with her would not have dreamed of so daring.

'Nay, no more did I, on Fomor; but, as you say, that was Fomor and this is Keltia, and it may be that I was permitted an action on Fomor that I am forbidden here upon my own ground. Well, perhaps I *should* have by now unlidded the Eye against the Marbh-draoi, used the other Treasures as well. And I may yet: I have delayed this long only out of hope that we might be able to win without needing their aid. They may work greater ill if they are used wrongly than if they are never used at all. It will be a fearful thing – '

'It is what you went for,' said Gwydion, his face stern, a hardness now to his voice.

Aeron glared at him. 'Do not think to try your bard-tricks with *me*, Gwynedd . . . But aye, as you so graciously remind me, it is indeed what I went for, though I had not thought I should so loathe the moment when it came. This delay of mine is but the hearkening-wind – that lull in a gale before the last destroying blast. It must blow, and it shall; but very many will wither before it. Maybe even ourselves.' She flexed her shoulders; to Gwydion's eye, it looked like a shiver. 'And so I say the Eye of Balor shall open with the sun; and you, my heart, must manage it.'

He bowed where he sat. 'And what to you?'

'To me, another task whose time I think has come.'

'But the other Treasures?' asked Elathan.

' – will fill each their proper task in proper time; though it may not be I whose hand shall be set to them.' Aeron slid down in the cushioned campchair, until she sat on her spine and her legs were stretched out in front of her. 'Mislike it however I might, in all good faith I can tarry no longer. One way or another, this matter will be settled before tomorrow's sun shall set.'

A little before dawn, Aeron stood with Elathan and Gwydion on a slope overlooking the Imperial lines. A few others clustered a little distance away: Rohan, Morwen, O'Reilly, commanders and officers of the royal household. The air was spring-cold and very still: the morning of the first of May. The grass was soaked with dew beneath their boots, and above their heads, mist hung in the hollows of the Loom, like steam rising from the flanks of a hard-ridden horse.

Aeron turned her head to look for the sun that was not yet up. In the east, it seemed as if the clouds themselves were drawn up in schiltrons, close-serried, awaiting their turn to move: first the low hill-scraping ones, then those farther behind and higher up the sky, thicker, puffed like bog-cotton, and highest of all the thin icy mare's-tails, so high that already they were catching the gold blaze from the sun that was still below the horizon. Off to Aeron's left, the Avon Dia was blue as sword-metal in the growing light, running high in its banks, strong and swift with snow-melt off the mountains to the east.

Gwydion came up behind her, and after a moment she felt his kiss upon her hair. Heedless of the many watching eyes, she smiled and reached up a hand to caress his cheek, a thing that once she would not have dreamed of doing in public. But that too had changed: After the first desperate violence of their reunion had been abated, they had discovered in themselves a new tenderness with each other, a heightened communion that, for all their double-souled closeness, had not been there before – a function perhaps of having nearly lost each other many times over, or a result of the evil haps that had befallen each of them in the months of their separation. Whatever its cause, and knowing too that all was dán and they could set their backs against that certainty, still there was a sense that never again would they take each other's presence as a given; that from now on they would trust to nothing save what they made between them for themselves.

'This is too grave an hour for such,' she said smiling. 'Keltia itself is today upon the counterpoise.'

'Then all the more reason for it. You are ready?'

'I am not; but I will act all the same.' She gave a teasing tug to the lock of hair she had twined in her fingers, and faced round to him. 'Tide what may betide, King of Keltia,' she said, voice so soft that he heard her more clearly in his heart than with his ear, 'know that I love thee.'

'And I thee, Ard-rían,' he said as softly in the High Gaeloch, and raised her hand to his lips. 'Go now.'

Her eyes, moving past Gwydion's shoulder, met Elathan's in a silent interchange that seemed to sum up all they had not said, nor needed to say; a quick glance for the others, then she was running lightly down a narrow track that led up onto the hill behind them, and was soon lost to their sight in the mist.

Gwydion looked after her a few moments longer, then

swung his glance across the valley, to where the Imperial armies were beginning to stir.

'Well, Fomor,' he said to Elathan. 'Now let the Eye of Fál behold its enemies.'

Far below Aeron as she toiled up the hillside, the battle began, the lines slowly flooding towards each other like rivers rising. She looked up, measuring the distance above her that had still to be covered, and sighed. The hill at the entrance to Nandruidion – Tallon Law, it was called – was far steeper than it looked, its green-turfed sides as sheer as a pudding basin. *And about as easy to climb*, she thought, winded by the effort that had brought her thus far. But this was the only hill that looked away unimpeded to the northeast; and, if all went according to expectation, that was the direction from which their help must come.

Aeron, reaching at that instant for a new and firmer hold, nearly came off the hill altogether as, below her and behind, a blaze of white fire shot out like some enormous arrow, straight and deadly, aimed at the heart of the Imperial camp. To look that full on would be like looking into a score of suns; even from the side, the light leakage was almost blindingly bright. She knew as if she had seen with her own eyes what had happened below: Standing behind it as she herself had shown him, using a hooked spear as the legends all commanded, Gwydion had raised the bronze lid of the Eye of Balor.

From where she clung now on the side of the Law, Aeron could see where the Eye did glance, the grass crisping and smoking in its wake, the ground blackening as she watched; could pray, vainly, that she did not see what was happening when living bodies were caught in that Eye's terrible glare. But she had an errand of her own that she must perform. Turning her face and her thought from the carnage, she called upon her last reserves of breath and strength to gain the top of the

Law; and fifteen minutes later, stood there panting, staring down at the battle.

The last stages of her scramble had taken her around the far side of the summit, and so for some time she had not been able to see what was happening below. From here, five hundred feet above the plain, the fight unrolled beneath her like a bloody tapestry. The armies had engaged in earnest now, and because of that the Eye had been shuttered, lest its baleful brilliance fall upon friend as well as foe. But threads of the tapestry crossed and ran and knotted with no regard for pattern: Kelts here, Imperials there, strands of other kind woven throughout – the few Fomori troops that had managed to win through to Tara, a sprinkling of the Protectorate levies brought by Aeron's cousin Kerensa, some of the Yamazai warrior-women, even. Yet as Aeron watched, a pattern began to come clear, and it was one she did not like.

She looked down at what she had brought with her to the top of the Law: a scrap of white silk tucked beneath her baldric – the Bratach Bán, the White Banneret – the Faery Flag that could be waved but three times to summon otherworldly help.

Twice had that flag been waved, and twice had that help arrived timely, as had been promised long ago, when a queen of the Sidhe had given it as tinnscra to a daughter of hers who had wed a mortal, with the pledge that thrice would it bring the help of the Sidhe to that princess's new kindred. Merlynn Llwyd, Arthur's Druid mentor, had waved it for the first time, to summon the Shining Ones to the defeat of Edeyrn; the second waving had been only seven hundred years ago, when Aeron's own great-grandsire to the eighth, the Ard-rígh Tigernach, had used it in his desperation, to bring to an end at last the bloody civil wars that had killed, one by one, his father Lachlan, his brothers Declan and Raonall, and his sister Angharad, each of them sovereign in turn over Keltia as another fell, and each falling in turn.

Now it had come time for Aeron to use it, for the third and last time of waving. Gwydion had been promised the help of the Sidhe by Gwyn their king, but it was for the Ard-rían of Keltia to ask for it; that she had known since first he had told her of Gwyn's promise. *And it is right and fitting that I should ask* . . . She unfolded the Bratach with careful fingers. No one knew for sure how old it was, but Merlynn had thought it ancient when it came to his hands, and that was fifteen hundred years ago; it had been in the keeping of Clann Graham ever since, and the new Master of Graham, Douglass's brother Aluinn, had proudly delivered it into Aeron's hands at Inver before they left for Tara. She stared down at it with wonder, and a little fear. A square piece of heavy white silk, close-woven and fine, its edges bound with remnants of heavy gold braid, it shone with a multicoloured iridescence that belied its name.

'I know not what words of ritual may unlock your powers,' said Aeron aloud, 'or what ceremony may properly go with this summoning. But bring us what aid there may be, for all our sakes.' She lifted her arm and swept the banner three times slowly through the air, hearing a faint shout go up from below as the Kelts saw her action, and the banner crumbled away to dust in her hand.

But the Imperials had seen too, and with some alarm Aeron noted the flashes off the lenses of the big siege guns – those that the Eye of Balor had not exploded – as they were swung to focus on her. She threw herself down the far side of the Law as the hilltop erupted around her.

Below, the fighting had grown savage, and no one now stood aloof from it. From the humblest foot-soldier to Gwydion and Elathan and Jaun Akhera themselves, every warrior who could still lift a sword raised it against the enemy, even if that warrior could no longer stand but must fight instead upon his knees.

But strange opponents were meeting now in the bloody press: Rohan, who had given over his usual place on the bridge of *Firedrake* to his brother Declan, had chosen to assume the cavalry command formerly held by Denzil Cameron – who had died in combat in Rohan's own service – and had been leading it brilliantly against the Imperial foot.

He was now extricating his horsemen from the assault, to regroup and attack again. Guiding his bay stallion with knees and voice alone, to leave his hands free for his weapons, Rohan suddenly saw from the corner of his eye a hatefully familiar face among the Coranian troops.

'Kynon of Ruabon – ' he breathed. 'Son of Accolon, I knew that I should see you one last time before all was ended.' Drawing his sword, he closed his knees on the stallion's flanks, and the powerful horse charged to his master's will.


A little way away, on the banks of the stream Velenryd, Gwydion stood in a bloody circle that his own sword had carved for him. For the moment, his opponents hung back, unwilling to be the next to fall beneath his blade, for none had yet come away alive after matching strokes with him.

The ranks around them churned, and when the swirl of battle had once more steadied, Gwydion found himself face to face with Pryderi. They had not met since Caer Sidi, and they stared now at each other across the detritus of slaughter.

'Well, Gwynedd,' said Pryderi at last. 'After all our time, it comes in the end to this.'

Gwydion shook his head. 'That end was settled two months since, at Caer Carrig Cennan, when you and your father found it in your hearts – and interests – to break the guest-law and betray one who had come to you in need. The penalty for that crime has never changed since first the Kelts left Terra.'

'The galanas, then? Well, take it; if you can.' With that word Pryderi came at him, sword already swinging in a blue arc.

Even then Gwydion held off until the last possible moment, then brought his own weapon up to parry, and the shock of the blades' contact nearly sent the Dyvetian off his feet.

Pryderi recovered his balance, cursing fluently under his breath. *Cythraul take him, I had forgotten how neat-handed a swordsman he is* . . . He lunged again, and again Gwydion casually parried, with a languid grace that belied the skill and strength behind it.

With a skill of his own born of his despair, Pryderi for some minutes and many blows gave good account of himself, and both of them were bloodied by the time Gwydion drew back a little.

'My sorrow, Pryderi,' he said, and there was true-sorrow in his eyes. 'I had thought this would be easy justice; but justice never is easy. Better for us both to end it swiftly.' His sword-arm rose and fell and backslanted in the air between them, too quick for the eye to follow, and Pryderi fell without a cry. The waters of the Velenryd closed over his face, running red downstream.

But skill of fence was not the only thing in play upon that field . . .

O'Reilly, who had been fighting side by side with Desmond, paused in a lull of the battle, then straightened suddenly, her attention caught by something on the far side of the glen. She pointed with her sword.

'Over there – what is it with those Coranians?'

Desmond looked where the blade was pointing. A small group of Imperial foot-soldiers, perhaps twenty at

most, seemed bizarrely plagued: They had thrown aside
their weapons and now were stumbling through the lines,
searching packs, tents, even the persons of the slain.
Wherever they found food of any kind, they devoured it
as if they were in the grip of excruciating hunger-pangs –
some of them were even stuffing grass and leaves.

'Are they crazed, or what?'

Desmond shook his head. 'Nay, the poor bodachs;
they have set foot upon the faer-gortha, the hungry grass.
It is a magic of the Shining Ones, that they use chiefly as
a defence against mortals. There must be a patch of it
hereabouts, left over maybe from the days of Ederyn.'

*The hungry grass* . . . O'Reilly felt a chill, and hitched
her tunic up around her neck. 'What does it do?'

'It sets upon such a hunger as no natural need could
cause, nor right feeding allay. As you see' – he nodded
towards the ravenous soldiers – 'they are driven by the
famishing to devour anything they can find, even grass if
there be naught else. They will die of the hunger in short
order, if they are not fed to break the spell.'

'Fed on what?'

'Bread and salted buttermilk – they are not like to find
it here, though every countrydweller in Keltia keeps some
in the cookplace against just such sudden need. It is a
hard way to die, by the faer-gortha, and Beltain the worst
day of all for the hungry grass to strike.' His eyes clouded
briefly. 'I must mention it to Aeron; after the battle is
done, Druids or Ban-draoi must find the place and purify
it, so that none of ours takes the hunger. But see, Sari-
fach, it is over.'

O'Reilly looked up reluctantly, to see the last few of
the afflicted Imperials stagger and fall, fingers still cram-
ming grass into choked mouths.

'Gods help them.'

A galloglass standing by overheard her, and said with

surprise, and respect also, for he recognized Desmond,
'But they are galláin, lady, and the enemy as well.'

'Gods help them,' repeated O'Reilly.

The sound, when it began, began low, almost beneath
the threshold of human hearing, and seemed to have
been going on for a long time: a deep harmonious
chanting in distinct parts, musical, rhythmic, strong – a
marching-chant, as though the gods themselves went
forth to war, out upon Achateny, the Field of Fire,
the battleground of the universe where shall be waged
Cymynedd.

Aeron, who had half-fallen, half-run down the steep
hillside only a few yards ahead of the laser strikes, came
now tearing around the base of the Law, and was caught
in mid-flight by Dafydd Drummond.

'Deio, let me pass – '

'Nay, Aeron, look!'

She stood motionless as he had seized her, staring
open-mouthed at the sight before her: The Sluagh Sidhe
were riding to the battlefield, even as Gwyn son of Nudd
had promised, and they were singing as they rode. How
they came there none could afterwards say: Some swore
they had come out of the north; others said not, that they
had ridden from the west, or the east or the south; or had
come out of the hills, or out of the air. One breath they
were not there, the next they were; and none was not
nearly frozen at their coming. Even the Kelts, who had
been warned what to expect, and who had been raised
for generations on tales of the Shining Ones and their
rades – even they would not have held firm in their lines
had they not been held there by Aeron's word and
Aeron's will, and by the love they held in turn for her.

'The Shining Ones,' said Dafydd in a near-whisper,
'you have called them by the Bratach Bán.'

Aeron heard his awe, and felt the same in her own

heart. All the old tales made much of the unearthly glory of the Sidhe in the moment of their twice-yearly transcendence, when they rode from their hollow hills at Samhain and again at Beltain; but no tale she had ever heard had dared to tell of them in their battle rage. Nor had she thought to find them so beautiful, and so terrible: Tall they were, fine-drawn and luminous, their hair of all shades from purest silver-gilt to darkest blue-black, their skin all of the same poreless pallor, white and flawless, and their eyes – But she could not meet their eyes, not yet, not if she were to fulfil the task she knew was only half-completed.

With a resolve she did not feel, she disengaged herself from Drummond's restraining arm and walked forward to greet her newest-come allies.

Others too managed to set aside their own fears and walk out in front of the armies, towards those who led the faerie host: Rohan, still on his big bay stallion, though now there was blood on the beast's front hoofs, and Kynon of Ruabon's head at the saddlebow; Elathan, who had fought alongside Niall O Kerevan, Tanaxio of the Yamazai and Haco Grex for one epic hour against a cohort of Jaun Akhera's personal guards; O'Reilly and Desmond; and Gwydion, who turned from the body of Pryderi and came, drawn sword still in hand, to stand with Aeron before the Sluagh Sidhe.

Mounted upon a gold-maned white stallion, Gwyn ap Nudd bowed very slightly to them from the saddle. From his place a little behind, Allyn son of Midna lifted his hand to Gwydion with a sparkling smile, and Gwydion gave a small start as of sudden gladness, instantly controlled. But Aeron's attention was held by the black-haired woman, sidesaddle upon a chestnut mare, at Gwyn's right hand.

Clad all in red, her raven hair bound by a silver fillet,

the woman heeded Aeron not at all. But looking at Gwydion, she lifted a golden branch from where it had rested in the crook of her left elbow, and shook it thrice. The tiny golden bells in the shape of apples that depended from the branch gave out a pure clear chiming; and meeting Aeron's eyes the woman spoke.

'Queen of Kelts,' said Etain, queen of the Sidhe, 'spancelled is your man.'

Aeron dragged her gaze away from the queen's face, as beside her Gwydion suddenly stiffened, as if he had been all at once turned to stone. She touched his cheek in utter disbelief: He neither moved nor seemed to breathe, and the grey eyes did not even blink at her touch; and Aeron turned on Etain with a face of thunder.

'Spancelled is your man,' repeated the queen, in a voice like the bell-bough or birds calling.

'Unfettered they that live the longest,' snapped Aeron in answer, and Gwydion shook himself all over, as one who has just come in from the rain or the deep cold, looking first at Aeron, then at Etain, in blank bewilderment.

Etain smiled. 'Were it not that you understood my meaning, and answered correctly, you had been less your lord.'

'Had I been less my lord,' said Aeron very softly, and now she too was smiling, 'no matter what help your own lord had given me, I had levelled your palace to the ground and sown the earth of it with salt and fenced it round with cold iron, and you and all your folk to be scattered whistling down the wind for an age and an age of this world.'

'Ah. It seems that Fionnbarr's daughter, then, is not entirely free of a vengeful spirit.'

'Not entirely; but let us not put it to the test.' Aeron looked then at Gwyn, who had watched the by-play between his lady and the Keltic queen with an amused air. 'Gwyn Nudd's son,' she said, only courtesy now in her manner, 'my greeting to you and your folk.'

Gwyn bowed again. 'And mine to you and yours, Aeron daughter of Dâna. We have come as I did promise.'

'And shall fight as you also did promise?'

He gestured. 'Look about you. We have already begun.'

Aeron scanned the valley behind Gwyn, where his sluagh had dispersed as at an unspoken order. Everywhere she looked, the faerie warriors were riding down the enemy; and as she looked more closely, she saw that the Sidhe warriors were unarmed. But it seemed that the Shining Ones did not need to draw weapon to rout their foe. The very terror of their presence seemed enough and more than enough. Wherever they rode they took fear with them, and the Coranian lines parted like water before them.

'We did not promise to win your fight for you, Aeron,' said Gwyn. 'That is your dán, not ours. But we came here to Nandruidion in fulfilment of two things: one a recent promise, the other an old – a very old – debt.'

He stood in his gilded stirrups and whistled; from between the silver-shod hoofs of the faerie horses threaded two red-eared, white-coated dogs. At sight of them, Aeron's wolfhounds, fearless in hunt and battle alike, whined piteously in their throats and retreated as close to their mistress as they could get; Aeron felt Cabal shivering against her leg, and laid a reassuring hand on the lifted hackles of the dog's neck.

'My hounds Bran and Sgeolaun,' said Gwyn. 'Given to me by Fionn, and to him by Arawn. Their rightful prey is traitors.' He made a small gesture; giving voice to three terrifying bays, the faerie hounds raced away down the hill, and they ran now in silence.

'One word more,' said Gwydion slowly. 'You spoke

406

just now of a promise, and that we know of; but you spoke of a debt also. What debt may that be, and to whom owed?'

Allyn son of Midna stiffened in his saddle, and even Etain the queen seemed to shrink a little at the question. But Gwyn only smiled.

'Ah, Prince of Dôn, I should have known that it would be you dared ask that question; and the answer I must make to it goes far and deep into the past . . . You know it was Edeyrn Archdruid, whose dún lay not a league from this place where now we stand, who first brought treacherously the evil of the galláin into Keltia: the same evil, and the same galláin, that you fight here this day. And it was Arthur of Arvon who did put him down. Know then that it was I who gave the Treasures of Keltia into Arthur's hand that he might do so: the Treasures that had been in my keeping for long years before; those same Treasures, Aeron, that I sent you in search of, so that the evil let in long ago by Edeyrn, and scotched by Arthur, might now be brought by you to a latter end. Daeth yr amser – Time is come – delay no longer. And when all is done, go to Caer-na-gael upon the Holy Mountain, where the circle will receive you.'

Aeron had stepped forward as Gwyn was speaking, and stood now at his stirrup, her eyes searching his face. 'Why do you, a king of the Shining Ones, trouble yourself with the sins of Edeyrn, and the evil of the galláin?'

Again Gwyn smiled, and gathering his reins began to wheel the white stallion in a caracole.

'Did you not know? Edeyrn was my brother.'

# Chapter Twenty-Nine

Though Gwyn had gone and Etain with him, as strangely and as suddenly as they had come, Allyn ap Midna yet lingered, as if he would have further speech with the rulers of Keltia.

Aeron herself had not moved, but still stood, deep in thought, where Gwyn had left her, eyes on the middle distance where a curtain of dust hid the battle from her sight.

At last she stirred, and looked at Gwydion. 'So that is why – '

He nodded, but it was Allyn who answered. 'My lord Gwyn is son to Nudd our king who was,' he said. 'And Edeyrn, to whom we were first to give the name of Marbh-draoi, was son to one Rhûn, a mortal Kelt. But both alike were sons of the lady Seli, she who was Nudd's queen. One day in anger she left the dún and her own lord; she was gone for a year and a day of our counting, and when she returned she brought with her – for our years and days are not in pace with your own – a boy of seven years' growth. She named him Edeyrn, which is to say 'golden-tongued', and he lived with us for seven of our own years, though in the outer world he had attained to full manhood's age. His mother sent him out then from our dún, to the hall of his mortal father; but what Edeyrn learned in his time with us he never forgot, for he was in part of our own blood, and in the end he turned it all to evil.'

'And so Gwyn his brother gave Arthur the means to destroy him.'

Allyn nodded. 'So he did, Prince of Dôn; and still the

evil was not ended, not completely. Therefore did Gwyn give you the words to set Aeron on the path that would, he hoped, bring her to the Treasures, to end Edeyrn's evil forever. There is no more that we can do.'

Aeron had been silent while the Sidhe lord and Gwydion spoke, but now she raised a hand, and Shane came quickly to her side from where he had been waiting with the others, some yards away.

'Gwyn has said it,' she murmured, as if to herself. Then more loudly: 'Daeth yr amser . . . Fetch now to me Fragarach, and the Spear Birgha. I will make an end.'

The ride of the Sidhe had reduced Jaun Akhera's forces as much by panic and disarray as by real destruction. He had watched, stunned and silent, as the faerie horsemen rode against his lines, scattering the terrified soldiery in all directions. But then all at once the Sidhe were gone, and wearily he prepared to rally his army once more against the Keltic schiltrons. Even as he did so, though, Jaun Akhera concealed the dismay and disbelief he felt. *What else can she have to throw at me*? he thought despairingly. *She must be the goddess Ananzanzu in human guise, whose sorceries are inexhaustible* . . . Still, even Aeron could not have many more surprises left, and if he could hold out until sunset – unless . . .

Jaun Akhera's face blazed with a sudden hope. Once before, Aeron had challenged him to fíor-comlainn; perhaps, now, he could offer her that challenge renewed.

A quarter-mile away, nearer the banks of the Avon Dia, Helior looked around in panic scarcely controlled, trying to see through the dust and confusion of maddened troops. *Where are my sons? Akhi, where are you?*

Out of the tumult she saw a familiar figure emerge, and forgetting her royal dignity, she ran after him like some street-waif, to grab at his arm. 'Lord Hanno – '

He looked at her as at some stranger, then his face cleared and he nodded. 'Madam? What is it? I cannot spare even a few moments from my command, the battle goes so ill – '

Helior felt a fresh wave of terror wash over her. 'My son – '

'I have just left the Emperor. He has decided on a course from which none could persuade him: to face Aeron in a meeting that may well decide all our fates . . . I must go now, Serenity; you will be safest if you remain here, you and the lady Tinao.'

*Tinao . . .* Helior realized that she had not seen the girl since the early hours of the day's fighting. *Where is she? Has she gone to Akhi? Nay, no doubt Indarrak is looking after her . . . And what of Sancho?* In her renewed fear and distraction, she began to run again, though she had no thought of to where, or from what. Then she saw before her in the eerie light Irin Magé's tall orange-clad form. The Cabiri priest was standing very still, his eyes seeing something a long way off, or perhaps it was not his eyes that saw . . .

'Well, priestling?' snapped Helior, fear sharpening her voice to contempt. 'What think you now of your counsel? What will you do to mend matters for my son?'

He looked at her from a greater distance than the merely physical. 'There is nothing I can do; or may do. I taught him, and I warned him, and now he must do for himself. No one else can help him here.'

'We shall see about that,' muttered Helior, and ran once more through the chaos of the Imperial lines, following Hanno's retreating form.

Powell of Dyved stood alone on a ridge above the battle. He had not shirked the fight – as more than one wound attested – and he had seen his only son fall to Gwydion's sword – as unconcealed tears had attested.

410

But the grief had been stanched even as the blood, and now his only thought was to emerge from this horror alive. Early on in the fighting, as soon as he saw which way it appeared like to go – between the Eye of Balor and the coming of the Sidhe, Aeron's way, not Jaun Akhera's – he had given secret orders for the Dyvetian troops to steal away from the Imperial lines as best they could; and now he was ready to attempt his own escape. He had ripped off his surcoat with its betraying blazon, and thrown away his riven shield, and in the seething battle-stour had withdrawn to the comparative safety of this ridge, whose other flank was a deep coombe through which, with luck, he could creep away unnoticed, to pass beyond Aeron's writ forever.

And beyond Jaun Akhera's as well; for by now, Powell knew, he was almost certainly hunted for a traitor by both sides alike, and the punishment for treachery was much the same no matter whose hand dealt it out.

*Almost safe*, he thought, *almost there* . . . Just over the lip of the hill, and down into the coombe's steep-sided safety, and then he would have more than a chance; for he had had the foresight to conceal a smallship, equipped for space, not ten lai away in a fold of the hills. Near sobbing with exhaustion and exertion, he gained the crest of the rise.

Powell never knew what caused him to turn, for there was no smallest sound, neither then nor later. But turn he did, and then there was no time for any sound of any sort, as Gwyn's white hounds Bran and Sgeolaun leapt for him in silence, in silence brought down their lawful prey, and, still in silence, tore out his throat.

In the few months of his acquaintance with Aeron, Elathan had thought himself grown inured – by sheer frequency, if nothing else – to any astonishment at anything his new friend might compass, though in truth her deeds even in that brief span had given astonishment cause enough. But the friendship they had so gingerly embarked upon had come to be a real and solid one in spite of such, the giving and taking on either side as free and open as it may ever be between true friends; though, given the stature of these particular participants, the scope of it was rather greater than most friendships can claim. Still, for all the galactic scale and interplanetary implications, at root it was two persons, not two monarchs, who were friends here; and it was as persons, even more perhaps than as monarchs, that each had acted.

So Elathan had entered wholeheartedly into Aeron's fight to reclaim her realm, as unstinting of himself and his resources – and of his own safety, even – as Aeron had been at Tory. And he had watched as Gwydion turned the trees to warriors, and as the Eye of Balor had been once again opened, and as Aeron had waved the Bratach Bán and summoned the Sidhe to Nandruidion. But through it all had run like a red thread the thought of Talorcan, and the dilemma that was twin to that thought: what, when he encountered his brother at last, would he do to him. Aeron had already once prevented him from shedding Talorcan's blood, had been willing to take even the guilt of that upon herself, though in the event it had fallen out otherwise. But here on Tara that problem was no longer hers, if indeed it had ever been, and Elathan knew very well that the knot of blood and betrayal between Talorcan and himself was his alone to deal with: to unravel, or to cut.

It was therefore less with shock than with a feeling of cold smiling inevitability – *dán to its last pinch*, he thought dully – that, watching Aeron and Gwydion speak to the Sidhe, Elathan saw down over the sloping ground to the west his brother standing among the officers of Jaun Akhera's high command. And it was thus less with personal hatred than with this new vast sense of being moved by fated forces that he now approached Aeron, knowing at last what he must do and how it must be done . . .

Allyn son of Midna had ridden away with his kindred when, obeying his cousin's bidding, Shane brought to Aeron the two things she had requested: the Sword, Fragarach, and Birgha the Spear. She had replaced her own glaive with the great leather-scabbarded longsword, and was about to take the Spear from Shane's hands when Elathan came up beside her.

She looked her enquiry, for in his face was no friendliness but only a rigid control.

He pointed to the Imperial lines. 'Talorcan is there. I think this quarrel is mine to settle.'

Aeron studied his flushed face, which paled again beneath her gaze; then she looked over to where Talorcan was a clear and recognizable figure in his red surcoat, and nodded once.

'Very well so. How do you choose to settle it?'

Elathan looked at the Spear in Shane's hands, its head still shrouded in the silver silk that had wrapped it for all the centuries of its slumber. Aeron, following his gaze, understood, and nodded again.

'To you then, King of Fomor.' She signalled to Shane to give the Spear to Elathan, and then withdrew a little, to see what he would do. *He has earned this; else the thought would never have come to him, nor the licence to use Birgha been granted him . . .*

Elathan looked down at the weapon in his hands. A beautiful thing; its slim ashwood haft was carved with baffling symbols – patterns that looked like broken wands and double-discs, combs and mirrors and grinning long-nosed beasts – and ringed below the point with findruinna. As soon as his fingers closed around it he felt its power; even wrapped in its silk veils, it pulled like a hound in leash. With sudden decision he ripped away the silk; the spearhead glittered in the light, seeming neither metal nor crystal, almost jewel-like in its translucence, but with a writhing cloudy fire at its heart.

Slowly he lifted the Spear to the level of his shoulder, feeling it balance itself almost against his will. From boyhood Elathan had been trained in the spear-toss, had excelled in it far above the average; but he was suddenly sure that this Spear would hit its mark by no skill of his . . . With renewed resolve he sighted down the shaft's length at Talorcan's distant red-clad figure, and the symbols on the Spear seemed to move and writhe in the corner of his eye.

The unexpected movement startled him, so that he faltered in the very moment of his release; but with no thought that he could afterwards recall, Elathan flung Birgha at his treasonous brother.

The weapon left his hand with such celerity – *alacrity, rather*, he corrected himself, staring after it – that it seemed he had not so much thrown the Spear as ceased to hold it back. Its flight kindled a stream of fire from the dusty air; and Talorcan, looking up too late, had not time even to flinch. As the Spear struck him through the heart and carried him backward to the earth, it roared.

And still Elathan did not move . . .

'"I am the Spear that roars for blood,"' said a low voice behind him: Aeron had come up quietly. 'So did one of our bards speak of Birgha, long ago on Terra.'

She followed his glance to where Talorcan, his figure diminished by distance, lay now upon the hillside, arms flung out to either side and the Spear upright through his chest pinning him to the ground. He lay alone, for all those standing near had fled as Birgha struck.

Elathan sighed and turned his back on the sight. 'He spoke rightly, that bard of yours . . . I am glad Cami was not here to see that,' he added. 'On Fomor it is the

King's responsibility alone to deal death to such as he and the law deem to merit it. But it is also the King's duty to ensure that it is justice that is being dealt, not revenge; and just now I failed in that duty.'

'Not so, King of Fomor,' said Aeron. 'If that were true, Birgha would never have endured even the grip of your hand. It was execution, and justice undoubted.'

'And mercy unmerited – a death richly deserved, though he was my father's son. He dishonours even the instrument of his execution.'

'Well, whatever else he was, he was of royal blood, and a death by Birgha's kiss is both fitting and cleansing. He will go on now to face what he has prepared for himself.' Aeron nodded towards the Spear. 'Call it back.'

He looked sharply at her, uncertain if she jested, but she nodded again.

'Aye so; call it. It will return to your fist like a falcon trained. You it was who sent it forth; now you must call it home again.'

Feeling as fearful as he did foolish, Elathan raised his empty hand, palm outwards, and in his mind summoned the weapon to him. And, across the valley, the Spear quivered as if a hand of flesh and bone had been set to it, then rose free of the body of Talorcan and blazed once more to Elathan's grip. Aeron quickly swathed the point once more in its silver silk, and Elathan dropped the weapon into her hands as if it had been a live laser blade, or a bar of white-hot metal.

Only then did those who had been watching come forward: Gwydion, Desmond, Grex, some others. Aeron looked at them questioningly.

'News?'

'For Elathan,' said Desmond. 'Those ones who came here with your brother are now also mostly dead – Dargato, Salenn and Grive chiefest among them – and the rest are taken. Shall we put an end to them?'

'Upon your peril!' Elathan was as surprised as the rest of them by the vehemence of his order. 'I am sorry, I am a little – overwrought. All the same, I do not wish them slain. Put them in some place of safeholding for now, and I will deal with them when the fight is done, or perhaps back on Fomor, as I think best.'

'As you wish,' said Desmond, and left to obey.

When they stood alone again, Aeron watched her friend covertly for a while in silence. 'Is it well with you?'

Elathan nodded, not looking at her, and ran a hand over his face, banishing his fatigue and his heartsickness alike. 'It is, now; or well enough, at any event . . . But that is the end, for me. You have still to deal with Jaun Akhera.' He glanced down at Fragarach, that hung from its baldric across her chest. 'Shall that be for him – as Birgha was for my brother?'

Aeron did not reply immediately. 'It might be,' she said then. 'Or again, it might not.'


And there came an hour between noon and sunset when the armies were balanced one for one, as if on the sword-bridge that spans the chasm-entrance to Annwn itself, so evenly matched that it seemed they fought in a mirror.

Aeron alone. The roar of the battle broke over her like waves on a rocky coast; she did not speak, not even to Gwydion who stood beside her, and she did not move, save that her fingers flexed now and again around Fraga-rach's serpent-hilt. She knew very well that those close to her were wondering, with impatience or compassion according as to how well they understood her mind, why she did not draw Fragarach, or open the Eye of Balor yet again heedless of the Kelts who might stand in its sight, or send the Spear roaring into Jaun Akhera's ranks, or into his heart; any or all of which would ensure victory for her and her allies. Knew just as well that she was free to use them if she chose, that the decision was hers alone to make.

*It would be victory, right enough, but, I think, not any victory worth having* . . . As she had told Morwen, so many weeks ago, before *Retaliator* had even come to the Morimaruse, it was an advantage she could not in honour take; as if it were fíor-comlainn, and she bore two longswords and her adversary only a table-sgian. This quarrel would be – should be – settled on more even ground than that, and she waited now only for the sign she knew would come.

It came as a call she alone could hear. The very air around her seemed to ring with her name, and she looked eagerly for the summoning's source. And saw Jaun Akhera, as she had known she would, alone, down beside the Avon Dia. Before Gwydion could move to stop her, she was running down the hill into the heart of the fight.

Jaun Akhera watched her come. He had seen what she had earlier perceived: that the armies were locked, and that therefore the struggle would have to be decided elsewhere. And that suited him as well as it did her; the private quarrels of princes should not involve their folk, and, beyond all the political trappings with which this war had been bedecked, behind all the masks of power and ascendancy and sway, this fight came down in the end to him and her only, and for more than merely the Throne of Scone. Even more narrowly than her battle against Bres, there was a clash of polarities drawn here between them, a contradiction of souls that could not be allowed to stand, and both of them knew it.

He sensed a familiar presence at his elbow. 'Mother,' he said gently, never taking his eyes from Aeron's approaching figure, 'you must stand away now. And whatever happens here, you must accept.'

'And I?' came a pain-soft voice, and a hand upon his cheek.

Jaun Akhera's features contracted briefly, as if she had struck him, not caressed him. 'Especially you, beloved.' He turned then to look at them – *perhaps for the last time*, he thought: Helior white and still; Tinao no less pale, but with tears on her face like a skein of jewels, glittering in the eerie light.

Jaun Akhera brushed away the tears, then kissed his tear-damp fingertips and pressed the kiss to her lips. He did not watch as Helior put an arm around Tinao's shoulders and drew her away.


The sun broke through the mounting cloudbanks, gold shafts splintering through to light theatrically the plain below, as Aeron made her way down to where her enemy awaited her. Running heedlessly, throwing off the hands that grabbed for her, ignoring the swords that slashed, she dodged through the press until she stood in an open space above the Avon Dia, Fragarach flaming now in her hand, and Jaun Akhera facing her not a dozen feet away.

Near enough to see his eyes: Their gold was changed now, something coiling darkly far inside; and as she looked into those baneful depths, Aeron felt her strength of body and of will running through her into the ground beneath her feet, like sand through a glass or water through a pipe.

'Well, Aeron,' said Jaun Akhera pleasantly. 'This then is the test.'

'There is no test,' she said, with a calm she was far from feeling. 'But once before you declined to take our quarrel to the sword between us two alone. Now I offer you that choice again.'

Jaun Akhera laughed. 'Though I flatter myself that I am a better man with a blade than your last royal opponent, I remember very well how you dealt with him, and I fear I must again decline. But I offer you a counterchallenge.'

'Of what like?'

He nodded at the blazing Sword. 'Easy enough, with such as that and its fellows, to face down and destroy any foe. But it would not be you that won the victory: The weapon, not the warrior, would do the fighting. You cherish your pride to face the fíor-comlainn, but where would be the truth in *that* combat? Would it not be merely Bellator over again, another unequal contest in which you held the strong hand uppermost not by reason of your own skill and merit, but by mere witchery? And would that be a thing worthy of the Queen of Kelts?'

Aeron made no outward sign, but she felt as if he had flicked her with a tip-whip on an open wound, and all the tiny barbs tugging at her flesh. How had he known? How had he reached so cunningly past all her defences, to seize upon the very reasons that had caused her to hold back thus far? *My guilt for Bellator, and the Aoibhell traha: What a pair of motives to decide this quarrel and to rule a queen . . . and they* will *rule me, too; he surely has the right of it there . . .*

'You argue as a plausible Kelt,' she heard herself saying. 'Past doubt but you have been here too long . . . Well then, what shall be the ground of our meeting?'

'Set aside that blade you bear,' he said, his eyes never leaving her face, 'and meet me armed only with your own powers, as I with mine. That would be a contest of honour such as the worlds have never seen, an equal fight between equal princes; the stakes equal also – my throne for yours. My challenge to you, Aeron, is magic.'

Aeron never hesitated. 'I accept for myself.'

'Only for yourself? Will your armies not be bound by the outcome?'

'It is usual with us that if the chieftain be slain the fight is over,' she said with a shrug. 'Though I cannot promise that Gwydion and Elathan will not keep the war alight should I fall.'

'I care nothing for that. To settle our score between us is enough for my part.'

'You seem sure of victory, Telchine.'

'And should I not be – Danaan? Whose magic was it defeated your folk's, on the last day of Amnael in the city of Lirias? Whose was it, not so very long ago, broke the Wolf Gate and took Caerdroia?'

Aeron smiled then, a real smile, open and guileless. 'Well, I can only hope my folk – not to mention myself – have learned somewhat since.'

Unslinging the baldric upon which she had carried Fragarach, she set belt and Sword reverently aside upon the grass. As her hand left the gleaming hilt, she felt, as if from an infinitous distance, a re-echoing of that feeling of rightness that had come to her once before, in her cabin on *Retaliator*, many months since: a reassurance like the sound of a far chime, faint, but true and clear-noted. *Ah, I was right then after all; this was indeed a test, though I said not so just now to the Marbh-draoi; and though it was lawful to allow the use of the Spear and the Eye, and, later, will be so to employ the Cup, for me to use the Sword to settle this quarrel would* not *have been lawful. Not so much because it is the Sword, but because it would have been I who used it. It was a geis and a test together, and by the grace of the gods I have been so far saved from failing – but then, it is barely begun.*

Straightening to full height, she pointed a little distance off to a patch of carse near a ford of the Avon Dia.

'Does the ground suit?' she asked in the formal challenge.

'It suits.'

'Be it so.' They took positions perhaps a score of feet apart, bowed their heads deeply and ceremonially to each other. Then Aeron stretched out her hand, and lines of blue-white fire ran east and west from where she stood, to meet in a ring of cold flame that shut them off from interference and assistance alike.

When it became clear what Aeron and Jaun Akhera were about to commence, an unspoken truce seemed to fall over their armies, like a ripple of stillness moving outward from a calm centre. And an unvoiced horror fell likewise over their friends: As the battle slowed and then came to an uncertain halt, those closest to the two adversaries hastened through the lines to be as near as they could be to what would be the deciding combat of this war, though they knew well there was nothing could now be done to stop it: Gwydion, Rohan, Elathan, O'Reilly; from the Imperial lines, Hanno and Garallaz, Helior and Tinao, Indarrak and Irin Magé.

And in the centre of all, Jaun Akhera and Aeron: Though the war had halted around them, waiting upon their contest, they were no longer of it. Within the riomhall, the protective fire-circle that Aeron had cast upon the carse, it was a different war that these two now did fight: a war that had been begun thirteen thousand years ago in Atland, a war that had continued even after both their races were free of the stars themselves. Once again it had come to Danaan against Telchine, and once again magic was their weapon.

To those who watched, tense with horror, from beyond the riomhall, it seemed that the two tall shapes within the perimeter were altering the very stuff of their own bodies: They rocketed through a bewildering sequence of transformations, preliminary ploys – bears and badgers, wolves and hounds, eagles and serpents, basilisks to griffins to columns of faceless flame. Then the shapeshifting was suddenly over, and they stood again in their own forms, both breathing hard, as if they had been running, and a little less firm upon their feet.

421

Aeron recovered herself first, pointed her right hand, the two middle fingers together. 'Áini thened, déini lóchet!'

A lance of light formed in the air and launched itself at Jaun Akhera, striking him full in the chest and hurling him to the ground. Yet even as he fell he was muttering a countercharm, and Aeron's head was suddenly knocked to one side, as if an invisible hand had dealt her a vicious slap. Before she could regain her balance, he had struck again; this time the unseen blow sent her to her knees in the grass, and blood beaded the corner of her mouth. Outside the circle, Gwydion willed himself to motionlessness, and Elathan closed his eyes.

But Aeron was on her feet again, and crying words in an unknown tongue she threw one arm up to the heavens. Lightning arced from her fingertips, and thunder answered in the shifting clouds. Then between them on the duelling-ground stood a giant black dog. Enormous and terrible, its smooth coat gleaming over rippling muscles and its powerful tail, thick at the base, tapering to a narrow tip, it crouched protectively in front of Aeron, and its eyes as it looked at Jaun Akhera were blazing red.

'The Púca,' whispered Desmond to O'Reilly, who had shrunk back against him. 'It is only partly in the world of form. It says much for Aeron's power that she was able to summon it, but whether she can command it . . .'

His voice fell away into silence as the faerie animal drew back its lips to show gleaming fangs, then loosed upon the air a long and terrifying bay. It began to move menacingly towards Jaun Akhera, but Aeron, feeling her control slip, spoke curt words; the beast, swinging its huge head to look at her, made a noise deep in its throat and was gone.

'I had thought you a better tactician than that, Aeron,'

jeered Jaun Akhera, 'not to call up what you cannot command.' But his voice was not so steady as his words.

So it went for many minutes, each countering what the other conjured: Jaun Akhera entangling Aeron in a hedge of thorns, she turning the inch-long curving spines into white flowers, though not before they had stabbed her cruelly; Aeron throwing round Jaun Akhera a wall of fire, he drawing snow whispering out of the clouds to quench it, though not before he had been badly burned; and other exchanges beside, and both of them grew weary long before it was done.

'Where is the magic that did so well for Bellator?' taunted Jaun Akhera, watching lynx-eyed for the first signs of her next spell. They had been fighting more than an hour now, and still they seemed evenly matched. *If I can anger her, so that she forgets her self-mastery for her wrath; and Bellator being to her a sharper thorn than those ones I conjured earlier* . . . 'Black magic once to such spectacular result, why not black magic again? You have grown soft as well as soft-hearted since then, Aeron; even Arianeira managed better at Murias than you do now.'

'That is as it is,' she said, voice low but very clear. 'I have made my choice not to use the Treasures to decide this; still less will I use the dark-knowledge, the eolas dubh. Not if I must perish for it and Keltia to follow me; but no working of Anghar, the Loveless Place, shall be wrought here by me.'

Jaun Akhera gave a deep mocking sigh. 'Ah, the neverending traha of the Aoibhells . . . but, as you will have it.' He made a curious sign with his left hand, and the writhing dark thing that had been in his eyes leapt suddenly out, assuming palpable form on the ground between them where the Púca had stood.

Aeron took an involuntary step backward, as a low vibration came from the shadow-creature and quickly grew to an unpleasant humming noise. A sick loathing mounting to nausea came over her as the humming waxed in strength; her vision blurred, and before she could move to defend herself the black thing was at her throat.

# Chapter Thirty

Gwydion had watched impassively as Aeron and Jaun Akhera came to first grips with each other's magic. *This is a thing neither of them has done before, matched spells for life or death against a foe of equal skill – It must be*, he thought, but he was desperately afraid, and he had no comfort for any other: not for Elathan, who had turned away at last, unable to watch any longer; nor for Rohan nor Grex nor even for O'Reilly, who had come running to him for reassurance as she had done once before in fear for Aeron. But this time he could give no courage to her, for he had barely enough for himself. *Aeronwy, if you come not alive and unhurt from that circle, I will choke out his life with my own hands, and care not for what may come after . . .*

Morwen, with Fergus and Ríoghnach and some others, had been standing a little to one side, and now she came forward to touch Gwydion on the arm. 'Do something,' she said, her voice utterly without inflection. 'It cannot go on so.'

He looked at her then, and she saw the anguish in the grey distant gaze. 'I can do nothing,' he said. 'Only she . . .'

'Do something,' begged Tinao, both hands clawing at Helior's arm.

'Nothing can be done,' said the Princess. 'You yourself heard Akhi tell us we must accept whatever befalls. Be silent now and watch, else you are not worthy of him.'

Defeated, Tinao lifted her eyes – dark, desperate, pleading – in turn to the faces of the others who stood there, mutely beseeching their help: Hanno, Inguari, Garallaz, Irin Magé. But the captains would not meet her gaze, and Sanchoniathon, who might have tried to help, and who surely would have comforted, was not there. Of them all, only Irin Magé the Cabiri would look at her, and Tinao found no shred of comfort in that, for there was both pity and pitilessness in his gaunt face. She turned away, shivering, and Indarrak put a gentle hand upon her shoulder.

'Oh, 'Darrak, he *will* be all right,' she said in a clear determined voice. 'You will see. He will be all right. He must be.'


As the shadow-thing came at her, Aeron instinctively flung her arms in front of her face; then it struck, with a force that knocked her backward to the grass. She could feel the weight of the thing: In shape it was something like to a badger or a monstrous talpa, ovoid and covered with dark silky shadow-fur, and it had no eyes that she could perceive. Though she sensed no personal hostility from the creature, she could feel it trying to leach away her power, drawing its shape and sustenance from her. And in that, she knew, it was but obeying its master, with no will of its own; if she could not throw it off, it would hold her there until she weakened, and then Jaun Akhera would place the final seal to their combat.

As if from a great distance, she heard Jaun Akhera cry out the words of a spell of augmentation, in a high ghastly voice: 'Kay o kam avriavel, kiya yakhé lo beshel!'

Her counterspell came quick as she would have riposted a swordthrust. 'Lezh-han, lezh-hon, bac'h an arer zo gant don!' A net of silver cast itself around the shadow-talpa, tightening in pulses that matched her own heartbeats; the more it contracted, the smaller the creature grew, until it was gone and the silver lattice with it.

Aeron got to her feet with care, head ringing, and

looked at Jaun Akhera. He was staring at her with fear plain on his face for the first time, for he had counted heavily on that spell. But as she looked at him, she saw, horribly, his face began to change: It was now Gwydion's, now Bres's, Haruko's now, Elathan's, Grex's, Strephon's, Morwen's, her own. In a silent explosion of clarity she saw a truth that cleared away all her weakness and steadied her on her feet; and the truth was that Jaun Akhera was her Shadow made reality and given form by her own fears, and she of course was his. Not the Shadow that was the other side of her soul's Light; that inborn darkness had long ago been absorbed as part of herself – her Self – and would not perish until she did; even then, it would only be unbodied, united with the rest of her soul. No, this Other who faced her here, all in white as she herself wore black, was rather the embodiment of all those things she hated most in the world, and she was that to him, and in that absolute difference they were utterly one and the same. There was no way to go on living sanely if the other also lived; dán had brought them to this place, in this time, and only death could free them.

After her bout with the talpa, Aeron had felt ready to drop, or howl, or both together; now there came a sharp stab of triumph to hold her up, rising through her weariness like a mast holding aloft the remnants of a tattered sail. *Now let the combat truly begin, for now we have each of us seen what we are fighting; thou, White Destroyer, and I . . .*

So it went, for another hour and more, there beside the Avon Dia; first one would have the mastery, then in an eyeblink the other would overmaster it again, and gradually their magics grew less subtle and more desperate, as they tried to defeat on a purely physical level what neither had been able to break on a higher.

By now they were both of them barely able to stand

427

upright. Jaun Akhera's left arm was useless, shattered in many places where a spell of Aeron's had closed on the bone like a chokevine; but he bound the arm across his chest with a strip of cloth torn from his cloak and chanted something heavy and dark.

And Aeron's sight was filled by nothing but sun-coloured rough hair. The mane of a huge lion was under her hands, and green-gold eyes without a pupil and three times the size of her own stared down at her.

She felt the lion's pads upon her shoulders, the claws digging bloody welts across her back, the immense weight and strength of the creature, and her arms that held off the beast's fangs from her throat began to tremble with the strain. With one mighty effort she flung back the magic; the lion was gone, and overbalancing, she fell to her knees before she could catch herself; but even as she fell she murmured a rann.

Jaun Akhera, taken off guard, found every joint in his body suddenly frozen; it took all his strength even to move his fingers, to blink an eyelid. His muscles were brass and his tendons lead, and his spine seemed a bar of cold iron.

Aeron's own back felt as if it were on fire, and she knew that the lion's claws must have left skin and tunic alike in shreds; knew too that she must strike now, while her enemy was still struggling against her meath-fhuar, the slowcold.

She drew a long sobbing breath. She was so tired, and no bone in her body but did not feel like bloody knives, and her mind seemed turned to mud. The words of yet another rann crawled now to the forefront of her brain, with a snaily slowness; she did not even know from where, but they came, and with the last of her strength, she dragged them forth.

'Daear a'th lwnc, dw'r i'th le – '

*Earth gapes, and water in thy place shall be . . .* Gasping out the Kymric syllables, Aeron sank back into the grass with her hands clasped between her knees, totally spent, but also strangely lighthearted that it was over at last. That was it. That was her last arrow; if it did not strike the inmost ring of the gold, she was lost, and Keltia with her.

Nothing happened for several seconds; then, with a roar like ten thousand lions, the earth behind Jaun Akhera seemed to open like two lips drawing back from bared fangs. The turf peeled away, then the soil, rust-red and volcanic, then the rock itself – skin and flesh and bone of the planet, all exposed now as if the ground had been slashed open by some sword of the gods, and in the cleft only black nothingness.

Gwydion, shading his eyes against the horror of that sight, saw now unbelievably in the sky behind Aeron's small forlorn form the towering phantom-shape of a Woman. She was leaning forward, drawing the pin of Her bronze cloak-brooch through the valley of the Avon Dia; the earth-gash was forming as She furrowed it. Her head was crowned with stars, and lightnings flickered in Her hair; rooted in earth were Her bare feet, and the hem of Her gúna seemed to brush against Aeron's bloody back.

*Earth gapes, and water in thy place shall be* . . . Earth had gaped, and now came the water: the Avon Dia itself, River of the Gods, joining in battle, gathering itself into a foaming fountain that grew every second thicker and higher, less translucent and more ominously dense.

Jaun Akhera, breaking from his immobility, lifted a face blind with awe, and with terror swiftly mastered. He raised his arm to Aeron in a gesture that was surrender and acknowledgement and final salute, and then with a smile he was gone. The water fell like a mailed fist, sweeping him down into the chasm the Ban-dia had opened to receive him. He did not go uncompanioned:

429

Helior and Tinao, Garallaz and Indarrak and Irin Magé, and many thousands more, went with him into darkness. Not a single Kelt, nor any Keltic ally, was taken by the waters; they had all been pulled back, by Gwydion's quick order, to the high ground where they now watched, numbed, almost as blind with fear as their enemies had been.

The roar of the avenging waters died, to be followed by a deeper roar as the earth split folded in upon itself, neatly as a seam being stitched. Where the gash had been, no living thing now stood, nor dead neither; no scar marked the smooth green turf, and the Avon Dia once again foamed whitely in its accustomed bed. Only, Jaun Akhera was gone, and most of the Imperial forces with him.

Aeron rocked back onto her heels, dirt streaking her face, her boots and cloak-hem soaked and draggled where the backwash of the water had swirled around her. The circle of fire, the riomhall, had died away, extinguished by the rival powers of earth and air and water. She was all but unaware of the few thousand Imperial survivors throwing down their weapons as one; through the smoke and tumult and buffeting wind her eyes sought Gwydion's.

Sanchoniathon and Hanno, and a handful of other officers who had been fortunate enough to survive the last few minutes by mercy of their distance from chasm and river alike, had come up behind her, their faces wild.

'Empress – '

Aeron turned and rose at the sound of Sanchoniathon's shaken voice, and already to his eye her posture seemed to hold a more than royal distance. First he, then, more slowly, Hanno and the other officers, went to one knee before her on the muddy turf, and across their bent heads she and Gwydion held each other's gaze.

"*Empress*," she thought, and the realization caused her

to sway a little on her feet. *Yr Mawreth . . . nay, it cannot be – it will not be . . .*

'Mae'r dial drosodd,' she whispered, and Gwydion closed his eyes, as if in pain, or pain's ending.

*Vengeance is done with . . .* The words sounded through his soul like the horn-cry that ends the long hunt, and every muscle in his body, so long strung for battle, seemed to unknot at the sound.

Aeron looked down then at those who still knelt before her; they had neither moved nor lifted their heads.

'Rise, my lords,' she said in Hastaic, and her voice seemed strange even to herself. She touched Sanchoniathon lightly on the shoulder, a tap that could have been an accolade, and he rose to face her as Gwydion came to stand beside her.

Sanchoniathon looked from one to the other, searching their faces, then drew his sword and presented it hilt-first to Aeron. Holding his glance, she touched the hilt and returned the weapon to him.

'To me?' he said blankly, staring at her. 'I do not understand – '

'No. Well, I do not understand either, not completely, and we will speak of it later, you and I. As for that name of Empress that you give me, it is no name of mine – neither claimed by me nor conferred upon me by another, or many others.'

'Then you do *not* declare yourself Empress?' gasped Hanno. 'But surely – '

'Have I not just now said so?' said Aeron impatiently. 'Imperial sovereignty is not what I made this war for; or did you not notice?'

'For what, then?'

'The Ard-rían of Keltia, and her friends the King of Fomor and the Queen of the Yamazai and the Ambassador of Earth, made this war upon the Emperor of the Cabiri in answer to his war upon her,' said Gwydion. 'To take her kingdom back from his unlawful grip; no more than that.'

Sanchoniathon smiled. 'Very well, both of you; believe what you like.' His eyes, so like his dead brother's, gleamed with sudden amber flame. 'But remember afterwards that it was I who told you first: Empire is a neverending temptation to anyone with the strength to win it and the strength to turn away from it. No shame in being tempted, or even in accepting the temptation. The only shame lies in pretending that you cannot be tempted in the first place. Do not forget that, ever.'

Aeron returned his look levelly, then nodded, and Desmond and Rohan came forward, at Gwydion's bidding, to escort the Coranians from the field to the castle of Tomnahara; though, as Aeron had shown by returning Sanchoniathon his sword, as guests and not as prisoners. She watched them go, then turned away, passing by unheeding the exultation and praise and triumphant joy of her friends and allies, and went up the rise to a place below the outer walls of Tomnahara where stood perhaps half a dozen aircars.

Gwydion caught up with her as she was about to climb up into the cabin of the nearest ship.

'Aeronwy – ' He caught her arm. 'Where do you go? Listen to them below there; you cannot leave them now, they are delirious with victory, theirs and yours alike.'

She leaned against the hull of the aircar, willing her exhaustion away and forcing herself to an explanation, for she loved him, and he deserved one.

'Do you not recall Gwyn's words? He said that when all was over, I must go to Caer-na-gael; that the circle would receive me. If I gave such heed to his words that I went blindly upon their strength to Afallinn itself, surely now I must heed them this little bit further, and go a few hundred leagues to the Holy Mountain.'

'And what of the people? Your friends, your kin, all those who love you – what will they say, when they see you have left them in the very hour of victory?'

'They who know me will understand. As for the others – ' Aeron looked up at him, and something of what the combat with Jaun Akhera had cost her was now there for him to see, though she had kept it hidden from everyone else. 'You heard Sanchoniathon just now, and Hanno – how they took it as given that I should assume Imperial sway for myself. And worse than that . . . Did you see just now, as I came up the hill, how my own folk kept clear of my very shadow on the grass? Any other time they would have come crowding to my side, talking and laughing and touching. Not now. Not after what I have done this day. They do not see that I had no choice; that it would have been less fearful for them, perhaps, had I used the Sword to settle the matter, but total perdition for me. But I am no empress, to take up Jaun Akhera's crown, and never am I a god, for my shadow to be kept clear of, and I will not be dealt with as either, Gwydion, upon my soul I will *not*.'

He heard the note of wildness, almost madness, that rang then in her voice, and he took her by the shoulders. 'It is but the moment they give way for, those folk upon the hill. They were afraid, and your manner of taking away that fear was perhaps a little – dramatic; hard for them easily to accept. They will treat you as they did; but they need a little time to remember that it is still you.'

Some of her old self-mockery came back then to her face, and she laughed. 'Well, let them be quick about remembering, then. They have only until my return from Caer-na-gael to jog their memories.' She turned then, grasping the metal bars to pull herself up into the control-seat of the aircar; as she did so, he saw her back clearly for the first time, and his mouth tightened at the sight.

'At least let Slaine tend to that before you go. Five minutes with a dermasealer – '

But she shook her head. 'Nay, it is in my mind that I must come as I am, straight from the battle . . . But do you attend to whatever must be done here. And do not fret: I will be at Caerdroia in time for the nightmeal.'

Gwydion reached his hand up to her; though she stretched her arm down as far as she could through the small port, only their fingertips caught – but they caught and held.

'Aeronwy – '

'Pendragon.' And the ship lifted from the grass.

The stone circle of Caer-na-gael, holiest place in all the Keltic worlds, stands beneath those twinned peaks of Mount Keltia that are called the Gates of the Sun: first of all points in the Northwest Continent to catch the light of the rising Grían. Alone on that high cold plateau is set Caer-na-gael, a double ring of rough-cut bluestone slabs laid out in the ancient pattern of trilithons and helestones common to all nemetons, brought to Keltia from Earth itself, and before that from the Danaans' lost home.

Aeron had landed the aircar on the edge of the plateau, and stood now at the entrance to the sacred circle, between two great carven pillarstones three times the height of a tall man. Behind her, the sun was setting in a mass of cloud – purple cloud, scarlet cloud, a cloud like a grey whale's tail – and the clear gold light sent her shadow streaming out before her across the width of the circle.

She took off her boots and walked forward, bare feet not even feeling the frozen stubbled grass. Around her, an odd susurration ran among the stones, as if the lithic giants themselves had sighed, or perhaps it was after all only the wind over the mountaintop.

Coming to the centre of the circle, she halted before

the majestic bluestone that lay like an altar at the nemeton's heart. She remembered well the only other time she had come to this place: the night before her coronation, when, like all the others who had preceded her as sovereign over Keltia, Ard-rígh and Ard-rían alike, she had kept vigil here from dusk to dawn, alone, fasting, half-frozen as much from fear as from the cold. And what she had seen then, what she had heard – and she had not been alone either, not really . . . She turned her mind from that memory, feeling suddenly her full grubbiness: the tangled hair full of dust, the black uniform torn and shredded and stiff with mud and blood, the sweat of battle still upon her; sensed too that it was right and fitting to come here so.

'I am come, whom you did call,' she said aloud. *Only the wind, as I thought . . .*

'And I, who did call you.'

She turned with a smile, for she knew that voice, though she had heard it only once before. 'Gwyn, son of Nudd and Seli,' she said, and, despite her attire, despite her weariness, despite the pain in her back, made a curtsy to the king of the Sidhe.

Gwyn bent his knee in return, and he too was smiling. 'So, Aeron,' he said then, and his voice that was deeper even than Gwydion's was merrier than when she first had heard it, on the plain at the mouth of the Valley of the Druids. 'You have won, and the Marbh-draoi is no more, and the last remnant of my brother's evil is lifted from this world. And now I return to you something I have had in keeping.'

He nodded towards the bluestone altar, and Aeron saw that there, where the stone had been empty, now rested the leather casket she herself had given Gwydion to bring to Dún Aengus, to deliver into Gwyn's hands. The coffer's lid opened, though no hand had been set to

435

it, and Aeron turned back with cold-stiffened fingers the purple velvet that shrouded the Copper Crown.

'Always it seems that by grace of the Shining Ones I am given some great gift,' said Aeron when she felt she could trust her voice again. 'The Bratach Bán and the help it brought; the horn you yourself gave to my lord, and the army it summoned; the way to the Treasures; the Treasures themselves, even; and now this . . .'

'Ah, nay! This at least was fairly yours before; and as for the others, well, they too were yours . . . But one thing more I will give you.'

He raised his hand, and a globe of misty light formed in the air above the bluestone altar. Dim shapes seemed to move within its depths; then at a quiet word from the faerie lord, the shapes came into sparkling resolution: a corner of the battlefield, an oak-grove below the walls of Tomnahara, near to the Avon Dia.

Aeron, leaning forward, lips parted in wonder at the sight, saw Gwydion with the Cup in his hands; he was setting it down upon a mossy bank beneath the ancient oaks.

'As you chose in the end not to avail yourself of the power of Fragarach,' came Gwyn's voice as from a very great distance, 'so he has chosen not to avail himself of the full powers of Pair Dadeni; and both choices were noble ones, and the right ones.'

They watched in silence as, within the magical sphere, Gwydion stepped back from the Cup. A silver mist began to gather around the bowl's graceful outlines, the pearls set into the knotwork rim glowing with blue-cream luminescence. Slowly, silently, the Cup became many times its size, expanding and overlapping itself like some eerie silver flower, until it stood the size of a great cauldron beneath the oaks, its mouth more than seven feet across, its depth perhaps three feet, the weight of it sinking its base some inches into the soft moss.

'He will use it to heal the wounded,' said Aeron, suddenly understanding. 'Though not the dead . . .'

'Nay, even though Pair Dadeni be the Cauldron of Rebirth, having the power to restore the dead to life, there are things worse far than the death of the body. Such use, even, could bring a kind of living death in very deathlessness.' Gwyn's dark eyes were soft with compassion, for he knew the bitterness of her present thought. 'Only the very newly dead, any road, may be restored by the Pair. Not lawful, to try to call back those who have already reached Tir fo Thuinn, Land-under-Waves, and commenced their next turn upon the Wheel.'

Aeron gave a gentle laugh. 'And no more would they welcome such a recalling from so glad a place as that, even by one who loved them in this life . . . But it is well thought of by Gwydion, and a thought such as he would have, to deal so with the wounded. I was myself given the grace of such a healing, and to deny it to others would be a grave offence against the Lords of Life and Death.'

'Even so.' Gwyn lifted his hand again, and the bright sphere died away. 'Think of this meeting here as the fágáil, the parting-gift of the Shining Folk; from now we shall meet only in dreams, I think, or by design of a Power greater than either of us. We shall have no place in the larger kingdom over which you and Gwydion shall rule; we are ever of Keltia, but Keltia will no longer be of us.'

'Say not so!' Her voice held real pain. 'What of Allyn's promise to Gwydion, that they should meet again? And did not you yourself promise that there should be closer bonds between your folk and their mortal kin? Friends are not so easily found, that even the Ard-rían of Keltia can afford to lose such a one as you have proved.'

'There are promises and promises,' said Gwyn, and now again he sounded as if he were withdrawing from the

437

stone circle and from her very presence, back into the fastnesses of the Hollow Mountains. 'Did you not make a promise that you would use no dark-knowledge to gain the mastery in your fight with the Marbh-draoi, though you died for it and Keltia fell? Did you not promise even to refrain from a victory that the Sword could have given you, though you endured so much to find it? Your friend Theo, did he not make a promise, that your hands should not again be stained with galláin blood – though your dán and his decreed otherwise? And that promise you and Gwydion made to each other and to Keltia in the circle at Ni-maen: That was a great and gallant promise, was it not? And all promises come due at the last.'

'And what promise may I make to you, King of the Sidhe, so that you will stay?'

But only the wind answered, and she knew that he was gone from the mountaintop. *Ah, son of Nudd, you have kept well* your *promise; surely all debts now are cleared; and, for all that, I think we shall meet again . . .*

Aeron leaned forward to lift the heavy leather coffer in her hands, prepared as she did so for pain in her lacerated back. To her astonishment, no pain came, not even a stiffness, and she reached round a hand to touch her back. Under the torn uniform, her fingertips encountered only smooth and unbroken skin, as unmarred and whole and healthy as if Jaun Akhera's sorceries had never taken lion-shape to score it. Unbidden, the image of the Cup transforming itself into the great Pair of healing rose before her eyes. *So again I have been healed by its power* . . . And by the power of Gwyn, and the power of Caerna-gael, and perhaps most of all by the power of letting go: a healing she herself had given herself, by relinquishing of her vengeance and by submitting the final contest to the judgement of justice and the gods alone.

She brushed reverent fingers over the beaten copper of the Crown and closed the leather lid. *And because of that, I have received my sovereignty here for the second time; and more truly, for the first time was by right from my father, and gift from the circle, and by no merit of my own. This time I have earned it; now, at last, I may go home . . .*

# Epilogue

Night at Caerdroia, and chilly for springtime, but there was Midsummer delirium in the streets of the City. The first of the victorious Keltic armies, with their Fomori and Yamazai allies, had come within sight of the walls before sunset, and the joy-maddened citizenry that had yet remained had opened all the gates and poured out to give them welcome.

On the little turret-walk outside her chambers, her hounds at her feet, Aeron stood leaning against the battlements, listening to the sounds of the revelry in Mi-Cuarta rising faint from below, and to the hushed murmur of the sea in front of her – tonight Manaan's white-maned horses did not ride. A beautiful night, with the summer stars beginning to wheel above the horizon and the Criosanna shimmering across their faces. *Sometimes*, she thought, *and more often than I did care to admit, I did not think to see this again* . . . Beneath her silken gúna, she flexed her shoulders experimentally, still marvelling. *Not so bad, to emerge from Cymynedd with not even a sore back to show for it* . . . Even as Aeron smiled at the traha of the thought, she felt the smile shadowed by the knowledge that the real wounds of the fight went deeper far than had those scratches, and they were by no means hers alone.

Still, even those wounds, grave and painful as they were, were scratches themselves by comparison to the gains this war had won for Keltia. An alliance with Earth, friendship with Fomor and Fomor's king, an end to the Cabiri Imperium; perhaps even, gods willing, an end to the hitherto endless enmity between Telchine and

Danaan, if Sanchoniathon's seeming change of heart was a true one. And why should it not be? Gwydion himself had remarked that Sanchoniathon and his late unlamented brother were more unlike than either of them knew; perhaps that too was an augury for a friendlier future.

And the greatest gain of all – the return of the Treasures to Keltia. *In the end, though I went to find the Treasures and brought them back, they were not meant for me to use. Gwydion and Elathan were permitted; but not I – and that was the true test all along: not the using, nor even the finding, but the refusing to use them, and the finding of the needed strength within myself . . .*

A noise of renewed merrymaking floated up from below, where the windows of Mi-Cuarta opened on the sea. They were all waiting down there for her to join them in a great ceili of celebration: Elathan, Grex, Morwen, O'Reilly, all her other friends and kindred, the leaders of the Protectorate levies and Fomori forces, even Queen Tanaxio of the Yamazai, who had led her women warriors to such terrible effect against the Coranians who had devastated their home planet.

She would go down to them presently: It was unthinkable that the Ard-rían not be with them this night; moreover, she had a need to rejoice every bit as great as theirs, setting aside for one night at least the thought of the staggering duties that awaited them all in the days to come. *If we are very industrious, and very lucky, perhaps by Fionnasa we just might be out from under the worst of it – and that will be a year since first the Terrans came to Tara . . .* But she had needed still more to come here first, to her own place, to give it reality in her own mind: that the battle was over; and that she was alive, and victorious over her enemy, and victorious over herself.

Behind her, a familiar step: without turning she reached

a hand to him. 'I have been waiting for you to come; why did you tarry?'

Gwydion kissed her hand and closed it in both of his, with a quiet word to soothe the demonstrative greeting of the hounds. 'Did I so? Well, it is only that empresses need time alone still more than do high queens.'

She looked up at him, green eyes glittering in the light. 'I thought we had not yet determined to take such title for ourselves.'

'No more have we,' he agreed, relinquishing her hand and settling himself comfortably on her stone bench, his cloak wrapped around him over his silk and velvet feast-garb – he was attired, as was she, for the festivities below. 'And I mind me well of Sanchoniathon's warning gibe . . . But I speak now as First Lord of War, and I advise the Ard-rían that she has little room for choosing. The Cabiri Imperium lies in ruin. Already Morwen has received petitions from some of its remnants for accept-ance as Protectorate worlds of Keltia; in the days to follow, there will be very many more. If there is ever a time when Keltia is to take up a position in the galaxy as a sovereign power beyond our Curtain Wall, that time is now.'

Aeron was silent for so long that at last Gwydion rose to his feet again and went to her where she stood, her face still turned to the sea.

'It is what you yourself said you sought, Aeronwy. Do you forget the day you told us all in Council?'

She shook her head. 'I said also that same day, if memory serves, that Imperial rule was no option I would willingly take. "Empress": It is too much change, and even the sound of it mislikes me.'

'Then stay Ard-rían, Aeron, if that sits better on your soul, but your sway will be no whit the less whatsoever you choose for title.'

'And you,' she said, all at once amused. 'If I defeated

Jaun Akhera's magic, then you as First Lord of War defeated his armies; and therefore half the Empress Aeron's victory is the Emperor Gwydion's.'

A look of unease passed over his face, and he gave her a rueful smile. 'I love the sound of that no better than do you,' he admitted. 'But already such sway is fact, will we or nill we; when the empire be already established, what differ shall it make to take the title as well? Even Elathan and Grex have urged you to do so – shall you be any less as Empress than you are as Ard-rían, or prove a worse than Strephon or Jaun Akhera? Too much change, you say; the adage has ever been "Change or die".'

Again Aeron was a long time silent, then: 'Did you see, at Nandruidion? I think perhaps most saw nothing, but surely you – '

He nodded, awed anew by the memory: the Ban-dia, the Mother Herself, clothed as Mâm Tarach, the spirit of the planet, drawing Her brooch-pin through the earth as easily as a child may draw a finger over a frosted windowpane.

'Many saw – sorcerers and sensitives for the most part, though O'Reilly and Elathan and even Grex were granted the vision – but the great run of the folk did not; hence did spring their fear of their own Ard-rían that you complained of.'

'And that still I complain of – by the gods, that will stop! I will endure much for the sake of this victory – even being Empress if so I must – but I will not be made to endure fear and reverence from my own Kelts . . .' Her eyes danced as she turned to look at him. 'Such is all very well for Keltia, where I am yet Ard-rían and my word is law. But how if the Empress shall disagree with the Emperor? Whose will shall then prevail?'

His hand playfully grazed the side of her jaw in a bladechop, a jesting touch as light as swanskin, his fingers turning to caress her cheek. 'Then we fight it out as

Fians, sword to sword. It will be the honourable thing to do. And more or less an even match.'

'Even! Nay, I shall give you a handicap – ' She was laughing, and Gwydion caught her round the waist and pulled her back against him. They stood a while in silence, watching the moons move across the Criosanna's arc.

'In spite of all,' she said at last, 'I cannot believe it is truly over.'

His mouth moved in the softness of her hair. 'You said it yourself, cariad. Mae'r dial drosodd – vengeance is done with.'

'And not an hour too soon . . . What is to come fears me almost as much as what has gone by. Since we seem to have been forced at the sword's point into an empire we never sought – It will be a tremendous task we undertake together, you and I.'

'Aye so, but we *shall* be together, Aeronwy, and Keltia with us; that is all that matters. As for the rest of it, when one must do a great thing, one grows to the size of it; and such matters very often appear more terrible from without than from within. When we are well into it, I think it will not seem so daunting as now. Still, I have thought, I shall cede Gwynedd formally to Elved, and perhaps yield up the Pendragonship as well, as my term has two years more to run. Have you had any thought as to Keltia?'

She stretched and moved away from him a little. 'Rohan as Regent, to begin with,' she said. 'Then, once our hold on the new Imperium is secure, and alliances are made, and matters settled with Earth and Fomor, and Rohan has established a line of his own, I shall confirm him as Ard-rígh.'

'And have you someone in mind, then, for his queen?'

'Surely I have.' But when he pressed her for a name, she laughed and shook her head and refused to tell; and at last, himself laughing, he went in.

Alone again, Aeron turned to look out once more over

444

the sea. So many there were who had shaped this present moment, and the choice she had just made – so many to whom she owed her thanks, for help and for friendship and even for opposition; but perhaps none had played a greater part than had Haruko. His face seemed to form in the moon-washed waves below. *Ah, Theo, I wonder what you would make of all this coil. Had you not come to Keltia, very like none of this would ever have come to pass. Keltia would be still at odds with Fomor, and with the Coranians, and ignorant of Earth as Earth of us, and Gwydion and I would by now be ruling peacefully over Keltia only, and not an empire in the making. But you changed all that for us forever; whether it be dán or karma, come soon back again, to see what you have helped to make . . .*

The big emerald of the Great Seal of Keltia, flashing in the light from her chamber behind her, caught her eye, and she held up the stone to the two moons. *It must be, and Gwydion has the right of it, as ever – to be Empress of the West, and Emperor, in true fact, and all the change that shall come with it . . . when the Alterator lifts his hand, nothing shall remain as it has been.* The very city below her would feel that change, for it would become the heart and capital of the new empire that would be –

But it was time now to go down. Once more she raised her eyes to the Criosanna, and spoke her thought of the future to the timeless witness that she wanted.

'Queen Rauni of Keltia,' said Aeron aloud. 'In the Gaeloch, the folk will call her Ygrawn.'

(Here ends *The Throne of Scone*, Book III of THE KELTIAD. Book II is *The Copper Crown*; Book I will be called *The Silver Branch*; it will deal with those matters leading up to Aeron's coronation: the wars with Fomor and the Coranians; the feud between Fionnbarr and Bres; the young Aeron; the young Elathan; the treachery of Bres and the vengeance Aeron took upon Bellator.)

# Appendices

# History of the Tuatha De Danaan and the Keltoi

The Tuatha De Danaan, the People of the Goddess Dâna, arrived on Earth, as refugees from a distant star system whose sun had gone nova. They established great city-realms at Atlantis, Lemuria, Nazca, Machu Picchu, and other centres of energy. It was an age of high technology and pure magic: lasers, powered flight in space and in atmosphere, telepathy, telekinesis and the like. There was some minimal contact with the primitive Terran native inhabitants, who, awed, regarded the lordly Danaans as gods from the stars.

After many centuries of peace and growth, social and spiritual deterioration set in: faction fights, perversion of high magical techniques, civil war. The Danaan loyalists withdrew to the strongholds of Atlantis, or Atland as they called it, there to fight their last desperate battle with those of their own people who had turned to dark ways. Atlantis was finally destroyed, in a fierce and terrible battle fought partially from space, and which resulted in a huge earthquake and subsequent geological upheaval that sank the entire island-continent. (The battle and sinking of Atlantis were preserved in folk-myth around the world; obviously the effect on the Earth primitives was considerable.)

The evil Atlanteans, the Telchines, headed off back into space: their descendants would later be heard of as the Coranians. The Danaan survivors made their way as best they could over the terrible seas to the nearest land – Ireland – and to the other Keltic sea-countries on the edge of the European land mass. There had long been Atlantean outposts in these lands, and they made a likely refuge.

But the refugees had yet another battle to fight; with the Fir Bolg and the Fomori, the native tribes currently in occupation of Ireland. Atlantean technology carried the day, however, and the Danaans settled down to rebuild their all-but-lost civilization.

After a long Golden Age, the Danaan peace was shattered by invasion: the Milesians, Kelts from the European mainland. War exploded; the new race was clever, brave, persuasive and quarrelsome. The Danaans, at first victorious in defence, were at last defeated by the strategies of the brilliant Druid Amergin. They conceded possession of Ireland to the sons of Miledh, and obtained sureties of peace.

The peace and amity between Danaans and Milesians lasted many hundreds of years; there was much intermarriage, informational exchange, joint explorative and military expeditions against raiding Fomori and Fir Bolg. Then a period of Milesian distrust turned to outright persecution, and the Danaans began to withdraw to live strictly isolated, although even then there continued to be marriages and friendships and associations. With the coming of Patrick to Ireland, bringing Christianity, the persecutions resumed with redoubled intensity, as Patrick and his monks called upon all to denounce the Danaans as witches and evil sorcerers.

Brendan, a nobleman of the House of Erevan son of Miledh, was also half-Danaan by birth – and more than half one in spirit. His mother was Nia, a Danaan princess, and he had been taught by her in the old ways. He rebelled against the persecutions, the narrow-mindedness and prejudice and condemnation of all the high old knowledge, and he resolved to relearn all the ancient lore, to build ships and take the Danaans back out to the stars, to find a new world where they could live as they pleased. All who felt as Brendan did might go, and did: Druids, priestesses of the Mother, worshippers of the Old Gods and followers of the Old Ways, all now so ruthlessly put down by the Christians.

After much study, instruction, construction and a few short trial runs, Brendan was ready at last, and the Great Emigration began. Following the directions of Barinthus, an old man who was probably the last space voyager left on Earth, Brendan and his followers left the planet. After a two-year search, they discovered a habitable star system a thousand light-years from Terra. He named it New Keltia; eventually Keltia, as it came to be known, would command seven planetary systems and a very sizable sphere of influence.

The emigrations continued in secret over a period of some eight hundred years, with Kelts from every Keltic nation participating in the adventure, and not human Kelts alone; the races known as the merrows and the silkies also joined the migrations.

After the first great voyage, or immram, Brendan himself remained in the new worlds, organizing a government, ordering the continuing immigrations, setting up all the machinery needed to run the society he had dreamed of founding: a society of total equality of gender, age, nationality and religion. He personally established the Order of Druids in New Keltia; his mother, Nia, who left Earth with him, founded the Ban-draoi, an order of priestess-sorceresses.

Brendan, who would come to be venerated by succeeding generations as St Brendan the Astrogator, became the first monarch of Keltia, and his line continues to rule there even now.

By about Terran year 1200, the Keltic population had increased so dramatically (from both a rising birth rate and continued waves of immigration from Earth) that further planetary colonization was needed. The Six Nations were founded, based on the six Keltic nations of Earth: Ireland, Scotland, Wales, Man, Cornwall and Brittany, called in Keltia Erinna, Scota, Kymry, Vannin, Kernow and Brytaned. A ruling council of six viceroys, one from each system, was set up, called the Fáinne – 'The Ring'. The monarchy continued, though the Fáinne had the ultimate sovereign power at this time.

This was the Golden Age of Keltia. The mass emigrations ended at around Terran year 1350, and the dream of Brendan seemed achieved. There was complete equality, as he had intended; a strong central government and representative local governments; the beginnings of a peerage democracy; great advances in magic, science and art.

It could not last, of course. By Terran year 1700, increasingly vocal separatist movements sprang up in each nation, and, a hundred years later, the Archdruid of the time, Edeyrn, saw in the unrest the chance to further his own power, and the power of the Druid Order. A fiercely ambitious and unquestionably brilliant man, Edeyrn succeeded in engineering the discrediting and ultimate dissolution of the Fáinne, in forcing the monarchy into hiding, and in installing those Druids loyal to him as magical dictators on all levels. Civil war broke out all over Keltia, and the realm was polarized by the conflict.

This was the Druid Theocracy and Interregnum, which was to endure for nearly two hundred unhappy years. Edeyrn and his Druids were joined by many politically ambitious and discontented noble houses, who saw in the upheaval a chance for their own advancement.

There was of course a fierce and equally powerful resistance, as many Druids remained loyal to the truths of their order, and joined forces with the Ban-draoi, the magical order of priestesses, the Fianna, the Bardic Association and some of the oldest and noblest Keltic families.

This resistance was called the Counterinsurgency, and it opposed Edeyrn and his Druids with strength, resource and cleverness for two centuries. Consistently outwitting the aims of the Theocracy, the loyalists managed to preserve the fabric of true Keltic society. Through the efforts of the Bardic Association, they also succeeded in salvaging most of the important lore, science, art and records of the centuries of Keltia's settlement, and the records from Earth before that.

The terrors of the Theocracy raged on for two hundred years, with the balance continually shifting between Theocracy and Counterinsurgency. The general population was sorely torn, but most did in fact support the loyalists, in their hearts if not in their outward actions. Then full-scale alien invasion, by the races called by the Kelts Fomori and Fir Bolg after their old Earth enemies, hit Keltia, causing enormous destruction and loss of life. But even in the face of this appalling new threat, Edeyrn continued to dominate, and some even said he was responsible for the invasions. Though he himself was by now ancient beyond all right expectation, his adopted heir Owain served as his sword-arm, and Owain was as twisted as ever Edeyrn was.

Though their most immediately pressing need was to repel the Fomori and Fir Bolg invaders, the Kelts had first to break free of the grip of the Theocracy; and in the midst of that chaos, a mighty figure began to emerge.

Arthur of Arvon, a minor lordling of a hitherto minor noble house of the Kymry, rallied boldly the forces of the Counterinsurgency. Arthur proved to be an inspired leader, and more importantly, a military genius, and he quickly smashed Owain's Druids in the Battle of Moytura. The Theocracy, its military power broken, caved in, and Arthur was named Rex Bellorum, War-Chief, by the hastily reconstituted Fáinne and the newly restored monarch Uthyr. Arthur then led the Keltic forces out against the invaders; the aliens were not prepared for such a concerted counterattack, and Arthur succeeded in utterly crushing the invasion.

But King Uthyr had died in battle. Arthur married the royal heir, Gweniver, and with her assumed the sovereignty of Keltia by acclamation. The wars behind him, at least for the present, Arthur turned his genius to political and social reform, establishing elective bodies of legislators, the Royal Senate and Assembly, restoring the House of Peers, formulating a new judicial system on the remains of the old brehon laws, and laying the groundwork for a standing battle force. He commanded a purge of the Druid Order, setting his closest adviser and old teacher, Merlynn Llwyd, to undertake the task, and he gave new power and prestige to the loyal orders of the Ban-draoi, the Fianna and the Bardic Association.

Arthur and Gweniver reigned brilliantly and successfully for nearly fifty years, and had two children, Arawn and Arwenna. Then, in Terran year 2047, he was betrayed by his own nephew, Mordryth, and the infamous Owain's heir, Malgan. Their treachery let in the invading Coranians, descendants of the Telchines, who had evolved into a race of sorcerous marauders whose savagery made the Fomori and Fir Bolg look like sheep. This was Arthur's first chance to test his reforms, and he was well aware that it might be his last also. He dealt with Mordryth and Malgan, then led a space armada against the Coranians, with devastating success. Tragically, he disappeared in the climactic battle, sending his flagship *Prydwen* against the Coranian flagship and taking both vessels and all aboard them into hyperspace forever. His last message to his people was that he would come again, when he was needed

In the absence of proof positive of Arthur's death, he is still King of Kelts, and all succeeding monarchs had held their sovereignty by his courtesy and have made their laws in his name . . . for who knows when Arthur the King might not return?

The monarchy, after Arthur's disappearance, became a Regency, the only one in Keltic history. Arthur's sister Morgan, his wife Gweniver, and his mother Ygrawn ruled jointly, until such time as Prince Arawn should be old enough to take the crown.

All three women were strong characters, skilled in magic, but Arthur's sister Morgan, called Morgan Magistra, was the greatest magician Keltia would ever see.

After taking counsel with the Ban-draoi, Merlynn's newly rehabilitated Druids, the Fianna and the Bardic Association, and with her own co-Regents, Morgan undertook the immense achievement of the raising of the Curtain Wall. There was no other feat like it, even back to the days of the High Atlanteans.

The Curtain Wall is a gigantic force-field, electromagnetic in nature and maintained by psionic energies; it completely surrounds and conceals Keltic space, hiding suns, planets, satellites, energy waves, everything. Once outside its perimeters, it is as if Keltia does not exist. Space is not physically blocked off, and radio waves and the like are bent round the Wall, but any ship attempting to cross the region is shunted into certain corridors of electromagnetic flux that feed into the Morimaruse, the Dead Sea of space, and now no one goes that way, ever.

\* \* \*

So the Keltic worlds and their peoples became a half-legend of the galaxy, a star-myth to be told to children or to anthropologists. But behind the Curtain Wall, the Regency carried on Arthur's work, and when in time Arawn became King, he proved almost as gifted as his parents. The dynasty he founded was followed in peaceful succession by the closely related royal house of Gwynedd, and that by the royal house of Douglas.

For fifteen hundred years Keltia prospered in her isolation – not a total isolation even then, for still there were out-Wall trading planets and military actions, and ambassadors were still received.

In the Terran year 2693, the Crown passed to the House of Aoibhell. Direct descendants of Brendan himself, the Aoibhells have held the monarchy in a grip of findruinna for eight hundred years, according to the law of Keltia that the Copper Crown descends to the eldest child of the sovereign, whether man or woman.

In the Earth year 3512, the probe ship *Sword* arrives in Keltic space. The Ard-rían Aeron Aoibhell, seventeenth member of her House to occupy the Throne of Scone, determines on an alliance with the Terran Federacy, and Keltia is plunged into war as a result of it. The tale of that war, and what followed, is told in *The Copper Crown*.

# Glossary

*(Words are Keltic unless otherwise noted.)*

**Abred:** 'The Path of Changes'; the visible world of everyday existence, within the sphere of which one's various lives are lived

**aircar:** small personal transport used on Keltia worlds

**alanna:** 'child', 'little one'; Erinnach endearment

**amadaun:** 'fool'

**amylle:** decorative water plant native to the planet Sannox

**an-da-shalla:** 'The Second Sight'; Keltic talent of precognition

**anderë:** (Hastaic) suffix denoting nobility used with a woman's name

**An Lasca:** 'The Whip'; the ionized northwest wind at Caerdroia

**anwyl, anwylyd:** 'sweetheart', Kymric endearment

**Annwn:** (pron. *Annoon*) the Keltic religion's equivalent of the Underworld, ruled over by Arawn, Lord of the Dead

**ap:** Kymric, 'son of'

**Ard-rían, Ard-rígh:** 'High Queen', 'High King'; title of the Keltic sovereign

**Ard-r*í*anachtas, Ard-ríghachtas:** 'high queenship', 'high kingship'

**astar,** pl. **astari:** gold currency unit of the Cabiri Imperium

**athiarna:** 'High One'; Fianna form of address to a superior officer

**aurichalcum:** (Hastaic) a type of metal-stone mined on the planet Alphor and used extensively in building there

**ban-a-tigh:** woman householder (*far-a-tigh*, male householder)

**Ban-dia:** the Mother, the Great Goddess

**Ban-draoi:** lit., 'woman-druid'; Keltic order of priestess-sorceresses in the service of the Mother Goddess

**bards:** Keltic order of poets, chaunters and loremasters

**Barna-baoghaill:** 'Gap of Danger'; historically, that part of a nation's borders where attack is most likely to come; by extension, the gap in the Curtain Wall (q.v.) created by the sorcery of the traitor princess Arianeira of Gwynedd

**barra-glaed:** war-shout given by army as it attacks

**Bawn of Keltia:** the space enclosed within the Curtain Wall (*bawn*: the area enclosed by the outer barbican defenses of a fortress)

**bee-bird:** on Fomor, name for the common hummingbird

**Beltain:** festival of the beginning of summer, celebrated on 1 May

**bodach:** term of opprobrium or commiseration, depending on circumstances

**braud:** Kymric, 'brother'

**brehons:** Keltic lawgivers and judges

**bruidean:** inn or waystation, maintained by local authorities, where any traveller, of whatever rank or resources, is entitled to claim free hospitality


**Cabiri:** (Hastaic) Coranian magical order of adepts, similar to the Druids or the Ban-draoi

**cam-anfa:** 'crooked storm'; violent localized cyclonic disturbance of the sort known on Earth as a tornado

**camur:** feral scavenger canine; usually runs in packs

**cantrip:** very small, simple spell or minor magic

**caoine:** 'keen'; lament or dirge of mourning, usually sung (cf. *coronach*, a lament that is played only, on the pipes)

**cariad:** 'heart', 'beloved'; Kymric endearment

**carlin:** shrew, hag

**cath,** pl. **catha:** military unit of 5,000 warriors

**ceili:** (pron. *kay-lee*) a dancing-party or ball; any sort of revelry

**chai:** (Japannic) beverage brewed from any of several different sorts of dried leaves or herbs in infusion

**chori:** (Hastaic) broad-leaved tree native to the planet Alphor (*alizachori*: tame white birds that feed off such trees, often found in formal gardens)

**Chriesta tighearna!:** lit., 'Lord Christ!'; name of the Christian god, used as an expletive

**cithere:** seventeen-stringed lap harp or lyre common throughout the Imperial worlds

**cithóg:** 'port', as on board ship (cf. *deosil*)

**clochan:** dome- or yurt-like structure used by the Fianna in the field

**coelbren:** magical alphabet used by Druids

**coire ainsec:** 'the undry cauldron of guestship'; the obligation, in law, to provide hospitality, shelter or sanctuary to any who claim it

**Coranians:** ruling race of the Imperium, hereditary enemies of the Kelts; they are the descendants of the Telchines, as the Kelts are the descendants of the Danaans

**Crann Tarith:** 'Fiery Branch'; the token of war across Keltia. Originally a flaming branch or cross; now, by extension, the alarm or call to war broadcast on all planets

**Cremave:** the clearing-stone of the royal line of St Brendan

**Criosanna:** 'The Woven Belts'; the rings that circle the planet Tara

**crochan:** magical healing-pool that can cure almost any injury, provided the spinal column has not been severed and the brain and bone marrow are undamaged

**crossic:** unit of Keltic money (small gold coin)

**cumal:** female serf, bondswoman; used as fem. of *bodach*

**curragh:** small leather-hulled boat rowed with oars

**cursal:** very fast light warship of the Keltic starfleet

**Curtain Wall:** the artificial energy barrier that encircles and conceals the seven Keltic star-systems (also known as the Pale)

**Cwn Annwn:** (pron. *Coon Annoon*) in Keltic religion, the Hounds of Hell; the red-eared, white-coated dogs belonging to Arawn Lord of the Dead, that hunt down and destroy guilty souls

**Cymynedd:** in Keltic mythology, the Last Battle, to be fought by gods and mortals both upon the battleground of Achateny, the Field of Fire; it will decide the fate of the universe between good and evil


**daer-fudir:** 'outlaw'; a legal term, used in banishment of a malefactor

**dán:** 'doom', fated karma

**deosil:** on board ship, the starboard side (cf. *cithóg*)

**dermasealer:** skinfuser; a medical tool that is used to repair flesh lacerations by means of laser sutures

**derwyth:** Kymric, 'oak-tree'

**dichtal:** bardic finger-language, often used as secret code

**Dragon Kinship:** magical-military order of Keltic adepts

**Draíochtas:** generic term for the body of arcane knowledge shared by adepts of the Ban-draoi and Druid orders

**Druids:** magical order of Keltic sorcerer-priests

**dubhachas:** 'gloom'; melancholy characterized by causeless depression and inexpressible longing for unnameable things

**dubh-cosac:** stimulant herb usually taken in powder form

**dúchas:** lordship or holding; usually carries a title with it

**dûhín:** (Lakhaz) the telempathic, tree-dwelling bipeds native to the Great Forest on Fomor

**dún:** a stronghold of the Sidhe, the Shining Ones (also *liss* or *rath*)

**dwnedau:** Kymric, stanzas of poem or chaunt (sing., dwned)

**earth-nuts:** any of several species of underground hard-shelled fruit

**Englic:** tongue of Terran Federacy; unofficial galactic Common Tongue

**éraic:** 'blood-price'; payment exacted for a murder by the kin of the victim

**-fach** (masc., **-bach**): Kymric, suffix added to a woman's name to denote affection

**fágáil:** 'bequest'; the parting-gift of the Sidhe to a mortal they have befriended

**faha:** courtyard or enclosed space in a castle complex or encampment

**Fáinne:** 'The Ring'; the six system viceroys of Keltia

**falair:** winged horse whose species is native to the Erinna system

**fetch:** the visible form taken by the spirit-guardian of a Keltic family

**Fianna:** Keltic officer class; order of military supremacy

**fidchell:** chess-style game

**findruinna:** superhard, silvery metal used in swords, armour and the like

**Fionnasa:** feast of the god Fionn, celebrated on 29 September

**fíor-comlainn:** 'truth-of-combat'; legally binding trial by personal combat

**fith-fath:** spell of shapeshifting or glamourie; magical illusion

**Fomori:** ancient enemies of the Kelts; sing., **Fomor** or **Fomorian**

**Fragarach:** 'The Answerer'. Also translated 'Retaliator'.

Historically, the magical sword borne by Arthur of Arvon; also, the moon-size laser cannon emplacement that defends the Throneworld system of Tara

**fudir:** 'criminal', 'outcast'; term of opprobrium


**Gabha-Bheil:** 'trial by Beli'; form of truth-test that requires the subject to walk barefoot through fire

**galláin:** 'foreigners'; sing., **Gall**; generic term for all non-Kelts

**galloglass:** Keltic foot-soldier

**gauran:** plough-beast similar to ox or bullock

**geis** pl. **geisa:** prohibition or moral injunction placed upon a person

**glaive:** (from Erinnach, *claideamh*) lightsword; laser weapon used throughout Keltia

**goleor:** 'in great numbers, an overabundance'; Englic word *galore* is derived from it

**grafaun:** double-bladed war axe

**gríanan:** 'sun-place'; solar, private chamber

**gúna:** generic name for various styles of long robe or gown


**hai atton:** 'heigh to us'; the horn-cry that rallies an army

**Hastaic:** the language of the Cabiri Empire

**hydromel:** sweet, extraordinarily intoxicating honey-wine


**iconoscope:** tube-shaped optical toy, activated by telepathic imagery, that shows constantly changing visual patterns

**immram:** 'voyage'; the great migrations from Earth to Keltia

**innaga:** (Hastaic) 'daughter', 'child'; endearment used by family or friends

**ion-besom:** machine for cleaning carpets, floors, etc., by suction of reversed ion polarities

**Justiciary:** voluntary interstellar court, located on the neutral planet Ganaster, to which systems may make petition for arbitrated settlement of grievances short of war; all participants must agree beforehand to be bound by the decision

**kenning:** telepathic technique originally developed (and used almost exclusively) by Ban-draoi and Druids

**kern:** Keltic starfleet crewman

**lai:** unit of distance measurement, equal to approximately one-half mile

**Lakhaz:** the language of the Fomori

**lithfaen:** 'lodestone'; quartz crystal, piezoelectrically charged, that can be keyed to various objects and acts as a homing device

**lonna:** light hydrofoil-type vessel used by Keltic navy

**machair:** 'sea-meadow'; wide grassland tracts bordering on the sea and running down to the high-water mark

**maenor:** hereditary dwelling place, usually a family seat

**marana:** 'meditation'; thought-trance of Keltic sorcerers

**Marbh-draoi:** 'Death-druid'; Jaun Akhera's epithet among Kelts

**merrows:** (Na Moruadha) the sea people originally native to Kernow

**mether:** four-cornered drinking-vessel, usually of wood or pottery

**Morann:** arid volcanic upland plain on the planet Kholco

**Morar-mhara:** 'lord of the sea'; title of chieftain of the Moruadha

**Morimaruse:** vast electromagnetic void; the Dead Sea of space

**nemeton:** ceremonial stone circle or henge

**ní, nighean:** 'daughter of'

**ollave:** a master-bard; by extension, anyone with supreme command of an art

**pastai:** small handmeal; a turnover consisting of a pastry crust filled with meat or vegetables

**Pheryllt:** class of master-Druids; they serve as instructors at the Druid schools

**piast:** a large amphibious water-beast found in deepwater lakes on the planets Erinna and Scota; the species was known to Terrans as the Loch Ness Monster

**pig-i'-the-wood:** children's game in which those in a 'safe' place are lured out by those who are 'it'

**pishogue:** small magic; cantrip

**púca:** mischievous, sometimes malevolent spirit of darkness; also, *cap.*, a spirit-dog, terrifying of appearance, the size of a pony, black-coated, with flame-red eyes

**quaich:** low, wide, double-handled drinking-vessel

**rann:** chanted verse stanza used in magic; a spell of any sort

**rechtair:** steward of royal or noble household; title of planetary governors; title of Chancellor of Exchequer on Keltic High Council

**ressaldar-general:** highest rank in Terran military establishment

**rígh-domhna:** members of the Keltic royal family, as reckoned from a common ancestor, who may (theoretically, at least) be elected to the Sovereignty

**saille:** Erinnach, 'willow'

**saining:** rite of Keltic baptism

**saining-pool:** another name for crochan (q.v.)

**Salamandri:** the Salamander-race, Firefolk; reptiloid race that inhabits the planet Kholco

**Samhain:** (pron. *Sah-win*) festival of the beginning of

winter and start of the New Year, celebrated on 31 October (Great Samhain) and continuing until 11 November (Little Samhain)

**schiltron:** military formation favoured by Fianna; very compact and organized, it is extremely difficult to break

**sea-pig:** semi-intelligent aquatic mammal, friendly, noisy and playful

**sgian:** small black-handled knife universally worn in Keltia, usually in boot-top

**shakla:** chocolate-tasting beverage brewed with water from the berries of the brown ash; drunk throughout Keltia as a caffeine-based stimulant

**Sidhe:** (pron. *Shee*) the Shining Ones; a race of possibly divine or immortal beings

**silkies:** (Sluagh-rón) the seal-folk originally native to the Out Isles

**Six Nations:** the six star systems of Keltia (excluding the Throneworld system of Tara), in order of their founding, they are Erinna, Kymry, Scota, Kernow, Vannin and Brytaned (or Arvor)

**skiath:** 'shield'; a force-field/pressure suit worn in hard vacuum, it generates for its wearer all necessary oxygen, gravity and protection against harmful or poisonous atmospheres

**slán-lus:** 'heal-herb'; specific often used in herbal compounds

**sluagh:** a hosting, as of an army

**Solas Sidhe:** 'The Faery Fire'; a natural phenomenon, similar to the will-o'-the-wisp but occurring over rocky ground, usually seen in the spring and fall; also, a magical wall of fire created by sorcerers as a means of attack or defence

**Spearhead:** the polestar of Tara

**Stonerows:** the lower circles of Caerdroia

**talpa:** blind, blunt-snouted digger animal native to the planet Kernow

**Tanist, Tanista:** designated heir of line to the Keltic throne

**Taoiseach:** the Prime Minister of Keltia

**telyn:** Kymric lap-harp

**thrawn:** stubborn, unreasonably perverse

**tinna-galach:** 'bright-fire'; the will-o'-the-wisp, occurring over marshy ground; especially noted for its appearances in the great marshlands of Gwenn-Estrad, on the planet of Arvor in the Brytaned system

**tinnscra:** marriage-portion given to a man or a woman by their families, clann, or (in the cases of royalty or high nobility) the reigning monarch (*tinnól*: the marriage-gift each partner gives to the other)

**tirr:** a cloaking effect, part magical, part mechanical in nature

**traha:** 'arrogance'; wanton pride, hubris

**usqueba:** 'water of life'; whisky, generally unblended

**vitriglass:** crystalline substance, its molecular structure reinforced by metallic ions; used in starship viewports for its extreme hardness and resistance to shattering

**water-acanth:** red-fronded riparian fern used as a decorative planting

**waterblanket:** cooling-device used by the Salamandri; large sheets of multilayered plastiweave linen, with hollow channels quilted into the layers through which water circulates to carry away excess heat

**water-elm:** medicinal herb with stimulant properties

**Yamazai:** 'Amazon'; warrior-woman race of a matriarchal system, whose homeworld is the planet Aojun

**Yr Mawreth:** 'The Highest'; Kymric name for Kelu or Artzan Janco, the One God who is above all gods

# Keltic Orders and Societies

## The Dragon Kinship

The Dragon Kinship is a magical and military order of adepts, under the authority of the Pendragon of Lirias. Members are the most accomplished adepts of all Keltia, elected strictly on the basis of ability. All professions and ranks are equally eligible.

All those of the Kinship are equal under the Pendragon; no formalities are observed, no titles are used, no precedence of rank is followed. The only other office is Summoner; chosen by the Pendragon, this officer is what the name implies – the person responsible for calling the Kinship together on the Pendragon's order.

The Pendragon is chosen by his or her predecessor to serve for a term of seven years; this choice must be confirmed by a simple-majority public vote and may be renewed only by a unanimous secret vote of the entire membership (not surprisingly, such a renewal has never taken place). At the moment, Gwydion Prince of Dôn is Pendragon; he was preceded by a farmer from the Morbihan, a poetess from Vannin, a weaver from the Out Isles and a bard from Cashel.

To call someone 'Kin to the Dragon' is the highest tribute possible. Most members are public about it, some prefer to keep it a secret, but all possess a certain unmistakable and indefinable air of apartness and assurance. It is a severely demanding society: More than any other power, save only the Crown itself, the Dragon Kinship is responsible for the well-being, the welfare and the quality of life and spirit of Keltia, on all levels. As a magical order, the Kinship takes precedence over all other factions: much of its membership, in fact, comprises members of other orders such as the Druids, Ban-draoi or the Bardic Association. It is truly a cross-section of Keltic society, for it reaches from royalty to farmers to artists to techs to soldiers to artisans to householders. There are no age limits either upper or lower, and no entry requirement save the possession of psionic Gift.

That Gift must include all psionic talents, and feature supreme proficiency in at least one: healing of body or mind; seership; broad-band telepathy, either receptor or sender; magical warfare – attack, defence or strategic; energy control; psychokinetics; retrocognition or precognition; shapeshifting; transmutation; pure magic; or any other magical discipline or talent. Members are recruited through observation and direct approach by a current Dragon. There are generally no more than ten thousand members at any one time, though in time of war or other great emergency the membership may be increased, if acceptable candidates are available.

The Dragon Kinship have their own brugh in Turusachan and rich lands on Brytaned and Dyved; their main training establishment, Caer Coronach, is in a remote part of Caledon. A Dragon is by tradition named the sovereign's Magical Champion, as a Fian is always named Military Champion.

## The Druid Order

The Druid Order is, with the Ban-draoi, the oldest order in Keltia, founded by St Brendan himself in the direct tradition of the Terran Druids. The Order is limited to men only, who may present themselves for membership beginning at thirteen years of age. As with the other orders, preliminary training is begun as soon as a child begins to show promise of talent, sometimes even as early as three or four years old.

The Druids are an immensely powerful body; they concern themselves with sorcery and politics, not necessarily always in that ranking. There are three degrees of Druidry: Novice, Ovate, Master. Head of the Order is the Archdruid, who is chosen by his predecessor upon his deathbed, and who then rules until his own death. The Archdruid sits in the House of Peers as Lord of Carnac, and is a member of the High Council which advises the monarch.

The training is long and intensive: all forms of magic, lore, herbalism, alphabets, correspondence, alchemy, psionics, chants, music, healing, seership, trance mediumship, and other occult disciplines. A fully qualified Druid is a master of magic, and very few can manage to withstand him when he puts forth his power.

There have been a few doubtful passages in the history of the Order, most notably the appalling two-hundred-year period known to infamy as the Druid Theocracy and Interregnum.

At a time of unusual political polarity and turmoil, the Archdruid, a brilliant and devious man called Edeyrn, saw in the divisiveness a chance to seize power for his Order – which is to say, for himself. A series of battles and massacres called the Druids' Wars followed, effectively demolishing all semblance of civil order in Keltia, and Edeyrn installed himself as magical overlord. He was supported in this by his fellow renegades and quite a few equally opportunistic noble houses. He was opposed by the remnants of the Fáinne, the Ban-draoi, the Bardic Association, the Fianna, most of the noble houses and many of his own Druids who had remained loyal to the teachings of their Order. This opposition was the Counterinsurgency, and they were very, very strong.

This horrific state of affairs existed for nearly two

centuries, with the balance of power continually shifting from one side to the other, until the invasion of Keltia by Fomori and Fir Bolg space fleets resulted in enormous destruction and panic. The Theocracy, now led by the ancient Edeyrn's heir Owain, tried to make a deal with the invaders but failed, opening the way only for full-scale war.

Arthur of Arvon, himself a Druid, rallied the Counter-insurgency in one great desperate throw and defeated Owain's forces at the Battle of Moytura. With the help of his chief teacher and adviser Merlynn Llwyd, who assumed the Archdruidship, Arthur went on to pull Keltia together and become King of Kelts, as has been told elsewhere. But throughout his long and glorious reign, Druid precepts remained Arthur's guide to action.

The Druids, under Merlynn Llwyd, began a period of severe purge and purification, and eventually were restored to their former high standards.

The current Archdruid is Teilo ap Bearach; the ranks of Masterdruids include Gwydion Prince of Dôn, Aeron's uncles Deian and Estyn, and her cousins Alasdair and Dion.

The Druid Order has a brugh of its own in Turusachan, and its chief college is at Dinas Affaraon on Gwynedd.


## The Ban-draoi

Equal in rank and antiquity with the Druid Order, the Ban-draoi are the evolvement of the incomparably ancient Goddess-priestesses of the most deep-rooted Keltic tradition. The Order was founded in Keltia by St Brendan's mother, Nia daughter of Brigit, who many said was of divine parentage herself, and who became the ancestress of the House of Dâna in Keltia.

Divine or not, Nia of the Tuatha De Danaan was brilliant, beautiful, foresighted, and incredibly gifted in magic, and the Order she established had power, respect and influence right from the start.

Open only to women, the Order of the Ban-draoi (the name is Erinnach for, literally, 'woman-druid') has as its chief purpose the worship of the Lady, the Mother Goddess; but they are sorceresses as well as priestesses, and their magic matches that of the Druids spell for spell. All women, whether initiates or not, participate to some degree in the ways of the Ban-draoi, as do all men in the ways of the Druids, since both systems are at their deepest hearts paths of worship. But the mysteries of the Ban-draoi are the Mysteries of the Mother, the things of most awe in all the Keltic worlds. Priestess or not, every Keltic woman shares in this awe, and every Keltic man respects it.

The Ban-draoi were never so politically oriented as the Druids, but when the Theocracy began, they became the chief focus of the Counterinsurgency and gave the resistance movement much of its force. Later, Arthur's mother Ygrawn and sister Morgan, and his wife Gweniver, were all three high priestesses of the Order, and gave him invaluable aid in his task of defeating both Druids and aliens. After Arthur's departure, it was Morgan who raised the tremendous energy barrier of the Curtain Wall, thus protecting Keltia from the outside worlds for fifteen centuries.

Obliged by circumstances to assume a critical political role, the Ban-draoi adapted, and have retained a position of political pre-eminence down to the present day. Aeron Aoibhell holds the rank of Domina, or a High Priestess of the Order, as does her sister Ríoghnach.

The training of a Ban-draoi (the word is both singular and plural) is as intensive as that of a Druid, and includes the same body of magical knowledge. Due to the heritage of Nia, however, it also emphasizes many branches of arcane lore known only to the priestesses. It is not so hierarchical as the Druid Order; an aspirant to the Ban-draoi is initiated as a priestess once her training is judged complete. If she wishes, and if her teachers agree, she may then seek the rank of high priestess, which carries with it the deepest knowledge of all and the title Domina.

The Chief Priestess is elected for life by a conclave of all the high priestesses; she bears the title Magistra, sits on the monarch's High Council, and sits in the House of Peers as Lady of Elphame. The office is currently held by Ffaleira nighean Enfail.

The Ban-draoi have a brugh of their own within the walls of Turusachan, and their chief training school is at Scartanore on Erinna.

## The Fianna

The Fianna is a purely military organization, comprising the most skilled and talented warriors of Keltia. To become a Fian, a candidate must pass a series of incredibly rigorous tests of his or her warrior skills: a test of knowledge, in which he or she must demonstrate mastery of a specific body of lore; a test of soul, in which the candidate must face psionic examination by a qualified inquisitioner, who may be Druid, Ban-draoi or Dragon; and finally a formal combat with a chosen Fian of the First Rank.

So rigorous are these tests, in fact, that it seems astounding that anyone at all ever becomes a Fian; but many do indeed succeed, and rightly are respected. Membership is open to all ranks, ages and professions; candidates must be at least eighteen years of age, for physical reasons, though training may often begin at age six or seven if a child shows talent.

Skills a Fian must learn include all forms of combat and martial arts: sword-mastery, both classic and lightsword techniques; fencing; archery; wrestling; four forms of unarmed combat approximating to Terran judo, karate, kung-fu and foot-fighting; boxing; riding; marksmanship with all forms of weapons; tracking; running; spear-throwing; and the piloting of all types of vehicles from starship to snow-yacht.

The test of knowledge requires extensive study in the fields of history, both Keltic and Terran; literature; brehon law; the arts; heraldry and genealogy; politics; and science, both pure and applied. Fians are expected to be able to speak all seven Keltic tongues, Latin, and as many alien tongues as possible (the minimum is three, and Hastaic, the Imperial tongue, is mandatory). In addition, Fians are taught the secret Keltic battle-language, Shelta Thari.

The test of soul could well be called an ordeal. It involves deep-trance, telepathy, and astral travel, and no candidate, whether pass or fail, will ever speak about it afterward.

The final formal combat is determined on an individual basis by the Captain-General of the Fianna; choice of weapon and combat form will vary, but there is always one armed and one unarmed duel for each candidate. The Captain-General also selects the First-Rank Fian who will oppose the prospective member. No allowance is made for sex or physical size: Women, for instance, are expected to know how to defeat a male warrior who vastly outmeasures them in height, weight and strength.

The Fianna have their own training establishment, Caer Artos in Arvon, and their quarters in Turusachan, the Commandery, are directly across from the royal palace. Military champions for trial-by-combat are always selected from the ranks of the Fianna; the Royal Champion is always a First-Rank Fian, and the monarch's personal bodyguard is made up of Fians.

The current Captain-General of the Fianna is Dónal mac Avera.

## The Bardic Association

The Bardic Association has a long and honourable history. From its founding in Keltic year 347 by Plenyth ap Alun, the society of bards has held without stain to its high principles and rigorous requirements, and bards of all degrees have traditionally been granted hospitality, honour and semi-royal precedence throughout Keltia.

Although bards receive a good deal of magical training in the course of their studies, it is not emphasized; the primary training of bards is words. Any and all literary disciplines: poetry, sung or spoken; satire; history; sagas; ballads; myths and legends; drama; genealogy; precedent – all belong to the bardic tradition. Unlike magical schooling, the bardic discipline may begin at any age; there are records of peers in old age handing over their titles to their heirs and going to the bardic colleges to end their lives in study.

Bardic aspirants spend five years as apprentices; five years as journeymen; five years as institutional bards. Having completed the fifteen-year training programme (which does not preclude other study; Gwydion of Dôn, for instance, is both Druid and master-bard), they are then permitted to take the examination for the rank of ollave, or master-bard, if they so wish. If they are successful in this bid, they may then present themselves as master-bards of the schools and seek the very highest employment. Not all bards choose to seek the status of ollave, however; and many do not remain even to become institutional bards. Any bard who has successfully passed the examination at the end of the journeyman term may serve as a teacher of children, and many choose to leave at this level to work in such capacity.

Bards of all degrees, whether journeyman, institutional bard or ollave, are much in demand throughout Keltia; they are employed by royal or noble families, or by merely wealthy families, as poet of the house and artist in residence, encouraged to recite the old lore and to compose creatively on their own. Exceptional bards of high degree are often entrusted with delicate diplomatic or social missions, including – not to put too fine a point on it – spying; though the last is done only in cases of the gravest national importance, for if too many bards did it, all bards would be suspect. The Ard-rían Aeron makes great use of bards, and gives them greater honour than they have had from the monarchs of Keltia for some years.

Bards have by law and custom several odd privileges: A bard may demand the nightmeal from anyone, in exchange for a song or a poem; the royal ollave (or ríogh-bardáin) has the right to a seat at the high table in Mi-Cuarta not more than seven places from the monarch's right hand; an ollave is permitted by law to wear six colours in his cloak (only the reigning monarch may wear more – seven, if desired).

The Chief of Bards is chosen by a vote of senior masters; he serves until death or retirement, and sits on the monarch's High Council. Chief of Bards at present is Idris ap Caswyn.

The Bardic Association has a brugh of its own, Seren Beirdd – 'Star of the Bards' – within the walls of Turusachan, and the Bardic Colleges are located on Powys.

# Partial Chronology

3400  Fionnbarr born at Caerdroia
3405  Bres born at Tory
3434  Emer born at Coldharbor
3438  Haruko born at Old Kyoto
3442  Quarrel of Bres and Fionnbarr
3455  Fionnbarr and Emer marry
3467  Jaun Akhera born at Escal-dun
      Roderick born at Kinloch Arnoch
3470  Gwydion and Arianeira born at Caer Dathyl
3472  Desmond and Slaine born at Drumhallow
3473  Elathan born at Tory
3475  Aeron born at Caerdroia
      Morwen born at Kinloch Arnoch
3476  Rohan born at Caerdroia
3477  Ríoghnach born at Caerdroia
3479  Fionnbarr's reign begins (death of Lasairían)
3480  O'Reilly born at Sandiangeles
3482  Kieran and Declan born at Caerdroia
      Melangell born at Bryn Alarch
3489  Fionnuala born at Caerdroia
3509  Aeron's reign begins (deaths of Fionnbarr, Emer and Roderick)
3512  Arrival of Earth ship *Sword* in Keltic space

Dates given here are in Earth Reckoning (A.D.); to find the date A.B. (*Anno Brendani*) or A.C.C. (*Anno Celtiae Conditae*), subtract 453 and 455, respectively.

The comparative ages can be misleading, as Terran lifespans average 100–110 years, while those of Kelts, Coranians and Fomori run to 160–200. Therefore, the 'younger generation' of protagonists (Aeron, Elathan, Jaun Akhera, et al) are very young indeed.

## Note on Age

The average Keltic lifespan is 160–175 years, and many individuals reach, even surpass, the two-century mark in full possession of their faculties both physical and mental. Physical development occurs at the same rate as in shorter-lived races, with full physical maturity coming between the ages of 18 and 21.

There is no single legal majority age. At 18, all Kelts, both male and female, are liable for military service; the mandatory term is three years. They may also vote in local elections and assume minor titles.

At 21, citizens may marry with consent (though marriage at this age is almost unheard-of – thus the scandal of Emer ní Kerrigan's elopement with Prince Fionnbarr as he then was; most marriages occur at around ages 30–35), vote in planetary elections, and hold minor public office.

At 27, Kelts may marry without consent, vote in major (system and national) elections, hold major public office, and succeed to major titles.

And no one under the age of 33 may hold the Copper Crown unregented.

# Note on Sources

Although THE KELTIAD is for the most part what we are pleased to call fiction, I owe a debt beyond acknowledgement to those sources from whom I have systematically – in the great Celtic tradition of cattle-raiding – pillaged elements to serve my story. For those readers who might be interested in these majestic, too-much-forgotten tales, or the work of the dedicated scholars who preserved them, here is a list of some of those books that served me best and longest:

*Trioedd Ynys Prydein* (The Welsh Triads), Rachel Bromwich, ed.
*Popular Tales of the West Highlands*, J. F. Campbell
*Celtic Invocations*, Alexander Carmichael
*Shadow and Evil in Fairytales*, Marie-Louise von Franz
*The White Goddess*, Robert Graves
*Visions and Beliefs in the West of Ireland*, Lady Gregory
*Old Celtic Romances*, P. W. Joyce
*A Social History of Ancient Ireland*, P. W. Joyce
*Legendary Fictions of the Irish Celts*, Patrick Kennedy
*The Mabinogion*
*Celtic Folklore*, John Rhys
*The Hibbert Lectures*, John Rhys
*Atlantean Traditions in Ancient Britain*, Anthony Roberts
*Myths and Legends of the Irish Race*, T. W. Rolleston
*The Tribal System in Wales*, Frederic Seebohm
*Celtic Scotland*, W. F. Skene
*Magic Arts in Celtic Britain*, Lewis Spence
*The Mysteries of Britain*, Lewis Spence
*Celtic Myth & Legend, Poetry & Romance*, Charles Squire

*Ancient Legends of Ireland*, Lady Wilde
*Folklore in the English and Scottish Ballads*,
   L. C. Wimberly
*Irish Folk Stories and Fairy Tales*, W. B. Yeats
*Mythologies*, W. B. Yeats

My chiefest borrowing is of course the famous poem attributed to the Welsh bard Taliesin, *Preiddu Annwn* (The Spoils of Annwn). For the version that appears in these pages, I used phrasing from the translations of Graves, Rhys, Skene and Squire (his translation a collation of itself), did some creative translating of my own and invented the rest to fit the demands of the action.

The other major borrowing I should like to acknowledge is another poem of Taliesin's, by way of the *Red Book of Hergest*, called *Câd Goddeu* (The Battle of the Trees). Elements used here are from the translations of Graves and D. W. Nash, with, again, additions of my own devising.